PRAISE FOR FREDERICK SCHOFIELD

FREDERICK SCHOFIELD

MEGASINO

THE 13TH CASINO

NEW HOPE BOOKS, INC.

Also by Frederick Schofield

The Boardwalkers

A Run to Hell

ABOUT THE AUTHOR

Former gambling-mecca trial lawyer Frederick Schofield colorfully represented casino executives to PhD's (Pimps, Hookers, and Dealers). He knows his turf – and which rocks to turn for gripping tales.

Also look for Schofield novels: A RUN TO HELL, a global adventure that delivers goose bumps with kisses, and THE BOARDWALKERS, a murder mystery that traces two love stories over sixty years at the seashore, while the tide turns crimson.

Frederick

Schofield

MEGASINO

The 13th Casino

Megasino: The 13th Casino

Copyright © 1999 Frederick Schofield

ISBN: 1-929625-13-8

Library of Congress Catalogue Card Number: 99-65924

Published by New Hope Books, Inc.
P.O. Box 38
New Hope, PA 18938
Toll Free Phone (888) 741-BOOK
URL: http://NewHopeBooks.net

Warehoused by Ingram

Printed in the United States of America

For Antonio DeBona,
loving husband to dear Lena,
doting father, killer, and Boardwalker

MEGASINO

THE 13TH CASINO

Preface

The 13th Casino

Joey A is one of the finest hoods who ever scared the peejezus out of me. Over dinner he simply asked me to pass the salt. That's all it took. He has a way with a lifted brow and the smile of a hungry carnivore. Recently released from a federal prison rap stemming from racket charges, Joey reviewed my works. He loved the honest portrayal of mob life in A RUN TO HELL, a story that mates fact and fiction. This tale troubled him. A different kind of page turner – one that rips for pure fun – touches stuff guys like Joey know about, but differently. This yarn mates fiction with innuendo.

Suggested by real-life battles between casino moguls Donald Trump and Steve Wynn, MEGASINO: THE 13TH CASINO places their conflict in fictional hands and heats their discord one degree. That's an amazing feat considering what's already happened in the Atlantic City marina district.

Wynn, that golden boy with Bill Gates' savvy and

John Travolta's looks, which is the preferable way to align those qualities, is chairman of Mirage Resorts, Inc. The gaming guru conceived plans for a colossal resort – the thirteenth casino in Atlantic City. Scaled with more grandeur than any classic wonder of the world, he even planned financing a tunnel to run miles, linking his game palace with the nearest expressway.

Trump, the most entertaining entrepreneur in the past half-century, developer and woman slayer extrordinaire, who never seems to have a decent haircut, opposed the complex rising so close to his bayside Castle casino. He and his associates challenged it in the courts. Trump obstructed and frustrated his rival.

Boys playing for huge stakes ripped off their white gloves to brawl. Published accounts have Wynn declaring of his vociferous opponents, Trump and Arthur Goldberg:

> It's very unfortunate for Atlantic City to be dependent on lightweight, second-string adolescents like Goldberg and Trump. Atlantic City, to a great extent, is captive to these two half-baked mentalities. And we are going to change all that straight away.

Bare knuckles raised to gnash square jaws. Now fictional counterparts launch those punches into lips that long for a different kind of mugging from softer assailants. Sit ringside for every blow.

MEGASINO: THE 13TH CASINO is a joyride for everyone, not just my hard-nosed pal Joey and his buddies. It melds tales from tabloids with gossip circulating under the glitter domes in Atlantic City and Las Vegas. There's fodder for great storytelling. Of course absolutely no truth ties anyone in life to the creatures stirring in this book. But the women and men you'll meet, as you turn these pages, are anxious to pierce your heart with a bullet or a kiss. Pucker up. Just don't turn your back.

Oh, yes. Joey heartily recommends you read this story. Better start fast as I passed the salt. And consider something else as you turn these pages. Shortly after Wynn picked up this book, he announced plans to sell the thirteenth casino to MGM Grand, Inc., in a 6.7 billion-dollar deal.

Chapter One

Money is the Prime Attraction

"The place is huge," she gasped.

Stuffed into stretch slacks, hips sashaying and top heavy, she clung to her man's arm. They were equally well gilded. Her golden-painted fingernails and toes matched the chains around his neck. Awestruck, they stopped in the main entranceway. Like pilgrims to Mecca, they had come, seen, and become true believers. Reverent words passed his lips.

"It's like a domed stadium."

"Are we on a cruise?"

Lofty ceilings simulated Caribbean night skies. Cushiony manmade clouds drifted. Twinkling lights formed a galaxy of electrically-charged stars. Beneath the heavenly portrait, a sea of playing tables and slot machines stretched to the horizon.

He dug for the diamond encrusted money clip buried in his pocket and pulled out a stack of thousand-dollar bills. The face on each screamed for action.

"Boys," he told them, "it's time to play."

Thunder clamored. A lightening bolt spear-chucked by Zeus zoomed from the sky at them. Both ducked as she squealed.

"That's the roller coaster!"

They watched it twist round on a single steel-tubular track. No one rode in the clattering coaster car. The MegaThunder thrill ride started outside and zipped upside-down above the casino's entranceway before roaring back outdoors. Distracted only momentarily, they straightened and sped toward the tables. Action beckoned, even so early in the day, with the allure of a nipple to a breast feeder.

Tommy "Buckman" Brucker watched bemusedly. He glided across the casino floor like he owned the place. He did. Constructed with everything he owned and every dime he could borrow, Megasino towered as the largest casino hotel in the world. He had built it in Atlantic City's Marina District, away from the main gaming tract where a dozen casinos jammed the boardwalk. By the tranquil bay, he had found acreage necessary for the colossal project.

"Shooter's up," came the cry from a crowded craps table. "No more bets!"

Tommy studied a player shaking the dice.

"Yhoa baby," the little man sang to one die. He hopped like a human jumping jack. "Yowsa, sweetie," he chimed to the other.

Fellow players awaited his roll. Tommy watched their eager faces hovering over the table. Some were big spenders everywhere. Others went through life with safety nets underneath them, afraid to put money into a chancy mutual fund but willing to drop a hundred each throw at the craps table.

"Come on, baby!" a burly man in a baseball cap shouted through teeth clenching an unlit cigar. He waved off an approaching cocktail waitress without ordering. Casino play was his intoxicant.

"Shorty, Shorty," called the little man's wife.

She stood close to him, her eyes glued to the green tabletop. With each leap he took the shooter sprouted up to where his larger mate breathed. He pulled back his fist, then hurled dice the way David launched slingshot stones at Goliath. Alabaster cubes banked off the wall at the table's far end. They spun back, rolled, and rested. Every eye instantly counted seven black dots. Unbridled cheers rose. The shooter was hot. Everyone was a winner and every voice shouted for his next roll. They clamored in unison for him.

"Shorty, Shorty, Shorty!"

Tommy marveled at his dream while the stickman collected dice and dealers paid. Sure, Las Vegas had more supersized casinos than Atlantic City, but Tommy's tremendous venture dwarfed them all and was surrounded East Coast money. More than just a gaming house, The Megasino was a destination-area resort with magnificent amenities. A marina docked everything from the worlds largest yachts to one-rider wave runners. Twenty-thousand-dollar a day high roller suites, fifty-dollar a day courtesy rooms, even waterfront townhouses and condominiums covered the lavish landscape. A shopping pavilion, movie theater complex, and day care center enthralled non-gaming family members. An amusement park sparked excitement. Its world-class roller coaster whipped round the property and above the main doors to the casino. Screams from thrill seekers on the "extreme ride" would magnify fervor on the gaming floor. Megasino had everything, but the prime attraction was money. Tommy knew that's what brought folks, so his final inspection had started in the casino where they would come for it.

The stickman handed dice back to the shooter. The little man studied the cubes as if there was a science, nay an art, to chucking them. Then he blew feverishly across the six flat surfaces of each die. The Buckman never missed a detail. As the shooter hopped again, Tommy saw his hair flap. The guy's toupee glue couldn't take the strain.

Tommy also observed a young dealer who hesitantly counted winning pays. Wrinkles furled in his forehead. Slow movements and nervous mannerisms revealed he wasn't accustomed to the pace of play. To fill the floor, Tommy had hired many experienced dealers from the town's other casinos. He had also recruited from Las Vegas. It wasn't hard. The Buckman had a unique reputation in the casino industry. He paid well and created a family atmosphere for employees. When his Vegas casino had a banner year, he had filled its parking lot with new cars, then told each manager to take one home. People itched to work for the Buckman. Yet sheer size of the marina property required him to hire some inexperienced staff members.

The shooter's wife stayed close to him, perched in pumps for a better view. She stuffed her crocodile-skin purse with her husband's winnings as if the reptile had come back to life with an insatiable appetite for hundred-dollar chips. Tommy knew the woman's motivation. She drooled for the big hit that would fuel a shopping spree. The first-class shopping center at the resort rivaled Rodeo Drive in Beverly Hills and Fifth Avenue in Manhattan. The next toss could send her there, knowing first hand that money won is twice as sweet as money earned.

At six-foot four-inches, Tommy stood above the crowd that jammed his casino floor for the weekend opening bash. His dark hair was perfectly trimmed and combed straight back. His broad smile was the brightest thing in the room. Wearing a two-thousand dollar suit like a man born in Armani, Tommy exuded warmth greeting casino employees and guests alike. Some said his charm had made him a multimillionaire. It had certainly helped him raise cash to build The Megasino as the biggest gamble of his life.

The little shooter hopped and threw. His hairpiece landed a split-second behind him. Dice ricocheted off the banking wall, twirled high, and landed hard. A call came from the pit, "Ten!"

Players hollered. Almost everyone had something to applaud. The stickman collected dice while dealers paid again. Only the heavyset cigar chomper at the end of the table complained.

"No, sir," the young dealer tried explaining. "You lost on that roll."

The Buckman grimaced. *A dealer never tells a player he lost*, Tommy thought automatically. *Sometimes players have an unlucky roll, but they're never losers*. He signaled the pit boss. A cursory nod was all it took. Instantly, the silver-haired gaming veteran approached to huddle. He clasped his hands together under his chin, displaying a professional manicure, as Tommy whispered in his ear.

"Get this kid back to the training room."

The pit boss raised his hand and called for a relief dealer. A less sympathetic employer could have fired the young man on the spot. Tommy glanced back at the bewildered kid and thought back to his own early days. He had risen from dealing cards to own The Fantasy, a grand casino on the Vegas strip, and The Megasino, his spectacular Atlantic City marina resort.

Tommy continued his inspection tour. Soon, the amusement rides would open to the public and he would take the maiden voyage on the roller coaster. Tommy feared heights. Still, like everything else on the property, he would sample the scream machine before opening it to the public. He chuckled at his own anxieties, knowing he was about to board a MegaThunder coaster car.

At the bottom of the roller coaster third hill, a man wearing maintenance fatigues examined a strand of piano wire. Head-on his face lacked distinction, but the profile had a definitive form. It manifested when he turned. The slender face, extended nose, and receding jaw, looked like a fish head. He spit a wad of chewing gum and ran his tongue over pointy teeth. Simply known as "the mechanic," the fish face knew what he was doing. He studied a strong steel wire that was safely affixed high above the rail. A small camera lens hung from it. The camera snapped digital photographs and electronically transmitted them to the end of the ride. As passengers disembarked, they could view their reactions captured along the way. Safety technicians also observed the images to monitor the ride in progress.

The mechanic's cellular telephone rang. He answered and spoke softly as if words came no louder through fish lips. Then he grinned and returned the phone to his pocket. His pronounced nose twitched from excitement. Tommy Brucker was walking to the boarding platform.

Now, the mechanic thought. *Time to lower the wire into a new position.*

The sharp steel strand was too thin for anyone on the thrill ride to see, but the Buckman was going to find it neck-high. The slender man moved efficiently, like the professional he was. Job done, he holstered his wrench in a tool belt and marveled at his handiwork. His index finger ran along the strand to test it. The wire lacerated his finger pad. The mechanic sucked his blood and savored the thought of how it would slice at breakneck speed. He pulled again, cut himself afresh, and licked his wounds.

"Here are the drop numbers from last night," Manny Levine called out.

Tommy reviewed the drop sheets without breaking stride. Manny kept pace by his side. At nearly fifty-years-old, Manny was slightly older than his boss. He was olive-complected with deep-set eyes. His thick brows often hid behind bookish reading glasses. But Manny was no ordinary bookworm. The compactly built desk jockey stayed fit by vigorously working out and playing racquetball with a passion.

Manny was the figure man. As Tommy's Chief Executive Officer, presidents of the resort's three divisions – casino, hotel, and amusements – reported to him. In turn, Manny reported to the Buckman. Tommy had lured him away from his position as CEO of the casino that had just become the town's second largest. He knew

Manny had come for more than just a higher salary and lucrative stock incentives. They shared a mutual admiration for each other's talents. Megasino was an amazing gamble. Together, with a little luck, they would make it work.

The casino required a million-dollar daily drop. They needed that volume of play every day to sustain it. Pre-opening figures on their test runs had exceeded prelaunch results at the casino that Manny had just left. Three years earlier, Tommy's bitter rival, Greg Conrad, had opened the boardwalk Pyramid Casino. Conrad publicized it as the eighth wonder of the world. Its opening week drop had astounded everyone in the gaming business. Tommy and Manny knew they would have to beat those figures at Megasino. And it looked like they would. Their opening bash would light up the casino industry like nothing gaming analysts and Wall Streeters had ever seen. They were a day away from the gala affair that would bring the biggest names in entertainment through the casino's doors. A show in the grand ballroom would enthrall a "Who's Who" list of high rollers. Afterward, they would all rush back to the casino floor.

Tommy looked forward to reviewing the post-event figures. He was also anxious to spend some special moments with one of the entertainers. An urgency had flared in her voice when she called. *What's on her mind?* he wondered. Tommy hoped he wouldn't be too busy. Timing had never been right between them.

He returned the drop sheets and caught Manny's good-natured grin. The figure man knew where his boss was going. As the Buckman walked toward the coaster, Manny pulled a cellular telephone from his breast pocket. He hit a key for a prearranged call.

"Send 'em over to the coaster, now," he said.

Show dancers, still decked out from their dress rehearsal, would accompany Tommy on the ride. Blow-ups from a photo shoot would bedeck the main lobby.

Tommy called over his shoulder, "I'm sure there's a seat for you."

"No thanks," Manny replied, still smiling. "Hairpin curves and 180-degree loops aren't for the faint of heart."

On the casino floor, the shooter hopped. His wife hung close. Her eyes fixed on the table. Her arms stretched with hands open to grab winnings. Players screamed for the roll.

"Shorty, Shorty!" they called.

And a single glue spot held the flapping toupee.

The mechanic finished soft-talking through another call and stuffed his cellular phone in a pocket. He worked for people who also had grand plans. Their schemes were smoothly unfolding in Atlantic City, Las Vegas, and the hills of Tennessee. Even Tommy Brucker was boarding the roller coaster on schedule. Soon, hell would reign.

He climbed to the ground and paused. His fish face turned in one direction, then another. Satisfied that no one had seen him, he strolled to the casino, then swam through crowds like a barracuda ready to feed on a school of unsuspecting sardines. He envisioned what the taut steel wire would do to riders taking the next trip. The sharp tips of his teeth emerged through a grin, reflecting fateful promise.

Dancers from the show room review surrounded Tommy. The women's sequined costumes revealed more than they covered. They had dancers' legs, strong and muscularly defined. Their waists narrowed to nothingness; fat didn't form on a hoofer's body. The work was too demanding. They removed headdresses that costume designers had adorned with faux jewelry to dazzle onstage. The headpieces would have whipped away in fast winds and heavy gravity pulls. Coaster engineers had told Tommy about the G-pulls that would smack him with the simulated force of a missile takeoff. Soon, he'd feel it first hand.

"Tuck your tushes into seats, people," a voice called. "That's it, darlings, tuck those booties."

Tommy looked toward the casino photographer, whose extended finger pointed the way, then boarded with the dancers. Six riders filled the car, two abreast in three seating rows. A power-operated drag would haul their car up the lift hill until they crested atop the first lofty peak. On the other side, they would descend at breakneck speed. A monstrous 3.5 G-pull would pin them into their seats. Tommy sat in the front row next to a dancer, who laughed nervously, as a safety bar latched them in place.

"This won't do," the photo flicker whined. He adjusted his lens and reset the scene. "Oh, Mr. Brucker! Sir, would you mind sitting in the back of the car? I can get a better picture of you there."

The guy wanted a better vantage point for the PR photo shoot and public relations was what it was all about, anyway. A ride attendant released the safety bar so Tommy could get out. He exchanged places with a dancer from the last row and settled into his seat.

Like a whistling teapot, the photographer spouted his final call before clicking away, "Smile, darlings!"

Then, with a jolt, the car zipped from the boarding platform and soared toward the sky. Even the power drag moved fast. Engineers had designed the ride for quickness to handle a heavy volume of riders. Too late to disembark, the drag clanked as they skyrocketed seven stories high. Tommy looked at the Atlantic City casinos his Megasino dwarfed. As the chain pulled the coaster car higher still, he saw north beyond neighboring Brigantine Island, a sleepy village that stretched four miles along the ocean, and south to Ocean City, a distant seaside gem with tamer attractions. He spied a Ferris wheel, no more than a speck, on its boardwalk.

Twenty feet from the crest of the first peak, it happened. The car stopped dead. A second later, it fell backward – in the wrong direction – down the incline. Anxious riders squealed in horror. Then, the car jerked to a stop and climbed upward again. Everyone laughed in nervous delight at the planned free-fall.

Tommy knew he shouldn't worry. The best engineers in the business had designed the track and preprogrammed safety features. They equipped each coaster car with computerized photocells and magnetic sensors to stop it if a mishap occurred. Still, his stomach knotted. He watched an airplane fly along the bay. It dragged an advertising banner for boaters. To Tommy's chagrin, he realized he was looking down at the plane instead of up at it.

As they neared the crest of the first peak, he quickly

surveyed his property. The show room stood separate
from the main casino tower, though it was attached to
the main building. That way, players stayed close to the
casino action even when they took in a show.

The car stopped at the peak for just an instant. Then,
it inched toward the first drop. Dancers squealed as
their car thundered down the wicked plunge. Air pounded
their faces at 75 miles per hour. The force of each G
tugged. They moved faster than their screams as the
car nearly scraped the ground and catapulted upward.
The crest of the next hill was almost underneath them.
Wind whipped their ears; tears filled eyes; hearts raced.
When they reached the second hill pinnacle, the car
slowed. The pause allowed them to look down at the
tortuous view – a curved two-hundred foot drop. Then
their rocket blasted straight down to earth.

Was he a bunny on steroids? Shorty hopped and
popped, dice exploded from his grip, and players feverishly cried. The cubes bounced off the banking wall
just as the shooter's toupee glue gave way. He didn't
notice his hairpiece fly above the craps table and float
downward. Dice still rolled as the hairy parachute hit
the table squarely atop a spinning die.

All action stopped dead. A dealer looked at the toupee and turned to his pit boss for directions.

A bespectacled player, quickly adjusting his horn rims
for a better look, was first to speak. "A rat's humpin'
the dice."

The man next to him articulated everyone's fear in a
single cry, "It better not end this hot streak."

In unison all the players chanted their earnest reprise,

"The roll counts! The roll counts!"

The pit boss beckoned his stickman with a curling finger and said, "Think you can lift that thing without turning the die?"

The stickman studied the table calamity uncertainly. His frown was a dubious indicator.

"The roll counts," the players continued screaming.

Like a Supreme Court Justice pondering a landmark decision, the pit boss weighed his option to disqualify the toss. He stroked his chin. Finally, he declared, "The roll counts."

His call detonated a blast of unbridled cheers. The stickman delicately inserted his stick under the hairpiece, while above the clamor, the shooter's wife screamed.

"Ya laid four grand on the table, but you only spent a hundred and fifty bucks on that rug, you cheapskate."

"Shut up," he hollered. "I got a hard six riding on this roll."

He watched the table intently, oblivious to glue marks spotting his shiny dome. Only one thought burned in his mind; everyone else wanted to know, too. What number was showing under the hairpiece? They needed a three. On the stick's tip, the mother of all dead rats slowly levitated.

The coaster car climbed to the third hill peak. It tugged against the tubular track as if yearning to break free. Tommy knew they were about to plummet down a vertical incline for the fastest drop on the ride and held his breath for the 3.85 G force to wallop them, unaware of what else waited below.

"Seven out," came the call from the relief dealer. The die showed a four; everyone lost.

A grandmotherly figure dropped her drink and yelled at the shooter, "You baldheaded son of a bitch!"

Players fixed to lynch him. The stickman pushed the toupee on the end of his stick toward the little man. The elderly woman sneered. Nostrils flaring, she grabbed the hairpiece, threw it to the floor, and stomped it with gusto.

The coaster car shot down track that twirled like the stripe on a candy cane. Violent gravity pulls wrenched back Tommy's facial flesh. Spirals turned his stomach. Head spinning, he leaned forward, fighting to avoid vomiting and having it blow back in his mouth.

Dancers cheerfully wailed. They approached the lowered guide wire at cataclysmic speed while the camera, affixed to the line, clicked photos of hair flying and face muscles drawn taut. With a whoosh the steel wire took its bloody toll.

The car roared up the next hill. From its towering peak, there were no more gleeful calls, no more sounds at all. Just silence filled the air, but for the wind whisking as a head plummeted to the ground.

The shooter and his wife made a fast exit to avoid the wrath of players who blamed them for the losing roll. They scurried to the casino's main doorway where they paused to catch their breath. Exhausted from their hasty retreat, she wheezed and hacked a smoker's cough;

he panted and silently vowed to undertake an exercise program.

A clanking overhead drew their attention. Safety mechanisms braked the coaster car. It stopped above them upside-down, safety bars locking riders into their seats. The shrill shriek from the shooter's wife filled the casino as crimson rain pattered. She collapsed in the little man's arms. He stood, transfixed, unable to take his eyes from the ghoulish sight.

A chorus of discordant screams stung his eardrums. Security personnel scrambled. People scurried in all directions, most not even knowing why.

As if frozen in space and time, the shooter was powerless to budge. Somehow, he supported his unconscious wife. Head tilted upward, all his senses focusing, he searched for movement in the car. He wished he could hear over the clatter. His eyes and ears strained as he wondered.

Is anyone up there alive?

Chapter Two

Pleasure Domes

The longest stretch limousine in Atlantic City sailed into The Megasino main drive. It cruised as if a shiny-white ocean liner had grounded itself and sprouted one front axle and two in the rear to support its extended load. A rotund door captain, resplendent in his red uniform, gawked, almost forgetting to signal on his caller. Hastily grabbing a grey pager, he watched it slip from his hand and bounce across the pavement.

"Damn."

Like a jumbo tomato being tossed in a salad, he skedaddled after the beeper, bent down, and clawed it.

"Umph," he groaned.

He straightened upright and signaled. Belt-clipped page receivers buzzed every available bag grabber.

The limo pulled up as a platoon of bellhops fell in line. They peered at the blackened windows but saw only their own reflections.

"Who's in that thing?" a rosy-cheeked rookie said.

The young man asked a tough one. With so many entertainers, sports stars, politicians, and high rollers scheduled to arrive, each bellman speculated.

"Politicos don't rate this treatment."

"Texas oil tycoon."

"Hong Kong businessman."

"Nah. It's an Arabian sheik with his entire harem."

Each offered their two cents, but they came up with less than a dime.

"Who's in that thing?" the kid repeated.

A tuxedoed chauffeur opened his door. Protocol dictated that hotel employees didn't dare open car doors until the driver signaled. Trained not to bother the rich until they were ready, bellhops waited as smaller limos backed up behind. The driver of a shiny Cadillac, unaccustomed to the lack of attention, honked his horn. Inquisitive onlookers formed a crowd.

The chauffeur opened a door midway back in the car. Two large black men emerged to survey the scene through silver-mirrored sunglasses. Muscles on the bodyguards bulged through identical Italian-designed mohair suits. One bore the flattened nose of a prize fighter. He had the size to have earned it in the heavy division, though it was difficult to imagine who could have given him the licking that broke his face. The other man looked small, but only by comparison. The stare he rifled at bellhops sent them retreating fast. They rearranged their formation ten feet from the limo trunk and waited.

Someone else waited two miles away. He stood, alone, in the casino he owned. Greg Conrad still promoted his Pyramid Casino as the eighth wonder of the world although another eclipsed it. His high-rise pleasure dome had no rival until Tommy Brucker constructed Megasino. On the highest floor of The Pyramid, which towered over the boardwalk, Conrad roosted atop his desk. Dance music reverberated through his office. His left foot tapped to a primal beat; his head jogged back-to-front in time. News of the Buckman's tragedy had aroused him, so he'd arranged a special diversion.

Greg Conrad hadn't been born classically handsome like Tommy Brucker. Instead, and unlike Tommy, he'd been born rich. Conrad looked good as money could make a man. A nose trim had fit his beak to his face. Surgical pinning had hammered down flapping ears. A crop of transplanted hair plugs sprouted over a receding hairline. Physicians had liposuctioned away love handles. Conrad squeezed his gut, feeling a roll that had found its way home.

"Fat has a memory," he reminded himself. "Time to hook up to a surgeon's Hoover again."

The mildly attractive man had strolled through life unequivocally proving wealth is a powerful aphrodisiac. Females of all ages, attractive ladies, even intelligent women, found him alluring. Clever enough to multiply the millions he had inherited into a massively greater fortune, he abounded in self-confidence that enhanced his appeal. Money even made his gruff demeanor and rough sexual proclivities easier to overlook.

He stood under a crystal chandelier his Euro-tramp wife had collected on an antique foray. Before their marriage, Francoise had been a French countess. She retained both her title and her accent. He called her a "count-ass" because counting his money was what her

ass did best. She shopped allover the European conti-
nent for worthless treasures. Conrad could afford her,
and he knew that was why she stayed with him. She
endured his indiscretions while he paid for the endless
shopping spree that had become her life. The chandelier was an ever present reminder of the price he paid to
play.

They flaunted a golden-couple image, a public persona familiar as the Conrad logo that adorned everything he owned. It crowned his casino. The trademark
decorated his Chicago skyscrapers and planes from his
independent airline that traveled between the Midwest,
Atlantic City, and Florida. The logo even garnished his
Euro-tramp. Francoise wore it on a diamond and sap-
phire broach that rested on a chain between her breasts.
The size of a Mercedes hood ornament, he could sell the
jewelry piece to feed a starving third-world nation for a
year, but that wasn't his style. Charity stayed home in
Conrad's universe.

From his glass-walled tower Conrad looked down
on everything – everything except The Megasino. He
gazed upwardly at the tower dazzling in the Marina District. The idea that Brucker's casino was bigger than
his own was emasculating until he remembered.

"The Buckman's dead."

With Brucker out of the way, the man's two casinos
were ripe for his takeover bid. An overpowering desire
drove him to acquire more property, wealth, women,
whatever. Brucker's casinos would sate a craving for
which his appetite was robust.

Contemplating Brucker's death roused libidinous instincts in time for soft door raps. His prey entered cautiously. *Come here, little lamb*, the big, bad wolf in him

thought. The door closed fast behind her. Automatically, it locked. He watched the young woman undo her top. His hand waved a message to stop her.

"Up here," he called huskily.

He would decide when and how those clothes would disappear. First, like reading a stock report with a good bottom line, he soaked in her charms. Long blond hair swung straight, loose, and free. Under a sheer chiffon blouse, creamy flesh called for him to churn a buttery spread. He savored her graceful strides as she approached. Standing beneath him on the floor, the open blouse previewed her treasures. He extended his hand and a delicate palm fell into his, one he tightly gripped, pulling her atop the desk with him. Conrad brought her close. An angel's essence peaked his senses, but a sense of omnipotent power firmed his uncircumcised manhood.

"Brucker's down," he whispered.

"What?"

"Rest in pieces, Tommy."

Her narrowed eyes and open mouth made it clear she didn't understand. How could a stupid hooker?

Their movements synchronized to music. Conrad danced gracefully for a man his size. Her spiked heels clacked on the marble desktop; her lithe form swayed. The face of a porcelain doll turned to his, her impish nose and hazel eyes bespeaking innocence she could hardly possess. The young woman had all the beauty her work demanded and time had yet to steal.

"Open your blouse."

One at a time she undid buttons on the tight leopard top. Her breasts peeked from inside, pink nipples jutting upward toward his eyes.

"Off with the top."

The young woman turned her back but instantly obeyed. She swayed to the beat and draped the spotted blouse over her treasures like a teasing veil. Then, it fell from her hand. The groove of her bare spine rhythmically twisted like a dancing serpent.

"Yes," he moaned. "It's time. Turn around."

Slowly, she revolved, teeny hands covering perky C-cups, fingers delicately parting.

He slapped her hard across the face; she didn't react. Bright red fingernails twirled over hardening nipple tips.

She took it on the chin, a strike with greater force. Blood emerged from the corner of her mouth. Her hands descended, caressing a bare torso, then rested above a silky skirt. Slits ran up its sides high enough to reveal she wore nothing underneath. Her hips reached to caress his loins; her cheeks met the open palm of his hand.

With each blow she breathed faster, harder, as if sucking for air that had vanished from the room.

"Lose the skirt."

She groped a waist-level clasp and tossed back long tresses. He came close, slowly and purposefully, as her eyes closed and lips parted for a kiss. Instead, he ripped the skirt and watched it slide down slender legs. She kicked it high into the air. From the corner of his eye, he watched its descent.

"Yeah," he said. "Brucker's head must have fallen this way."

His mouth raced to cover hers. His tongue probed. Their bodies merged, hips undulating, she quivering in his arms, then shuddering when he jerked back. She twitched spastically but never moved as he raised his

fist. The punch sent her reeling backward. She stumbled backward, lost her footing on the desktop, and fell
to the floor bottom-first.

"Get out!" he roared.

Seated on the carpet, the young woman covered her
face with both hands.

"I told you to leave. Now, get the hell out of here!"

She scrambled for her clothing until he leaped down,
grunted, and rushed at her with eyes wide, lips sneering.

She screamed and sprinted naked to the door. Frantically she twisted the knob. Locked, it didn't budge.

"Out, vermin!"

She tugged the doorknob. Her tender face, moments
earlier fresh and winsome, was swollen and distorted.
She cried for help, unaware no one could hear from the
fully soundproofed room.

Conrad returned to his desk, stood beside it, and
breathed deeply, watching her struggle, all the while stroking himself. Then, with a surge, he was fulfilled. He hit
a button under the desk and the door latch buzzed. The
door opened.

Out the young woman scurried, sobbing, "Someone,
please, help me!"

His staff would stop her before she could leave the
suite. Conrad opened his desk drawer for a sterile tissue kept there, soaked in astringent. He wiped himself,
then reached for a soft terry cloth to pat dry.

Conrad gazed out plate-glass windows. The lofty
office offered panoramic views; he rotated to catch them
all. Looking north, he viewed churning inlet waters. A
flotilla of pleasure crafts traversed the passageway between the bay and the ocean. Eastward, ocean surf

pounded the shore. Gulls hovered over waves hoping
to snare tasty treats. To the south, Ocean City basked
in pristine sunshine, while to the west fishing trawlers
and pleasure crafts harbored in marinas. He turned all
directions, yet his attention focused only one way. Eyes
burning with covetous purpose, he stared at The Megasino.

"A golden apple ripe to pluck," he mused with satisfaction, "with Brucker buried. Good for me – and good
for the worm population."

At Megasino, Manny Levine hustled. The CEO over-
saw financial operations. Tommy Brucker had always
handled public relations. Guests and stars expected the
Buckman's famous smile and familiar handshake to welcome them to the weekend kickoff affair. Never a greet-
er, Manny contemplated the new role circumstances dictated he undertake.

"What the hell," he said to himself, "nothin' to it."

He pulled what he wanted from his lower desk drawer. Before he mixed with the crowds, he would mingle
with a good buddy, his old friend Jack Daniels. Booze
made it easier to schmooz.

Manny was a product of his generation. He was old
enough to have been drafted into the Marines when they
wanted a few good men for Vietnam. How well he remembered the stares his busload of drafted recruits drew
at the Parris Island training camp. In 1968, they had
assigned one of ten draftees to the Marine Corps. The
attention focused because Marines had always volun-
teered; draftees were something new to the corps. So
was a bus packed with proud New York Jews whom

the Marine Corps promptly trained and sent overseas.

Vietnam had been a drug store. Whatever you wanted came at discount prices and Manny had seen firsthand how drugs consumed good men. He never wanted a part in the drug culture. Young executives worked
the casino floor with flake stinging their nostrils, but
that wasn't for Manny. His singular indulgence was
one his strict upbringing precluded from ever becoming
an overindulgence. It originated at a historically certi-
fied distillery in Lynchburg, Tennessee, population 361,
so the label read. Manny poured a glass of Jack Daniels
Black Label and called to his personal assistant.

"Did you reach Darnel?"

"Not yet, Mr. Levine," Lisa called back. His efficient
aide sifted through ledgers at a desk just outside his door.
She set them down and ran her fingers over the tips of a
short, blunt-cut 'do, instantly sweeping mousy-brown
hair into place.

Darnel Halloway would have to help Manny handle
The Megasino opening bash. Darnel would also know
how to keep the morning disaster under control. Atlantic County's Chief Prosecutor had already sent investigators to examine the MegaThunder mishap. That didn't
make sense. What were they looking for and how did
they get there so fast? All of Manny's instincts screamed:
something's wrong.

"Try him at home again," he called to the outer office.

Manny picked up the bottle for one more pour. He
thought of the dear friend who had introduced him to
Black Jack. Yet, while he swallowed, his mother's
words stung his ears as if she were calling from the
next room.

"You're not having a drink, are you, Emanuel? Remember how drunk your uncle was at your cousin's bar mitzvah? That could run in the family."

"Mom," he would reply whenever he heard the story, "that was twenty years ago. Uncle Louie hasn't had a drink since."

His father would pat his arm and console him. "It's okay for a man to have a drink," he would intone, "in moderation."

Manny loved his parents dearly. His mother wasn't just a Long Island *yenta*. She was a woman fixed in her ways with a good heart. Her folk wisdom was so ingrained that, at the age of forty-nine, he still felt guilty going out on a school night. He wished he had listened to her when she'd warned him not to marry Tina, though. She was reason enough for any man to drink. Manny put her out of his mind as he set down his glass and called to his assistant.

"Time for me to walk the property and check on folks."

The blond telephoned her service in tears. Prell took the call. She supplied hookers to the elite and never faced a business lull. For a hefty price, her women satisfied any need, straight or special. In return, she pampered and protected them. Prell even provided them health care benefits. The service advertised as a temporary employment agency, so a handful of legitimate secretaries and paralegals accepted real work under pseudonyms to give each hooker a cover. Prell cared for her ladies. That's why the young woman's call bothered her.

Verbal and physical abuse were Conrad's shtick. He paid well, but she couldn't let him get behind; he liked to bargain down the tab. Prell didn't take those calls. She assumed he was getting off while he haggled. And she no longer turned tricks, not even over the telephone.

"Miss Prell," the young woman cried, "He –"

"Don't say it," Prell cooed. Her deep voice evoked sensuality that could never be feigned. "I know. The guy's scum, honey."

"Mr. Conrad said something about the Buckman goin' down."

Prell had trouble deciphering words that emerged through little girl whimpers.

"Tommy Brucker? What'd he mean?"

"Dunno, Miss Prell."

Prell paused.

"Conrad beat me bad."

"Come on home, sweetie." Prell's husky tones soothed the way piping-hot chicken soup remedies the common cold. "Momma's gonna take care of her baby."

Prell set down the phone and reflected. Tommy was one of the few truly decent men at the top of the casino industry. She wondered if he was all right. Prell had connections in town. She picked up the phone to call around.

At the Megasino main entrance both bodyguards looked satisfied. The chauffeur stood by the rear door of the elongated limousine. The casino cameraman waited in front of the crowd, lens aimed, finger ready to snap. Then a dark-suited sentinel gave the word.

"Now."

The chauffeur opened the door. A long black-stockinged leg emerged. The crowd pushed nearer as a demure Manalo Blahnik high-heeled pump glistened with toes pointed straight down.

"It's her!"

The call rose from the crowd. Concerned looks on her bodyguards were just hype; she intended her entrance to be grand. The larger guard gallantly extended his arm, which she took like the lady she had become. Standing next to the brawny man, she looked small. Certainly, the songstress wasn't overpowering as she appeared on stage or on her album covers. She almost disappeared inside her full-length sable coat.

"Look over this way please, Miss Halloway," the photographer called, snapping away.

She was stunningly beautiful, face expertly made up, blushed, and highlighted. Her eyelashes were long enough to whip a man lucky enough to stand in their way.

"Again please, ma'am. Look this way."

Her complexion was rich mocha with heavy cream. Full ruby lips kissed the crowd whenever she glanced in their direction. High cheekbones suggested elegance as did her every graceful movement.

"Can I have an autograph, please?" a woman shouted. "I've got everything you recorded for the past thirty years."

Susannah stopped for an instant only, then rushed away. For her, rushing was an art form. She always appeared to scurry as she took her time passing fans she had cultivated over a long career. That day, however, she was genuinely anxious to see Tommy.

Why isn't he here to meet me? she wondered.

"Miss Halloway," a well-dressed man called. "May I speak to you a moment, please?"

His demeanor connoted worldly refinement while a trace of Long Island lingered in his accent. She looked him up and down. He wasn't tall, but he was physically fit. Susannah Halloway liked that in a man. With his olive skin and pronounced facial features, she couldn't tell whether he was Jewish or Italian.

"I'm Manny Levine," he introduced himself, "Mr. Brucker's CEO for this property."

She spoke hurriedly. "Where's Tommy?"

Manny told her and Susannah stopped in her tracks. Slowly and deliberately, her words came.

"Get Darnel here."

The voice that never sang offkey quivered. Her son would know how to handle things. Susannah's relationship with Tommy went back to the beginning of her singing career. He had taken her boy under his wings and taught him the casino business. Darnel would have to take charge for the man who was his mentor.

"We're trying to reach him, now."

As her thoughts focused on Tommy, a lone tear stained her blush. Shocked, the crowd noise grew dim, then silent in her ears.

An unrelenting intercom buzz roused him from a daydream.

"What the hell?"

Greg Conrad cussed for his own benefit; being bothered filled him with self-importance. He took the call over his speakerphone.

"Sorry to interrupt, sir," a secretary said. "I thought

you would want to know right away."

"Know what?"

"Tommy Brucker is alive. They only had one fatality in the roller coaster mishap. Mr. Brucker's been sedated, but he's not seriously hurt."

Conrad's face reddened. The revelation raised his body temperature. Bullets of sweat shot from his pits and down his sides. His lungs fought for clean air; everything smelled. Tommy Brucker had cheated him — the bastard was alive.

Conrad picked up the telephone without thinking, started dialing, then regained his senses. Never could he make that call over an open line. He cradled the handpiece and grabbed a porcelain ashtray next to it. The trinket from the casino gift shop bore the omnipresent Conrad logo. His grip closed tightly, his knuckles glowing an alabaster hue as he boosted the pressure. Overhead, the chandelier from hell mocked him. Conrad pulled his arm back and pitched a fastball that smacked its crystalline target. The lighting fixture clanked and swayed.

He would have to meet the people who would finish off Brucker. Getting close to them was risky, but he had no choice. Those people would see that Brucker died. They'd take care of The Megasino, too. Conrad chuckled. They claimed they could literally take the place down. He pondered. How could anyone topple that size building and make it look like an accident? Hoods like them had run mob operations silently in the resort town for more than a hundred years, but snuffing a life here and there was their business. Taking down a superstructure was something else altogether. He wondered aloud.

"Can they really do it?"

Soon enough, Conrad realized, he would learn.

Chapter Three

The Snake Cemetery

Darnel Halloway felt ready for whatever the day might bring. He peered out his kitchen window over the back-yard swimming pool. Spiny cacti, stems reaching for the sky, baring white, yellow, and purple blossoms, surrounded sparkling aqua water at his personal oasis. Never had dawn come with greater splendor. The Nevada morning sun out dazzled even the famed casino lighting displays that blazed on the Vegas strip, just a forty minute drive away. Freshly brewed coffee filled the whole house with its potent aroma. He set down his mug as Jasmine called to him.

"Sweetheart. You ready yet? Your limo's outside."

"That's what I like about being a casino president. Your driver waits while you enjoy a second cup of coffee and a second helping of –"

Jasmine laughed and pushed his eager hands away. "That's thirds on me and you've already bagged your morning limit."

Love's afterglow still fresh on her face, Jasmine straightened her husband's necktie. His work dictated late hours, so morning was their time together. Often he would kiss slumber from her eyes and wrap himself in her inviting embrace. Together, they would rush toward heaven. Afterward, she'd rest contented but never long. Jasmine would rise to brew java and to hold him again before he left for the day.

One of the youngest men ever to serve as president of a major Vegas casino, Darnel enjoyed presiding over the Buckman's place, The Fantasy. He had the energy of youth for the long hours it took to manage its operations smoothly and the savvy to run it profitably. Tommy Brucker's close relationship with his mother had made the older man a natural mentor. Tommy had taught him the business from the ground up. During college and law school, Darnel spent his summers working in both the hotel and casino ends of the industry.

He looked the part of a casino executive. Tailored clothes clung tight to his well-toned musculature. Tall with cropped hair, Darnel was a handsome man of color. His luminous green eyes were as incisive in the boardroom as they were evocative in the bedroom. He pulled his wife back to give those eyes a feast.

Jasmine had cover girl features. She was an ebony beauty with dark-curled hair that fell to her shoulders. He knew her every gentle curve. Soft-spoken and demure, she was the woman he cherished.

They had met when she came to Vegas for a fashion merchandising convention. Darnel had spotted her and instantly knew he would love her. He wasted no time proposing; Darnel hadn't wanted the woman to slip away. She'd given up a promising career of her own as a fashion buyer to marry him. About to celebrate their third anniversary, their love remained genuine and deep.

He felt a tug at his pant leg and looked down. A pair of dimples tilted upward. The little lady beamed. Tracy was a two-year-old charmer like her daddy, but the dimples came from Momma. Darnel wondered if the child Jasmine carried inside her would be blessed with them as well.

"Are you getting to that meeting on time, Mr. Casino President?"

Her arms still held him. Darnel didn't want to leave her embrace, but he had planned a teleconference with Tommy's Atlantic City casino. From the conference room in the Fantasy, he would place an audiovisual call to the boardroom at The Megasino. They would coordinate efforts to kickoff the Atlantic City operation. With so much happening at Megasino, Darnel knew they would probably ask him to fly there. They had given high rollers from The Fantasy invitations to The Megasino's grand opening, and he would have to court those players.

The lifestyle excited a guy so recently graduated from law school at the University of Nevada - Las Vegas. He often wondered how life would have differed if he had joined his classmates in the practice of law. He had loved his legal studies and would have made a good lawyer. Something about the casino business boiled his blood, though. Darnel enjoyed the rush. He wouldn't trade it for any career in the world.

The telephone rang. Jasmine answered and put the caller on hold. "Sweetheart," she sang, "it's Manny Levine's secretary calling from Atlantic City."

Darnel looked at his wristwatch, knowing he was

running late.

"Tell her I already left for the office."

Manny often forgot that Atlantic City was a few hours ahead of Las Vegas time. Frequently, his calls came a little early; usually they could wait. Besides, Darnel would talk to him during the conference call.

As Jasmine conveyed the message, he planted a kiss atop his daughter's head and lifted the toddler into his arms. Tracy squealed with delight until he gently set her down and Jasmine came to him for a goodbye kiss of her own. Then Darnel scurried out the door.

With the desert heat scorching through his clothes, Darnel picked up the pace, dashing between air conditioners. A uniformed chauffeur stood at attention beside the black car. The man opened a rear door and quickly closed it behind Darnel to keep cool air inside from escaping. As the limo drove away, Darnel waved goodbye to his two ladies who stood on the doorstep.

"Where's Mike?" he called to the chauffeur.

The man turned his head and spoke through the opening between the driver and passenger compartments. "Your regular driver took the day off, sir. His wife had a baby last night. Mike got caught up in the celebration. He's probably sleeping it off."

Darnel smiled. He had almost done the same thing with the birth of his child. His regular driver had spoken of his wife's pregnancy when they shared small talk on the road. Tommy had also taught him how to know the people who worked for him. That type of caring was always returned in kind. Darnel was happy for the young man and made a mental note to have his secretary send a newborn's gift.

"You haven't driven me before. What's your name?"

"They just call me Scratchy, sir."

The slightly-built man lifted his chauffeur cap to itch his scalp, while Darnel picked up his newspaper, realizing the drive to work afforded his last non-hectic moments of the day. They pulled from the posh residential development. Stately homes congregated where all the sprinklers allowed by local zoning ordinances made small grass plots and plantings so green. Water conservation was always a concern in the desert community. The rest of the ride to the casino strip wouldn't be so sumptuous.

He just finished studying market reports when the limo left the main highway for an unfamiliar stop. They pulled into a small gas station with Darnel wondering why. Limos were always gassed before going into service.

"What's the problem?" he called up to the driver.

"Water light came on, sir. We may have a broken engine hose."

Darnel checked his wristwatch. "I have a meeting in twenty minutes."

"Just need to take a fast look under the hood, Mr. Halloway. Don't want to break down along the way."

The driver walked to the front of the vehicle where a uniformed service attendant joined him. Darnel observed antiquated gas pumps on the driver's side of the car. Out the passenger-side windows he saw someone had boarded the door to the gas station office and the garage door to the repair bay. The place looked deserted. With the limo hood raised, he never saw the driver and attendant grab weapons strapped inside the engine compartment.

Scratchy pulled out a Smith & Wesson 10-millimeter

semiautomatic pistol. Its bullets were larger and more
lethal than .45-caliber ammunition and the weapon delivered firepower at an amazing rate of speed. The service station attendant clutched a sawed-off 20-gauge
shotgun. Loaded with Number 12 cartridges, the short
double barrels were ready to discharge two-thousand
searing pellets. At close range the gun could flail a human into a shredded carcass.

Both men held their guns behind their backs as they
sauntered around the driver's side of the limousine. The
chauffeur returned to his seat while the attendant walked
behind the pumps.

"What's the problem?" Darnel said.

The rear door flung open and the barrel of the attendant's shotgun poked Darnel's chest. Simultaneously,
Scratchy reached through the opening between the front
and rear compartments of the car, aiming his semiautomatic directly at Darnel's face.

Darnel instinctively looked toward the passenger-side
door for a means of escape. Out the window he saw a
red-haired ball of fire. The tiny woman in towering high
heels and gold lame minidress sprinted toward the limo.
Immediately, he could tell. Two hoods and a hooker
were taking him.

Why? Darnel asked himself.

The service attendant pulled the barrel of the shotgun from his ribs. Darnel saw the man was huge, flabby, and hirsute. A forest of brown hair ran up his arms
to his short sleeves and sprang out his wide-open collar.

"All right," he addressed the driver more calmly than
he felt. "What do you want?"

He didn't see it coming. The butt of the big man's
shotgun smacked Darnel in the side of the head.

Cindi studied their captive as he woke hours later. Never before had she seen a black man with green eyes. Eyes had always attracted her and those were precious emeralds. *God, he's adorable*, she thought. He had what it took to jump-start her imagination. She fantasized about what laid hidden beneath his expensive business suit. In the heat, he wouldn't wear it much longer.

Cindi Rella was her street name. She wasn't drop-dead gorgeous, but she had a good shtick. She would offer to bed a man and circle his erogenous zones with a magic marker for $1.50. Every guy asked the same question.

"That's all it costs? Just a buck and a half?"

She'd get them in bed and go to work.

"Now what?" they would ask.

"I play inside each hoop for fifty bucks a pop. It'll cost ya one-hundred dollars to put anything we circled in me. Cash up front, sweetie."

Cindi's act worked well on Prince Charmings who were too eager or too intoxicated to make their way to legal brothels situated outside the City of Las Vegas. She would have preferred working for a high class escort service, but Cindi was freelancing the strip until something better came her way. That's where she had spotted her two mob pals, Scratchy and Sludge. Cindi recognized them from having dated a wise guy in their Atlantic City crime family. Surprised to find the boys in Vegas, she quickly teamed up with them.

Mob guys know how to treat a woman, she realized. Their girlfriends always got the best of everything – shopping sprees, fancy dinners, and big nights out. Mobsters were great boyfriends, but lousy lovers. *You get a mob guy in bed*, she thought, *and the whole time he's talking about what horse to play, what number to pick, and who he has to whack.* They never talked that way to their wives. Those women never knew about their husbands' business. But girlfriends heard it all.

Cindi had accepted their offer to join them on a vacation and quickly realized she should have asked where they planned to go. She hadn't counted on spending time in a tin-roof shack. The "Helliday Inn," as she referred to it, was on a dusty road. It had no swimming pool, no plumbing, no electricity – just an old mine shaft out back. The two hoods sat at a wobbly table, playing cards while she sulked. In the middle of nowhere, they hadn't even brought booze.

"Don't you boys have any angel dust for your little angel?"

"Sorry, sweetheart," Scratchy said. "This job's too big to screw up. We didn't bring nothin' to entertain us but you." He had taken off his shirt in the heat. The rat-face wore blue jeans and the chauffeur cap that never seemed to leave his head. He lifted it for just an instant to wipe perspiration from his bald scalp. Then, he pulled the cap down over his sweat-slick dome and checked their hostage.

Cindi couldn't figure their plan. They wouldn't tell her, but it had to be something big, all right. She recognized the man they were holding from pictures in local newspapers. Casino presidents often hit society pages. She wondered if they had kidnaped The Fantasy president for ransom money. Tommy Brucker had a reputation for caring for his employees and would probably pay a fortune to get the guy back.

"Come on over here, honey," Sludge called while patting his chunky knees.

As Cindi's eyes sponged his mammoth form, her lips curled down. She swallowed hard and plopped atop a cushiony lap. A student of the anatomy, Cindi surveyed his furry hands and arms. He removed his sleeveless undershirt. "Italian tuxedos," she called them. His chest hair was long enough to part. Quickly, his fleshy frame looked like a road map, baring the markings of her trademark felt-tip pen. Unhappily, she was back at work on a gorilla.

"How much longer do we gotta hang out here?" she whined.

The two hoods exchanged furtive glances. Cindi didn't like the look of them.

Sludge broke the silence, "You and me can drive into town together later, baby. I gotta make a call to check our orders."

She remembered the western "town" where they had stopped for bottled water and basic provisions miles back on a lonely road. A small building there housed a combo diner, grocery store, and post office. A single gas pump rusted in front. The place was virtually a ghost town, but Cindi knew she was with the real ghouls. The mob soldiers whom she'd sallied up to were crude and tough. Death's glimmer shone in their eyes. She wondered if they would kill the casino honcho. Cindi pondered over something else, too. If they whacked him, would they have to whack her?

They had pulled a fast one on her. She couldn't afford to be less than accommodating to their carnal urges for fear she would be left there, dead or alive, in the middle of the desert, one-hundred miles from Vegas. If she could get to a phone, though, maybe she could make something out of the mess. She knew a woman who ran a topnotch Atlantic City escort service. Prell was friendly with Tommy Brucker and she would be grateful to get information Cindi could deliver. As a reward, maybe Prell would put her on the payroll. Service work beat turning tricks from the street. Cindi Rella had a chance to find her glass slipper and she intended to grab it.

"Can't you just make telephone calls from the limo phone?"

She asked for her own benefit. Cindi hoped to sneak into the limousine and place a call to the Atlantic City's madame.

"Nah. Not here, sweetheart," the furry creature beside her replied. "We're too far from any roam zones. Out here, cowpokes don't use cellular telephones. They use CB radios. Now, how 'bout twirlin' my hula hoops?"

"All right," she cooed. "Let's tickle what you need scratched." The sooner they finished, the sooner she would find a phone.

Light pressure of her touch evoked giggles from her gorilla. Sludge's belly rolls jiggled as she fished for trouser trout. Cindi looked around the one-room shack and laughed to herself. Those guys sure didn't care about atmosphere. A little wine would've been nice. She nuzzled and worked; he grunted and sighed. Between his rumbles, woeful words escaped her lips.

"Damn, I could use some candlelight."

Far away, a single candle flickered. Crushed-velvet drapes sealed out the light of day. The flame barely illuminated that small room situated on the Atlantic City boardwalk. In smoky mist, where air reeked of old age's stale bouquet, a wrinkled face faintly glimmered. A dark scarf wrapped what was left of the woman's hair. Her teeth were in her pocket.

Letitia DeLuca engaged in the art form her family's women had practiced for generations. Pulling tarot cards from a silk purse, she shuffled them by placing the strange deck facedown on the table in a center spread. Under faint flickers, she swirled pictorial keys to the future. Ritualistically, her left hand collected the deck in a single stack. Then she cut three piles and picked them up left to right. At last they were ready to tell their story.

The first card hit the tabletop. Her lips parted for a gummy grin and Letitia spoke with her customary economy of words.

"*E' piu giovane.*" He's younger, she observed.

The cards painted a portrait for the man seated across the table, concealed from view by darkness. They were telling him what he needed to know. For years, he had come to her before carrying out his deadly business. Even as boss of the Atlantic City crime family, he observed his strange liturgy. No matter whether he believed, he paid homage to the superstitions fostered in the Sicilian hills of his youth. Letitia analyzed the card, but its symbols told her no more. She laid another face-up and studied it in the faint candle glow.

"*Denaro.*" So much money, she saw. Something very big was afoot.

"Get on with it, old woman," he bellowed.

He startled her. As always, the giant hid in shadows. Letitia couldn't see him, but she sensed his mood whenever he was near. She could feel his anger stir. Letitia's hands shook. The deck dropped from her grasp, all the cards falling facedown on the table. She reached to collect them and shuffle again, but he clutched her wrists. Her frail and arthritic bones ached as if caught in un-yielding steel clamps. Only his hands glimmered in the dim candlelight as he relentlessly squeezed.

"*Dolore!*" she called out.

"That's right, old woman," he said. "It's going to hurt more if you don't give me an answer fast. Pick from the cards on the table. Tell me what I need to know with the next card drawn."

Tears welled in her eyes. The tarot cards had told her why he had come. He wanted the answer to a single question. Was it time for the young man to die? Letitia surveyed the cards spread about until she spotted the only one to pick.

"That one," she said, her head pointing at what her hands couldn't touch.

Her tormentor released her so she could draw it. Letitia rubbed her wrists to circulate blood. Quickly, she flexed her fingers, then lifted the card to her eyes.

"What do you see, old woman?"

She laid the card on the table faceup. A skeleton in a top hat smiled.

"*Pericolo di morte*," she observed in raspy tones, mortal danger.

"*Bene*," he simply replied.

Relieved that he was satisfied, she took a deep breath and sat back in her chair. Letitia knew what he was thinking. *Omicido*. Murder filled his dark heart. She would have told him more if he hadn't frightened and hurt her. True, mortal danger had manifested. Yet the way in which she had drawn death's portrait made her uncertain. Was it the death of the young man she had seen? Perhaps, but it could have been the death of another. Maybe she'd even seen death for the one whose eyes couldn't tolerate the light of day. As the big man left, Letitia spit into the seat of his chair and picked up the cards. Slowly and deliberately, she shuffled again. The strange deck would let her know the answer and she would keep it to herself.

Cindi studied the magazine rack at the only store in town. Outside, a dust storm kicked. Winds howled. Sand and sage brush blew, peppering the clapboard walls of the building and clouding the moon.

"I'm gonna use the phone," the gorilla said.

That was her chance. The public telephone was near rest rooms in the rear of the store. As he walked toward it, she looked for a private line. She would entice the shopkeeper to let her use it. The place was empty except for the three of them. Sweet-talking the old-timer, who sat in a rocking chair behind a counter for the cash register, would be a snap. Cindi opened buttons that went up the front of her dress and pulled the top apart. Her hands pushed up her breasts as she confidently strolled toward the front doorway. With a wink, she leaned over the countertop to give the storekeeper a good view.

"Hey, cutie," she warbled. "You have a private telephone that a girl can use? I'll be glad to pay for the call."

The old timer raised his head slowly as if he had been dozing. "Nep," he replied. "Ain't no need. Got me a

pay phone by the rest rooms and a CB in the back office."

Damn, she thought.

Her single question opened floodgates to the old timer's mouth. A man who had seen a lot, but no longer
had anyone to tell, let it all out.

"Don't have no one to call round here no more. Not
many folks left in this old town. Nearly all of 'em plum
left when the silver mines ran dry. Once, silver was big
business here. Now, this store's the heart of town.
Graveyard across the street is its soul. Its tombstones
bear the names of miners like Shag Ugly Stevens and
Grubby McRotten. They even buried a couple of horses and snakes in there."

Cindi nodded her way out of the local history lesson
to stroll around the store. She would have to let the
gorilla make his telephone call, then say she was using
the bathroom. She could sneak to the pay phone and
place her call while he waited for her in the front of the
store. Scanning the magazine rack, Cindi grabbed a
couple things to read back at their encampment, then
saw Sludge approach.

"You ready to go, doll?" he called.

"Gotta use the ladies's room. Will you pay for these?
I'll just be a minute."

She didn't even know what she handed him. Cindi
had just picked up as much junk as she could find to
keep him busy. As he sauntered to the cash register, she
hustled toward the rear of the store, rummaging through
her pocketbook along the way. An information operator
in Atlantic City could supply the escort service telephone
number. Then, she would need enough change to dial
Prell. Cindi counted nickels, dimes, and quarters, fe-

verishly praying to the Almighty she had enough and letting him know how she felt when she didn't.

"God's a faggot," she moaned. She hoped the escort service would take a collect call.

Cindi looked back over her shoulder and breathed easier when she saw the gorilla was out of sight. She dropped a quarter into the telephone and waited for a dial tone, but the phone stayed silent. Cindi looked down and saw why – somebody had cut clear through the wire connecting the receiver to the phone.

The CB radio, she thought. *Where's the office?* Maybe she could patch a CB call through to someone who could deliver a message for her. Once, she had diddled a truck driver in the back of his cab. He'd shown her how to work those things. Afterward, Cindi spent an entire night lining up tricks by CB. Truckers are good ol' boys, but they don't carry much money and rarely have time to bathe on the road.

"Think, Cindi," she mumbled. "How do these things work?"

Through the open door to the office, she heard a radio squawk. Cindi entered and saw the radio atop a wooden filing cabinet. She picked up the handset, then cried aloud.

"No, it can't be."

The gorilla had cut the wires to the CB, too. She knew she was in danger. Mind spinning but no ideas churning, Cindi started toward the front of the store, feeling like a death row inmate walking the last mile. She saw the limo through window panes on the rickety door. Wailing winds swirled sand around it. The big man sat inside the car, honking its horn. She had no choice. Cindi had to go with him. The shopkeeper couldn't protect her. She called to the geezer as she drew near the counter.

"Hey, pops! Did my friend pay for the magazines?"

The shopkeeper didn't answer; he was asleep in the rocker with his head down. *Nap time*, she thought with a smile. Cindi opened the door. All at once, wind, sand, and a thought struck her. She slammed the door and turned to the old dude. Maybe she could say something to him, so he could send the local sheriff or whoever the law was in those parts out to their camp.

Cindi popped open the top of her dress again and called louder to rouse him. Then, she noticed. Her fingers fumbled over buttons as she tried redoing them. Cindi's eyes fixed on the old man's throat, slit ear to ear, draining blood that covered his shirt like a red bib. Her pals didn't want witnesses to their sojourn.

A honk from the limo jarred her; the gorilla was heavy-handed on the horn. She couldn't run from him and she couldn't keep him waiting.

"What in hell can I do?" Cindi asked herself.

Were there any options? She would have to pretend she hadn't seen the murder or he could slice her throat open, too.

"Hold onto your pants," she called out to him. "I'm coming."

She took a deep breath and ran to the dust-covered limo fast as she could. Sand blasted her face, nested in hair, and filled both ears. Leg muscles weakening, her knees turned rubbery. Somehow she had to reach the seat before she fainted. Cindi plopped into the front of the car next to the big man. She spit out grit and wiped her eyes. Suddenly, she leaped, pounding her head into the roof.

"What's the problem, doll face?" Sludge said.

His hairy paw had wrapped around her knee and scared the daylights out of her.

"No problem," she lied. "This ghost town just spooks me."

As they drove off, she glanced at the cemetery again. A thought stung like a smack in the puss – she didn't want to die there. Cindi didn't want to lie in that graveyard next to a snake or a horse.

Chapter Four

Gramzie Brown

The open hand of the wiry man walloped her cheek.

"You worthless piece of poop," she screamed. "Hitting a grandmother. . . ."

Her foot sank into his groin. The twisted expression on his face let her know that Chichi's head was spinning. Stars shined in his sky and they were in a windowless basement. She watched a full plate of pasta come back on him.

"Now you did it, puddin' for brains. You threw up on the floor I gotta sleep on."

Chichi's lips curled underneath a trimmed beard and mustache. Jet-black hair was slicked straight back and flipped up in a ducktail. His oily top coverage and whiskers framed bulging brown eyes. They had the twinklies, all right. He groaned and muttered under his breath.

"How am I gonna explain to the boys that a dame kicked my ass? Jeez, I hate hillbillies."

The skinny man circled inside the tiny room holding

a dinner plate in one hand and his groin with the other. Then, leaning against a wall for support and sounding decidedly out of his element, he moaned, "Tennessee sure ain't Atlantic City."

Wearing a black silk shirt, pegged jeans, and ankle-high dress shoes that looked like designer booties, he was an urban pigeon in a field for country crows. The diminutive black woman was glad to see him in pain. He deserved that and more.

"You ain't no grandmother," Chichi proclaimed. "You're the Antichrist."

"Watch your mouth," she blasted back.

His balled fist swung, but she ducked out of its way and hit the floor. He took the dish that he had used to bring her meal and tipped it over her.

"Dinner is served," he said as he left.

Gramzie Brown heard her captor close and lock the door. She fought a powerful urge to cry. Gramzie didn't want them to see her breakdown when they peered through the slot cut into the door. They had confined her in a twelve by twelve-foot furnace room. The basement floor, next to an empty coal bin, was her bed. Dampness chilled her. The concrete floor smelled of vomit, and she had no stomach for the meal she wore. Repeatedly the question raced through her mind. *Why have they taken me*? Gramzie couldn't figure it. She picked herself up and brushed goop from her blouse and skirt; the tough lady wouldn't lose her dignity.

Gramzie wasn't old. Her famous grandson was twenty, but she was just slightly over fifty herself. Child bearing came natural and early to country folk. She wasn't sure of her exact birth date, but she was still looking fine. The name "Gramzie" was one she took with pride and a bit of a grin.

"I sure don't look like no grandmother," she always told herself.

The world agreed. Her waist was trim, her breasts monumental, her bottom full and man-pleasing. Her sweet face had classically beautiful Afro-features and few wrinkles to reveal her age. She felt her own hair was too nappy so she kept it short, always wearing an oversized wig outside the home. She had dozens of them in varied shapes and styles, all big. The four-foot ten-inch countrywoman looked more like a black Dolly Parton than the grandmother of a basketball superstar.

She was born on a Tennessee tenant farm and grew up working in its tobacco fields. Some would call her life hard, but Gramzie saw it as a good and clean Christian one. She was a God-fearing woman who lived for two things: one was rollicking with her choir at the First Black Baptist Church of the Holy Deliverance, Redemption & Salvation; the other was basketball. She had kinfolk all over the country hills, but it was her grandson the world knew. He was the boy she'd raised and the reason everyone called Grace Brown . . . Gramzie.

She laid her head on the pillow they had left and wrapped her body in a thin summer blanket on the concrete floor.

"I'll get them for this," she whispered.

Gramzie was hurting and indignant. She joined her hands together and prayed aloud.

"Please, Lord," she beseeched, "smite the men who've done this to me. Deliver me from this Hell. And, oh yes. The one that just came in here and spoke blasphemy – give that devil cancer, cancer of his swollen testicles, if you would. Praise Jesus. Amen."

She closed her eyes and thought of what had brought her there. It had started nearly twenty years earlier with a bus ticket that had taken her north. For the first time, she had left the rural county where she'd been born. The trip had taken her to Detroit to save her daughter.

"Mrs. Brown, don't you be goin' up there alone," her pastor warned her. On the front steps of their church, as the congregation ambled in for Sunday worship, he thrust his pointer finger toward heaven. Round-faced Reverend Harris waived that poker the same way he shook it while delivering sermons. "You don't know what trouble you'll find. Get some family to travel with you. I'll find help if you need it."

"No time for that now, Reverend. My little girl called last night and cried. Something's wrong. I'm bringing her home if I gotta drag her back on a bus myself."

The pastor was a good man, but too patient for her likes. A demon was riding her little girl's back, and she was leaving right after services to find the child. Grace should have never let the little girl chase that dream on her own, but the child was pigheaded. Once Deserie had decided she was traipsing to Detroit to be a pop singer, nothing could hold her back. She was chasing the dream of many young black girls from rural footholds and inner cities alike.

Deserie wanted to join the recording stars she heard on the radio. She had natural talent. The little girl packed a booming voice. It had risen above the rafters and stood out from the choir Sunday mornings. And Deserie loved to sing. Even as a little girl, she'd stood up at parties and family get-togethers, then lip-synced to songs made famous by girl groups of the sixties. Their sweet and soulful sounds crossed over the color line from the black music to white. They filled a musical void between the times of Elvis and the Beatles. Groups like The Shirelles, The Ronettes, and The Dixie Cups delivered coquettish love songs like "Soldier Boy," "Be My Baby," and "Chapel of Love."

Often little Deserie had belted out their tunes, accompanied by a record player or radio. Afterward, she'd curtsied and passed a hat, collecting money for singing lessons she took two days a week after school. Deserie had decided she was going to be a star like her personal hero, the young woman who had sung as lead for The Ecstasies until she left the three-girl group to sing solo hits. Someday, little Deserie Brown always promised, she would be another Susannah Halloway.

After she had graduated from high school, her Momma couldn't hold her back any longer. Deserie had packed all she could into a single suitcase. She had taken all the money Momma had put aside and peered into her wallet. Deserie had cash for a bus ticket and enough to get started until she found a job to support her dream. Then, the little had girl climbed onto the bus that would take her northward.

"Life is too short to be poor," Deserie had said with a smile. "I'm gonna be a star. Then, I'm coming back here to take care of you, Momma."

The last words the little girl had uttered before the bus departed were expressed with all the brash naivete of youth. They rang in her Momma's heart.

She had settled into the Maynard Projects where Susannah Halloway had grown up herself. By the time Deserie had arrived, however, the projects weren't the same as when Susannah was a young lady with her own visions of stardom. Once, it had been a safe community, a good place for poor blacks who'd often arrived to escape uncertain futures in the South. In Detroit they had obtained steady employment in factories. Back then, they'd found themselves financial security and good lives, but the subsidized-housing project in the late-seventies was a dangerous place. Those, who could leave, fled to the suburbs. In their place came tough black gangs with names like The Slammers and The Hoods. With them rose an ever-escalating wave of violence, crime, and drugs. That was what Deserie had found, but she never told her Momma. She only called with good news, reporting on wonderful friends she was making and of course the big break that was always just around the next corner.

When the calls came less frequently, Grace became concerned. When they almost stopped coming altogether, it was time for action.

"What's really going on up there?" Grace asked herself.

Each night she prayed for the daughter she had raised alone, asking the Lord to look out for her little girl. Her maternal instincts told her something was seriously amiss.

"What can be so wrong that a little girl can't even tell her Momma?"

Grace would find out. She bought a round-trip bus ticket for herself and a prepaid one-way ticket home for Deserie. Nothing would hold her back. Grace headed toward the motor city. The bus rolled through the night, every mile bringing her closer, all her instincts telling her that time was running out.

By daybreak, the bus rolled into a terminal. Grace

pulled a wrinkled scrap of paper from her handbag and checked the address she had scrawled. She adjusted the wig atop her head and looked for a taxicab. She didn't have enough time to take a city bus. Besides, she didn't know their routes. She screamed for a cab with a mighty blast and jumped inside the first to heed her call.

"Where to, honey?"

"Don't you be givin' me that look," she reprimanded an admiring cabbie.

Men were something else. It didn't matter how haggard you might be. If you had a pair of breasts, they just came on to you.

She handed the driver her paper with the address and sat back.

"Whoa, girl. Whatcha goin' there for? That ain't no safe place to be."

That's what Grace had assumed and feared. It wasn't the secure neighborhood her daughter had claimed.

"Get me there fast, and don't you be looking at me in that mirror of yours. Keep your eyes on the road."

The driver chuckled and took off with a jolt, heading toward the projects. She was lucky to have arrived after dawn as many cabbies only drove there in daylight.

The city grew rougher. Graffiti covered walls; storefronts were boarded. Winos hung outside liquor stores that never closed, swigging from bottles still in the bag, while the homeless huddled inside cardboard boxes.

She wondered, *just where does my little girl live?*

The cab pulled into the project and she studied the uniform rows of housing units.

"Sure you want to go in here, ma'am?"

"Just get me to that address."

The man shook his head and drove onward. All the while she thought of her little girl. As they neared, something told her she'd arrived too late.

"This is it, but I wouldn't go in there alone," the cabbie said.

She didn't even hear him. Grace just dropped the rest of the cash she'd brought onto the front seat to cover her fare. Then, she ran toward the broken-down building baring the address she sought. She entered and looked for her daughter's apartment. Thieves had removed light bulbs and entire lighting fixtures from hallways reeking of urine. She stumbled over the body of a man who was sleeping it off in the dark.

"Watch where you're going, bitch," he slurred. The drunk started to rise, but he didn't scare her none. The guy was too out of it to make it to his feet. He just fell back to the floor and began snoring.

She rounded a bend and saw her daughter's door. Stopping before it, words escaped her lips on a worried breath. "Please, sweet Jesus," she prayed, "let me be here in time."

She knocked, but no one answered. "Please, Lord." She knocked again. Still, no one answered. Grace twisted the knob and tried pushing the door open.

"Locked. Damn."

She studied the rotting door frame and wondered. *How hard could it be to break this thing down*? The little woman pulled her big wig down tight over her head. She leveled her shoulder against the door and turned the handle. With all her strength Grace slammed into a door that was no match for her. It swung open fast. She stumbled into the room, falling on her face.

Grace lifted herself up slowly and adjusted to her surroundings. *Deserie, you're living in a dump, child*, she thought. A foul odor filled the room. *The toilet must be backed up*. The living room was in total disarray. Battered furniture was overturned as if there had been a fight. Cigarette ashes were strewn across the floor. *Since when did my Deserie smoke?*

Her eyes continued to scour. There had to be a bedroom somewhere. She saw an open door down a narrow hall. Slowly, she moved toward it, fearful of what she might find.

Grace looked inside and tears cascaded down her face. There, uncovered on the bed, laid her little girl. Deserie's deep-sunken eyes stared listlessly at the ceiling. Her left arm was still tied with a rubber cord. The needle that had found a vein still jutted from her arm. Track marks stretched from one end of the little girl's lower arm to the other. Grace cried the tears of a mother who knew she was watching her daughter die. She fell to her knees beside the girl and brought her hands together. Grace looked up to God.

"No," she cried. "Please don't take this child from me."

Whimpers shook her body. Her chest heaved with each breath.

"She's all I got, Lord. Please don't leave me alone."

Even as she prayed, she knew it was too late. Her little girl already had the stench of death as she drew her final breaths. Without so much as a sigh, Deserie left this world. Grace's tears stained her daughter's face as she took her lips close. Tenderly, she planted a final kiss.

"Alone now," she moaned. "God's taken my sweet

child and left me alone."

Grace stayed on her knees with hands clasped, praying for God to accept her child into heaven. She prayed aloud, faster and with greater volume, until her whole frame shook. Shivering and perspiring at the same time, Grace suddenly stopped. She thought she heard something. Someone else was crying. The sound came from the floor on the other side of the bed.

Slowly Grace rose. She lowered her hand over Deserie's eyelids to shut them. Ever so cautiously, she rounded the bed and looked to the floor. There, she saw it wrapped in a dirty blanket, squalling. The baby was skinny, hungry, and clamoring for attention. It seemed to see her and bawled even more forcefully. Grace had never heard anything like that baby's cries. You could hear those wails across the room and probably around the world.

She gently lifted the infant into her arms. The baby was foul. She tickled its nose, brown like a little berry, then stuck her finger in its tiny mouth to suck.

"Just how long have you been laying here?"

Instantly the child grew calm. It looked up with loving eyes and she knew what she would do. She'd raise the baby as her own. She rocked the infant in her arms and softly sang to it.

"I'll never let you stray from home," she promised. "I'm your Grandma."

She tweaked the child's cheeks and watched it beam with joy.

"That's right. I'm your Gramzie." She pulled apart the dirty blanket and studied the naked child. "A little boy, that's what you are, a beautiful little boy."

She looked at the child's feet, so huge already.

"I don't know who your daddy is, but I got a feeling that you're going to be a big boy someday. Whooie," she exclaimed. "Look at the size of these things! These feet are gonna make you big and move you fast, little man."

The ball moved down the court too fast for the defense. The big center leaped from the hardwood floor sky-high into the air. Gracefully he spun around, as if in slow motion, stuffing the hoop so hard that the backboard yelped in pain. No high-school player in Tennessee could slam-dunk like "Stuff Daddy" Brown. Already, they called him that. At 7'3" he was as big as any big daddy, and he could stuff slam-dunks oh so sweetly. The boy was a natural.

Gramzie Brown, as everyone came to know her, watched all his games. She was his biggest fan, sitting courtside-center through a high school career that had been unparalleled. College coaches had called upon their home since his freshman year. The University of Tennessee Volunteers wanted him badly. Coaches from the big basketball schools in nearby North Carolina courted him like eager suitors. They offered full scholarships with all the perquisites. All he had to do was play the game that came so naturally to him. He would be the biggest star the college game had ever seen.

Dion "Stuff Daddy" Brown couldn't decide which way to go. With so many hands extended and so many mouths promising to make all his dreams come true, he had decided to make no decision at all. He'd just play the game he loved and leave the decision to the person he trusted most. Gramzie would make the call.

She watched her grandson steal the ball from a boy who stood bewildered on the court. The kid was still wondering what had happened to the ball as her grandson stuffed it through the hoop again. Dion would easily score fifty points with a bevy of scouts in the stands. All of them drooled at the prospect of having the soft spoken, respectful, and overwhelmingly talented young man play for their team in the coming year. They represented every major college, but Gramzie had already decided. Her boy wasn't going anywhere. She wouldn't lose another child. She'd found a way to keep him close to home. It was a gamble, but the boy had the talent and the strength of will to pull it off. She had raised him to be God fearing. He was a good boy and if she kept him close to home, he'd be all right.

The coach of a professional expansion team had convinced her it was the thing to do. Dion was skipping college to join a new professional franchise. They would play all their home games just 56 miles from home. He'd play for big bucks. Even coming out of high school directly to the pros, he'd be a top draft choice the Tennessee expansion team would eagerly swoop up. Not only was Stuff Daddy a local boy who'd draw fans, he was the most promising player basketball aficionados had seen in years. Dion had the size, strength, and skill to be a "franchise player" like Michael Jordan or Shaquel O'Neill. Who knew how far the kid could take a team?

Gramzie looked at all the offers her grandson received from colleges and other professional teams. They were all good, but that one stood above the rest. Besides the money that would instantly make her grandson a multi-millionaire, the contract contained the killer clause. It gave her the one thing no other offer matched. Just a country drive from home, she'd have courtside-center seats for every home game the Nashville Wildcats would ever play. She'd watch over her grandson. The child would stay safe and never move away.

"Wake up, Granny," the skinny man called through the slot that he and his hoodlum pal had made in the door.

"I ain't asleep." Gramzie remained sprawled on the concrete floor.

"Thought you might like some news."

"Don't want no news from you."

"We just spoke to your grandson."

Gramzie jolted upright.

"He's in Atlantic City for a casino opening. We let him know you're here at our little party. We also let him know what he'd have to do if he ever wants to see you again."

"What are you talking about?"

"Oh, he's gonna work for us to get you back, granny."

"What do you want from my boy?"

Chichi laughed.

"When the time's right, you'll find out."

The man walked away.

Gramzie knew that Dion had gone to Atlantic City for some kind of affair. He went with a couple of players on his team so it seemed safe. They had time off between playoff rounds. She kept wondering though.

What do these hoods want from my grandson?

Gramzie lowered her head back to the pillow. She was worried and mad at the same time. Somehow she would get even with those devils. She wanted to plan an escape, but was too tired. Gramzie had been too hungry not to eat the food that they had dumped on her. Afterward, she realized they must have put something in it to make her drowsy.

"So tired," were words that fell from heavy lips.

Without strength to resist, nighttime beckoned Gramzie to sleep.

Chapter Five

Dream Girl

In the middle of the night Tommy woke with a start. *It's been a bad dream*, he thought until he looked round the bedroom of his casino suite. A bottle of pills that had sedated him was on a mahogany night table. His head throbbed. He pulled back satin sheets and reached to touch his scalp. Instead he felt the six-inch long gauze bandage covering a wound that had closed without sutures.

"You're all right, now," a silky voice cooed.

That speaking voice came smooth as the songs she sang; he was waking to a dream girl. Tommy tried to focus across the expansive room. At the far side, she came into view, reclining on a cushiony loveseat, lit only by moonlight, which streamed through bay view windows, into his private living quarters. Even in the glimmer of night, Susannah's beauty shone.

"You look like last week's leftovers," she said.

He chuckled and realized she must be right. Tommy

sat upright in bed and felt an ache in his hips. The steel bar that had locked him in his coaster seat upside-down had pinched tightly until they had finally routed the car forward to remove the injured. They had pulled him out, blood covered – but mostly from dancers who'd been more seriously hurt. Tommy looked down at himself.

"You're all there," Susannah assured him. "Something grazed your head, but you're alive, honey."

"Come over here."

Susannah approached. She sat on the bed beside him and brought her lips to his for a gentle kiss.

"Go to sleep," she said, stroking his hair back from his eyes.

Her touch was warm and familiar. Tommy looked into her eyes. They were naturally wide, but something dimmed their radiance. He had hoped he wouldn't have seen the signs. She still popped pills.

"The doctor said you'd better rest through the night."

Tommy wanted to drift back to sleep, knowing he would be on the casino floor no matter how he felt in the morning. Too much was at stake for bed rest.

"Darnel," he whispered.

"They've called for him," Susannah said without mentioning that her son still hadn't been found. "There's nothing to worry about. Sleep, now."

Before he'd allowed himself to be sedated, Tommy had put his staff in action. He was counting on Darnel's assistance with the tragedy, but knew he would still have to muster all his own strength. The next three days would be critical. He would meet grief-stricken family members of the dancer who had died and see to their needs. He would also visit the women who'd been injured. Then, he would deal with the press and resume his role as host of the biggest party ever planned on a casino floor. He had no choice. The affair was too big to cancel. They had to continue with some measure of respect paid to the woman whose life had ended so abruptly.

How the hell could that have happened? he wondered. Engineers, who had designed the coaster, were being flown into town. They would examine the thrill ride to find answers. Tommy couldn't allow anything else to go wrong. What had looked like a sure thing was turning into a craps shoot.

He turned to Susannah and thought about what might have been. She had twice divorced and run through a series of brief relationships. His only marriage had long ago ended in acrimony that scarred him. That was the one gamble he would never again risk. Tommy remained married to his work; love wouldn't burn him. Once, though, fiery romance he and Susannah had shared almost crushed both their meteoric careers. Timing just hadn't been right, but embers of their once forbidden love would always kindle in his heart.

Susannah returned to the small sofa across from his bed. Her long legs crossed and Tommy savored the view. *This woman could bring a man back to life from the dead*, he thought.

She remained lovely as the day they had met in Las Vegas twenty-five years earlier. Beauty could never mask her pain from him, though. It showed in her eyes. Pills she popped like candy glazed them. Concerned to see her that way but still under the influence of his own medication, Tommy closed his eyes and drifted.

Susannah watched him rest. Although she never liked sharing the limelight, she would help Tommy by taking the casino's stage with other performers for the kickoff bash. Susannah remembered the early days of her career when she had no choice. Lord, that had been so long ago. Memories flared as if she were reliving them. Her pills kicked in hard, sending her to that magic place where daydreams came in Technicolor with Dolby surround sound.

In the Summer of 1962, no one outside the motor city had heard of The Ecstasies. Three high school girls made up the act with Susannah singing lead. They boarded a bus chartered by their recording company. The black-owned and run enterprise took several acts on tour through the South. That was Susannah's first foray before live audiences. It was also the first time she had been to the deep South that hadn't been integrated. The famed marches led by Reverend Martin Luther King had yet to generate the Civil Rights Act of 1964 that would end segregation. In Detroit Susannah attended a racially mixed public school. In the South she learned that signs for "colored bathrooms" and "white only restaurants" were meant for her.

Susannah remembered peering from backstage before her first performance on the road trip. A rope ran down the center isle, separating Negroes on one side from Whites on the other. She turned to the president of her recording label who stood by her side.

Mr. Benson was a worldly-wise black entrepreneur who had risen far above his humble southern roots. By maintaining a sharp eye for talent and a keen ear for popular sounds, he had collected a stable of rhythm and blues acts. Part talent manager, part father-figure to youngsters on his label, but foremost a shrewd businessman, Mr. Benson groomed his artists into recording giants. His musical family created an identifiable sound that gripped national attention. Susannah turned to him and whispered what was on her mind.

"They're divided down the middle, Mr. Benson. Are all the theaters in the south going to be this way?"

"Alabama isn't Detroit, sweetheart."

His quiet but somber tone let her know he spoke from long experience he didn't want to share.

"Just stand in the middle of the stage," he counseled, "right where the rope is. Your backup girls will be centered behind you."

Susannah heard her cue and felt Mr. Benson's gentle shove push her onstage.

The MC's bark filled the theater. "Give it up for a dynamite act from the Soul City, Susannah Halloway and The Ecstasies."

Mr. Benson's voice called from behind her. "Remember, don't sing to either side more than the other."

Susannah spotted the chalk mark fixing stage center. Planting her feet astride it, she realized how easily members of both races could be offended when they were separated and pitted against each other. Susannah closed her eyes to the ugly specter of racism and lighted the crowd with her group's first gold-record hit.

Back then, no one knew what to make of the three-girl act. They were black, yet they sang songs both black and white folks liked. Moreover, Susannah's voice always puzzled them. People continually asked the same question.

"Is that girl singing through her nose?"

By the time she'd graduated from high school, her voice had matured. It maintained the nasal quality that was her trademark, but Susannah's sound had grown smooth and sultry. The group turned out one chart topper after another. Before long, they were in demand. Ed Sullivan booked them. Dick Clark wanted the group for a tour. The Ecstasies placed three hits on Billboard's pop chart at the same time. They weren't hot; they were on fire. Still, Susannah's happiness wasn't bliss. She loved to perform but from the start didn't like sharing the spotlight. Inevitably, the group would disband.

"Susannah doesn't have a group mentality," her sister Ecstasies complained.

"That's right," she replied with a smile.

Susannah was on her own and on her way. She took her solo act to the road and when she pulled into The Oasis Casino in Las Vegas, she met the man she had to have. She spotted him across the crowded casino floor. Amid slot machines clinking and ringing, players hooting at the game tables, and a thousand voices babbling, Susannah hollered to a cocktail waitress. At first the woman didn't hear, so Susannah grabbed her arm and yelled in her ear.

"Who's the handsome guy with the million-dollar smile?"

The woman didn't turn to look. She was too busy. All the women who slung drinks were. They had aching backs and sore feet from working in high heels for eight hour shifts. Their arms ached from holding drink trays high. She didn't even need to glance, though. Only one man fit that description. Cocktail servers knew everything about the guys on the floor. They measured men by two things, the size of their wallets and the size of their dicks. The guy measured up in both departments, though certainly more so in the latter category at that stage of his career. On top of it all, he had the handsome looks and million-dollar smile.

"Tommy Brucker, Miss Halloway."

I'm going to get that man, Susannah promised herself.

Businessmen in bland jackets and ties surrounded Tommy, beckoning for his attention. Suddenly something distracted him. She realized he must have seen her and was walking in her direction. Her heart quickened. Susannah turned her head and moistened her lips with the tip of her tongue. When she turned back, he stood beside her. She wilted as he took for her hand, lifted it to his lips, and kissed it. At that instant Susannah Halloway discovered the man she was ready to love for the rest of her life. She wasn't sure where the moment would take her but sensed she'd get there fast. Susannah opened her heart and let the suave stranger enter.

Susannah woke from her daydream. *Love walks in so smooth when it doesn't stand a chance*, she reminded herself. Yet, times were different and so was she. Susannah had a plan. After the show, she would dine with Tommy in her suite, just the twosome. That was the sole price she would charge him for her stage appearance. She planned to tell him something long overdue. Susannah wanted love, his love. She needed it more than ever, more than fame, more than wealth, even more than a handful of pills.

Her eyelids grew heavy. She slipped into a trance that grew troubled. The pills took her temperature down. Susannah shivered. That was the price she paid to make it through the day.

Tommy rose to spread a blanket over Susannah's frame. He looked at her, cuddled and shaking on the sofa. What had happened to the woman he had met so long ago? Why did she do that to herself after attaining success? She'd once had more strength. He remembered the vitality that had shone in her face the day they met.

He had traveled across the casino floor to introduce himself to the pop singer, then held her hand after he'd lifted it to his lips. Tommy was making a name for himself as a floor person who knew everyone. He greeted performers and casino guests with the charm that was fast becoming his trademark. People liked Tommy because they could tell he liked them. Whom he knew made a name for him in the business. He had a good book, a list of high rollers who called for him alone, and they would follow Tommy to another gaming house if he ever left. That wasn't lost on management. His mentor at the Oasis Casino was its president. Grant Taylor was a Mormon who had already pegged Tommy as a possible successor someday. Tommy let Grant know he was anxious to become a vice president. Grant was ready to move the young man up the corporate ladder but didn't want to part with a stock interest the ambitious young man demanded.

In the midst of their negotiations, Tommy met the demur songstress when she entered the casino for her first solo appearance. As they spoke, it never occurred to him to let go of her hand. They stood on the floor and talked. It wasn't until her bodyguard interjected that he realized how much time they had spent standing there.

"Miss Halloway," the big man said, "shouldn't you go upstairs. You'll want to rest before your show."

Susannah didn't seem to hear. The budding of love is a powerful magnet and her attention was singularly drawn. She looked into Tommy's eyes until he lifted her hand to his lips again, parting with the promise to meet after her midnight show.

She sang two sets. After the ten o'clock show, she had a forty minute break. A stage hand had let Tommy know what happened. Having given everything she had to her audience, Susannah came off the stage mopping her brow. She had sung all The Ecstasies' songs with a two-girl backup group and belted a string of solo hits. She returned to her dressing room for a wardrobe change looking like she badly needed to kick off her shoes. Shoulders slumped, she opened the door and a sea of peach roses smacked her in the face. They filled the entire room and overflowed into the hall.

"My Lord," Susannah squealed, "are there really this many peach roses in Las Vegas?"

That was all it took to revitalize her. Backup singers and dancers from her review walked by and laughed. The sight was amazing and everyone recognized the hand-iwork.

A dancer called out, "There's only one man who can find so many roses in the middle of a desert."

Their late evening together was everything either could have imagined. So was their time alone in her suite afterward. Tommy wasn't a man to disappoint a woman.

They spent all their free time intimately, but those

moments were hardly enough. He sensed they were both searching for an excuse to stay together longer as Susannah's singing engagement came to a close. Sitting close in a quiet corner of the top casino gourmet restaurant, an opportunity arose. It was served on a silver platter, like the northern Italian cuisine they savored amid massive Roman pillars that supported a domed ceiling.

"Mr. Wu invites you and Miss Halloway to join him this evening," a tuxedoed waiter said. "After dinner, he has special plans."

"Who's Mr. Wu?" Susannah chimed.

Tommy's answer was almost somber.

"He's wealthy, mysterious, and scary. Some say he's one of the world's major drug traffickers – shipping from Thailand. But, when he comes here, he's just a Hong Kong businessman who's solid gold to the casino."

"Tell him we're busy tonight."

Tommy let out a breath that whistled. "Tell that to a thousand-dollar-a-hand man? In Vegas, Mr. Wu gets treated better than the pope."

Susannah looked uncertain until Tommy explained.

"His holiness doesn't play for a thousand dollars a hand."

Tommy turned from Susannah's eager face and looked across the room to the diminutive Chinese man. He sat next to a Marilyn Monroe look-alike twice his size. The aloof Mr. Wu seemed comically out of place with the boisterous woman, who towered above him, waving her hand at a waiter and calling for second helpings.

"What's he have planned?" Tommy asked the waiter.

"Wedding bells," the man replied. "He's going to marry the blond and take her back to Hong Kong with him. He'd like you and Miss Halloway to act as witnesses."

Susannah burst out laughing. Tommy just flashed his smile and lifted his champagne glass to toast the couple.

"Tell Mr. Wu we're delighted."

Tommy had a telephone brought to their table. He made some calls and wedding bells rang.

They stood in line at the "Twenty-Four Hour a Day Chapel of Love." Elvis Presley was getting married ahead of the Wu party. At least that's how it seemed. In a town full of Elvis impersonators, a man adorned in a glittery-white outfit with full cape and white boots stood ahead of them saying, "I do."

"You may kiss the bride," a bearded chaplain informed the eager couple.

The groom responded with an earnest rendition of "Love Me Tender" in tribute to his bride and his rock 'n' roll king.

Vegas had a slew of marriage factories providing prompt and complete service. The chaplain approached, his hand extending for cash, his voice bellowing above the offkey wedding march cranked out on a dying eight-track tape deck.

"It'll be one-hundred forty-nine dollars and ninety-nine cents, Mr. Brucker. That includes a wedding photo, floral bouquet, and ring. I assume the casino is comping the loving couple."

Tommy took the ring and removed its cellophane

wrapper. With a grin he placed the cheesy glass gem on Susannah's finger and told her, "The groom already picked up a bauble for his bride."

A seven-karat canary-diamond number emerged from deep in Mr. Wu's coat pocket that sent his bride into a tizzy.

"Oh, Mr. Wuuuuuuuuuu," she exclaimed.

Tommy and Susannah laughed as they envisioned a wedding night where the big blond would passionately call her new husband "Mr. Wu" in the marital bed. The groom beamed and focused attention on his bride. A head taller than him, the buxom beauty gave him a face full of mountain view.

After the three-minute ceremony, the Wus departed for their honeymoon. Tommy and Susannah joined them in their limo to see the newlyweds off at the airport. A sharp curve sent Susannah reeling into Tommy. She tightly grabbed his arm as the bride across from them hugged the groom she dwarfed.

"We're honeymooning in my Hawaiian cottage before flying back to Hong Kong," Mr. Wu said. "We'll only be there a few days. Perhaps you might like to use it after we leave. It's humble, but from Diamond Head you have a lovely view of Waikiki."

Tommy knew the man was being exceedingly modest. Diamond Head was prime realty. Whatever the "Hong Kong businessman" did for a living, it provided the means for an extravagant lifestyle. Something about Mr. Wu didn't seem right. Though soft spoken, his voice had an edge. Tommy could tell the man never had to raise it to accomplish his ends. He was likely part of the increasingly prevalent Hong Kong criminal element lured to Las Vegas by gaming action. For some reason,

the man chilled Tommy. He tried to think of a polite
way to decline the offer.

"We'd love to go," Susannah exclaimed.

Tommy knew he had no choice. Susannah was already planning what to wear with the bride who hadn't
had time even to pack a bag.

"Whatever you need or desire shall be yours, my
lamb," the groom cooed. "We'll buy it there."

"Oh, Mr. Wuuuuuuuuuu!"

At the airport they said their goodbyes and watched
Mr. and Mrs. Wu stroll toward a plane. The blond leaned
over and rested her head atop her husband's. His arm
wrapped her waist, then lowered to a globose derriere.

What's this young woman walking into? Tommy won-
dered. He pondered the same thing about himself and
Susannah. He just didn't like the idea of being in Mr.
Wu's debt. Concerned words escaped his lips.

"Strings are always attached to this kind of invitation."

Excitement lit Susannah's face, though. *Innocent
eyes never see danger*, he realized.

"You heard him," she said assuredly. "It's only a
humble cottage."

Tommy and Susannah reclined on lounge chairs beneath Diamond Head, the extinct volcanic crater rising
majestically behind them, ocean surf churning in front
of them. Beside them, pool waters rippled from a breeze
that stroked palm branches and tropical flora indigenous
astride the tropic of Cancer. Mesmerizing as a Hawaiian
rainbow, dazzling floral petals encircled them – pink and
purple orchids, showy hibiscus in pastels encompass-

ing long golden stamens, red bougainvillea sprouting from vines, fragrant white gardenias clustering on shrubs, and scarlet poinsettias blooming among red and white lined leaves.

A macaw, whose clipped wings confined him, uncaged, to a golden perch, was their constant poolside companion. The large bird poked its hooked bill through red saber-shaped tail plumage. He scratched himself, then screeched his familiar call.

Mr. Wu staffed his sprawling estate with a maid, houseman, and grounds keeper. So far as Tommy could tell, none of the Chinese servants spoke English. Somehow, they disappeared into the lush background, yet were always there to serve. For he and Susannah, though, needs – but for each other – were few.

They spent days strolling Mr. Wu's private beach and relaxing poolside. Nighttime brought rapture in each others arms.

Whispering in his ear over the sound of pounding surf, she let him know, "Heaven can visit earth."

Tommy peered into wide eyes that were clearer than the crystalline waters kissing the shore, then felt her breath, so hot, so moist, as if rising deep from within Susannah to offer the promise of love's fulfillment. He shared her sigh, realizing their bliss came not from moon glow over the Pacific, nor from palm branches swaying in a tropical breeze. Enchantment rose from finding each other completely.

"A beloved," he vowed, "is the true center of paradise."

The vow became theirs, sealed as lips joined, arms bound, and two bodies merged into one.

Tommy returned to Las Vegas with the taste of her

kiss lingering. Susannah was cutting an album in Detroit, but they had big plans. Tommy was going to marry the songstress and they would make Las Vegas their home. The only thing holding him back was the elusive promotion he would demand with even stronger resolve. Grant Taylor would either move him up or he'd take his book to another gaming house.

Tommy strode into the casino president's office, then traipsed thirty feet from the door toward Grant's desk. Thick burgundy carpet felt spongy underfoot. The leather chair he sank into was soft, but Tommy was ready for hard talk. Grant's tight-pinched lips and narrowed eyes let Tommy know the older man was equally prepared.

Grant just stared, squaring off as if implacable. Motionless in his high-back chair that spanned out at the top like a throne, his silver hair glistened in sunlight streaming from the large window beside them. A rich tan covered his wrinkle-free face as if his flesh were immune from aging. Somehow it remained unweathered though soaked in ultraviolet rays on golflinks he frequented. Outside the plate glass, stretched the casino strip. If Tommy didn't get what he wanted, he would walk that street until another casino offered the opportunity he knew he deserved.

What he didn't know, however, was that he was about to get hit. Reality was firing a double-barrel blast. At the same moment, in Detroit, Susannah was about to be shot by it, too.

She sat with Gordon Benson, her record label president. The fatherly figure stroked his chin as she settled into a chair across from his desk. The full-bodied black man was beginning to show grey in his sideburns. Susannah expected he would cover it, trying to look youthful in a young man's business. Yet, perhaps, he was above those kinds of worries. His name was synonymous with soul music. And he possessed confidence that came from unparalleled success in the recording industry. She sat back and let him do the talking.

Hundreds of miles apart, Tommy and Susannah were reminded that life is not lived in Elysian Fields.

"You know I have nothing against these people," Grant began.

"What are you talking about?" Tommy said.

"The Scharvtzes. They don't bother me personally."

Tommy had never heard the man use the word. The straight-as-an-arrow Mormon was usually more direct, preferring to call a spade a spade.

"That's a Yiddish term, isn't it, Grant?"

"Yep. It's a Heeb word. Heebs and Niggers, they're all the same to me."

"What are you getting at?"

Grant took a deep breath and paused.

"Well, you see, Tommy, the casino looks out for its own. You're part of our family. We don't want you make any mistakes that might interfere with your advancement. You understand Las Vegas has very provincial attitudes. Hell, we didn't even let Negroes onstage in this town until five or ten years ago. Even a couple of years ago, we wouldn't let Negro entertainers use the swimming pools. We were afraid white players wouldn't go in after Negroes took a dip."

Tommy knew it was true. Frank Sinatra had been big enough to see that his buddy, Sammy Davis, was the first black entertainer ever permitted to take a room in a white casino hotel. There, Sammy had a steamy relationship with Kim Novak. The story was that mobsters had a stake in the white starlet's career. When Sammy announced his engagement to the actress, hoods kidnaped him. They took him to the middle of the desert where they told him that he'd either break the engagement or they'd blow his brains out. Two days later Sammy married a black cigarette girl who worked in the casino where he was staying.

Tommy knew all the stories. He also knew where Grant was taking their conversation. He didn't like it.

"Susannah, you've got a string of hits and a career that will make you one of the entertainment industry's biggest stars."

She listened intently to Mr. Benson. He was more than just the president of her record label. He had taken her under his wing as an eager high school girl and molded her into the star she'd become. The genial black man had often provided wise counsel and had never let her down.

"Your records sell in both markets, honey, R & B and pop. Black folks and white folks are buying. They buy because they like your songs and they like you. We've designed an image for you, just like we have an image for every artist on this label. It's a clean image.

We don't want your star tarnished."

"What do you mean, Mr. Benson?"

"I want you to rethink your relationship with this white boy in Vegas. Look at these things."

He handed Susannah a pile of tabloids.

"We can't keep your names out of these papers any longer. All the rag sheets picked up the story."

"So."

"Honey, don't kid yourself. Look in the mirror. You're a star but you're not white. No one's ready for you to zip around with an ivory Galahad. Not only are you hurting your career, you're hurting everyone here. All our acts have worked hard to keep this label clean. We've never had a scandal and don't want this to be the first."

"I'm not giving up Tommy Brucker."

"Susannah, think. What choice do you have? You're destroying him, too. What do you think his chances are going to be out in Vegas with you on his arm?"

A tear streaked Susannah's face.

"I'm just asking you to slow this thing down, honey. Times are changing. You're just moving faster than of the rest of the world, right now."

"I can't give him up," Susannah choked out. "I'm pregnant."

"Is it too late for an abortion?"

She nodded.

"Oh, good God."

"Tommy, here's your contract."

Grant slid papers across his desk. Tommy studied them. Grant's signature boldly graced the dotted line.

The deal gave Tommy everything he wanted – bigger salary, new title, stock options, and bonus bucks. All the contract needed was Tommy to ink it, but he knew there would be a catch. They'd ask him to give up the woman he loved. Tommy spoke with more confidence than he felt.

"I'm not giving up Susannah Halloway for a contract. You know I keep one of the hottest player books in town."

"Indubitably," Grant replied. "High rollers follow you."

"I can ink this deal with a half-dozen game houses on the strip."

"You probably can – if you don't carry Aunt Jemima in the door with you."

Tommy had heard enough. He rose from his chair. He had never been comfortable with that kind of bigotry. Maybe it was time to leave the place.

"Sit a minute," Grant beckoned. "Let me say one last thing to you."

"Honey, I'm not surprised. You're already beginning to show. That's why I called you in. Someone's outside my door who wants to talk to you. Jake Tanner wants to marry you. He'll raise that baby as his own."

"Jake Tanner! That man beat the daylights out of me when I dated him. No way I'm going back with him."

"Jake's moving up. He's not just a record promoter anymore. I've made him the number two man in the company. The two of you will make a good couple. Most important, he'll be able to raise that baby for you."

Susannah instantly read between the lines.

"You've promoted him to marry me. We'll be a good couple because we're the same color. And he can raise my child because the baby will be black."

Susannah knew black bigotry was no less unsavory than white.

"There's something else you should know, Tommy. While your lady's been recording her new album, she hasn't been sitting home."

Tommy fired back, "What the hell are you talking about?"

"Word is . . . she's having an affair with a record promoter back in Detroit. Ask her. She's carrying the guy's baby."

Tommy picked himself up.

"Take this with you," Grant said, sliding the contract across his desk.

Tommy hesitated before grabbing it and rushing to his own office. He called Susannah through the day until he finally reached her. When they spoke, her voice was soft and muffled. It sounded as if she had been drinking, but that wasn't like her.

"No," she said. "I just took something for my nerves." The phone was silent, then she told him. "My life's in Detroit. You've been busy in Vegas and he's been close. One thing led to another and, well, we're getting married."

Tommy didn't say anything. He just held the telephone to his ear.

"I'm going to have his baby, Tommy."

He hung up the phone without saying another word. The contract waited on the desk in front of him. Tommy picked it up. Without another thought, he signed the pact that would someday make him a wealthy man. On her wedding day, he sent a single peach rose.

Tommy watched Susannah turn under her blanket. Her shivering subsided. Then, he walked back to his bed and collapsed on the mattress. His head sank deep into a pillow. He would rise early in the morning but wouldn't catch the dawn the way another man would.

Somewhere nearby, a man who worked in the shadows was busy even as Tommy's eyes shut. That man would have the advantage of time over those who rested in the night. He'd also have the advantage of surprise. Tommy wouldn't see him coming.

Chapter Six

Boss of the Boardwalk

Joey faced dawn on the boardwalk. Quick stepping along, his ears rang from waves that crashed on the beach. His nostrils filled with salt air carried to shore on gusty breezes.

"Another sunrise," he mumbled, as if it were a curse.

Teko covered his back. The underboss was a loyal shadow carrying .38 caliber protection. Of average facial features, height, and build, he blended into every background, like a chameleon with artillery to flash at any threat. Joey watched the smaller man scurry to keep pace with his larger steps. Then the sun emerged far east where the sea and sky met, exploding like a torturous fireball over the horizon. Joey needed shelter fast. Even the dark eyeglasses he wore didn't spare him from daylight's agonizing glare. The big man held both hands over eyes that couldn't adjust.

He hadn't always been that way. Rivals had blinded him with battery acid in the rear of a gas station. Sur-

gery at Wills Eye Hospital in Philadelphia had partially
restored his vision. The procedure had allowed him to
break his walking cane. And he had shattered it over the
head of a man who'd held him. Each of his attackers
had died with his mark. They'd been found with eyes
roughly gouged from their skulls. Many more were about
to die but not for revenge. Business was at hand and he
dealt in death.

"Teko," he called over is shoulder. "Time for a familiar visit."

"You still see that dame after all these years, boss."

Joey barely nodded his accord. Like a baseball player, who claims not to be superstitious while reaching for
his lucky bat, he traipsed to the old woman again. She
was both a habit and an indulgence. Joey always met
Letitia DeLuca before he killed. Some things never
change, he realized, while others can't stay the same.
The boardwalk he had walked all his life was a place his
sore eyes had seen transform.

"Once, my friend," he called to Teko, "I walked these
boards past grand hotels." Joey glanced with disdain at
the casinos that had replaced them. "Now," he exclaimed
in a drawl filled with resignation, "legit casinos suck
money from suckers faster than vacuuming their wallets."

He turned as if looking for times long gone to reap-
pear. Carny barkers no longer called from side shows.
Diving horses, midget boxers, and bearded ladies appeared only in his daydreams and memories. He laughed,
knowing he was one of the few freaks left – he and the
old woman he was about to meet.

Joey "Boner" Bonivicolla had taken over the Atlantic
City crime family upon the passing of Tony DeBona, a

tough geezer who'd called himself the "Boss of the Boardwalk." Joey had fought to control the resort crime family with assistance from the larger Philadelphia mob. The
five New York families waited on the sidelines. None of
them could allow the others to control the seaside town,
so they simply watched the usual drama unfold.

The power struggle hadn't been bloodless, yet spotting the winner in that kind of fracas was always easy.
He was the one who survived. Joey took the dead don's
moniker as the new boss of the boards. It became a
sign of disrespect for anyone to call him by his former
nickname. And few were foolish enough to taunt him.

He strained to peek at the ocean. A lone seagull dove
into the waves, then reappeared, squawking proudly with
a fish flapping in its beak. The boardwalk boss smiled
at so auspicious an omen. *This thing will go my way*, he
thought, as he entered the card reader's shop alone. His
trusted man waited on the boards, protecting his back.

Inside the darkened parlor Joey's vision gradually focused and the aches that came like ice picks to his eye
sockets subsided.

"*Si avvicini, per favore*," the old woman welcomed
him.

The man, who suffered the impairment of one sense,
drew more strongly upon others. Joey realized his keen
ears had grown accustomed to the terse dialect of the
province where she'd been born, yet his nose had never
acclimated to her garlic-laden breath. He joined her at a
card table and watched the tarot deck shuffle in her
hands. Then the first card struck the tabletop.

"Bones," he said.

A skeleton in a top hat smiled bizarrely on the card's
surface – the death card. She dealt another. Death

grinned again. In one day's time, he would deliver those death cards to the grand opening of Brucker's casino.

Her lips parted. *"Pericolo di morte,"* she observed in raspy tones.

"Si," he said. He too saw mortal danger in the cards. The mob boss picked up her telephone and dialed. When a man answered, Joey simply said, *"Fa catuda."*

A voice at the other end of the line repeated the instruction to confirm the go-ahead, *"Fa catuda,"* it's falling. His *capos* would move their crews.

So simple was the order; so tremendous would be the carnage when The Megasino tumbled. Officials examining the disaster afterward would never know what happened. The catastrophe would give his family the one thing that had eluded them. For the first time, organized crime would gain foothold in a legitimate casino at the seashore resort. The boardwalk boss would take the Buckman's empire apart in Atlantic City and Las Vegas. Then, he would hand it over to a man who was willing to pay the price to topple Tommy Brucker's dream. Greg Conrad would open the doors of Brucker's casinos to the crime family that had asked for only a small piece of what it would deliver him.

Everyone knew Tommy Brucker was leveraged tight. A calamity in Atlantic City would also jeopardize his Las Vegas operation. The Megasino and The Fantasy would become ripe for takeover bids placed by Conrad with financing Joey's family arranged. Three forces would then control the casinos. Greg Conrad would be the front man while Joey's family and the financiers stood silently in the wings.

Conrad didn't realize his new partners weren't compliant as the women he had the reputation of abusing.

In time, he would learn the bedmates he had chosen in the venture had lethal agendas all their own. They would keep Conrad as their front man, but taking over the Buckman's casinos was only part of their game. They wanted Conrad's Pyramid Casino on the boardwalk, too, and they were prepared to take it with the spilling of blood.

Joey gambled for his own huge stakes. Success would bring him and his crime family billions. Failure would be absolute. He was about to unleash mob violence on an unprecedented scale. The stronger families in Philly and New York wouldn't want him around if his scheme fell apart. They couldn't allow any man to live who failed after committing mass murder in the mob's name. They would whack him to avoid investigations and prosecutions that might unmask or interfere with their own ventures. Big stakes indeed, but the odds were stacked in his favor. Tommy Brucker would never suspect a thing until it was too late.

Letitia dealt another card. Death smiled again. "*Fiume di sangue*," she said.

"*Si*," he agreed, "soon a river of blood will flow."

Chapter Seven

Star Filled Nights and Days

Tommy surveyed the huge crowd and quick-paced action on the casino floor. It told him The Megasino would recover from its single mishap. His head still throbbed, but he had removed the bandage. Fortunately, the gash didn't show under his hair line. Flashing his familiar smile, Tommy extended his hand to everyone. Comfortable with a Wall Street millionaire or the bar porter who lugged glassware, Tommy treated his players like royalty and his employees like family. That was the Buckman's inimitable touch. He turned to Manny and spoke with confidence restored.

"If you want to make money in the casino business, own one. If you want to make more money, own two."

"True," Manny said less forcefully, "so long as our daily sheets keep showing that million-dollar drop."

Tommy kept his eyes on the surrounding action.

"You're right," he had to admit, "but God help me, I love to gamble high."

Suddenly, a disturbance erupted on the casino floor, people hustling, pressing toward the casino entrance-way to the main doors.

"Not again," Tommy said. His eyes peered over the crowd.

"Are you sure that's who it is?" a woman shouted.

The woman's equally enthralled companion yelled back, "It *is* Courtney!"

"Courtney Wymann?" Tommy said. Superstars arriving for the evening gala were setting off the commotion. Fast as he worried, relief swept over him, relief quickly replaced by another concern. "Get her off the floor."

Manny looked perplexed.

"She's only nineteen," Tommy explained. "Usher her out before casino control people pick her up for being underage."

"Wait a minute. I don't listen to much pop music, but I've seen her pictures. She can't be nineteen."

"Manny, you haven't listened to pop music since it asked: 'Who put the sham in the sham-a-lama ding dong?' She's a knockout, but she throws punches that are two years underage for these play tables."

Manny moved toward the demure young woman, whose flowing blond hair and curvy form evoked sensuality, while she maintained a reputation for strict virtue. The kid could also belt out a tune. Tommy was looking forward to hearing her at a performance showcasing three generations of talent. Susannah Halloway represented the golden era of pop from the 1960s and 70s. She still packed concert halls on rare occasions she booked a date. Courtney Wymann was the top pop diva of a new generation, while EnCor, an early-nineties hip hop group, rounded out the show. Three female vocal acts would light up the stage. A magician would even excite younger tastes with some quick illusions. And during the star filled nights and days, showbiz and sports personalties would continually filter through the casino.

There had been a time when only two attractions guaranteed luring high rollers – heavy weight championship fights and Sinatra. The crooner had truly been "chairman of the board." He had once inked a $10 million-dollar deal with the Golden Nugget to appear for a handful of shows over three years. He also received a stock interest in the casino. It was an unbelievably sweet deal – for the casino. Nobody attracted players like Frank Sinatra back then. Yet the days when guys with big Cuban cigars toked cocktail servers with twenty-five dollar tips and called them all "doll" were passing.

Tommy catered to a new multigenerational pool of players. He was betting they would come to a family attraction, a casino that had something for everyone, and he was proving himself right. The place was filling to capacity. By evening, they would rope off entrances to limit admission. Those lucky enough to snare show tickets would see the casino review of a lifetime. Then, they'd race back to play. In the morning, Manny would hand him the largest daily drop sheets any casino in the world had ever recorded. Tommy smiled as he and Manny walked toward the show room to check preparations for the evening event. He moved with confidence, knowing his dream was about to payoff.

Beneath the show room floor the mechanic held a

flashlight to scrutinize handiwork baring his mark. Actually, it had begun when they laid the foundation. The Atlantic City mob controlled all concrete jobs in the town. They ran the trucks that delivered and poured. No one had ever built a casino in the resort city without contributing to their coffers. The mob kept a low profile while making money from every large structure that went up. They had even scored from construction of the town's new police administration building.

The Megasino had been a special job. Before they had laid the foundation, Bonivicolla had consulted builders from Sicily who had special talents. They knew how to put up a building on sandy soil close to water. They also knew how to take it down. They didn't need to topple the entire casino. Ripping down the separately constructed show room would bring the mob what they wanted. In ten hours the show room would be packed to capacity. Then, what they had planned would rip the place apart.

The fish-faced man stuck a flashlight between his pointy teeth and aimed its beam at electrical wires stemming from the concrete. He tugged them gently. *Ready*, he thought. The mechanic moved around the dark corridors, surveying the site. One explosive charge was set under the stage and another was under the audience. Both were ready to blow.

The soft, wet ground would help them bring the show room down. Buildings stood better on hard rock as opposed to softer rock, clay or sand. On soft ground the earth's solid bedrock was far below. Supporting a superstructure could be problematic, especially when groundwater was present. Water could make soft and sandy soil turn to quicksand and give way. All that worked to the mob's advantage.

Architects and structural engineers, who had designed the show room, had argued the merits of divergent theories. The professionals had bandied their notions, considering the best way to construct the super high-rise tower and separate show room on the bay. While one school of thought suggested supporting the mammoth structures with tremendously deep anchors, the other recommended utilizing a "floating foundation." The technique had gained acceptance in many soft earth areas. Proponents spoke of how Mexico City sat atop the mud bed of a once vast prehistoric lake. They claimed the city would have better survived the crippling 1985 earthquake had floating-foundation technology been employed. After the disaster, the restoration work in Mexico City utilized that method to avoid future cataclysms.

Over the objection of some governmental inspectors, Tommy had constructed Megasino with a combination of the two building techniques. The foundation to the main tower that housed the casino and hotel was anchored deep into the bedrock. The separately constructed show room had a floating foundation. Tommy had lobbied to gain final government approval for the design. He had satisfied the State Department of Environmental Protection that his plan would be ecologically sound for the waterway. On the other hand, the Municipal Board of Licensing and Inspection refused to grant approval. A tough city engineer had opposed the show room's floating foundation proposal. At a series of public hearings, he had heatedly argued that the design was unsafe. In the end Tommy had masterfully pitted the DEP against L & I to get exactly what he wanted. That was the fastest way to get the buildings up. Besides, he .

believed his experts when they told him that both foundations would be sound. They would have been right – if the concrete had been poured to specifications.

The mechanic was satisfied. Explosive charges had been set into the foundation during construction when they had poured the concrete. At a given moment that evening, the show room would cave-in atop thousands of victims. No one would ever detect the charges amid the rubble. Inspectors would fault the design plan. The inspectors, who would make that finding, were already on the mob's payroll.

It'll be showtime soon, the man in maintenance fatigues thought. He beamed a smile that nearly ran out of room on his slender face. When the curtain went up, that place would tumble down.

An attendant in a maid's uniform sifted through the star's wardrobe. Susannah sat before a lighted stage mirror, already preparing for the evening performance. She no longer entertained for the money. On the rare occasions Susannah sang in public anymore, she performed for the unparalleled thrill of appearing on stage. Only then did she feel the rush that made life full without reaching for a bottle of little helpers.

She thought of what she'd tell Tommy as they dined after the show. *How will he react?* she wondered.

"Is this the gown you'll be wearing tonight, Miss Halloway?"

"What? Oh, yes." Susannah quickly refocused her attention. "I'll wear the Bagley-Mischa tonight. We'll keep the Richard Tyler for tomorrow's performance."

Her dressing assistant looked confused.

"Purple beaded tonight. Black tomorrow."

The dresser studied the purple gown. "It's ripped down the back, ma'am."

Susannah smiled, realizing she should have brought her own wardrobe people. "It's not ripped, sweetie. You'll sew me into it after I put it on."

The gown was form fitting. To get into it, she couldn't even eat until after the show. That, she reflected with eager anticipation, was how she had planned her dining arrangements anyway.

Susannah checked the clock on her dressing stand. It told her to get working. *Three hours until showtime*, she thought. A lot of labor went into being a natural beauty and time was ticking down.

Someone else counted down. He counted and ducked all at once. A lamp smashed against the wall behind him and a tear-choked voice screamed.

"How could you?"

His Euro-tramp was in excellent form. He figured the curvy blond package could pitch another six innings. Stairmaster sessions had tightened her buttocks and fortified her stamina. Another lamp hit the wall. He was getting frustrated.

"You're so friggin' smart. You know everything," he shouted at her. "You should go out, right now, and get a big tattoo on your new tight ass that says 'fuckin' rocket scientist'."

An antique vase shattered into a million pieces. One piece for every dollar it must have cost, he surmised.

"*Rat d' egout*! *Batard*!" she exclaimed in her native tongue.

"Just once," he howled, "I'd like to have a conversation with you that doesn't start or end with the words 'you rat bastard'."

Her accent and occasional retort in French were things he had once found endearing. All too soon, the accent became grating. When she spoke in French, he wanted to drive steel nails into his eardrums.

A chest of drawers crashed onto the floor. Francoise stood defiantly beside antique wreckage. Her own grandiose chest heaved as she panted for air. Full bosoms raised as she inhaled and sunk as wind raced from her pipes.

"Do you buy this junk just to break when you're mad at me?"

"*Oui*," she whispered, nodding her head affirmatively.

Francoise slowly reached for another vase. She looked tired. Smashing everything in sight was an exhaustive endeavor. Before she could break it, too, they heard a knock on the door. Conrad held up his hand, calling for a timeout. His count-ass was hyperventilating but somehow sufficiently in control of her faculties. She held the vase in both hands, suspended in midair. The raps sounded again. Conrad walked toward the door and wondered if he should open it.

What a sight we make, he thought.

Conrad surveyed the living room of their casino hotel suite. Every lamp laid in pieces. Every picture was down.

He turned to his wife. Her blond sixties-style bouffant hairdo was in total disarray. Mascara flowed with tears down both sides of her face. She looked like the Bride of Frankenstein.

Door knocks sounded again.

Who has the nerve to interrupt this fracas? he wondered. Conrad picked up a piece of the broken mirror that had once been the focal point of their foyer. He looked into the glass and jolted back. If his wife was the Bride of Frankenstein, he was the monster. His hair also flew wildly about. Francoise had nearly pulled out his transplanted plugs. He tried combing them down with his hand, but the effort failed miserably.

Knocks, ever so persistent, reverberated.

Conrad opened the door. There, beneath sultry bangs that fell heavier on the left side, an auburn-haired sex pistol put him in her sights. Tina Levine's eyes darted from his head to toes. They moved deliberately enough for him to discover what it was like on the other side of an abusive stare. It came, as always, with her sheepish grin. He breathed heavily. Still catching his wind, he had to force out words.

"Mrs. Levine, tell me you have *really* good news."

"I always bring good news. I know you didn't hire Manny Levine's wife just to produce your dance reviews."

"Tina, you couldn't produce a bowel movement. That's why I've got a fag with talent backing you up. Just keep bringing me information and I'll keep you on the payroll."

Tina began to speak, but he wasn't listening. Instead, he struggled with a dilemma. *Should I warn her or not*? It wasn't a battle of conscience so much as a balancing act. Did her value to him outweigh the risk of telling her? If he warned the woman to leave The Megasino show room, would she surmise he knew of the calamity in advance? Whatever the woman was driveling about wasn't weighing in her favor.

She had first come to him while Conrad was trying to lure Manny Levine to the Pyramid. Conrad badly wanted Manny as CEO and wondered what the guy's wife wanted. As it turned out, she wanted a job, too. Tina handed Conrad a resume with impressive credentials. It showed she had undergone classical dance training in Europe and had earned a Fine Arts degree from Manhattan's famed Julliard School. Conrad's private investigators later discovered she had actually been a topless dancer in a Follies review. Before she had met and married Manny, she'd even turned a few tricks. Her husband didn't know about his wife's sordid past and Conrad didn't care.

Tina wanted to produce stage reviews at the Pyramid. Conrad offered her the job provided she convinced Manny to become his CEO. Her work wouldn't require an abundance of talent. All the damned reviews looked the same anyway. She didn't want the position for money; her husband would earn plenty of that. She wanted prestige. She delivered Manny and Conrad gave her a contract that was twelve months longer than her husband's. If Conrad wanted Tina out of the casino, he could simply payoff the balance of her salary. On the other hand, if he wanted her around, she and her husband would have no choice. The personal service contract bound Tina and irritated her husband like a freshly lanced boil.

What excellent payback for the little prick who abandoned me, Conrad thought.

As for corporate espionage, the woman thought of herself as Mata Hari, the famed World War I spy who had been an exotic dancer. Tina's slender legs weren't made for dancing, but she expertly sold her husband's secrets.

Finally, Conrad resolved his quandary. "Tina," he said, "when the curtain rises tonight, I want you to leave The Megasino show."

Tina's eyebrows arched. "And miss an evening with my husband." Sarcasm coated her words with the subtlety of a dayglow paint job.

"Sneak out with any excuse you can manufacture and get back here. I want a report on who's in that show room, right away. List the high rollers on the front rows. I'll want them, here, at a bash I'm planning. "

"I can get their names next week after marketing people do a wrap-up."

The woman's disloyalty to her husband knows no bounds, he thought. She had given Conrad her soul. More than once, Tina had offered her body as well. With the intimation of subterfuge that enthralled her, she had also offered to replace Francoise "permanently."

"I don't want to wait for marketing reports. Leave when the lights dim. Don't even wait for the curtain to rise."

Tina came close. He felt her breath as her lithe body began grinding against the door he held between them. Conrad's attention shifted downward.

"Is your pelvis devouring my doorknob?"

She pouted as Conrad studied her hungry hips. His eyes traced the contours of her slender form upward. Under rich curls that ran the spectrum of shades between red and brown, her face was drawn tight by a surgeon's knife. She'd also lied about her age on that resume. Most women played with a few years; Tina dissolved decades. The lips inviting his kiss could never be trusted to tell any man the truth.

Conrad shut the door and turned to Francoise. She hadn't moved. The vase still languished in midair as if levitating. Thoughts of mayhem about to unleash on Tommy Brucker aroused him. He walked toward Francoise purposely. Like a carnivore ready to pounce on prey, he sensed her fear. The vase fell from her hands, shattering as she scurried into the bedroom. Francoise slammed the door. He heard the key turn in the lock from the other side. Conrad studied the only obstacle separating them. He had taken down many doors during their brawls and decided to do it again. He leveled his shoulder against the formidable impasse but heard the key turn again. Slowly, the door opened. No one was in sight. He entered cautiously, as a history of head lumps warned him to be wary, and spotted Francoise sprawled seductively on the bed.

"*L'amour force toutes les serrures,*" she said. Love laughs at locksmiths.

Conrad glanced at a clock that had escaped their fury. Time ticked away. A single thought excited him: *At showtime The Megasino is going down*. He stripped his belt, folded it in two, and gripped both ends. Then he snapped the leather straps together. They cracked like a bullwhip as Conrad closed in on her.

Tommy Brucker sat behind his office desk, leaning back in his chair. He swallowed an antibiotic and a pain reliever for his scalp wound as he thought it through. Manny had brought him the news, then asked what he should tell Susannah.

"Lie to her," Tommy finally said while massaging his temples. "Convincingly, Manny. Darnel's her only child."

He knew Manny would reluctantly obey. Lying to anyone was an unnatural act for Manny Levine, but he would carry out his orders. He would tell Susannah her son was on a flight to Atlantic City. That was the lie. Tommy knew the truth. Darnel was still missing. They couldn't find the man who was usually connected to The Fantasy Casino twenty-four hours a day. His responsibilities tied him to the casino like an umbilical cord. Cellular phones and pagers always linked him. He always let his office know his whereabouts and regularly called for messages. Where was he? No one had seen or heard from Darnel for thirty-six hours. Worse yet, the dispatcher at the limo company under contract to The Fantasy had given chilling news. Someone had called to cancel Darnel's scheduled pickup. No one knew who had driven The Fantasy president away from his home. Manny had carefully approached the police and hospitals for fear of creating a public stir. They hadn't heard anything. Thankfully no "John Does" had turned up on the police blotters, in the emergency rooms, or on a morgue slab.

Darnel's wife was frantic. Jasmine claimed there weren't any problems at home. Her husband was simply missing. Tommy knew Darnel was too solid a man to just takeoff. It was difficult to avoid the conclusion that he had met foul play.

Tommy's thoughts turned back to Susannah. He sensed she was too fragile for the news. Still, if they didn't hear something soon, he would be forced to tell her. Tommy knew he could never keep it from her over the intimate dinner they had planned. He would have to tell her after the curtain came down. That didn't give them much time. Tommy lifted an engraved invitation that his marketing department had circulated for the event and realized how little time there was. Soon the show room doors would open and people would take their seats.

The mechanic shimmied in the tight quarters of a bathroom stall removing his maintenance fatigues. Once changed, he shoved the uniform in a trash can and checked his fish-face in the mirror.

Coulda used a shave, he thought.

He had to stay close. The radio-transmitted signal that would ignite the explosives came from a miniature transmitter in his pocket. It looked like a small black-metal box. He would attend the show to make sure the arena filled, then leave when it was time to set off the blasts. First, though, he was hitting the game tables. Filled with the kind of cockiness that so often accompanies trouble, the mechanic was feeling lucky.

Chapter Eight

Showtime!

"One hour until showtime," a doorman called.

As the theater doors swung open, the crowd filed inside, eager for a show that would light up the stage. No one was more anxious to see those fireworks than the mechanic, who soured for a seat. He spied what he wanted, a long table near the rear of the room, which provided quick access to an exit, and had a maître d' lead the way. Following along, euphoria twisted the corners of his mouth into a grin.

Sevens and elevens, he thought.

The man with a barracuda beak loved the irony of it. Seven thousand people would meet their doom at eleven o'clock. Everything was rolling his way. Even the dice had turned in his favor and he had left a craps table with pockets full of chips. He wasn't even cashing out. Instead, he would keep the tokens as souvenirs of the night the casino rolled itself craps.

The maître d' pulled back a chair at the table, which

the mechanic would share with a dozen strangers, none of whom would have an inkling of what was about to happen.

"Is this table to your liking, sir?" said his guide.

The mechanic pulled a hundred-dollar token from his pocket and flipped it as a tip. He enjoyed watching the man's eyes bulge at his good fortune.

"Lucky night at the tables, sir?"

"For some," the mechanic said, "more than others. You can bet on that."

He settled into his chair and boldly set his black box atop the table. A curly-haired waiter studied the box as he took the mechanic's drink order. The mechanic loved watching such an obsequious peon stare at the strange contraption. His quizzical scrutiny added to the thrill that escalated with each passing moment.

"Sir," the waiter said, "management won't permit you to record the performance. The casino strictly forbids it because of copyright laws."

The mechanic knew all casinos ran a warning at the start of their shows. "Ain't a tape recorder," he said with a smile unveiling his pointy teeth.

"You can't take photographs either."

"Ain't a camera neither."

The waiter took his order and left with a disconcerted look. The mechanic knew what the guy must be thinking. If the little box doesn't hold a tape recorder or a camera, what's in there? That jerk would never learn. The killing device sat in plain view, but no one had a clue of what was coming so soon. *People are such morons*, he thought.

When the waiter returned, he brought the same stupid look on his face and a pair of strong cocktails. "Your martinis," he said. "Doubles, sir." He glanced at the box again before leaving.

The mechanic enjoyed giving him the creeps. He savored a cocktail, then checked his wristwatch, realizing how soon it would happen.

Backstage, the festivities had already begun for "The Amazing Meriden." The magician savored champagne someone had delivered in cases. With a glass never far from hand, he ran through his routines for anyone who would watch. Exotic birds popped out of dancers' headdresses, a fifteen-foot python slithered around his waist, and Bert the Lion paced in his portable cage. During Meriden's stage allotment, he would place his female stage assistant into the cage, cover it with a blanket, then remove it. Magically, Bert would appear in her place.

Having so much fun entertaining the dancers, Meriden didn't notice Bert seemed upset. At ten years old, the lion was normally tame as a lamb. That night, however, Bert wouldn't stop pacing, almost as if natural instincts told him disaster loomed.

Meriden's assistant had to pass the animal in the trick cage as they exchanged places performing the illusion. The leggy brunette watched Bert tread back and forth.

"I don't like the looks of this," Peggy said. "I don't wanna get close to a four-hundred pound cat that looks so antsy."

She checked herself in a mirror and tugged on her seamed stockings to straighten them. Then Peggy turned back to the cage and watched Bert pivot, march, pivot, and march again.

"Shouldn't we tranquilize him?"

Meriden barely looked at the animal. "Nah. It's probably just indigestion. Bert's stomach isn't what it used to be. You know that."

His assistant blinked and stared at the beast. "Do you think he's trying to tell us something?"

"Bert? Sweetheart, he's never told me a damn thing. Don't worry about it."

Back into his act, Meriden lowered the zipper on his trousers. Gingerly, a parrot poked its way out. The bird flared bright green plumage, flew around the room, and returned to land on Meriden's shoulder.

"You don't have anything to say, do you?" he asked his feathered pal.

He had trained the parrot to reply, but it didn't say a word. It, too, seemed out of sorts. The bird just sat on Meriden's shoulder and snuggled to his ear, as if clinging for protection.

"Hey," the magician called to his assistant. "Put this guy back in his cage. We'll use the cockatoo, instead." With a shrug, Meriden poured himself more champagne, then roamed the crowded dressing area.

The backstage area only had two private dressing rooms for stars. Naturally, Susannah Halloway took one; Courtney Wymann took the other. Four women, who harmonized so well as EnCor, resented having to primp next to dancers and the magician. They guzzled champagne to sooth their injured egos and tossed each bottle they drained to the floor. Alcohol stoked their fiery rages, and they were ready to burn the women whose stars outshone their own. The smallest was fastest to sear the solo song birds with her acerbic tongue.

"Who the hell do they think they are?"

"Halloway has been around longer, girl," another group member offered. "She usta sing from caves to the dinosaurs."

"So you gotta be on social security or what?" The smaller singer reached for another bottle and didn't let up. "And what about the kid?"

"Hottest girl act in the country."

"It's that 'no sex before marriage' shit. That's what it is. Keep your legs closed, tell the world, and become a superstar."

The women of EnCor were hot. Their recording label had defined a sophisticated image for the racially mixed act, two blacks, one Hispanic, one white, and all beautiful. In their videos and on their CD covers they appeared sassy and demur. Spicy and street-tough was the truer picture. The foursome primped, drank, and spewed venom until the smallest expressed the question they all had.

"You think that Courtney's really a virgin?"

Courtney savored the warmth of an embrace. Her center-part hairstyle, extra glossy from a shine serum, was brushed from the side of her face with tender fingertips, sparking an electric shiver. Bobbie's pitch-black hair and olive complexion came in striking contrast to Courtney's long blond locks and fair skin. As teasing fingers traced the contours of her neck, then swirled lower, she relished playfulness that never went too far, for she carefully maintained her virtue, even behind closed doors.

"Ten minutes, Miss Wymann," came the call outside her door.

Dancers would open the show, then Courtney would appear as the first singing act, followed by EnCor. Susannah Halloway would close. Dancers would also entertain in between the singers.

"You should have been the closing act," Bobbie said. "You're the biggest star here."

"Doesn't matter," she replied. Her tone conveyed conviction – it didn't concern her. Despite overwhelming talent, good looks, and fast-found fame, Courtney remained true to her image as a down to earth girl-next-door. It was hard to find faults with the immensely popular young woman, save one she fought to keep under wraps. Whenever interviewers for fan mags asked if she would like to change anything about herself, she told them innocuous things like: "my hair's too thin" or "I think I have ugly toes." But Courtney knew her real problem was guarding a temper that flared like fireworks on the Chinese New Year. Afterward, she was always contrite, but watch out til afterward.

"Well, it's not right," Bobbie was still saying of Susannah closing the show. "Just pussy politics. Everyone knows Halloway had a thing with Tommy Brucker. She screwed her way to close."

"Help me with this necklace," Courtney said, changing the subject by picking up a dazzler that could never outshine her.

Bobbie fixed the clasp behind her neck, then came round with moist lips puckered.

"*Baby, one more time*," Courtney sighed, closing her eyes for the kind of kiss that only came from a woman.

Manny watched Tommy walk into the show room to squeeze hands. Half in jest the Buckman had once told him, "Wine them, dine them, and never break them the first night." His boss knew how to greet guests with fanfare and how to keep them happy. People were enjoying drinks at long tables. Though the stage would showcase enough talent for a three-hour review, everyone would be out in fifty-five minutes. The idea wasn't to entertain players there for the entire evening. The show was only bait that would close fast to send everyone back to the tables.

As Manny studied chairs along the first twelve rows, he realized enough money filled those seats to payoff the national debt. Some players wore tuxedos and fancy gowns. Others sported casual attire. They came dressed all ways, but they all packed big bucks. For them, corks popped from complimentary bottles of Dom Perignon. After the show, cleanup crews would pour ten-thousand dollars worth of champagne in half-consumed bottles down the drain. It didn't matter. The casino could collect the tab from one card hand played by the whales – the high rollers who sometimes dropped a hundred thousand or million during a stay.

"There's Tommy Brucker," Manny heard a woman shout.

"Where?" someone else clamored.

"Down there. He's the one with all the money."

Manny smiled. Sure, Tommy was wealthy, at least on paper. But the real money sat near the stage. He watched Tommy greet it. People never brought their own money there. Once they walked in the door, their money belonged to the casino. It was just a matter of how long it took the casino to get it.

Manny's eyes scoured the show room, looking for his wife. He hadn't seen Tina all day. *We've both been too absorbed in our careers*, he thought. After that weekend, he would establish a more normal routine. Consumed preparing for the Megasino grand opening, he felt sorry for Tina who had been so busy closing out her contract at the Pyramid. Tommy's lawyers had reviewed the personal service contract she'd signed with Greg Conrad. Ironclad, she had no way out until it expired in a couple of months. Between their obligations, Manny realized he had been spending too many nights alone with his buddy Jack Daniels.

The mechanic's waiter delivered him another round, still looking suspiciously at the black box on the table.

"Sir, I have to remind you. No recording and no picture taking in the show room."

"Fuck off, frizz head," he replied.

"Hey, watch your mouth," a man across the table exclaimed. "There's ladies and children here."

The stranger couldn't have realized whom he was admonishing. When the mechanic was drunk, he had killed men for being less curt. He studied the guy. Soon, he would kill him along with everyone else in the room. The mechanic just lifted his glass in a toast to the jerk and his jerk-faced family sitting at the table. His wife was a porker and his two children were little piglets. The youngest, looking about five, sat next to the mechanic. The kid reached for the black box.

Sneering as if venom tipped his pointy teeth, the mechanic pulled a plastic sword from his drink that held a martini olive. He flicked the olive at the boy who ducked out of its way. Undeterred, the child reached for the box again, while the mechanic used his martini sword as a saber, trying to stab the little hand.

Laughter surrounded Tommy. He heard movement behind the curtains. So close to the stage, he could hear the crews scurrying. Musicians in the orchestra fine-tuned their instruments.

"Two minutes 'til showtime," someone backstage called out. Stage jitters hit some, but most of the entertainers were pros. Only the animals seemed out of sorts. Bert the Lion paced faster, the birds squawked, and the Amazing Meriden didn't know why.

"Shut up your faces!" he shouted to them.

It was tough enough to stick a bird down his trousers without having the thing flapping its wings and sounding off. He watched Bert and the jittery birds. Maybe they were trying to tell him something. Exasperated he asked them, "What's wrong with you guys, tonight?"

The mechanic pulled a key from his pocket and inserted it into the metal box. Once unlocked, he removed the lid and studied two buttons inside – one to set off the charge underneath the stage; the other to set off the charge underneath the audience. Almost time to pickup and go, he realized. He would put the box in his pocket with his fingers resting atop the buttons. He needed to remain within the transmitter's range of the detonators, so he would push the buttons just outside the show room when he left. Then, he'd sprint away. The mechanic started to rise but fell back into his chair.

Man, I've had a lot to drink, he thought.

He had been comp'd to drinks as he gambled. Caught up in winning, he had lost track of his drink count. Afterward, he polished off more cocktails in the show room. Drinking a little while he waited to do a job always settled his nerves. He realized, too late, he had over drunk. Rising from the chair was going to be difficult. Walking with his fingers over the buttons, without setting off the explosions too early, was going to be torturous. One slip and he would blow himself to hell along with everyone else. He looked up. Through a fog, he saw the waiter returning with a uniformed security guard.

"Sir," the waiter said, "you'll have to turn that device over to me. We'll see you get it back after the show."

The mechanic looked at the two men hovering over him and wondered what to do. If he gave up the box, he couldn't set off the explosion. *Maybe I should take 'em out*, he thought. He could handle the waiter easily. One whack would knock the guy's perm straight. But the security guard was a load of muscle. *Instead of force*, he thought, *I'll try diplomacy*.

"Fuck off," he told them. Seeped with gin, his diplomatic skills were ebbing.

"Hey," the guy across the table said. "I warned you about that kind of language in front of my wife and kids."

"Sir, give us the box," the security guard pressed.

"The MegaTheater welcomes you to tonight's star-filled performance. . . ."

The stage announcer's voice filled the room. The mechanic's head spun. Through a mental fog he tried figuring how to make his move with the security guard so close.

As the curtain began rising, Tommy heard the lion's thunderous roar. He knew stage hands had pushed the animal's cage on rollers toward the wings and wondered what had set off its chilling call. Tommy didn't know much about animals, but could tell that growl was genuine. It generated nervous laughter from the crowd as musicians took their cue.

Tommy looked around and observed with satisfaction, *not one empty seat in the house*. Then he walked toward the rear of the show room where he and Manny would watch. Afterward, they would greet folks returning to the casino floor.

Onstage, dancers leaped from their markers into the opening number as the orchestra blared. Backstage, Courtney hustled through the main dressing area toward stage right, knowing how she stunned in her shimmery cutout gown with ample fishtail train. The sultry dress, a tad mature for the teen sensation, lent the appearance of sensuality that blended with her wholesome looks, befitting her stage persona.

She saw the four young women of Encor sizing her up and heard them whispering. As she smiled to them, one rushed up, blocking her path, while the others surrounded her, the smallest behind her.

Pointing a finger under Courtney's nose, the woman in front lambasted: "So you got cobwebs up that virgin thing of yours or what?"

Courtney looked for stagehands to assist her, but everyone was busy, handling their part in a show underway. She thought of calling Bobbie, but she had already left to take a seat out front.

"Virgin, my ass," another woman assaulted.

Unwanted feelings began to surface as Courtney's blood boiled. *Guard your temper, girl*," she told herself. She pushed past the four women, felt a tug behind her, then heard a tear. As she spun round, she saw the smallest member of the singing group standing on the torn off fishtail from her gown.

"Oops," said the teeny singer with a smirk.

That lit Courtney's rockets. Her rage flared as she squared off against the woman with long fingernails set to strike.

The security guard had called for backup on his walkie-talkie. Two more guards stood behind the mechanic. The guy across the table sat with his arms crossed and a smirk spread wide, inviting trouble. The well-lubricated mechanic rose, but his head was whirling. In an instant, he fell back into his chair so hard it tipped. A guard caught it just in time to keep him from tumbling to the floor.

"Just take that box from him," another guard said.

"Nobody's takin' nothin' from me," shouted the mechanic.

If he didn't set those charges off, Bonivicolla would put a contract on his life. *I gotta knock this place down*, he thought.

First, though, he wanted to take a swipe at the smirker. The mechanic leaped to his feet and sunk his fist so

far into the man's mouth he wasn't sure he'd get his
hand back. The guy's wife shrieked.

"Snuggums! That man hit my Snuggums."

"Grab him," a guard shouted.

The waiter ducked as all three security guards leaped
atop the mechanic. They dragged him, kicking and
screaming.

"Give me my Goddamned box!"

He screamed for it, again and again, as they hauled
him away. Somebody had to hit the buttons on that box
to set off the explosion. Otherwise, the mechanic realized with stone certainty, he would be the only one to
die. His boss would have him whacked.

"I want my friggin' box!"

The orchestra stopped playing. Dancers, who had
completed their opening routine, wondered what to do.
They all thought the same thing.

Where's Courtney Wymann?

Again the lion roared, but no one heeded its primal
warning call.

The conductor tapped his baton, set his arms in motion, and performers took his cue. Musicians started a
second dance number they had scheduled between acts.
Dancers shrugged their shoulders and began moving.
They would have to stall until a singer appeared in the
wings.

Backstage, Courtney's five-thousand dollar Marc
Bouwer gown was shredded. The quartet had teamed
up against her, yanking satin and tearing seams. She

examined what they'd done. Her face flushed an angry purple; her eyes filled with fire. Unbridled emotion burst in a Vesuvian eruption. Four women saw her crazed expression and screamed while sprinting for cover.

"Oh, shit!" the smallest member of the troublesome quartet shrieked.

"Harmonize to this, bitches," Courtney wailed with outstretched claws.

In the rear of the theater, Manny gave his boss a showbiz kiss on the cheek to congratulate him for putting everything together. It looked like they were going to pull off the night.

Tommy laughed good-naturedly and pushed his CEO away, all the while wondering: *Why's the first singer taking so long to get onstage?*

Snuggums nursed his jaw. His wife leaned close to nuzzle, then attended to her own discomforting needs. She removed her shoes to massage mammoth bunions. Their chubby five-year-old held the black box in his hand. Snoopy little fingers toyed with the buttons. His mother saw what he was doing and called out.

"Get your hands off that thing, Mickey. It belongs to that awful man who hit your father."

"I wanna play with it."

"Mickey, don't you dare."

"Leff him," the kid's father said.

"What?"

His wife held her hands up, palms pointed upward, indicating she couldn't make out what he was saying.

The orchestra played loudly, and his lips – swollen to
the size of horizontal bananas – muffled his words.

"Leff him play wit' it," the man struggled to say.

The woman appeared uncertain if it was a good idea,
but their child seemed attached to his new toy, wrapping his hands around it protectively.

"Oh, all right. Play with it if you like," she conced-
ed. "I just want to watch the show."

Dancers didn't draw the kid's interest; red buttons
on the box did. He placed chubby little fingers over
them. Just then, another tiny hand jerked the box away.

Mickey wailed.

"Now waff?" his father screamed.

Too cool to resist, Mickey's brother had taken the
box. Both boys began to scream.

"Mine."

"I'm older. Let me see it!"

"Ma said it's mine."

"Hey, Snuggums," someone called from another table. "We're trying to enjoy the show. Can't you keep
your brats in line?"

"Fuff you," the father called back. He was mad at
everyone. He was mad at the guy who had slugged
him. He was mad at the casino cops who didn't protect
him from the blow. *I'll sue for this*, he thought. He
was mad at the jerk who was yelling at him. Yet most
of all, he was mad at his two sons who were pulling the
box back and forth in their struggle to take it from one
another. He rose and slapped both their faces with a
single stroke. They stopped dead.

"Puff it down, now."

"What?" the boys cried in unison.

"Puff it down on the table!"

They set the black box on the table between them. "Waff the show."

They turned their faces toward the review. Dancers still flew across the stage without any signs of the singing sensations everyone had come to see. Snuggums gently touched his stinging lips, then jolted his head back in agony. Still angry and hurting, he peered at the stage.

God, these shows are boring, he thought. He had promised his wife he would take the family to the casino review. That was the price he had paid for attending the opening bash. He longed for action on the casino floor. His mind wandered; his eyes drifted, focusing on the black box that had intrigued his children. Curiosity killing him, he wondered, *What the hell is this thing, anyway?*

He brought it near to inspect and set it on the table before him. The two red buttons fascinated him. *What are they for?* There was only one way to find out. He picked it up.

"Ow!" he screamed. His tongue had run over his banana lips, causing a surge of pain. The lion roared again but that didn't distract him. His fingers touched the buttons. It only took an instant to press down.

A muffled rumble rose from the bowels of the earth. Reverberations gently massaged the feet. Cocktails on tabletops began shaking, then spilled over the rims of glassware. Thunder rolled as if from afar but fast growing closer and louder. Strangely, it came not from the heavens; it rose from hell. That time the lion's roar came as a wail, like a lamentation announcing impending demise. Every eye grew wider scouring the room; every mind wondered.

What can it be?

Then an agonizing blast pounded every eardrum.

Chapter Nine

Midnight Kisses

Nothing is silent as the desert at night. Darnel Halloway heard no sound until he heard vermin; that's what he called the two men and their woman who kept him bound and gagged. The redhead's voice buzzed in his ear.

"Shush," she whispered. "I'm setting you free."

Duct tape wrapped his legs like a cocoon and strapped his arms together behind his back. She tugged the strip of tape covering his mouth and gingerly removed his bindings.

Hushed words rushed from his mouth. "Why are you doing this?"

Cindi whispered again in his ear. "I heard them talking while they thought I was asleep. They received their orders. They'll kill us both in the morning."

Ten feet away the larger hood slept soundly on the floor. The smaller guy, who was supposed to be standing guard, sat on the floor with his back propped against thin wooden planks serving as walls. His chauffeur's cap tipped downward, covering peepers that had closed tight.

Cindi peered into Darnel's green eyes and plastered him with an unexpected kiss. Then, she stuck something folded like a map between his lips. Silently, so as not to wake the sleeping mobsters, she used scissors to slice the duct tape binding him. He yanked the map from his mouth and flexed muscles that felt cramped and sore. She looked into his eyes again and pressed her lips to his. Cindi's breath sizzled like a Death Valley noon and warmed off the desert midnight chill.

He broke away, struggling to stand. Then with a jolt, they stopped moving. Sludge rolled from one side to the other. He adjusted his pillow on the wooden floor, let out a deep breath, and commenced snoring. Like a chain saw cutting green timber, guttural jags ripped through the cabin. Darnel feared they would wake the smaller man, but Scratchy simply itched his stomach as he snoozed.

Both hoods slept by their guns. Sludge's arm wrapped his shotgun like a longtime lover. Scratchy's semiautomatic pistol rested on his lap. Their weapons must be loaded, he figured. Two rounds were chambered in that shotgun for certain. Just as surely, both men had unlocked the safety mechanisms on their firearms; they weren't safety conscious. The weapons were powerful lures. Darnel moved toward them. Suddenly he felt Cindi's grip on his arm and hot air fill his ear as she feverishly whispered.

"Don't think it. If you wake 'em up trying to grab a gun, we're dead." She dangled a pair of car keys before his eyes and pointed to the door. "I snatched these off the table."

"Good. Go for the limo."

Cindi slipped out the door with Darnel close behind. The dust-blowing winds had stopped raging at dusk as if that were their bedtime. Overhead, a full moon and one-thousand stars shone bright. Beneath them, sand and sage brush, stretching to the horizon, turned the landscape into a surreal vision of lunar terrain.

Cindi jumped into the limo front passenger seat. Darnel slipped behind the steering wheel. Without warning, Cindi's lips assaulted his again. Her tongue recoiled and surged like a striking viper. He tried pulling away, but her arms wrapped him tightly. He was still weak from being bound and surprised by the strength she unleashed from a petite but perfectly toned frame. Her determined moves told him she was wrestling for more than kisses.

"Keys," he managed to say. "Let's get out of here."

She turned over the keyring and he glanced at the two keys on it.

Which one? he wondered. Darnel tried the first. It didn't fit. He tried the second futilely. Then, he looked at both more closely and spotted the problem.

"There's no such thing as a Chevy Nova limousine. You swiped the wrong keys."

"Road map," she said. "I picked it up today in town. We're gonna need it. I don't know where we are and we'll have to make a run for it."

Darnel glanced at the map. It read, "Underground Treasure Trips."

"Damn," he blurted. "It's not a road map. This thing's a tourist map to the deserted silver mines, out here."

Cindi turned white. "They're supposed to dump our bodies in the one behind the shack."

"Hey! Where the hell is he?" Darnel heard Sludge yell inside the cabin. "The broad's gone too. Wake up, you dick lick!"

A burst from Scratchy's semiautomatic pistol rang. Darnel had been right. Both men had slept with the safety switches unlatched and the little guy set off the firepower when wakened with a start. Bullets seared thin cabin walls and its tin roof.

"You moron," Sludge screamed. "Don't shoot us. Let's go out and whack these fucks."

Cindi and Darnel jumped out of the car. His eyes darted, scouring the vacant landscape for a place to hide.

"Sorry, hon'," she whispered to him.

"Sorry?"

"Sorry there's no such thing as a whore with a heart of gold."

Darnel cocked his head uncertainly.

"Help!" Cindi screamed toward the cabin. "He's fuckin' kidnaping me. He's out here."

He suddenly realized she would try sweet-talking her way out of the mess at his expense.

"Help," she screeched again. The redhead sprinted back toward the cabin, one hand flailing in the air above her head, the other hiking up her soiled minidress to ease athletic leaps and bounds.

The two hoods, racing from the cabin door, stopped when they spotted Cindi Rella. The big man's gunsight zeroed in on gold lame shimmering in moonlight, then a single shotgun burst exploded. At such close range it blew her off her feet and high into the air.

"We shoulda whacked 'em soon as we got the order," Scratchy chirped.

"Hey, we both agreed to wait until morning so we could do the broad again," Sludge said. "We'll find him. A full moon in the desert lets you see for miles."

The little man tugged his cap down on his head while peering all around for Darnel. The lunar glow reflected on barren turf. "Look," he said, pointing to the ground. "It's bright enough to cast our shadows."

"Let's lay out that casino honcho in his." Determination filled Sludge's voice. "You go around the cabin to the right. I'll go left. If we don't see him, we'll search the mine out back."

"I ain't goin' in there. Those places freak me out."

"If we don't spot him, we're both going in. The truck's gonna be here by sunrise. We better find that a-hole before it gets here."

The two hoods stalked like commandos on patrol. They knew what they were doing; hunting desperate men was their business. Darnel would be easy. He was unarmed and had nowhere to go. They circled the cabin and met at the mine's opening. Then, both spotted it simultaneously – Darnel's necktie. He had stripped it to run. They smiled, realizing with no place to hide, he had entered the mine where he would die. They had read the tourist map. The mine had only one way in and out. Twenty feet into the cavern, a hole opened. A ladder went fifteen feet straight down. From there, a single trail wove under the earth one hundred yards. There weren't even side passages, just a single winding tunnel, a path that would lead their victim straight to hell.

"Let's just seal him inside alive," Scratchy suggested.

Sludge stroked his flabby chin. "No, we gotta verify the hit. Get our gear from the shack."

The smaller man collected what they needed. Each donned a miner's helmet with a battery-powered lamp aimed forward to light the way. They entered the tunnel and marched to the ladder. Their eyes peered down the shaft their prey had descended.

"This place has a smell," the larger man said.

"Like a tomb."

"You go down first."

The little man moved uneasily toward the ladder. His hands gripped its rails; his feet alighted its rungs. With a gulp that made his Adams apple bob he disappeared into the hole. Sludge followed.

When they collected their bearings at the bottom, Scratchy pointed the only direction anyone could roam. Sludge walked point. He moved inside the tunnel no more than fifteen feet at a time with Scratchy covering him. Then, he stopped while the little man came forward to cover his advancement again. Gaining confidence with each step, the larger man chuckled at the thought of the casino executive feeling his way through the dark, not realizing how soon he would run out of room to scurry.

At a sharp bend Sludge stopped and waited for the smaller man to catch up. He pulled his finger away from the trigger and flexed his hand to stay loose. Then, nodding to show readiness, he wrapped his finger around the hair-trigger again. The slightest pressure would splay blood and man-meat across the cavern walls. He thought of the truck that was coming. Its cement load would seal the tunnel and no one would ever find the corpse.

The smaller man called, "This is it. The tunnel ends around this corner."

They knew how they would find their sniveling quarry. He would be shaking in the dark, crying for mercy they'd never show, and praying for his soul.

"Yeah, we've got him," Scratchy said with a trigger finger itching to shoot.

Above ground, while the sun began to rise, a cement truck drove up the dirt road. Its mixer turned with a chugga-chugga, rotating a logo on its side that read, "Bananos Construction." As the truck approached the shack, two blasts from its mighty horns filled the air. The unexpected sounds jarred him from underneath the limo dashboard, and Darnel banged his head on the steering wheel.

He had never gone into the mine. Instead, he had circled back around the shack and hid under the limo while the two hoods equipped themselves to search the cavern. He watched them enter the mine, then tried hot-wiring the vehicle. Without tools to open the steering column, he tugged at the panel under the dash. A dozen wires fell out and he wondered which ones to cross. His fingernails scratched the plastic coating from wire after wire. He touched one against another, but sparks didn't fly.

The truck horn bonked again.

Darnel didn't have time to finish. He knew he could have figured it out, but the cement mixer was too close. Brain racing in overdrive, he asked himself, "What can I do?"

He sprinted to the mine opening and found something to try camouflaging his appearance. The little guy must've dropped his chauffeur's cap when he donned the miner's helmet. Darnel wondered if it would work. The two hoods had east coast accents. Maybe the eastern dudes hadn't met the truck driver. If the driver knew them, he was out of luck. As the cement mixer pulled up, Darnel placed the cap on his head. He pulled its bill down over his face and buried his hands inside his pockets. Dust the truck kicked up settled as the driver called from his cab.

"Where do you want this load dropped?"

Darnel nodded downward, right where he was. He would put the cement at the mine's small opening to seal it.

Inside the tunnel, the two stalkers reached its end.

"Where is he?" the little man squeaked.

"He was never in here," Sludge bellowed. "The bastard tricked us!"

Fear slammed them simultaneously. Looking at each other through bulging eyes, they shared the same harrowing thought. Scratchy shouted out.

"Did that son-of-a-bitch lift the ladder from the hole?"

As they scampered back toward the mine entrance, the big man bounced off a vertical beam supporting a header above the narrow passageway. He fell backward atop his smaller buddy. Dirt tumbled down on them. The old mine looked ready to cave-in. Just as quickly as they'd fallen, they leaped to their feet and scurried to the only exit. When they rounded the last bend and saw the hatch, the little man was first to cry out.

"Jesus to peezes! The ladder's missing."

Both looked up.

"Stand on my shoulders," Sludge yelled. "See if you can reach the top and pull yourself up. If you find the ladder, send it down. If not, get some rope from the car trunk."

Scratchy tapped his pants pocket. He felt his keys and jumped onto the larger man's shoulders. Just then, they heard it. The cement truck roared outside. It sounded like someone was backing up to the mine's entranceway. They realized it was readying to drop a load.

The little man puffed as he climbed up his companion. "I can't reach the top," he wheezed.

"Shout," Sludge roared. "Shout or we'll be buried alive down here!"

In unison, both men screamed, "Help! Hel-l-l-p!" Their vocal chords stung; their lungs ached.

The truck driver leaped from his cab. He had poured for the mob before and knew better than to ask questions. Yet something about the job seemed strange.

"I thought this guy was supposed to be hit, already," he said.

"What difference does it make?" Darnel replied.

The calls for help grew louder.

"That one guy or two in there?" the driver said.

Darnel's voice came muffled from under the chauffeur's cap. "One guy. It echoes in there."

Desperate screams rang from the mine again.

"Sounds like two guys."

"You wanna go inside to find out?"

The driver went back to business without saying another word. He didn't like Sicilians, and that dark one scared the daylights out of him. He pulled a steel lever to drop the load. Cement filled the opening, silencing cries from inside forever.

Darnel zipped along the highway in his hot-wired limousine. He placed a call from the car phone when he reached a zone for cellular service. Jasmine and his daughter were fine. Silently, he thanked God. Whatever was happening hadn't put them in jeopardy. Jasmine placed the telephone to Tracy's teeny mouth.

"Daddy, guess what I'm doing?"

He could only see his ladies with his heart. The longing to be with them was irresistible and would only end when they were in his embrace. First though, he had something to do. Darnel laid out his plan to Jasmine. She would have to go along as if she hadn't heard from him and he counted on her to be cool.

"Get your butt home," she urged him.

"Soon, sweetness," was all he could say. "Soon as I can."

His second call brought surprise. The phone rang repeatedly. *How come*? Someone had to answer at The Megasino. He was dialing the main number.

A recorded message came on the line. "No calls are being placed through to The Megasino Resort Casino Hotel."

What's the problem? he wondered. He had dialed the right phone number. Darnel tried again just to make sure.

"No calls are being placed through to –"

He hung up. Just as he'd met foul play, something

was wrong at the new casino. He had to reach Atlantic City fast. *Be careful*, he reminded himself. People wanted him dead. *Who?* They would quickly realize something happened to the hoods who had been sent to kill him.

Darnel even feared calling his office. He would have to sneak into Atlantic City to learn what it was all about, but he couldn't take a plane. Goons might be waiting for him at the airports. Darnel slammed the gas pedal to the floor and felt the sand-covered limo accelerate.

"A lot of country to cross," he said, "and little time to do it."

Chapter Ten

Temple of Ruin

Panic is the word they use, but infectious terror is what occurs.

A stage dancer, bedecked in golden plumage, felt her jeweled headpiece shake. Donna froze amid her routine. She heard a muffled boom and detected shifting ground. The leggy survivor of a California quake realized she was reliving the experience on a more horrific scale.

One at a time, musicians stopped playing, though their conductor never missed a beat. The elderly orchestra leader waived his baton, oblivious to stage lights that began to shake, rattle, and explode. Finally the baton-swinger glanced upward and stalled, as if transformed into a biblical pillar of salt. Donna peered to see what he saw. Her eyes followed a single light fixture, falling like a shooting star. Its target was a tuba player. As if sensing danger, the man looked up, causing his instrument to tilt backward. With a kawoosh, the light sailed into his big horn, knocking him to the floor, feet pointed up, as a hailstorm of electrical appliances poured.

The stunned audience watched fireworks erupt onstage. Then, a single scream trumpeted and a thousand answered its call. Everyone moved everywhere at once – all but Donna, who stood like Satan's designated witness, watching hell break loose.

Ceiling panels plummeted, whizzing from above as a roof section above the stage cracked, then ruptured under stress. Chunks plunged, opening a cavity to starry skies. Like a machine gun blast, rivets popped at roof beam joints until, with a thunderous boom, steel support joints at the roof line split apart. Exterior concrete columns bent like plastic. Interior arches with lesser ductility shattered. Walling behind the bandstand caved inward, then tumbled. Musicians, some carting their instruments like mothers protectively cradling their babes, others fast abandoning them, darted for cover.

As severed electrical lines caused lighting outages, darkness, the magnifier of the fear, turned the crowd into a mob. Donna watched them scoot like so many blind mice, and prayed to survive in the temple of ruin. Battery-powered emergency lights activated, radiating an uncanny amber glow. Their beams shone through dust particles that floated like gritty clouds.

She saw something move stealthily in the shadows. Huge and inhuman, steely-yellow eyes fixed on her. The lion, free from its cage, stalked her. Donna shrieked for help knowing no one would hear.

"Snuggums! Where are you?" the full-figured woman shouted.

When disaster had struck, she'd been massaging her bunions. She climbed under the table, searching for her shoes. She felt around in the dark, but couldn't find them. When she came back up, she couldn't find Snuggums or her children. The woman moved with the surging mob, bewildered and barefoot. Shards from broken cocktail glasses sliced her feet.

"Somebody, find my children!" she called out.

A slow rumble garnered momentum until stage flooring ripped apart. Natural gas lines underneath ruptured, discharging noxious fumes into the tumult. Sparks from fallen lighting equipment ignited gaseous plumes of skyrocketing flame. Crowds swarmed with greater urgency, pushing harder and moving mercilessly. Somewhere in their throngs, she went down.

"Help me," the woman screamed.

A man in a tuxedo walked close. His foot came down her arm. She watched her wrist bend and snap under his weight. No one heard her squeal.

Rumbling ground tremors intensified, stirring then shaking the earth, until another gas line burst, launching a second fiery plume beside stage curtains. Intense heat began melting the fireproof fabric, while thousands of screams grew louder.

As if spewing from the bowels of the earth, a geyser whooshed from a pierced water main. It shot from under the stage, upward toward the hole that had opened in the roof, and fell like misty rain, helping contain some stage fires, but flooding the wreckage. The edge of the stage became a waterfall, spilling to the show room floor. Some still near the stage slipped and desperately leaped to avoid drowning in fast forming pools.

Yellow eyes of the stalking lion glared. Fifteen feet from Donna the big cat stopped. It set back on its rear haunches, ready to pounce and seeming to know she wouldn't move.

"Please, no," Donna screamed.

Her shrill wail was lost in the chorus of surrounding cries. The beast leaped at her with eight-inch fangs exposed and flesh-shredding claws outstretched.

Manny Levine started dashing into the theater to help. Tommy grabbed him by the lapels and yelled over the clamor.

"Find a phone. Fast! Have the police send every car in the city. Get fire and rescue personnel here."

"What the hell is happening?"

Tommy peered into the show room. He could only wonder, too, as a long rumble turned into a boom!

Both ducked, Tommy still holding his CEO. "Manny," he said, "every hospital between here, Philly, and New York better be ready."

As Manny dashed to make calls, people staggered out show room doors. Tommy took a deep breath and entered the mayhem to help anyone he could. No one ever wants to walk into an inferno, but Tommy knew he had no choice. Saving even one life would be worth the risk.

Inside, he saw the magnitude of the disaster and realized hell could visit earth. Tommy fought his way through crowds and looked toward the stage. Above it, the roof's hole had opened wide. *Thank God*, he thought. The aperture let smoke escape. So many lives could have been lost to smoke inhalation.

"Please help," a woman cried from the floor.

Tommy looked down. Careful not to grab the crooked left arm she cradled in her right hand, he carried her piggyback. *God, she's a load*, he thought.

All around him, heroes emerged. He saw firsthand that human tragedy always produces more heroism than cowardice. State police officers, assigned by the Casino Control Commission to the property, were already in action. Beverage servers and good Samaritans from the crowds helped the injured, the young, the aged, anyone they could.

Tommy looked toward the side exits. Building the show room separate from the main tower provided an abundance of emergency exits, so crowds dispersed to safety directly outdoors. Thank God they didn't all have to all leave through the casino.

He carried the woman on his back to the casino floor where workers were ushering anyone, who could walk, out the casino main doors. Tommy screamed loudly enough for all his people to hear.

"Get the injured up and out of the way. Put them on the playing tables if you have to."

He turned to a floor person by his side.

"Sarah, get any help you need, but make sure all the emergency exits to the theater are opened. I want everyone who's nonessential outside and far away from the show room as possible."

She ran, taking a handful of dealers with her.

"Robby Vee," he called to his burly security chief. "Wait outside for the cops."

"I've got my crew guarding the cashier's office and chips on the tables until we get them under lock and key," said Vandegrift.

"We're saving lives first. Jump on it. I want to talk to the police and fire department commanders. Bring them to me. We'll coordinate their efforts with the utility companies. We have to control gas and water leaks."

The head security officer took one fast look at the tables before rushing to his newly assigned task. Fortunately, blasts from the show room had scared most players out casino doors fast. Millions of dollars in chips laying on tables could've been easy pickings for looters. Robby Vee's men collected tokens as watchful security cameras maintained surveillance. The cameras connected to hundreds of video recorders running on backup power with main electrical lines to the surveillance department severed. How long they could maintain power throughout the casino was impossible to tell. Even back-up lines could fail in a disaster that size.

Tommy called to a pit boss. "Joe, have South Jersey Gas shut off natural gas lines coming into the Marina District until we have this under control."

"You want water mains shut down too, boss?"

"Hell, no. We won't have any way to put out fires. Find our maintenance chief. See if he can control broken water lines without shutting down the whole system. And make sure he cuts electricity inside the show room. We have battery-powered emergency lighting. There's no reason to fuel an electrical fire."

Tommy watched his workforce jump into action. They were good people, but how could anyone have prepared them for that calamity? Sirens wailed outside the casino's doors. As emergency personnel arrived, an unnerving thought crossed his mind.

Susannah. She had been in her dressing room backstage when the disaster erupted. Only as he considered her did panic strike his heart. *My God*, he thought. *Is she alive?*

In urgent tones, Greg Conrad yelled into his office intercom. "Get the damned thing ready for takeoff, now! I want a pilot in my helicopter and I want it ready to fly in five minutes."

He knew what was happening. From his office windows, he watched black smoke eerily rise from The Megasino toward the moon. Sirens sounded throughout town as police cars, fire trucks, and ambulances descended on a single site.

What a great night to pull off a robbery, he thought. The city's entire police force would be at the disaster zone. Conrad had no thoughts of robbing any bank, though. He already had a plan in action. Conrad was heisting an entire casino right under the nose of every cop in town.

He wanted a better look from the air. The black helicopter with his logo on its sides would takeoff from The Pyramid rooftop helipad. He stroked his chin and thought, *What a terrific view!*

Conrad buzzed his night secretary again on the intercom. "Sally, delay that takeoff twenty minutes and call my service. Have them send over a companion." The action charged his sexual energy. He'd unleash it in the air while the drama unfolded beneath the chopper.

Snuggums moved fast, bumbling and mumbling along. "Now, ya did it, aw-white," he said through his swollen lips. "Ya set off dat ex-posion somehow wiff dis ding." Knowing he had ignited the calamity with the little box, he feared being blamed for the disaster. *They'll either put me in jail or sue me for this. How was I to know?* He had simply pushed a button on the black box and heard rumbles. Somehow, he had caused the stage to fall apart. "Twouble, twouble, twouble," he groaned.

Thank God I didn't push the other button, too, he thought. Who knew what it would've done? He could have landed in even deeper trouble.

The box was still in his hand, having scrambled with it from the show room when fireworks erupted onstage. He had run so fast and furiously he'd forgotten his wife and kids. Snuggums would worry about them after he ditched the thing.

He scurried among crowds outside the casino. Some people laughed in nervous relief; some asked the same question, repeatedly.

"What happened?"

Others just walked in stunned disbelief.

"My Arnold's in there," a woman called with a blank stare on her face. "Has anyone seen Arnold Stubin?"

She grabbed his arm and asked him, too. Snuggums shook her off, knowing he had to dump the box before someone caught him with it.

Damn, he thought. *I bet my finger prints are all over this thing.*

There was only one thing to do with it. He hustled to the marina and set foot on the docks. Snuggums followed a path of wooden planks past yachts with names like "Lucky Lady" and "Come 7 and 11." Many boaters had returned to their pleasure crafts and a party atmosphere emerged among those who found safe refuge from harm. Drinks flowed. People shouted to one another. Some shared camaraderie of survivors; others continued parties that had started when they had docked their boats.

He quick-stepped along the dock as far as it went into the bay. Finally, Snuggums stopped and studied his black box a last time. He wondered what the other button did.

What the hell, he thought. *Who's going to catch me out here?*

He pushed down and waited. Nothing happened. He tried again. Nothing. The transmitter was out of range.

"Fuff it," he said.

With a mighty heave, he tossed his box into the bay. It splashed and bobbed on the surface.

Sink, he thought, *sink!*

It wasn't going down.

"Hey, buddy," a partygoer behind his back called, "want a cold beer?"

Snuggums grabbed a can and placed the chilly metal on his banana lips. All the while, his eyes fixed on his box bobbing atop the water. It floated back toward the docks with an incoming tide.

The man rested his elbow on Snuggums' shoulder and spoke to him face to face. "Man, look at your mouth. Did a truck hit you or what?"

Snuggums had heard enough. He pushed the guy into the bay, watched him splash, then swigged his beer. The cool can had a soothing effect. He held it against his inflammation to relieve swelling, while his eyes fixed again on the bobbing box. They remained glued to it until the thing finally submerged. What he'd done would remain a secret.

Finally, he thought.

The only evidence to prove an explosive device had caused the disaster joined the clams.

Donna struggled to her feet. She hadn't moved when the big cat attacked. It had leaped as a chunk of roof fell in its path, nicking her but striking the lion squarely on its skull.

On wobbling legs, she surveyed the huge, huge and motionless, feline sprawled before her. For an instant, she thought she saw the tail twitch and realized she didn't have strength to run.

No, she thought, *it's just my imagination*.

Still, there was no reason to dally. What if the beast wasn't dead? Donna let out a long breath and lumbered toward an emergency exit, half an eye still looking back.

"We can't contain the flames," the city fire chief explained. "A lot of initial fires are out, but secondary fires are spreading fast," he told Tommy and his crew. "They're going to reach the casino and take the tower down."

"Put 'em out," Manny said.

"We can't," the chief replied. "Water pressure went down when the mains ruptured. Our pumper trucks only carry five-hundred gallons. Suction hoses we're sticking in the bay won't be running in time. That leaves us depending on the Coast Guard fire boat. It's only operational on the building's bay side and can't tackle a fire this size. It's like using a water pistol."

Tommy turned to his maintenance chief. "What can

you do?"

"Nothing, boss. Only the public utility company can repair the ruptures and that would take hours. Besides, you have to figure ruptures are underneath the show room. There's no way to reach them until the fire's out."

"In fifteen minutes, twenty tops," the fire chief observed, "the casino tower will ignite. You're going to lose it."

Tommy glared. "We're not losing this casino."

"Maybe there's one thing we can do," his maintenance chief suggested. The man scratched the top of his head as if scraping a thought free. "Blow the water tank on the show room's roof. It's holding millions of gallons."

The fire chief thought, then nodded. "We have people who could try."

"Have we evacuated everyone from the show room?" Tommy said.

"It's hard to imagine anyone alive in there, now," the fire chief replied.

Tommy weighed the options and realized he had no choice. He nodded to the chief who put a specially-trained fire department team to work. Six firefighters would climb to the rooftop.

As Tommy watched the blaze, he asked his security chief a question. "The performers backstage . . . does anyone know if they got out?"

"Don't know, Mr. Brucker," the man said. "The fire took off in that direction awfully fast."

Again, Tommy's heart raced to Susannah. He wanted to find her, but knew they needed him where he was. He was responsible for every life on the property, yet he could think of only one. Susannah would be on his mind until she turned up, alive or dead.

Susannah tripped in the dark, but caught herself before going down. Behind her, Courtney carried handfuls of hair. She had yanked hard at the two nearest members of EnCor and ripped off matching wigs just as mayhem had unleashed. Amid the havoc, she'd forgotten to let go and carried the hairpieces like pompons. All the singers had gathered by Susannah's dressing room door and heard clamor from the stage area. Then, the lights had gone out. The backup system never activated in the backstage hallway, so they had to feel their way through it. Not knowing where they were going, they just followed a long and winding hall away from the stage area. Susannah's larger bodyguard took the lead. She, Courtney, and the four women of EnCor followed. Susannah's smaller guard, who had been watching the show from the wings, had disappeared somewhere in the darkness. Suddenly the big guard stopped.

The teeny singer from EnCor immediately called out, "What's wrong? Why are we stopping?"

"Can't go any farther," the big man said. "We've run into a dead end."

"I can't see anything." another member of the quartet complained.

The bodyguard lit a match, illuminating a steel door that blocked their passage. They looked for a way to open it, but the match went out.

"Damn," the guard said. "I've only got one match left in the pack."

"Light it," Courtney said.

"When it goes out, we're stuck in the dark," he replied.

"Light it and hold it up for me."

He struck the match and raised it. Courtney placed one of her pompons over the match and watched it ignite.

"Just like I thought," she said with a smile, "slow burning. We'll light the other one when this one begins to go out."

Susannah and her bodyguard tried to budge the door. They leaned into the bar handle and pushed, but something was jamming the door from the other side.

From the stage area, they heard crackling flames. Smoke was making its way down the long corridor. They knew they didn't have much time. Even if flames didn't reach them, smoke would poison their lungs.

"Push harder!" The quartet screamed in unison.

Jose Rodriguez looked calmer than he felt. Special training and ten-years experience qualified the lean firefighter to lead what the department good-humoredly called their "commando force." He and his men tackled tough jobs, but they had never handled anything so big. An aerial-ladder truck extended a sectional ladder upward. He and his team would ascend it. A pyrotechnics expert carried an explosive charge. With luck, they would blast the rooftop tank apart.

Rodriguez reached for his St. Christopher's medal, then remembered he no longer wore it around his neck. Even under flame-resistant protective garments, the bright orange overalls worn by all members of his team, the medal would burn skin when close to so a large fire's intense heat. His three youngsters had given it to him as a father's day gift to keep him safe, and he never had the heart to tell them he couldn't wear it where his dangerous profession took him.

His chief grabbed his arm and asked him directly, "Can your team blow that thing?"

Rodriguez looked up. His dark eyes scoured the roof-line they would have to ascend.

"Is it worth taking the risk?" his commander pressed.

The ladder perched on a steep angle to keep the fire truck safe from flames. Its incline was dangerous. If the building gave way, their truck wouldn't support the ladder long. They had to move fast and hope for the best. There was no way to answer his chief's question without trying.

Above the roof, Rodriguez saw all the air traffic. Helicopters hovered over The Megasino's helipad. Rescue birds airlifted seriously injured to Camden and Philadelphia for treatment as casualties overburdened local hospitals. News copters roamed alongside military choppers that had been pressed into medivac service. Rodriguez knew what he had to do. He turned to the chief and said, "Get those choppers out of the area before we blast."

Blades on Conrad's helicopter spun loudly. Though the sky was crowded, a perfect view below riveted his attention as the intercom buzzed.

"Mr. Conrad, air traffic control is ordering all crafts to remove themselves from the rescue zone," the pilot called into the passengers' compartment. "They want everyone out of the area."

"Everyone?" Conrad shouted back. "Everyone never means me."

The pilot spoke with conviction. "I'm sorry, sir, but we'll have to –"

"Unless you really want to be sorry," Conrad interrupted, "turn off your radio and hover. Later, just say it went out."

"Sir, that's a violation of –"

"Turn off the damn radio and shut down the intercom. Now!"

Greg Conrad watched flames rise from the theater's stage area until his companion's cheery call diverted his attention.

"Want to play 'slutty stewardess and bad little passenger' with me?"

Conrad grinned at his perky playmate. She sat beside him with hair cropped so short it never saw a comb. Freckles covered the pug nose dream. She looked innocent as an angel and it was time to spread her wings. The helicopter, which normally flew high rollers and casino executives, was designed for comfort. He lowered his oversized seat into position. Conrad's slutty stewardess opened his shirt as he admitted, "I've been a *very* bad little passenger."

From atop the show room, Rodriguez studied flames consuming the roofline as his five men worked beside the huge water tank. He peered through openings where the roof had collapsed. Smoke had engulfed the theater. Anyone trapped inside was dead, he figured.

Their pyrotechnic expert double-checked explosives affixed to the tank's underside. Without time to set backup charges, they would try to break it open with a single detonation.

Rodriguez called to him. "Almost ready, Maloney?"

The man kept working without answering. Smoke billowed into the sky. The blaze inched toward them, cooking the rooftop.

"Jimmy, are you almost done?" Rodriguez hollered.

Sweat streaming down his face, the blast man signaled thumbs up.

Their boots stuck in roofing tar as they scurried to the ladder that extended six-stories high from their fire truck.

"Get down the ladder," he ordered his team.

A firefighter called back, "This ladder won't hold more than two men at a time."

Rodriguez knew the man was right. At its steep angle leaning against the building, they couldn't trust the ladder to support all their weight, but they didn't have time to descend in pairs. With fire racing toward them, all six team members had to alight at once. They would test the ladder's strength to its limits. Rodriguez also knew the ladder operator would be anxious. He'd be checking ground jacks spanning outward to keep the fire truck from tipping as six men took their only ticket out of harms way.

"No time to wait," Rodriguez declared. "Everyone goes, now!"

He watched the first firefighter leap onto the ladder and climb downward. Beneath them, beacons on hundreds of emergency vehicles rotated. Police had moved crowds back. Still, Rodriguez could sense eyes – thousands of them – focused upward, watching the firefighters' silhouettes as flames seared their backs. As team leader, he would leave the roof last. The roof began vibrating as he watched his team descend. Just one more man had to step onto the ladder before he could start his own descent. His pyrotechnics expert handed him the radio-transmitted detonator, then grabbed the ladder's rails to climb down. As team leader, Rodriguez was responsible for assuring the blast went off.

As he looked toward the water tank one last time, the roof section where he stood reverberated, cracked, and collapsed. Rodriguez leaped and squeezed a ladder rung with one hand while holding the detonator in the other. His feet shimmied for a rung to support his weight. The wall beside him crumbled. An exterior concrete column bent inward. Interior arches gave way and the wall went down with six firefighters still clinging to the ladder. Only the truck turntable supported the ladder. It would never hold. Straining under the firefighters' weight, the turntable locking mechanism slipped. The ladder jolted downward ten degrees, shaking off one firefighter, who tumbled headfirst, screaming toward ground. Five men still clenched the ladder with all their might. It jarred downward again. Rodriguez glanced at the detonating device and a thought instantly crossed his mind. *If I fall, I have to detonate that explosion before hitting the ground.*

As they reached the bottom twenty-five feet, the lowest men on the ladder slid down side rails rather than climb rungs. Rodriguez and his pyrotechnics expert were still five stories high. Again, the ladder dropped. If ground jacks on the truck gave way, the ladder would collapse into the fire and they'd be roasted. On the ground, firefighters with safety nets tried scooting underneath, but the steep angle had placed them out of range.

Rodriguez called down to his pyrotechnics man. "Do we do it now?"

Maloney's sweat-drenched face looked uncertain. Rodriguez knew if he exploded the charge underneath the water tank, the aftershock would hurl them off the ladder. On the other hand, it might be their only hope to extinguish the fire without any further loss of life. His pyrotechnics expert didn't answer, so Rodriguez decided. He was ready to detonate the blast and send the fire straight back to hell.

Inside the casino another of manifestation from Hell lurked. A squat man wove through the few workers who remained in the building. He had clipped a county identification badge to his lapel. Peering here and there, he searched the casino floor, carrying papers he would serve on Tommy Brucker. His office had obtained a court order from an emergency judge of the Atlantic County Superior Court. Even if fire didn't take the casino down, he would close the place.

Horace Grender was the county's Chief Prosecutor, reappointed to the position four years after he had left the office in disgrace. Grender had gone into private practice until his successor took a Superior Court judgeship. That man was on his way to the Supreme Court bench someday. Grender had less-grand ambitions. The vacancy in Atlantic County's top law enforcement slot was a prize he quickly snagged. Having regained his position with the influence of special friends, the kind people in his position normally prosecuted, Grender had debts to pay and he would cancel them out by simply doing his duty. He would see that The Megasino, as the sight of two separate calamities, was closed so long as it remained in Tommy Brucker's hands. Grender strolled the casino floor. The casino was big, all right, and it was going to be big and empty.

Rodriguez was sliding down the ladder for the last fifty feet. Hands of three firefighters waited to cushion his landing. Eyes looking upward darted toward the truck turret as it cracked under so much stress, then toward the ladder, which collapsed into flames that instantly consumed it. Rodriguez jumped off and dropped toward earth. He heard something snap when his boots landed, and groaned as pain shot from his legs to his brain. The impact fractured his ankles. The detonating device was still in his hand. *Time to blast this baby*, he thought. His fire chief rushed close and knelt beside him as EMT personnel injected him with strong pain relief. He knew he only had a few lucid moments before he would pass out, but Rodriguez had to see if they could get the fire out. He started to turn the detonator over to his chief.

The chief shook his head. "This one's yours," he said. Then, he stood and shouted, "Is the show room empty?"

"So far as we can tell, Chief," one of his men replied.

"How 'bout the casino?"

"There's still a few people inside who haven't cleared out."

The chief thought for an instant only. "They take their chances. We gotta control this fire."

Rodriguez saw crowds were out of the way. Air

traffic was diverted except for one helicopter continuing to hover.

"Sound the alarm," the chief said. "This thing blows in sixty seconds."

Horace Grender approached Tommy and Manny by the casino doors leading to the show room. "I'm looking for you, Brucker," he called. Naturally high pitched, his voice almost sounded like a pig squeal.

Manny turned to Tommy and said, "What's the county prosecutor doing at a fire scene?"

Tommy didn't know either. He immediately recognized the man and wished there were repellents for that kind of scum. "I don't have time for whatever you want, right now, Grender," he said. "Talk to my CEO later."

Grender came close and poked his finger in Tommy's chest. "Oh, I'll be talking to Mr. Levine later," he said earnestly. "I'll talk to him in front of a grand jury. Someone always takes the fall for a disaster this size. It's going to be you, Brucker. I'm going to indict you for charges ranging from reckless endangerment of human life to homicide."

Tommy's back went straight and rigid. "What are you talking about?"

"Officials warned you the design plan for your show room was unsafe, but you went ahead, anyway. You put this place up fast, without a thought for safety. Now you've had casualties on an unsafe thrill ride. You've got more in your show room – the show room you guaranteed would be safe in sworn testimony before a planning board."

Grender paused to take a handkerchief to his brow. Wiping beads of sweat, he smiled wide, too wide for Tommy's likes, as he said, "Looks like putting up this town's thirteenth casino changed your luck, buster."

"We make our own luck," Tommy answered automatically.

Grender started to fold his handkerchief, then grimaced as if it were too wet to place back in his pocket. He dropped it to the floor and focused on Tommy with eyes that flared with conviction.

"You made your own luck, all right. And it's all bad, asshole. You're going to pay for putting up this death trap. You'll serve twenty years, Brucker. I may even seek a death sentence."

Susannah prayed to live, still trapped in the dark hallway with nowhere to go. In front of her, the jammed steel door wouldn't budge. Behind her, flames crackled louder. As fear gripped her, so did something else, another feeling that rose from the pit of her soul. Whether it was anger borne of self-recrimination or just plain remorse, she couldn't stop chastising herself.

I waited too long to let Tommy know, she thought, *and may never have the chance, now.*

She could tell fire was nearing. The opening above the stage had let most of the smoke escape harmlessly. Yet, as fire meandered down the hallway, thick black billows crept in their direction, stealing oxygen from the air.

EnCor's four women sat close to her on the floor. Courtney held the last burning wig. When it smoldered out, she collapsed too. Susannah and her guard continued to bang the door, desperately trying to break out. As life-draining smoke seeped into Susannah's lungs, she dropped. Susannah covered her nose and mouth with her hands, futilely attempting to shield herself. Violently, she coughed and hacked, while her bodyguard leaned against the door, lamely pounding with one fist.

The bomb blasted. Then like a dam burst, water billowed across the show room roof toward openings, poured down, and doused flames. Searing steam replaced black smoke. The theater filled with rivers that rushed out open doors, crashed through closed ones, and raced down halls.

"What's that?" Courtney blurted.

Susannah's bodyguard smacked the door one last time. "Sounded like it came from above us," he said.

Another wham sounded, less loud, but just as clearly . . . and closer. It sounded like a sledgehammer on the other side of the door, pounding faster and harder with each blow.

"Someone must have heard us banging," her bodyguard offered.

From the other direction, Susannah heard rumbling like a freight train. One of EnCor's women rose to her feet and shouted.

"Something's coming at us from down the hall."

Water cascaded round the last bend in the hallway like a tidal wave, sweeping everything in its path. Just then, the door cracked open. *Clean, fresh, breathable air*, Susannah thought. The opening wasn't wide enough for anyone to push through, but Susannah could see a firefighter working frantically. Face flushed, he swung his sledgehammer into fallen debris blocking the passageway. Her bodyguard threw his weight at the door.

Susannah felt water pound her. It whipped her into the steel door, forced it to fly open, and washed Susannah outside with her bodyguard. Courtney and the quartet followed, swirling in surging torrents. Frantically, Susannah clawed for anything to anchor her in the raging waters. Then the flow ebbed. She rose to her feet and staggered.

"Thank you, Lord," she prayed. "Amen."

Her desperate prayer was answered. Susannah looked up to the sky, grateful to see stars. Exhausted, she grew faint, then fell facedown in a pool of water and began to drown.

The pudgy prosecutor handed Tommy the papers he carried. "Consider yourself served with process, Brucker. Your casino's closed by order of the Superior Court."

Grender smiled smugly. The Buckman smiled back, realizing Grender had his back turned and didn't see it coming. Tommy and Manny watched water surge through the entranceway between the show room and casino. They waited for it to grow near, then jumped onto a craps table behind them as Grender washed away. The prosecutor slid headfirst into a playing table leg.

"Craps," Tommy said softly. Grender supported his weight with his hands. His arms stretched straight; his legs lay flat. Another surge of water washed over him. Grender jiggled his head to shake it off – like a trained seal waiting for a fish.

"He'll be back on his feet," Manny said.

Tommy shook his head in agreement. "To beak us." He studied the court order. Grender had exercised the full authority of his office to close The Megasino. Tommy knew what that meant. "We need the casino's daily drop to keep this operation alive," he said. "Without it, we're done. And we're done fast."

Chapter Eleven

Champion on the Line

Nothing moved swifter on the court than Dion "Stuff Daddy" Brown. He burst open on the breakaway and drove alone under the hoop. Palming the basketball in his right hand, the big man readied to slam-dunk an easy two-pointer, but a referee's whistle blew to stop the play. Normally, that was the only thing that could stop Dion, but the night hadn't been normal.

"Traveling," the official called.

Another careless mistake turned the ball over. All evening Dion had played a lackluster game and it showed on the scoreboard. Nashville's Wildcats trailed 88-72 with seven minutes remaining in the game. They headed toward losing game one in the best of seven series. With the championship on the line, oddsmakers had heavily favored them. Bookies were going to take an enormous hit all over the country. Even the legitimate sports books were in trouble, and no legal betting parlor had more money on the line than The Fantasy Casino in Las

Vegas.

A whistle trilled again.

"Time out," the referee called.

The Wildcats coach needed time to regroup. His starters circled around him tight; bench players gathered behind. As a former player, the coach was tall as most of them. He had put on weight since his playing days that showed up waist high. His hands rested a small pot belly that jiggled as he yelled over cheers from hometown Chicago fans.

"What the hell is going on out there?"

He looked to all his players. He didn't have to say it. Each knew what he was talking about. They were playing for the championship. Everything they had fought for all season was at stake. They knew how important it was to win the first game of the series, but they were letting Chicago walk away with it.

Coach Walton didn't reprimand. He challenged his players. He put it to all of them rather than to any one man – though it was clear what the problem was. Their star center didn't have his head in the game. He had missed easy baskets. He didn't take shots he had sunk all season. Instead, he passed off the ball to teammates who weren't even in position to receive it. Dion was a champion on the line, and the young man was faltering badly. Charlie Walton wondered if his team could pull it out.

"Ten seconds," an assistant coach called.

It was time to send his starters back to the floor. "Now, do it!" he called out to all of them. He slapped Stuff Daddy on the butt. *Maybe that'll wake him up*, the coach figured, as he watched his players set into their positions.

A whistle sounded to signal resumption of play. Nobody had expected his team to fall apart. Afterall, Chicago's biggest star, the man who had taken them to repeated championship seasons, had retired before the season had even begun. Perhaps his team was just feeling game one jitters.

Scanning the crowds, Charlie observed a familiar face was missing. He had expected to see her at the road game and wondered if that was what bothered his superstar.

Where's Gramzie Brown?

The game came in fuzzy on their twelve-inch black and white TV. Chichi had found the old television in a country store selling "used notions and such." The set only picked up two channels in the rural hills of Tennessee. He adjusted the aluminum foil antenna they'd fashioned as rabbit ears atop it.

"Yeah, that's better," Petey "Pets" Petrillo called from across the room. Chichi's partner was mightily moussed and heavily needled. His hair curled in rigidly set ringlets. Three golden loops in his left lobe crested over a diamond stud. Tattooed forearms displayed a zippy Road Runner on the left arm and a surly coyote on the right. They emerged from a tee shirt he wore untucked over baggy black sweatpants.

Chichi returned to his seat.

"Nah," Petey Pets mumbled. "You gotta stay there."

"What?"

"When you leggo of the antenna, the picture goes fuzzy. You haveta hold the foil."

Sometimes Petey Pets garbled words. The golden

spike piercing his tongue turned him into a mush mouth whenever he didn't take time to enunciate.

Chichi studied the fuzzy picture again. They could make out forms in motion as the camera panned up and down the court. The picture sucked, but the sound came in fine.

"I ain't standing here like a moron while you two watch the friggin' thing," Chichi said. "Let her hold the antenna."

Both hoods turned to their captive. They were letting Gramzie watch the game, but Chichi had tied her to a wooden chair and taped her mouth closed. Gagging was the only way to keep her quiet. Throughout the first half of the game she had prayed aloud for Almighty God to smite them with various inflictions – testicular cancer, festering face warts, and bodacious rectal blockages. Her seemingly endless a list made the two nonbelievers uncomfortable.

Chichi sat gingerly, still nursing the injury he'd suffered when she kicked him. He studied the woman, who was finally under control. He had told her they wouldn't let her watch the game if she didn't keep herself in line. They threatened to throw her back in the basement furnace room of the rented country cabin. The small room had become her dungeon, and the threat seemed to do it. Gramzie wanted to see the game even if she didn't like what was happening on the court.

Stuff Daddy was working for the mob. They had recruited him to throw the series. The mob knew they would never tempt the superstar to throw the games for cash; he made mountains of money already. Besides, the kid was too honest to go for any scam. They also knew how close he was to the fiery woman who had

raised him, so they had kidnaped her as leverage to collar the big man.

The Atlantic City mob was doing more than just
throwing a championship series. They were putting the
final nail in Tommy Brucker's coffin. They had mustered big bucks to place into the legal sports book his
Las Vegas casino ran, betting on underdog-Chicago to
win the series. Huge bets were placed through a number of sources to keep their identity secret. The Fantasy Casino would take a major hit if heavily favored Nashville lost the seven game series.

Amazingly, no one had ever pulled it off. Not since
crime overlord Arnold Rothstein had fixed the 1919 World
Series, had anyone thrown a major sport's championship. Naturally, Rothstein's baseball scam had fallen
apart. Too many players have to be involved to fix a
baseball game. One player out of nine wouldn't have
enough impact. Basketball was different. If you fixed
just one player, you fixed one out of five athletes on the
court. And if that player was a superstar like Stuff Daddy Brown, who was responsible for 38 per cent of his
team's scoring output, you controlled the outcome.

Ironically, the mob would use money they scammed
from The Fantasy sporting book to help buy The Megasino at a fire sale price. Joey would funnel winnings
with other funds to the stooge who was acting as their
front man. They would hand it to Greg Conrad with
loans structured from offshore investment banking firms.
The mob's foreign partner in the venture was advancing
the credit. Essentially, Tommy Brucker's own money
would help the mob buy his Atlantic City casino at a
discounted price after they had caused the two separate
calamities. The mob even controlled the prosecutor who

would see that The Megasino remained closed so long as Brucker kept it in his name. It was a sweet deal for the Atlantic City crime family, and Stuff Daddy was helping them pull it off.

The whistle blew again.

"Foul number four called on Dion "Stuff Daddy" Brown," the announcer called out.

Things were going Chicago's way. Chichi felt good knowing everything would roll their way through the series. He watched Gramzie's head tilt down. She knew what was happening. After Chichi and Petey had picked her up, the mob had collared her grandson in Atlantic City. He had walked into their backyard when he arrived as a special guest at The Megasino grand opening. They had put the superstar on the telephone to talk to his grandmother, just long enough for the big man to verify they held her. Gramzie was their insurance policy and they would place her on the phone again if her grandson wavered. True sports heroes care how they perform, and they couldn't allow pride to mess with his head.

"Game one's over," the announcer called out. "It goes to Chicago. Stay tuned for a wrap-up."

Chichi turned off the television. It was time to stick Gramzie in her hole. He untied her from the chair while Petey Pets kept a pistol trained on her. They had learned to watch the woman closely.

"Move," Petey barked.

She trudged down basement stairs ahead of them and slumped as she entered the damp chamber.

"Stand still," Chichi said. "I'm going to pull the tape off your mouth."

He tugged fast and smiled when she grabbed her lips.

Chichi didn't remove it out of compassion. They didn't want the woman to suffocate on the basement floor.

"Nighty night," Petey called as they locked her inside.

They didn't want her to die – not yet, anyway.

Chapter Twelve

Love Comes Once

Waking in a strange room, Susannah tried rising but aching muscles and stiff joints didn't cooperate. A form approached, a woman's form, it seemed.

"You're in the Avery-Davis Clinic, Miss Halloway."

"What?"

Susannah tried focusing on the uniformed attendant, then on her surroundings. Thoughts raced through a mind that drew blank spots. She didn't remember anything after a tidal wave had washed her out the door.

"How long have I been here?"

"They admitted you last night. A doctor gave you something to make you sleep."

Susannah wondered what it was. "I feel rotten."

The nurse drew close and raised Susannah's arm to check her pulse; it was a small gesture, yet one that let Susannah know she was, at last, safe. She studied the woman — middle-aged, wearing a fair amount of make-up, unlike so many in her profession who looked scrubbed, hospital clean. Her soft voice soothed like a tonic.

"The doctor will arrive shortly. I pushed a call button for him when you began to stir."

Susannah ran her hands along her arms, then flexed her fingers. Everything worked at half-speed.

"You're fine, but you'll probably feel weak for awhile. You didn't break anything, but you are badly bruised."

Susannah tried stretching her legs, then groaned instead; moaning was lots easier than moving.

"Nurse, I want something for pain. Tell the doctor I need something strong."

The woman frowned. "Take two of these," she said, handing over pills in a small paper cup.

As the nurse poured a glass of water from a pitcher on a silver bedside tray, Susannah noticed something. *This place is pretty plush for a hospital*, she reflected. The walls were pale blue, rather than stark hospital white, with soft-colored framed prints hanging. No, she observed, they were oil paintings.

"How did I get here?"

"Ambulance. Rescue personnel saw you fall into a water pool. You're lucky they grabbed you so quickly."

Susannah studied the pills through eyes of a skilled observer. Familiar with all kinds of pain killers, as a regular part of her diet, she could identify most by shape, size, and color, but those were strangers. *Maybe my eyesight is out of whack*, she thought.

"What are these?" she asked.

"Muscle relaxants. They'll ease your movements."

"Good afternoon," came a call from the doorway.

Susannah looked across the room and spotted a bearded black man, approaching at a brisk pace.

"I'm Doctor Simons. How are you feeling?"

The nurse handed him Susannah's chart.

"I feel like catfish after it's been fried."

The doctor smiled as he glanced through entries.

"You'll feel that way for awhile from the soft tissue injuries. We'll start some light physical therapy. Nothing too aggressive. Sooner you begin, though, the better."

"Doctor, I didn't bring my pills with me. They were in my room when this happened. Could you get me –"

"Miss Halloway," the physician interrupted, "after you eat, we can talk about our overall treatment goals."

"What do you mean? I just want something strong to kill the pain."

The doctor took a small flashlight to her eyes. His stethoscope momentarily chilled her chest. While he poked and probed, he spoke.

"Local hospitals were very busy last night. Firefighters alerted Mr. Brucker when they found you and he arranged your admission here. We principally treat people who suffer from alcohol and drug dependencies. We can't keep you here without your consent, but. . . ."

That sly son of a bitch, Susannah thought, realizing what he'd done. Tommy had once encouraged her to check into the Betty Ford Center. So many stars passed through their treatment programs that dependency problems became chic. Susannah knew she needed help. Needing it and wanting it were different.

"I'm getting out of here, now," she said.

Susannah rose, her head spinning, her bones aching, her entire body revolting against being upright. *This ain't getting it, girl*, she realized. Collapsing backward, her head anchored into a downy pillow. Soft sheets enveloped her frame as the nurse covered her. Tucked between them, Susannah knew she wasn't going anywhere.

"Don't try too much too soon," the doctor said. "I'll be back, later. Meanwhile, nurse Tilles will see to your needs."

Through half-open eyes, Susannah watched him leave. She'd walk through the same door soon as she mustered enough strength. She was mad . . . and anger would be the driving force to set her on her feet. Tommy had pulled a fast one on her, but she would check out, fast. Susannah had been on pills with the help of her own doctor too long to stop.

It had started as a way to deal with Jake, the man she had married so many years ago, the man who had lived down to all her expectations. With a style slick as grease, Jake was one slippery weasel. Their work had often sent them in separate directions, which had been the single blessing holding their marriage together. She had gone on tour while Jake promoted records around the country. His ceremonial title as "the number two man" in the recording company was merely glitter; Jake's responsibilities hadn't changed.

Jake had done what he liked. Being a husband to Susannah or a father to her child never interfered. His tastes ran to ladies and fast living. Whenever she had reminded him he was wed, Jake took to her with vengeance, shouting the same thing.

"You remember why I married you, don't you?"

Their arguments had always escalated to fistfights that weren't fairly matched. It wasn't that he was much bigger than her. Jake was wiry and tough. Growing up in streets had cast a mean streak he hid under a smooth smile and easy talk, meanness that unleashed violently. Mr. Benson at the record company had found a doctor who administered special care she needed afterwards. The pasty practitioner looked like the grim reaper and had a bedside manner befitting his appearance.

"Miss Halloway," he would blandly fawn, "I'm so sorry to see you this way again."

Susannah knew those words were no more sincere than the grin twisting his thin lips. The physician made money from her misery, piles of it, paid by her record company. He kept its superstar beaming when she had to smile bright – and assured the scandal of her loveless and abusive marriage didn't leak.

"Why don't you try some of these?" he had once offered. "They'll make you feel better."

Susannah had barely glanced at the narcotics. Pills eased her suffering, but a single prescription couldn't cure the pains of her heart. The longer she had stayed married to Jake, the more medication it took. She had been Jake's punching bag for ten years. When he had left her for a younger woman, Susannah lounged in a drugged stupor and didn't even hear the door slam behind him.

Her second marriage had been right in every way but one. Susannah never loved the guy. Again, pills had helped her sail through the day. Darnel had been her solace, but her second husband had insisted on sending the boy to boarding school. Reluctantly, she'd agreed. At least with Darnel away, he hadn't seen how her habit ruled her. The marriage never stood a chance.

Maybe true love only comes once in a lifetime, she thought. Susannah had instilled that lesson in her son. When Darnel had found love, he jumped for it fast and didn't let go. She was glad he didn't make her mistake. *Darnel*, she thought with a start. *Where is he?*

His limousine still carried desert dust down the highway. Darnel drove hard as he listened to the radio. Game two of the series was underway.

"Chicago has stripped Dion Brown of the ball again," the commentator called. "Oh, baby! This is not his day."

Wildcats were fast becoming an endangered species. They were far behind and about to go down in the series, two games to none. Listening to the game was painful. He was rooting for the Nashville Wildcats because he identified with the scrappy expansion team and its youthful star. Being a young executive, Darnel knew what it was like to come up against big boys who'd been around awhile. He also rooted for Nashville because he knew how much money The Fantasy had taken in bets placed on Chicago to win the series.

The vice president who handled their sports book had come to him with a concerned frown. That wasn't like their customarily optimistic sports guru.

"We're getting heavy action on the finals," Dave had explained. "Big money's on Chicago to take the series."

Darnel looked at the figure sheets Dave handed him, and said, "Homers?"

"Hometown fans placed some of it, but big bets are coming from everywhere. Nobody expects Chicago to win so odds are heavy on the longshot. That's what bothers me. We could take a shellacking if Nashville loses this series."

Darnel had to make the call. "Adjust the odds, but

keep taking bets," he said. "The house should do fine."

After game one, sports prognosticators were surprised as him. The Wildcats' superstar was choking. Maybe Dion Brown was in over his head. If Nashville lost, Darnel realized, people would think the same about him. His judgment call could kill The Fantasy just as Stuff Daddy's play was killing his Wildcats.

"Time out," the announcer called. "Nashville will try to regroup again."

Too late for that, Darnel realized. The game was lost. He turned the radio dial to a news station. Reports on The Megasino disaster still flooded the airwaves.

"Pittsburgh, 17 miles," a road sign read.

Darnel was getting closer. He picked up the limo phone and tried calling the casino again. The same recorded message greeted him.

"No calls are being placed through to –"

Telephone lines were still out. With each mile he drove, Darnel wondered: *What is going on in Atlantic City?*

Chapter Thirteen

Aftershocks

Tina Levine crossed her slender legs, deliberately letting the hem of her dress rise to expose more view. She sat in Conrad's darkened office, calculating her gestures as they scrutinized each other from opposite sides of his oversized desk. Tina had ears long as her gams. She'd heard stories of what happened on that marble desktop. It thrilled her to fantasize about what she would let Conrad do to her there. It stimulated her even more to dream of what she would do to him if the tables ever turned. She, too, enjoyed being in control.

In a far corner, another figure sat in darkness. Tina couldn't see his face but knew who he was. The mob boss didn't scare her. Instead her excitement piqued, knowing she was part of their plans. Big things were about to happen and she could play a major role. Tina fought to conceal how anxious she was to join them. They needed her and she was bargaining for all she could get.

"My proposition's very simple," Conrad said. "Just do what you've done all along. Bring me information once I make an offer."

"Yes," she agreed, "simple." Tina's head clicked through its cognitive process. A hundred-million cranial cells fixed on selfish purpose and delivered a message calculated to tease. "But the value of information you want me to collect in my boudoir has dramatically increased, wouldn't you say?"

She watched Conrad turn toward the mob boss. Though Tina couldn't see his reaction, she knew both men were thinking the same thing. She was squeezing them. The trick was to squeeze hard enough to get what she wanted without clutching so tightly the mobster felt compelled to pinch back. She knew his reputation; he would strangle her. She directed her conversation to Conrad but kept a bit of her eye focused across the room. The faintest stir from that man could signal her to back off.

"The Megasino is the sight of a major disaster," she said. "You're making an offer to take it off Tommy Brucker's hands. He'll have to consult Manny. You want me to bring information I'll snare from my husband in our bedroom. That's a fairly intrusive imposition on my marital relationship, isn't it?"

A sly grin crossed her lips. "You should be able to steal that property, right now. Manny's told me how much money Brucker borrowed to open the place. It should be very valuable to know how bids stack up if he decides to sell."

Her fingernails rapped on the desktop. Glossy-red talons gave her a predatory look. "Let me think," she mused, all the while watching Conrad squirm in his chair.

"To get that kind of information from my husband," she said with a long pause for emphasis, "I suppose, I'll even have to fuck him."

Tina chuckled at the idea of giving Manny what she denied him. She'd just visited her gynecologist who confirmed how fit she was. *I have the dick snapper of a twenty-year-old girl*, Tina mused. *Manny may get a sampling, but he'll beg first.*

"You'll be well compensated for your services, dear," said Conrad.

"Dear," she reflected. "I like the ring to that."

"Brucker will have to sell fast. It's unlikely anyone else will have the money it's going to take on short notice. Information you provide will be useful but not essential."

She knew he was just trying to downplay her significance to lower her price. *I'm no fucking dope*, she thought. She could save them tens of millions, maybe more, with inside information. Opportunity presented a chance to get exactly what she wanted and she intended to grab it.

"Greg, can I talk to your partner a moment?"

Conrad bolted upright in his chair, his eyes darting toward the dark corner, then back to her. He had never introduced her to the man in the dim. Certainly, he'd never intimated the guy was a partner. Tina guessed and Conrad's reaction told her she speculated correctly.

"The gentleman is just an associate. He's not a partner in this affair."

She could see through his lies. The mask Conrad wore in business dealings was transparent to her.

The man across the room beckoned her. "Come close," he said.

His voice startled her. Those were the first words he had uttered. She rose and walked with trepidation toward the man in darkness. Why did he want her close? What would he do to her?

"Sit," he told her. His face remained in shadows. Only a large hand, which patted a chair seat next to him, was visible.

Tina sat and panicked. Was she about to make a fatal mistake? Perhaps she was pushing for too much.

"What does one so lovely want?"

She realized his hushed tones were meant for her alone and her answer shouldn't reach Conrad's ears. She had just learned where the real power lay. *This guy runs the show*, she thought. *How far can I push*? Tina decided to shoot for it all.

"I want a new name, *Missis* Tina Conrad. That's what it will take."

There was silence.

If I could only see his face, she thought. Tina didn't know what he was thinking. Suddenly she wished she could retrieve her words. She had demanded too much. The mob boss was a killer. She should never have been so bold. Tina sat so close to him, she felt wind escape his lips. His breath wasn't warm. Instead, it chilled. She shivered in silence until he spoke.

"Agreed," was all he said.

The man stunned Tina. Could all she dreamed for come so easily? What of Conrad's wife? She wondered what would happen to Francoise.

"I'll need assurances," she insisted. "I won't feel comfortable until something's done with his wife."

He brought himself toward her, emerging from the shadows. Tina jolted back as pustulate lesions, which

oozed murky milk across ruptured facial flesh, grew
nigh. Cobwebs of micro-scars crisscrossed his eyeballs. Their pupils loomed like a matched pair of rotting
black olives while mucous brimmed in the corners of
deep sockets.

The man whispered for only Tina to hear. "Do all
we ask, and you shall have my family's word on your
betrothal. His wife will be no concern. Fail and you'll
have a face like mine."

He held her shoulders in his powerful grip and brought
his face even nearer to hers. Tina tried turning away.

"Look at me," he said. "Fail us . . . and this shall be
your reflection."

Tommy checked himself in the mirror. He was shav-
ing when he heard knocks on the door to his suite. A
final razor stroke finished the job and he cleaned away
excess lather with a towel. Knuckles rapped the door
again. Faster and harder, they beat an urgent sounding
call.

He strolled through the apartment he had built for
himself in the casino hotel as an exact duplicate his suite
at The Fantasy. He had identically furnished them and
even maintained duplicate wardrobes at the properties.
That way Tommy felt at home in either casino. Only
the views differed. In Vegas, he overlooked hotels along
the strip and out to the desert. The Atlantic City vista
was of their marina and Absecon Bay. Neither suite had
a kitchen. World class chefs delivered anything he wanted, anytime. Fine living for a bachelor, but more frequently he considered the price. His dreams came at the
cost of a normal home life.

Tommy opened the door and his CEO delivered news every bit as urgent as his raps had indicated.

"Boss," Manny blurted, "we have to vacate the property."

"What are you talking about?"

"A sheriff's deputy just served another court order."

He handed it to Tommy. "Order to Show Cause," it read.

Tommy whistled. "That scumbag," he said.

Within an hour of the show room disaster, Grender had obtained a court order from an emergency judge closing the property to the public. Apparently, he wanted to hit harder. Grender obtained a second emergent order barring casino employees from the property as well. It permitted only security personnel to remain, "a staff of no more than six members." Instantly, Tommy deputized himself and directed Manny to call their security chief by walkie-talkie.

"Tell Robby Vee I'll stay here as part of his team. Have him rotate five guards at a time on six-hour shifts."

Tommy realized they needed to restore communications in the hotel quickly as possible. Depending on walkie-talkies and cellular phones was problematic. Transmissions were often garbled in the steel-framed high-rise.

Power lines, which had been laid near the disaster site, were also out. A huge backup generator serviced the property, but they had never put it to that kind of test. Designed for short term outages, rather than a regular power source for the huge facility, it went down sporadically, leaving them in darkness.

"Any word on when telephone lines will be back up?" Tommy asked.

"No way to know. This court order even keeps utility companies from entering to make repairs. Grender
has us by our guzungas."

Tommy wondered what was happening. They had
roped off the show room as a crime scene. No one
could enter it until the prosecutor's office and the fire
department completed their investigations. The disaster
had barely touched the casino. It only suffered minor
water and smoke damage that poured from the show
room. Essentially the hotel tower, which also housed
the casino, was fine.

"Manny, how much time do we have to clear out the
hotel?"

"The order gives us three hours."

"Get our local lawyers here. We'll meet them in the
conference room. They have a hearing in front of a
judge Monday morning. I want to talk with them before
they appear in court trying to relax these restraints."

Manny picked up his cellular telephone to make the
call.

"Damn," he said. "The call didn't go through." Manny walked to a window and dialed again.

The disaster had been brutal. What Grender was
doing to them was equally disruptive. He impeded ex-
peditious restoration of vital services. The court orders
he delivered so quickly came like aftershocks. Tommy
held the latest one in his hand, studying it and hoping his
lawyers would bring brighter news.

"First," the white-haired attorney, drawled, "I advise
you and the casino to get independent counsel, Mr.
Brucker."

Tommy looked up with a start.

"What are you talking about? I own the casino."

Lights momentarily flashed off in the mahogany paneled boardroom. When they returned, the attorney continued.

"You're the principal stockholder, but the law recognizes your interests may conflict with those of other shareholders. Frankly, they may wish to take civil action against you to distance the company from criminal charges the county prosecutor promised to file against you."

"I have an attorney whom I'm comfortable with if it comes to that," Tommy said. He didn't believe the words even as he spoke them. He could depend on Darnel to be loyal to him, but the younger man never had any real courtroom experience. Besides, right now, they couldn't even find him.

He and Manny sat at a conference table across from their lead counsel and his younger associate. Douglas Hooper was a self-proclaimed "elder gentleman of the bar." The seasoned attorney headed the largest law firm in Atlantic City. Because the local legal system was known for parochial quirks, Tommy kept Atlantic City lawyers on retainer. Hooper's firm represented many casinos, but Tommy had never seen the man act under fire. He wondered how effective the distinguished-looking gentleman would be. The man's demeanor was reserved as the grey Brooks Brothers business suit he wore with penny loafers. Sparks never flared from him, and Tommy demanded more from an advocate.

Hooper hadn't introduced the associate, who accompanied him, until Tommy asked for the young woman's name. *Helen DeMarco*, Tommy thought. He made a

point of remembering that name. The young lawyer
seemed more than a mere brief case carrier for her boss.
Her every dark hair was in place. Short bangs and a
blunt flip in the front framed strong facial features, which
were lightly dusted with powder, rouge and lip gloss in
brownish hues, lending her an appearance of determination without a trace of masculinity. Dressed in a navy
business suit with a long skirt, she looked sharp and
spoke with refreshing directness.

Confronted by big stakes, lawyers often hedged their
bets. Men like Hooper were afraid to stick out their
necks. Tommy wanted a clear idea of what to expect in
days ahead. He needed to know his chances of quickly
reopening the casino. He also wanted to know how his
lawyers intended to do it. The restraints in Grender's
court orders had to be relaxed fast or his Megasino venture would fail.

It didn't take long for Tommy to rate Hooper as too
cautious. The older lawyer didn't want to promise much
for fear of later disappointing a major corporate client.

"Douglas," Tommy finally said out of exasperation,
"it's time for you to earn your retainer. Every day the
casino's shut, it loses a million-dollar drop. We can't
afford to fall any further in the hole."

The older lawyer pensively stroked his chin.

"We'll try lifting these restraints Monday morning,
but it's hard to speculate what a judge will do. You have
to expect a conservative decision. Safety is at stake.
No judge will expose the public to a potential hazard. If
another disaster hits the casino before they hold safety
hearings, the judge would have his head handed to him
by the press. No jurist wants to go through that."

"Who's the judge?"

"Mel Hastings."

"What's he like?"

"Could be worse," their chief counsel muttered.

"But only if blood or marriage related him to the prosecutor," the younger lawyer added.

Her words were crisp and lively. Tommy liked hearing from the younger attorney. Hooper's voice seemed to emerge from a tomb rather than a mouth. The pessimistic prognostications of their chief counsel had grown tiresome.

"What do you mean?" Tommy said.

"Melvin Hastings is prosecution oriented. He came to the bench as a former prosecutor. He's got a built-in slant on how he sees things. We're better off delaying our hearing until Tuesday. He'll be away at a state bench convention most judges will attend. That leaves the county with only two judges in the courthouse. Either would be less biased."

Tommy saw the young woman had spoken out of turn. Her boss scowled. Tommy didn't care; the logic was sound.

"What do you think, Douglas?" Tommy said.

"Well, I'm not so certain that –"

"I am," Tommy interrupted. "Push our hearing back a day. Say I'm not available. You're a lawyer; lie like one. Just say cleanup efforts are consuming my time. In a case this size, the casino owner should be able to attend."

"Well, it's unlikely a judge will consider any testimony at this stage of proceedings. If the court takes testimony at all, it'll come at a plenary hearing within the next ten days."

"What judge handles that hearing?"

"Same one who hears the emergency application."

"Then we go Tuesday," Tommy declared. "When I draw a card, I don't like the deck stacked against me."

The two lawyers left. Again Tommy wondered if the elder gentleman was aggressive enough. He didn't have time to consider it, though. The casino was emptying. Soon, just he and five patrolling security guards would remain. Communication systems were still down. Who knew how long they could count on their backup power system? The night was going to be long and lonely.

Conrad rose as Tina left his office. He didn't rise out of gentlemanly courtesy and certainly not out of respect. He rose to sit next to Joey. Conrad had to remind the hood who was in charge. He didn't like the way the man had spoken to Tina privately and decided to stop that kind of thing.

As he settled into the chair in which she had sat, he felt the warmth of her fanny, an unnerving sensation that made him strangely tingle. Without thinking, he leaned forward, lifting his bottom to rub a hand across the cushion, as if brushing aside unwelcome feelings. Then Conrad sat back, turned to Joey, and blustered.

"From now on, I'm a part of everything that happens. Understand?"

"What are you talking about, my friend?"

Conrad was not to be blown off. The mob couldn't make its move without him. Conrad wouldn't let them walk on him – not now, not ever. Their agreement entitled the local crime family to a fair piece of action for helping him make the deal, but not more.

"Joey, who's going to run this casino venture?"

"You are, of course."

"We can stop, right now, if there's any question about that."

"Don't concern yourself with the young lady," the older man said. "She and I just had a little chat. At my age, one takes comfort in bringing a lovely woman so close. I had a few fatherly words for her. Now, let me share some with you."

What's this guy up to? Conrad thought.

"It will behoove you to be, shall we say, receptive to her charms – at least until we have the information we need."

Conrad considered the man's words. As the mobster spoke, Conrad recalled Tina's straightforward advances. Her allure had a keen edge, but she was too assertive for his tastes. Joey was nudging him into something Conrad feared would lead to trouble.

"A little tenderness," the mob boss said, "is all you need to show."

The hood paused, lifted his hands to his eyes, and massaged them before continuing.

"That's not too great a price to pay to enlist her full cooperation, is it?"

Conrad appraised Tina's feminine charms. He had never seen a pair of hungrier hips. They would devour a man if he wasn't careful. He would act cautiously, but the hood was right. They needed her, at least for the moment.

"I'll lead her along for a while," he finally said.

"Good. Then, all is well."

"So long as she gives me what I want, I'll keep her happy.

Conrad reflected, then spoke aloud as he rationalized.

"We need an inside track on Brucker's thinking. He's a tough negotiator, even when he doesn't have much to work with."

"You may not have to deal with him at all," the hood said. "You may deal directly with Mr. Levine. That would make his wife's cooperation all the more valuable, would it not?"

"What do you mean?

"His casino's a very dangerous place. Mr. Brucker may not be disposed to conduct negotiations. That's all I'm saying."

Conrad's intercom buzzed. It distracted him before he could pursue the mobster's insinuations. The thought quickly flashed through his mind, though. *Does the hood plan to have Brucker killed?* Already, the mob had spilled too much blood for Conrad's tastes.

"Mr. Conrad," his secretary called over the speaker, "the gentleman you are waiting to see is here."

Conrad rose. He strolled to his desk and pushed a button to speak.

"Show him in."

He had never met the man. Joey would introduce the third partner in their operation, the man who controlled offshore funds that would make their deal possible.

The financier entered Conrad's office slowly. His blue pinstripe suit lent the appearance of a businessman, but Conrad sensed he was more than that. The hood's longtime acquaintance extended a hand that disappeared inside Conrad's bigger mitts.

"Mr. Conrad," Joey began, "allow me to introduce

you to my dear friend, Mr. Wu."

Chapter Fourteen

Deadly Disciples

At midnight a dozen khaki-uniformed sheriff's deputies checked their weapons. Armed with semiautomatic pistols, which were capable of firing rapid bursts from 9-millimeter ammunition clips, and some carrying high-powered rifles, they were ready for their assignment. The garage where they gathered was dimly lit. Where they were going would be darker still, so they carted infrared military night-goggles in their back packs to help them see.

The highly-trained officers practiced working without words. They flashed hand signals. On cue ten deputies climbed into the back of a van and took seats on steel benches. Two closed the windowless rear doors, then took their own seats in the cab. The deputy in charge sat shotgun, checking paperwork as the driver reached to start the engine.

The dull-grey van prominently displayed the words, "Atlantic County Sheriff's Office," above the county law enforcement insignia. Like most county vehicles, the truck had plenty of wear.

A bang cracked in every ear. Each man grabbed a weapon, ready to shoot. It banged again, the old truck backfiring and sputtering as its engine revved. Just a false alarm, they realized. No one smiled though; they were all business.

The garage door opened and the van hit the streets.

The five guard shift shuffled at Megasino. Four men and a woman wearing navy-blue security guard uniforms relieved the crew that had worked the six-hour shift ahead of them. Everyone on the retiring crew was glad to leave. The big place was so empty it was spooky. The main electrical-power system fluctuated off and on as if it had its own mind. Even backup generators operated sporadically, meaning darkness could blanket the property anytime.

The shift captain manned the main entranceway. His command desk was situated inside a corridor between two sets of locked doors. Captain Brosz could unlock the outer glass doors by punching a number into a keypad. Anyone wishing to enter the casino walked through that corridor. The outer doors would lock while he inspected their ID. If it checked out, the captain could punch a second code into the keypad. That would unlock a second set of metal doors at the corridor's other end, which opened into the building. The casino was secure as a jailhouse.

Guards on duty covered a lot of ground. One patrolled the huge casino floor. A man strolled through the outdoor thrill rides and docks, while another watched the restaurant and shopping area. The female guard took the surveillance room.

Hundreds of monitors in the surveillance room connected to cameras inside the casino and all around the facility. When the system functioned, cameras could fine-tune on playing tables to detect a the value of a card or the denomination of a playing chip. Video screens in the surveillance room spanned an entire wall. Normally twenty surveillance technicians manned them, but not that night. Fortunately, there wasn't much to see with the place deserted.

No one patrolled the hotel room floors. Elevators and fire stairs to the hotel tower were locked-down to make sure no one entered. Only Tommy occupied his suite. The property wasn't secure, but they did the best they could with the limitations imposed by Grender's court orders.

Tommy tried to sleep. He monitored the security guard channel on a walkie-talkie kept on a bedside night table. Next to it rested a cellular phone. Without regular telephone service, the cell phone was his lifeline to the outside world. A .38-caliber revolver sat in the night table drawer. Reluctantly, he had taken it from his security chief.

"If you deputize yourself to stay in the casino, you'll have to carry a weapon," the burly man had said.

Tommy had looked at the handgun. He didn't want it and instantly replied, "Robby, even your guards aren't carrying guns."

"Not all of them. But the captains on duty will have pistols and I'm giving you the rank of honorary captain.

Keep the gun. Believe me, you'll feel better. This place will be lonely after the sun goes down."

Robby Vee was right. Tommy couldn't imagine needing the weapon, but it felt good having it near.

The cellular telephone buzzed and Tommy checked his wrist watch.

Who would be calling at one in the morning?

He didn't bother turning on lights. Instead, Tommy fumbled in darkness with the phone until he hit a button to answer the call.

"Mr. Brucker, this is Security Captain Brosz at the front door. I just wanted to report that —"

The line went dead.

"Damn it," Tommy said.

The steel-framed structure created too much static interference. He picked up the walkie-talkie and tried reaching the captain, but the thing just squawked. Maybe he wasn't working it right.

The cellular telephone rang again. Tommy walked to a window where he took the call. That time, it came in more clearly.

"Yes, Captain."

"Mr. Brucker, there's a truck load of sheriff's deputies outside our main door. They say they're here to help with security."

"On whose authority? We're strictly limited on the number of personnel allowed on the property."

"They have a court order, sir. The guy in charge gave me a copy. Here's what it says. 'The county sheriff and his deputies are to assume responsibility for security of the property commonly known as The Megasino until a full hearing is held before a judge of the Superior Court.' You should see these people, Mr. Brucker. They look like commandos."

"Do they have proper ID?"

"Yes, sir. They're wearing badges, and photo-identification cards are clipped to the breast pockets of their uniforms."

"Well, we can use all the help we can get. Let me talk to the deputy in charge."

After a pause, a new voice came on the line. His tones were crisp and military-like, making Tommy feel like he was talking to GI Joe.

"This is Deputy Matthew McMullen, sir. At twenty-three hundred hours, the Atlantic County prosecutor delivered a court order to the County Sheriff's Office. It directs our deputies to maintain security here. The prosecutor instructed me to give you a warning. If you obstruct our entry, you'll be brought before a judge in the morning to explain why you should not be held in contempt."

"That sounds like a mouthful, deputy. Look, we're grateful for any boost you give us. Put my security captain back on the phone."

Tommy heard Captain Brosz pick up the line and clear his throat.

"Let them in the casino, Captain."

"Mr. Brucker, about these people. . . ."

There was a long pause. Brosz had been a master sergeant in the Military Police and still wore a flattop haircut he neatly shaved on the sides. The guy was a devoted employee, but at that late hour Tommy was impatient waiting for the man to finish his thought.

"Captain, what about these people?"

"Sir, they just seem awfully well armed for sheriff's deputies."

"Does their paperwork look genuine?"

"Yes sir."

"Cooperate with them. I'll check their story with a telephone call."

Tommy dialed another number that rang and rang.

Sheriff's deputies lined up inside the corridor leading to the casino's main entrance. They waited for Captain Brosz to open the second set of doors by punching the code into his keypad.

Brosz looked them over again. As a retired military man, he appreciated professionalism. It was unusual, though, seeing paramilitary performance in the ranks of men who conducted routine tasks. Those deputies normally provided security at the county courthouses and jail, transported prisoners, and delivered court papers. The deputy in charge was young to have so much authority. But with the face of an altar boy and a confident demeanor, he seemed both trustworthy and competent. The kid knew all the right questions to ask.

"Where do you have your guards deployed, Captain?"

Brosz didn't like telling, but he had orders from Mr. Brucker. He pulled property diagrams from the duty desk and discussed the casino's layout. One by one, he showed the whereabouts of his guards.

"Is there anyone else on the property?"

"Mr. Brucker's in his suite."

"What's the room number?"

Why do they need to know? Brosz wondered. Something was wrong about those people. The deputies never talked, smiled or flinched. Brosz eyeballed the eager young man in charge. His name tag said "Matthew Mc-

Mullen," but his dark hair and features made him look more Italian than Irish.

This kid must be black Irish, he thought.

"The room number," Matthew repeated.

"Suite 711," said Brosz. "The Buckman always goes for lucky numbers."

"Where's the electrical power room?"

"Why do you need to know?"

"We have a man with some experience handling power systems and backup generators. Stationing him there might be helpful."

Brosz wondered. Since when did a sheriff deputy have electrical training? He pointed to the maintenance room on a layout sheet.

"Surveillance room?"

Brosz pointed. "I have one of my guards there, but the system crashed. She's trying at put it back on line, but they don't train us for sophisticated repairs."

"Maybe my men can help."

Brosz didn't know why, but he didn't think those people came to help anyone.

"Where's the cashier's vault?"

Brosz pointed again. Matthew's men were covering every key location in the property.

"What frequency are your guards using on their walk-ie-talkies?"

Brosz told him. Matthew immediately conveyed the information to his deputies. Each took a walkie-talkie unit from a belt clip and tuned into the casino channel. Brosz noticed something peculiar.

"Your people carry two walkie-talkies?" he said.

"Backups," replied the deputy.

Brosz realized the casino security lines would be monitored by deputies who would also be talking on a separate channel his guards couldn't access. He didn't like it. He watched the deputies place on headsets with dual-eared headpieces. Brosz surmised one side listened in on the guards' walkie-talkie channel while the other side monitored the deputies' own channel. The headsets had thin plastic tubes extending in front of their mouths so they could communicate without having to lift the walkie-talkies from their belt clips.

"Captain, I'm going to assign two of my men to the hotel tower. My deputies will need room passkeys."

Brosz handed over plastic cards with metallic back strips. "We use an electronic locking system here," he said. "These cards are coded like passkeys to open any door on the property."

Matthew handed them to his men. "Does the system work during power blackouts?"

"Yeah. There's battery powered backup as a safety measure."

"Perhaps you should let your people know we're coming onto the property."

Every suggestion this kid makes sounds like an order, Brosz thought. He resented the younger man's tone and the way the kid flaunted his authority. Captain Brosz picked up his walkie-talkie and called his personnel. He noticed Matthew was careful not to dispatch his deputies until each of the casino security guards had confirmed receiving the message. Then, Matthew gave a final instruction.

"Open the casino's inner doors."

Captain Brosz punched keypad numbers as Matthew watched. The inner doors unlocked. One deputy held the door as others entered. Matthew and two of his men remained behind.

Tommy had almost hung up his cellular phone when a groggy voice finally answered. At first, Tommy wasn't sure he had dialed the right number. It just didn't sound like the elder lawyer, so he asked.

"Douglas Hooper?"

"Who's this?"

"This is Tommy Brucker calling. Sorry to wake you. Look, we just had a dozen sheriff's deputies arrive at our main door. They have a court order directing us to let them enter for security purposes. Do you know anything about this?"

"What time is it?"

"One o'clock or so, Douglas."

A long pause followed. Tommy couldn't tell if the man was thinking or if he had fallen back to sleep.

"Yes. That sounds about right to me, I guess," the man finally said. "Grender would probably want some people in an official capacity to supervise the site. Afterall, the prosecutor's office regards it as a crime scene, right now."

Tommy still wondered. "The Atlantic City police have already assigned patrols to what's left of the show room. They're making certain no one enters the area. Why would the prosecutor need county deputies here?"

"Dual jurisdiction, Mr. Brucker. City cops have an obligation to monitor the fire scene for safety purposes. The county prosecutor wants to preserve any evidence that may be found for prosecution. He's got his own men on the job."

"Are you guessing or do you know for certain? From

what I understand, the sheriff armed these people like they're about to reenact the Gulf War."

"What time did you say it is?"

"One o'clock."

"Oh, yes. That's right." The lawyer paused again. "I'll check on this for you. Don't worry about a thing. If there's any problem, I'll give you a call."

"Do you have my cellular phone number? That's the only way you can reach me."

"Yes, Mr. Brucker. Good night, now."

The cell phone clicked in Tommy's ear. He thought for a moment. Was the old guy really going to do anything? Tommy started to dial another number, then stopped.

Maybe I'm just getting edgy in the dark, he thought.

Tommy climbed back into bed. He needed rest and grabbed what would help – a bottle of sleeping pills from his night table drawer. With a quick swallow, two went down. As he set the bottle back, the pistol in the open drawer stared up at him.

"Oh, why not?" he said to himself.

He tucked the handgun under his pillow, then swaddled in satin sheets, at first cool to the touch, then warm like a toasty cocoon, a place where sleep came swiftly and peacefully.

Captain Brosz saw Matthew give a hand signal to the two deputies who had remained behind. Calmly, they raised their semiautomatic pistols. Instantly, Brosz realized they had muzzled the weapons with silencers. One aimed at his face while the other aimed at his body.

My God, the thought flashed through his mind, *they've*

even preplanned where they'll shoot me.

He drew his handgun from its holster. Bullets whizzed through smoking muzzles. The deputies appeared to rise above him as Brosz slunk to the floor. His reflexes made him writhe involuntarily. Brosz didn't feel the point-blank gunshot wounds. In fact, he didn't feel anything at all as he gaped upward and watched a deputy come close. A gun barrel stared Brosz in the eyes, then a single flash of fire burst. For Captain Brosz, the lights went out forever.

Matthew's men holstered their weapons, then went to the dead man. Each shooter clutched the body under an armpit and shoved it under the duty desk. Matthew took Brosz's chair at the desk and propped his feet on the still warm corpse. That time he punched numbers into the keypad. The shooters entered the casino while Matthew waited for walkie-talkie calls.

Two deputies walked into the maintenance room where power lines entered the building. Matthew had been right: one man was well versed in electrical operations. He surveyed the facility and went directly to the main throttles, then pointed out switches that regulated power mains to his companion. Silently, they shut them down. Lights went out through the casino then quickly came back on as the backup system activated. They would shut that system down on Matthew's order.

Three deputies marched to the cashier's main cage,

walked directly to the rear, and stopped in front of the vault. Each carried a different set of tools in his backpack. Without a word, they laid them on the floor.

One man studied the safe. Tackling it wouldn't be hard. Like a surgeon inspecting instruments before an operation, he studied the tools then grabbed an industrial drill equipped with a diamond-tipped bit. With a tug on its trigger, a powerful motor surged. Two men held the monster as it drilled holes into the safe, while another waited to insert plastic explosives.

Matthew had assigned one deputy to each of the patrolling security guards. Stealthily and with singular purpose, the khaki-uniformed assassins tracked down their blue-uniformed targets.

The two men, who had gunned down Captain Brosz, strutted to the seventh floor. They found the Buckman's suite and pulled out their plastic pass card. Whenever Matthew ordered, the two men would enter suite 711 with guns drawn. They exchanged glances. Suddenly, the suite number didn't look so lucky for its occupant.

Matthew picked up his walkie-talkie and beckoned from the casino main entranceway. "Roll call, my holy men."

Deputies checked in one at a time. They had assumed the identities of Christ's twelve disciples as call names for the operation, but they were ready to do the devil's work.

First came the call from deputies in the maintenance room. "John the Baptist and Peter, ready," they reported.

"Andrew, James, and Philip, ready," came the next call from the cashier's office. They crouched under steel desks away from the vault.

"Bartholomew, ready." He'd found the security guard on the casino floor and stalked him on his rounds.

"Thomas, ready," the man said in hushed tones. Thomas lurked in the restaurant area, spying on a heavy-set guard who had found an inviting kitchen. The guard sat at a table with a seven-course meal. He had even cracked open a two-hundred-dollar bottle of wine. A linen napkin was tucked under his chin to cover his blue uniform from spills. As Thomas watched the guard indulge, he felt hunger pangs.

"James, ready." He had found the surveillance room. The door was open and James could hear the female guard cussing as she focused her attention on malfunctioning monitors. *We better move fast*, he thought. *If she gets that system up, we'll be discovered.*

"Thaddaeus, ready," came the next hushed call. He was outside in the marina where a security guard strolled the docks. Boats belonging to guests had departed when the place shut down; only vessels owned by the casino languished in the harbor.

"Judas Iscariot and Simon, ready." They stood outside the door to Brucker's suite with their pass card, fingers ready over triggers.

Matthew watched his illuminated digital wristwatch countdown in its stopwatch mode. Each deputy had seven minutes to complete his assigned task and return to the corridor. That would give them ample time to leave, even if cops patrolling the show room fire site happened to hear something.

He spoke into his microphone, clearly enunciating: "Blessed are those whose hearts are pure, for they shall see no darkness."

The disciples in the maintenance room, John the Baptist and Peter, pulled switches on backup power generators. Darkness cloaked the property. Battery powered lights activated only in halls and stairways. Matthew waited for his wristwatch to tick down thirty seconds while each deputy strapped on infrared goggles, which would allow them to see in the dark. Then, Matthew called into the walkie-talkie again.

"Blessed are the persecuted," he intoned. "Theirs shall be the Kingdom of Heaven."

Simultaneously, each disciple moved.

Andrew detonated the plastic explosives set in the safe. A mighty blast blew the door off its hinges. Desks, chairs, and papers flew. With the burst still ringing in their ears, Andrew and his fellow disciples swam through smoke, spreading their arms as if breast stroking to clear the air of floating debris. Tears streaming from eyes irritated by particulates, they entered the huge vault. On one side of the room, they spied shelved cash. Three smiles widened as the holy trinity stuffed cash in large denominations into canvas sacks, loading as much as they could carry.

Bartholomew placed the guard on the casino floor in

his rifle sights and squeezed the trigger. "Ah," he sighed, satisfied with an accurate aim.

As the security guard in the dining room poured himself a second glass of wine, Thomas fired his rifle. The holy man's victim dropped his bottle on the table and slumped forward. Blood pumped from a single bullet wound in the skull, blending on the white table linen with a rich Bordeaux.

James burst into the surveillance room with his semi-automatic pistol roaring. He let loose a clip of twenty rounds, blasting everything in sight of his infrared goggles. Video monitors shattered. Secondary fires rose from electrical equipment. In two seconds, James dropped his empty clip and inserted a loaded one. He fired again. James didn't know when he took out the female guard. He couldn't hear her screams over the gun bursts and didn't see her fall. She laid in a corner of the room, bleeding from a half-dozen random wounds. James liked taking out video screens, so the disciple loaded a third clip and fired again just for the hell of it.

Thaddaeus strolled up to the guard on the docks. He waved to the blue-uniformed man who peered back quizzically. When he was six feet from him, Thaddaeus raised his pistol. A single round zipped through the silencer on the gun barrel, nailing the security guard squarely between the eyes. Thaddaeus watched him fall backward into the bay with a splash. The body sank, then rose to the surface. The disciple genuflected as the tide took it out. If the corpse reached the inlet, it would float to the ocean.

"Fish food," Thaddaeus muttered.

Simon and Judas nodded to each other, then Simon slid their plastic passkey into the door lock mechanism. They heard the bolt slide open. Suite 711 was theirs. They smiled and walked in calmly. Judas covered while Simon peppered the suite's living room with a clip from his semiautomatic pistol. Pictures fell, lamps smashed, and windows shattered.

Pausing to scan the room, they spotted no signs of Brucker. Judas nodded and took the lead, walking further into the suite while Simon dropped his empty clip and slipped a full one into his handgun.

They walked toward a hallway and stopped before entering. That time, Simon covered while Judas emptied a full clip. More pictures fell. Bullets randomly hit their marks. They paused again. Still, no sign of Brucker appeared. Judas dropped his empty clip and reloaded. Simon retook the lead.

They stopped at a closed door to the bedroom. That was it, the disciples realized. The Buckman was inside. Judas stood on the right side of the door; Simon took the left. Both disciples tapped the bottom of full ammunition clips to assure they were locked in place. Their pistols pointed upward in the ready position. Judas tipped his head and Simon nodded back.

They blasted the door lock with one shot each. Judas kicked the door open and they entered with guns blazing. Firing in a spread pattern, Judas fanned to the right and Simon to the left. Feathers from down pillows flew faster than the geese they'd come from had ever moved. A television screen exploded while windows shattered out of their frames.

Eerie silence filled the room as both disciples reloaded at the same time. Their ears rang from the blasts; their nostrils filled with the sulfuric scent of gunfire. Squinting through gun smoke, floating feathers, and particles of debris, they searched for Tommy's corpse.

"There he is," Judas pointed.

Simon nodded with a smile. Through infrared goggles, they saw Brucker laying in a corner. Both pumped twenty rounds before taking off their goggles to verify the hit. As they neared the corpse, Judas took a deep breath. The adrenaline rush that accompanied the kill had winded him. Suddenly, though, the sweet taste of murder turned sour.

"We just took out a loveseat," the disciple said.

Simon looked at the bullet-riddled lounger and asked what both were thinking.

"Where is he?"

Judas used the walkie-talkie. His coded message was simple.

"Jesus wept."

The disciples had just learned the captain at the front desk had lied; that wasn't Brucker's suite. They'd have to track him down.

Matthew didn't like it. He wanted the twelve-man crew out of the casino, but they still had a job to do. He dictated fast orders over his walkie-talkie.

"John the Baptist, pull up the truck. Peter, stay by

the power station in the maintenance room. Everyone else, find our patron saint."

"Where do you want us to look?" Judas Iscariot called.

"Search the suites on the penthouse level. He's gotta be up there." *That's where we should have looked from the start*, Matthew thought. "Sweep the entire floor."

The confident edge in his voice was faltering. He didn't want to report failure. They had to make the Goddamned hit.

Tommy woke in a haze thinking he heard something. Standing by a large window, he strained his ears and soaked in the water view from his penthouse suite. The night was perfectly still.

The moon over Absecon Bay caused his mind to envision quiet nights he had spent on Hawaiian shores under Diamond Head so long ago. Thoughts of those evenings with Susannah came like a lullaby. As sleep called, Tommy yearned to hear her soothing voice. It would be awhile before he could talk to her at the treatment center. While patients detoxified, they weren't permitted to make or receive telephone calls. Too often, patients used phones to contact their suppliers during drug withdrawal stages. Tommy wondered if she had the strength to fight her dependency.

Yawning wide, he felt the effects of his own medication. Sleeping pills punched out his lights as he returned to bed. Tommy lowered his head and his face bumped against the pistol.

Damn, Tommy thought. *This thing could go off in the middle of the night*.

He put the gun back inside the night table drawer and

shut his eyes. Tranquility filled his soul and sent him into peaceful slumber.

Chapter Fifteen

Rendezvous in the Nighttime

Rendezvous pendants la nit, Francoise fantasized, rendezvous in the nighttime. Alone in the back of a limousine, she conjured thoughts of an enchanting late-night escapade with a secret lover. God knew she was ripe for a *tete a tete* with the tender hand of love. If only it were to be. Instead, a different kind of engagement awaited.

Elegant in slinky black, a couture gown hugged her every curve. She twisted strands of lustrous pearls between her fingertips, necklace gems manufactured by mollusks, which had toiled their lifetimes spinning calcium carbonate round grains of sand. *Sad*, she thought. They worked so hard manufacturing something so beautiful. Beautiful, too, was she – polished, primped, and decked for a meeting long overdue.

The car slowly rolled through traffic from her husband's Pyramid Casino, yet the garish lights illuminating its grand marquee quickly disappeared. Turning onto busy Pacific Avenue, she watched tourists hop between boardwalk casinos, like her, looking for a change in their luck. Her eyes lingered on brassy street walkers, who owned corners, if only for a night. Strutting their wares in heavy makeup and scanty attire, raw sexual allure was their snaring magnet. Had it been hers, too?

Francoise closed her eyes, again imagining she was en route to a paramour, pretending youthful exuberance had not deserted her. Perhaps she was paying for those carefree times. Turning another corner, she realized she would not be lingering at Monaco's famed American Bar in Hotel de Paris. Francoise was sneaking to a beer and black eye joint in Duck Town, the longtime heart of blue collar Atlantic City.

Stopped for a red light, she spied ragged row homes flanking both sides of the street. A pair of stray mongrels nosed through a tilted garbage can. Suddenly, the larger mutt, the size of a German shepherd though more wolflike in appearance, bared menacing teeth. It growled at the smaller pooch, which reluctantly backed away, eyes fixed on what both hounds desired. Supreme and defiant, the stronger dog settled to gnaw a bone that the other lacked courage to sample. As the light changed to green, the diminutive mutt let loose a woeful howl. Sounding almost human, the cry chilled her, as if it were her own.

Her car proceeded down the block and stopped in front of a shabby corner tavern. Its neon sign simply read, "Open 24 Hours." The driver jumped out and opened her door, but Francoise didn't budge.

"We're six blocks and a lifetime away from the world I know," she mused.

"Would you like me to take you back to the casino,

madame?"

She didn't answer. Francoise stepped from the car and into a dimly lit bar where cracked vinyl seats atop rusty stools greeted her. Two drunks quarreled in a corner, while a lonely soul searched the juke box for a tune to match his mood. Behind the bar area, a pool room with two tables stood empty. Torn velvet topped one, bespeaking its abandonment, while the other displayed a rack of balls, calling anyone to play.

A grey-haired bartender lit a knowing smile and tipped his head deferentially. Unkempt and clothing mussed, the man fit the place. "Follow me, ma'am," he called. "I'll give you the nickel tour."

His gait was uneven, as if old age had taken a toll on his hips. Yet, despite awkward strides, he moved briskly from the bar to the back room, stopping only to point out highlights.

"This joint was a speakeasy, once," he said. His frame straightened with pride as he recalled grander days. "The backroom became a gaming hall long before they legalized gambling in Atlantic City. All the bigshots played here. I saw 'em. Sinatra shot dice whenever he sang at Skinny D'Amato's 500 Club. Jolson crooned from that corner." The man pointed with a finger that advanced years made tremble. "Marilyn Monroe stood right where you're standin' when she was grand marshal for the '52 Miss America pageant."

Francoise glanced at faded photographs hanging in dusty frames. The stars who'd partied there had signed them. She almost shared the thrill of days long gone, until they turned round the next bend. She entered a dark hall smelling of mildew. An exposed pipe ran along the wall. At an elbow joint, slow but steady drips splashed on concrete. At the end of the hallway they entered a small office. Her guide motioned for her to sit by tapping the back of a wooden chair. She lowered herself into it and studied the scuffed desk in front of her, wondering what kind of business had been transacted there. Behind it, a chair with a well-worn cushion waited for the man she would meet. A bare light bulb dangled on an electrical cord hanging from the ceiling. Its glare was about to dim.

"I hope you don't mind," the man said as his feet shuffled toward the door. "I have to turn off the light."

Francoise didn't want to be left alone in the dark. Trembling, she rose to leave.

"Don't worry," he said. "I'll wait outside the door and keep it open until he arrives."

She was uncertain. Perhaps she had made a mistake coming, but what could she do? The clandestine meeting was Francoise's singular opportunity to extract herself from the miserable existence that had become her life. Still, as she sat at the gateway to hell, she couldn't stop contemplating. How had she come to find herself there?

Francoise was born to be rich the way Monet was born to be a painter. The youngest of three children, she was Papa's favorite. An exquisite beauty from the moment of birth, naturally she had received his doting attention as a little girl. Too young to notice the jealousy of her older brothers, Francoise eagerly aimed to please her devoted father.

Papa ran a banking house that had been in his family for generations. Located in the Swiss financial center of Zurich, the bank provided her family a life of privilege to which the youngster was oblivious. Little Francoise knew only she was happy, especially when Papa was around. She would run to his lap to receive his earnest affections. There, she was secure, sheltered in his strong embrace and comforted by the touch of his fingertips. Ever so gently, they ran through the blond curls that cascaded to her waist.

"You're lovely, my little one," he would constantly remind her.

Her earliest memories were those of anxiously waiting for him to return from work. For Francoise, Papa always brought a gift – candy or a toy – to light the smile on her face. She would rifle her father's pockets until she found what he'd hidden. Her mother quietly watched their games. *Mere* didn't receive so much as a cursory kiss until Papa and Francoise completed their ritual.

Later in the night, so often alone, he would come to her room to say good night. It was then that they shared their secret. One night always stood out in her childhood memories, though, the night their secret was discovered.

"*Quel amour d'enfant*," he said softly, what a love of a child.

He kissed her forehead, then brought his mouth lower to kiss the tip of her nose. She could smell brandy on his breath as he combed her hair with his hands. Without warning, his lips covered hers.

"I don't like that," she said. "Please, don't do it again."

Her father had a strange glint in his eyes.

"Don't you wish to please your Papa?"

She wished for nothing more and smiled upward as

his fingers stroked her curls.

"Your flaxen locks," he said, "are more precious than all the gold in the world."

He came toward her again. She remembered wanting to flee but at the same time wishing to please. His lips covered her tiny mouth. They were moist rather than dry. His hands stoked her wee frame and lingered in private places.

"*Batard*!"

The cry came from *Mere,* who rushed into the room. Her mother screamed the word over and over, swooping Francoise from bed. The cries brought servants whom Papa quickly ushered away. Francoise remembered thinking the same thought repeatedly. *What have I done wrong*? She wondered why her mother was so upset and why Papa slunk away. Her mother held her tight, sobbing and rocking her, all the while squeezing tighter.

"You're hurting me," little Francoise said.

Then, something even more peculiar happened. Her mother dragged her to the bathroom and frantically searched a cabinet above the marble sink. Still whimpering, she approached Francoise with long scissors in hand. Her wide eyes and fast breaths terrified the child. Instantly, the little girl knew what her mother was thinking.

"*Bonne Mere*. Please," she cried, "don't kill me."

Her mother's face twisted, as if in some dark alcove of her psyche an instinct told her what had sprung from her womb would steal her man. Fraught with the abomination of motherhood that lay on the flip slide of paternal desire, her *mere's* eye's lit with primeval urges for survival, those born of beast, deeply supplanted by humankind.

"Please," a small voice begged, "please don't."

Words so tiny carried no weight. A father's twisted lust for a child was no less a sin than a mother's snuffing of life she cursed for having suckled her breasts. Light from the chandelier above a marble bathtub glistened on the shears.

"*Batard*," her mother cried, bastard.

Her mother pulled her round and forced her little head down. Guilt-ridden tears filled Francoise's eyes as she saw her beautiful golden locks fall to the floor. Her mother sheared her hair to the scalp.

Never again did her father greet her the same way. She could only continue wondering, *What have I done wrong?*

Afterward, her parents rarely spoke to each other with warmth. A winter chill settled over their big house that Spring didn't chase away. She saw her mother's scowls whenever Papa neared. Her mother flinched at his touch until he no longer approached her at all.

When Francoise was of age, she attended boarding school in the fashion of wealthy Europeans. Only then did her mother allow her to grow long hair again. When Francoise returned home for holidays, her mother kept a close eye on her. Francoise's love for Papa became unrequited. While he maintained his distance, her mother and brothers blamed her for troubles the family bore.

The old bartender walked into the darkened room.

"I just received a telephone call, ma'am. It won't be much longer until he arrives. Can I get you something from the bar?"

Francoise shook her head. She only wanted to complete her business quickly as possible. The bartender left her alone again with her memories.

She had known love three times. *No*, Francoise thought. *Now, I'm lying to myself.* First came Papa, then Pierre, and finally Gregory. Yet in so many ways she had really loved the same man thrice.

While her brothers prepared to take charge of the banking house, her parents had groomed her to find a suitable young man. Capable and bright, her education and talents lay wasted as a byproduct of the times. Francoise became a fixture in continental high life – especially in Monaco where she had no trouble attracting men. Like most Swiss, she was multilingual. Her family was of French origin, but she was equally fluent in French and English and could speak a smattering of German and Italian. Well bred, blond, and beautiful, her allure enticed men of all nationalities. Intelligent and discerning, she discovered few held her interest. Her family's wealth turned life into a carnival. Francoise found no way off its carousel until she found Pierre.

The older Frenchman held the title of Count. Napoleon had conferred the station upon an ancestor as a tribute. While purely ceremonial, the bestowment had entitled the first recipient to lands in the fertile *Bordeaux* region. Title to the realty had vested in a trust. It passed to lineage who inherited the title. Pierre held the property, upon which vast vineyards had once produced fine wines, but he lacked resources to cultivate them. Even the great chateau on the grounds had fallen into disrepair.

When time came and as protocol demanded, Pierre approached Francoise's father, seeking permission for her hand in marriage. She, Pierre, and Papa sat in her father's study. A raging fire stirred in the fireplace that winter day. Papa looked into their eyes and spoke frankly.

Disparity in the lovers' ages was of no concern to him. Indeed, he was many years older than Francoise's mother. However, the nobleman's lack of wealth disturbed Papa. His daughter had needs only a rich man could afford. He had instilled them in her as surely as he had created her with his seed. What her father said surprised Francoise. It was not that she disagreed; she had just never contemplated a financial need. For her, wealth existed like fresh air.

Then, Papa spoke with the candor of a man who knew he had little time to live and a wrong to right before meeting his maker. His fortunes, too, passed in trust to male lineage. He expressed concern that Francoise's brothers would cut her off from the family fortune when he died. Francoise dismissed the idea, but her father was unequivocal. Perhaps, he suggested, a marriage to Pierre could guarantee her comfort.

Pierre and Papa agreed to terms as Francoise observed. The shrewdness of the scheme wasn't lost on her. Papa would endow their marriage generously, so the newlyweds could cultivate Pierre's untended vineyards. The lands would generate fine *appelations* to support his daughter in years to come. Although she had no right to inherit the property upon her husband's death, the trust would go to their first born son. Pierre and Francoise would immediately embark on creating an heir.

After Pierre and Papa shook hands to seal the betrothal, her father took her in his arms for the first time since that nightmarish childhood incident. He held her tight, planting a single kiss on her forehead and a kiss on her nose. In that moment she felt tender affections that had been so elusive over all the years. Papa waved the couple away and retired to a chair before the fire. As she slowly closed the door, Francoise saw Papa weep with his head held low. At last the chill, which had pervaded their house, dissipated.

Papa died shortly after her marriage. As he had predicted, her brothers cut her off from the family fortune as if she had died with their father. The plan made that wintry day failed, though. Her union with Pierre produced no progeny and she was childless when he, too, died of injuries sustained in an auto accident. The lands passed to one of Pierre's distant cousins as his successor. Francoise was left with the only things her men had conferred upon her. Pierre had bestowed her with the title of Countess. Papa had given her beguiling beauty and quick wits to put those gifts to good use. She raced to Monaco, searching for a man to fulfill her dreams.

In the famous Monte Carlo casino, Countess Francoise won a hand of baccarat. She collected her chips and sipped champagne from a crystal goblet. Looking around a room reserved for the ultra-rich, she surveyed the well-to-do and the titled, who – like herself – sometimes clung to threads of spent purses. Amid decor befitting the gilded palace of Louis XIV, she caught a pair of peering eyes and realized she had also won the attention of a tuxedoed gentleman. He approached with the enthusiasm of an overanxious suitor. The flamboyant American tycoon wasted no time. Gregory Conrad swept her aboard a magnificent yacht his eight-member crew harbored there. She joined him for an impromptu Mediterranean cruise and fell in love before she had time to ponder the single incident that should have alerted her.

Once as they made love in the master berth, it had happened. With the shimmer of moon glow reflecting on calm waters and the sound of gentle ripples reminding them they were cast on heavenly seas, he smashed her face with his fist. She nursed her jaw, uncertain. Had she seen a demon in his eyes – or was that just moonlight flickering so brightly?

He passed off the madness as a regrettable anomaly. "I just had too much wine," he stammered embarrassedly.

Francoise wasn't so sure, but the moment was forgotten. They harbored at one beatific port after another, til in Cannes he proposed. They married and she came to the United States as his bride. Only later, did she learn the true nature of the beast inside her husband.

Beatings were elemental to his "lovemaking." Francoise suffered his raw attentions until she took a separate bedroom and locked the door. Even that didn't protect her when he had drunk too much.

Power in their relationship lay in the wealth he controlled. So long as she was pliant and turned her head to his infidelities, she was free to spend his money as she chose. Often, she did so just for spite.

A prenuptial agreement, which his lawyers had sent to their love boat, chained her to a cold and abusive relationship. He had married her, he relentlessly proclaimed, for reasons that seared her heart.

"As a countess, you were important enough to be my wife, but your beauty's fading, no matter what sor-

cery your plastic surgeons concoct. We'll see how long
you last around here."

She came to know him too well. He had married her
for the same reason he possessed so many things. Francoise had been collected for the thrill of the acquisition.
Conrad savored wielding authority over lovely things.
The "count-ass," as he mocked her, was a minion to his
desires.

All her life Francoise had been beholden to a man. At
long last, she was prepared to take charge. The deal she
could make in that dismal bar might accomplish her end.
And she was prepared to pay any price for what she
wanted.

Francoise heard heavy feet thud in the hallway. The
man who sat behind the desk was coming. In low tones,
he spoke to the bartender outside the door. She couldn't
make out his words but could tell he had dismissed her
aged guide and caretaker. The old man's slower and
lighter footsteps shuffled away. She and his boss would
meet alone.

The man filled the door frame. She saw only his
huge silhouette as dim hallway lighting illuminated him
from behind. He entered and closed the door. As her
eyes adjusted to near-total darkness, she saw his form
settle into the chair behind the desk.

"*Buona sera*," Joey Bonivicolla greeted her.

"I'm afraid my Italian isn't so good," she lied. "Can
we speak in either English or French?"

She knew he was testing her abilities that she intended to conceal. Later, putting her rudimentary knowl-
edge of Italian to use might be convenient. She might

pick up something from the mobster if he spoke to an associate in his native tongue.

Francoise felt the man scrutinize her as they sat silently in the dark. She wanted to study him, too. Francoise pulled a cigarette from her purse and opened a lighter. With a flick, the small torch illuminated his grotesque disfiguration. Francoise felt strangely compelled to stare into those hideous eyes. Without thinking, she rose but not to flee. She approached the man and looked down at him in his chair. Still holding the lighter like a torch for a clearer view, Francoise bent the same way her father had when she was a little girl. Gently, she ran her fingers through slick hair on his scalp. Softly, she planted a kiss on his forehead, then one on his nose. Francoise returned to her chair, lit the thin cigarette, and waited for his reaction.

He uttered not a word. Instead, he pulled a small tape recorder from the breast pocket of his suit. He laid it on the scuffed desktop. Francoise realized she was about to learn what kind of business was done there. The man's big hands fumbled with the play button. Then, she heard his voice and two more converse. He must have surreptitiously recorded the conversations. Francoise knew all the participants. The big man seated across from her spoke first to the Levine woman, who worked in the casino, then to her husband. When the tape finished, Francoise posed a question.

"Why did you play this for me?"

"Your husband and this woman plan to acquire certain properties in which my family will have an interest. They are, shall we say, in an advantageous position to make the acquisitions."

He paused. She could tell her calm reaction to his

horrific features still astonished him. Her compassion had somehow reversed the tables. He was the one who felt ill at ease.

"Once the properties are in your husband's hands, it will behoove my family to have a more reasonable partner controlling the business operations."

"You wish to install me as head of the casinos – the Pyramid that my husband owns and Brucker's two properties."

"You would be a natural choice if your husband should find a reason to retire."

"And what of his betrothal, as you promised, to Tina Levine?"

The big man paused again. She knew what he was thinking. He had already told her a great deal. Too late to stop, he would have to tell the rest. If she didn't agree to join him, she wouldn't walk out alive.

"I'll keep my word. Your husband and this woman will be joined; their betrothal shall come in death."

Francoise drew on her cigarette to gain time for reflection. She pulled it from her lips, surprised it didn't quiver in her hands, then expelled a long puff of smoke that crested above the man's head. In the murky dim, it appeared to rise satanically from the monster. His offer could only end with her in charge of her husband's holdings or with her dead. She fought to prevent anxiety from surfacing. To muster composure, Francoise concentrated on whom she was.

The countess held out her hand. The big man took it in the European fashion. She allowed him to raise it to his lips. His mouth opened. At first, she feared he might bite. Instead, he displayed affection, almost gratitude, for the compassion she'd shown in approaching him without revulsion. Francoise had sealed a pact with the devil.

Chapter Sixteen

Gauntlet

Twelve disciples carried out their unholy mission to murder Tommy Brucker. Matthew still manned the security desk in the corridor entranceway. Knowing how much was at stake, the efficient young man in charge redoubled his resolve to steal the casino owner's last breath. Peter stood by the main power switches in the maintenance room. John the Baptist sat in their van, ready to extract the team of executioners after they hit their target.

Nine armed men infiltrated the hotel tower to sweep the penthouse level. Quickly, they designed an impenetrable gauntlet that made Brucker's escape impossible. When they were ready, Matthew gave the order to activate electric power in the casino and hotel. With Brucker contained, lighting would make it easier to track him.

One man guarded the bottom of the elevator banks. He watched a large panel that lit the floor numbers of the elevators as they traveled up and down. If Brucker managed to enter one, he would gun him down. Two men waited at the bottom of the tower fire stairways, ready to take out Brucker if he descended them. Two more men marched up the stairs with guns ready. James returned to the surveillance room. He would try activating parts of the system he had so gleefully shot apart.

Five men ascended in an elevator to the hotel penthouse level. Judas, as the family's top hammer, directed that crew. He stationed one man at the elevator doors so Brucker wouldn't have a chance to sneak past them. Then he sent two men leftward in the hallway to sweep suites in that direction. He and his partner went to the right. They would enter each suite with weapons drawn, ready to shoot anything that moved or breathed.

Tommy woke to a buzz. *The alarm clock*, he thought. He reached for it on the night table beside him and slapped the top. Yet the clock didn't stop buzzing. Sleeping pills had made him so groggy he didn't remember having set the thing. He slammed hard again; still, it buzzed. Realizing that meant electric power had returned, Tommy turned on a table lamp to check the clock. He put his hands to his eyes and rubbed. *Wake up and focus*, he told himself.

Suddenly, it occurred to him. The buzz wasn't coming from his clock. Someone had tripped the security alarm. Whoever had triggered it was entering the front door to the suite. Who it was it? *Wake up*, he told himself. *Think*. It couldn't be security guards. They would've called on the walkie-talkie or telephone to alert him before entering. He heard voices from two men. Whoever they were, they weren't concerned about making a surreptitious entry. Those men were loud and confident.

"What's the buzz?" Judas asked.

Simon instantly replied, "Security alarm."

They looked at each other knowingly. That had to be Brucker's suite. It would be the only one with a security system activated.

Judas sniffed and smirked. "I smell blood."

He sprayed the living room with a full clip of ammunition. Twenty rounds zipped out of his weapon. Simon flicked on a light switch and they surveyed the damage. With no sign of Brucker, Judas reloaded and nodded. Simon took the lead to the suite's hallway. There, he fired a full clip of ammunition.

Simon's weapon smoked as he dropped his empty clip and inserted a full one. Both knew where they'd find Brucker. He had to be in the bedroom. The door was directly in front of them. Judas touched the doorknob and slowly turned it. Unlocked, he realized. Underneath the door they could see traces of light from inside. It would be easy. Brucker hadn't even thought to conceal himself in darkness.

They held their guns upward in the ready position, primed to rip their target apart. As the security alarm relentlessly buzzed, their hearts pounded faster, their palates tasting blood they were about to spill.

Judas turned the knob, Simon kicked the door open wide, and they saw him. Brucker stood directly in front of them, his hands at his side, his head bowed as if he had resigned to die. Instantly, their weapons roared. *This is great*, they thought simultaneously. *There's noth-*

ing like the rush that comes from a kill.

Tommy fell to the floor as two intruders shot out his reflection in the mirrored bedroom wall. He went to one knee and lifted his pistol. At point-blank range, he fired. Simon collapsed without a sound. Judas squirmed on the floor, bleeding from his chest. He moaned, looked up, and pointed his handgun in Tommy's direction. Tommy scrambled to him and kicked the disciple's wrist. As the gun sailed across the room, Tommy stomped the man's head into the floor. The moans stopped dead.

Gun smoke filling his lungs, Tommy tucked his revolver into his belt, then went to the night table. He picked up his cellular telephone and walkie-talkie. Faint sounds of a walkie-talkie came over the headset that had fallen off a deputy when he went down. Tommy realized other assassins were lurking and knew he had to leave the suite fast.

Sprinting into the main hall, he headed toward the elevators. As he rounded a bend, he saw an armed man standing in front of the elevator doors. The guy called frantically on his walkie-talkie for support. Quickly, Tommy backtracked. There had to be another way out. He rushed to the fire stairs, but heard footsteps rising. A voice called from a landing below.

"There he is!"

Gunfire echoed off cinderblock walls as Tommy darted away. He ran down the hallway to a door marked, "Service Personnel Only." Tommy inserted his pass card to enter the utility room used by the housekeeping staff, entered, and slammed the door closed behind him. His eyes scoured and settled on a trash chute. Instantly, he

opened its wall-mounted hatch.   Barely large enough
for him to enter, Tommy stuck his head inside and stared
downward. Each floor had access to the chute that
went straight down to a ground-level trash incinerator.
The chute was too dark to see down. His eyes scanned
the room again. Trash bags, which housekeepers hadn't
tossed out in the fast evacuation, rested in a corner. Next
to them, he spotted a room service cart with remnants
of a half-devoured meal.

"I have to wake up," he mumbled.

The sleeping pills were still making him drowsy.
Somehow, he had to clear his head. He studied the meal
cart. *Thank God*, he thought, spying a full coffee cup
with a cigarette stub floating on top. He flicked the butt
and gulped the foul brew. Ashes tickled his throat on
the way down.

He raised the walkie-talkie to his lips, then realized he
couldn't use it. His conversation could be picked up by
any of the men who were after him. Instead, he took
the walkie-talkie to the trash shoot, dropped it, and waited
for the sound of it hitting bottom. The sound never
came. It was a long way down from the penthouse
level. The chute was a black, bottomless pit.

Tommy tried dialing 911 on his cellular telephone.
The call didn't go through; his phone wasn't working
there. He had to move closer to a window where he
could call out. Tommy looked to the door leading back
into the hall and realized he couldn't walk out there. The
man at the elevators must have obtained assistance. More
armed men were likely searching the halls. There was
only one way to escape.

Reluctantly, he climbed partway into the trash chute,
feet first. He clutched the rim of the hatch and spread

his legs out wide, pressing them hard into the slick steel sides. One slip and he'd fall all the way down to the trash burner. Whenever Tommy mustered courage to drop, his hands and arms would have to grab into the sides of the steel shaft, somehow. Otherwise, he'd fall to his death. He wondered if he should do it. Every fiber of his being told him not to move any farther into the hatch.

"I can't do this," he told himself.

The door to the room burst open.

"Found him!" a voice cried out.

Tommy let go and heard semiautomatic weapon fire as he slid downward. First, he fell slowly, as he extended his arms out to the sides and his hands scraped along the steel walls. Then, his left hand hit something sharp.

"Damn," he blurted.

The gash went into his palm. He jerked his hand away, and his jet-propelled descent began. Tommy couldn't see a thing. He just knew that he was speeding down from the penthouse level to the ground with nothing below to cushion the fall. His hands grabbed in the dark. If he didn't find something to grip quickly, he would pick up too much speed to stop his fall. His hands groped, yet all he felt were slippery walls.

Semiautomatic weapon fire burst out above. He looked up to see flashes from a gun barrel. The man who'd rushed into the trash room was firing down. Bullets whizzed and ricocheted off the steel walls.

Both his hands found something at the same time, a ledge. He grabbed tight, his weight pulling his body down until he stopped with a jolt. Tommy's arms felt like he'd ripped them from their sockets, but he knew he had to lift himself up while he still had strength. As he tried to chin himself upward, his grip gave way. Tommy's hands slipped. Suddenly, he held by only his fingertips.

Another burst of gunfire rang. More bullets bounced off the shaft's steel walls. Tommy felt a round zip past his face and realized how close it had come to striking the top of his skull. That was all the impetus he needed to try lifting himself up again. Aching muscles tugged; perspiration soaked his brow; his palms grew slick. He couldn't hold much longer. His only hope was to reach the ledge where a hatch would open to another floor. Panting, he raised himself and banged on the door. It didn't budge. Far above, two voices spoke by the hatch at the penthouse level.

"Find something big to toss down," he heard one man say.

If anything hit him there, he would plummet with it to the bottom. He banged against the closed hatch again. Looking upward, he saw light from the opened penthouse-level hatch, then total darkness. Tommy realized they had tossed something down the chute and it was racing toward him. He pounded again at the hatch, and its door sprung open. He pulled himself through it just as filled trash bags zipped down the chute, past him, toward the incinerator.

Tommy reached for the cellular telephone to try calling out again. "Damn," he blurted. The phone was missing. He must have lost it in the downward free-fall. Tommy walked to the doorway that led to the hall, put his hand on the door, and wondered if anyone was waiting for him on the other side. Patting the pistol still tucked inside his pants, he wondered how many bullets were still in the thing. He hadn't thought to count rounds while firing them.

Tommy turned the knob and slowly opened the door. No one was there. He poked his head into the hallway. It was empty. With his pistol drawn and pointed straight ahead, Tommy walked through the hall. A room number told him he'd fallen four floors. Still a long way to ground level, he wondered if he should try hiding on that floor. His passkey would let him enter any door, but the rooms were death traps. He couldn't count on escaping the same way again if someone found him. He had to get out of the casino fast and there were only two ways down.

Do I take an elevator or a stairway?

The question begged for an answer. Both ways were risky. Someone could be waiting for him at the bottom of either. Tommy decided. He went to the elevator in the center bank, pushed a button, and waited. He pointed his pistol at the doors, ready to fire if someone was aboard. The doors opened slowly.

"Empty," he sighed with relief.

Tommy boarded and pushed a button for the ground floor. The elevator descended. Again, he wondered what he would find. All the elevators were glass-walled on the far side. They opened to the lobby area for the lower five floors. From the fifth floor down he'd have a view to ground level, but he realized something else: anyone there would be staring back. The elevator sped downward, too fast, he feared. Tommy watched floor numbers light above the door as the elevator passed each. Ten lit, nine, eight. . . .

Starting at the fifth level, his eyes scoured beneath him. Instantly, he spotted something. Another man dressed as a sheriff's deputy aimed a rifle up at him.

Shots rang as Tommy became the target in a human shooting gallery. Bullets shattered the glass wall. He ducked under a shower of crystalline shards and desperately jabbed the elevator buttons, hoping to halt the descent to his doom. The elevator stopped. Its doors opened and he scampered off.

Third floor, he thought. *Where can I hide?*

Tommy ran toward the surveillance area. If he could make it there, he would be able to see over the entire casino floor. The surveillance department had steal catwalks, narrow pathways with thin steel safety-rails, that supported personnel who meandered them. The catwalks crisscrossed over the playing area. Personnel and cameras could look down over games through dark glass that served as the casino ceiling. From the casino floor, looking upward, the ceiling looked like it consisted of solid dark squares. The tinted panes of glass only allowed visibility in one direction. From the catwalks, Tommy could plan his next move.

"He's on the third floor," the disciple at the bottom of the elevator banks called into his walkie-talkie. He lowered his rifle and waited for orders.

"This is James in the surveillance room," came the next call. "I just heard someone enter the catwalk area above the casino floor."

Matthew called out on his walkie-talkie. "Did any of our people enter the surveillance catwalk area?"

There was no response, just dead air and static.

"I repeat. Did anyone enter the catwalk area?"

Again, nobody answered.

"Good," Matthew said. "Now we know where to

find the son of a bitch. John, wait with the van. Peter, maintain your station in the power room. Bartholomew, stay at the bottom of the elevator banks. Keep two men with you so Brucker doesn't backtrack. I don't want to lose him in the tower again. The rest of you . . . swarm the catwalks and take the guy out."

One at a time, men called Matthew to confirm receiving his order, all except the two whom Brucker had killed. Ten men stalked one.

Tommy didn't see anyone on the brightly lit casino floor. If he could only get down there somehow, he could try reaching a door. Outside the building, he might stand a chance. Cops guarding the show room weren't far, if only he could get to them. Suddenly, a harrowing thought gripped him. *Are they really police officers?* The men pursuing him were dressed as sheriff's deputies. How would he know the uniformed officers patrolling the show room were actually Atlantic City cops? He'd have to take that chance if he could only make his way outside.

He heard the door to the catwalk area open. Someone entered. Another man dressed as a deputy instantly spotted him. Tommy raised his gun and aimed. He pulled the trigger. A single shot whizzed past the man who raised his own handgun and fired a burst of semi-automatic weapon fire. Glass panes under the catwalk, where Tommy stood, shattered as bullets took them out.

Tommy aimed to shoot again. He pulled the trigger and his gun hammer struck an empty chamber. Tommy squeezed again. The pistol was empty. He tossed it at the man who ducked out of its way, smiled wide, and walked closer. Tommy spun around. The catwalk took a dead-end behind him. *Nowhere to run*, he realized, *no place to hide*.

The man approached, striding purposefully like the skilled assassin he was. His short breaths came loud and quick. His face flushed crimson – either from the chase or perhaps from exhilaration, realizing he was about to kill their quarry. As he approached for an easy shot, Tommy looked down through the glass panes to the playing floor. Three stories beneath them an oversized twenty-foot roulette wheel spun on electric current. A banner above the promotional piece called it "The World's Largest Roulette Game." A pea-ball the size of a basketball bounced around in it. Tommy wondered if he should just jump through the broken glass pains. *If I break my legs on the fall*, he thought, *this guy's going to have an easy target*.

More men dressed as sheriff's deputies entered the catwalk area and called out, "Shoot him!"

Expertly, the assassin removed an ammunition clip and reloaded. That was Tommy's chance. He dove at the man. They locked in a struggle for the semiautomatic. Suddenly, the gun blasted. The other deputies sprinted toward them as Tommy and his red-faced pursuer tumbled over the thin metal support rails. They crashed through the glass, still struggling. Tommy lost the tussle for the gun as they plummeted. The barrel plunged into his open mouth. Tommy couldn't turn away.

They thudded on something solid before the guy could let loose with another burst of fire. Tommy laid atop the man, who had cushioned the fall, as they turned round and round, making Tommy dizzy.

"Uhhhhh," the man groaned. The crimson color drained from his face. Tommy had the wind knocked out of him and still couldn't move. Something jabbed his stomach. The gun was still in the guy's hands and his eyes stared wide open.

Why hasn't he shot me? Tommy thought.

He rolled off the man without strength even to fight for the weapon. Then, he saw the same thing that the men above must have seen. They had landed directly on top of the spinning roulette wheel. The oversized center shaft of the wheel had speared the guy. It stuck straight through him and grazed Tommy's belly. Tommy felt his own stomach. Blood covered it, but mostly from the man who was skewered like a pig on a roasting spit. Tommy climbed off the wheel and watched the lifeless body rotate.

Gunfire thundered from above. Bullets zinged like lethal raindrops, ripping apart the roulette wheel and tearing up the floor around him. Tommy dashed from the casino. He only had one hope. He ran toward the indoor amusement ride area. Maybe there, he could find a way outside. If the power stayed on, maybe he could activate an electric door. Tommy held his hand to his stomach wound and darted fast as he could. Blasts of semiautomatic fire filled his ears. Glass panes smashed above as disciples chased along the catwalks and fired down.

"Where the hell is he?" Matthew called into the walkie-talkie.

"Running toward the indoor amusement area," one man on a catwalk called back.

"You won't be able to track him from the catwalks," Matthew screamed. "I want everyone in the surveillance area and hotel tower to converge on the indoor rides. Now, Goddamn it!"

Tommy heard a rifle fire. A bullet breezed by his head and he ducked to the ground. He reached the indoor ride area but couldn't make it to an outer door. Where could he hide? In front of him, at the entrance-way to the cup and saucer ride, a twelve-foot plastic clown held a sign that read, "Killer Kups." Each of the ten cups on the ride was big enough to seat six riders. He would try hiding inside one and hope for the best. Tommy jumped in and slunk to the bottom, knowing his pursuers neared.

"I saw him head over this way," one of them shouted.

"Check the cups," another called.

Tommy poked his head up and saw four men searching the amusement ride with guns drawn. Another climbed into the control booth, peering downward.

"There he is," the man in the booth called out.

"Where?"

The man pointed at Tommy's cup. As he did, the guy leaned forward onto the control panel. Inadvertently, his chest hit the start lever and the ride flew into motion. Tommy's eyes darted, scanning for a way off somehow.

Men, who were standing beside the cups, leaped into them to avoid being run down.

"Arrrguh!"

Tommy heard the scream of one who hadn't leaped

fast enough. A cup smashed him, splattering blood across the "Killer Kups" sign.

A single rifle shot rang. The bullet missed Tommy as his cup jerked in another direction, instead nailing another man whose cup spun to where Tommy's had been. They twirled in circles and twisted in all directions at breakneck speed. All the while they flew toward one another as if to crash, then quickly jerked away.

Tommy's hands gripped the rim with his head peeking out. He wanted to jump out but they moved too fast, spinning him toward a cup holding a man aiming his semiautomatic pistol. Its deadly fire erupted.

Tommy's cup darted away as a long fire burst escaped the weapon. The guy swirled in his cup and inadvertently took out two of his cohorts. Men dressed as deputies dropped fast while the ride lived up to its namesake.

"Stop firing," the man from the control booth screamed. "Stop fucking firing!"

No one heard him over the clanking cups and roaring motor that powered them. Frantically, the man searched for a stop button. He pushed everything in sight, trying to bring the ride to a halt. Nothing worked. Instead, the ride whipped faster still.

Sounds of gunfire filled the air, and another deputy caught an unintended bullet. He grabbed his shoulder and howled.

Another burst of gunfire roared, wiping out the plastic clown's groin.

In the control booth, the frustrated operator found the throttle. He pulled back on it hard. The ride slowed. Gradually, it was coming to a stop.

They'll get me now, Tommy realized. He stumbled

out, dizzy from the frenetic turns. A deputy jumped out of another cup and staggered up to Tommy with his pistol ready. He fired but twirled in a lethal pirouette, bullets flying in all directions until he collapsed. Tommy seized his chance to sprint toward the exits.

The disciple in the control booth spotted Tommy. He looked ahead and saw where their prey was dashing.

"Matthew, this is Luke," he yelled into his walkie-talkie.

"Not so loud. Your transmission's garbled."

"He's headed toward a doorway."

"Where?"

"The revolving door to the outdoor amusement park area. Looks like it's closed down."

"Goddamn!" Matthew's urgent cry reflected fear. Their mission might fail; Brucker could escape them. "He may be able to activate that door. It's electrically operated," he exclaimed. "Peter, shut down all the power systems again, fast."

Tommy saw the door. His plastic passkey would start it turning, and he was almost there.

Just thirty feet and I'm out of here, he thought. *Twenty, ten.*

He made it. Tommy stuck his security pass in a slot beside the doorway. Glass doors began spinning. That was his chance. He was going to make it.

Suddenly, electric current fluctuated. Lights went out. The doors stopped. He looked at the immobilized glass doors. So close, he'd come to escaping.

A rifle shot zipped by his ear. Tommy dove to the ground. He turned and saw four forms moving in the dark, khaki-uniformed men approaching fast. They had him. He had no way to escape except through the doorway that the power outage paralyzed.

Like a ray of hope, lights flashed again. The doors turned. Tommy realized the backup system had activated. He picked himself up and darted into the revolving glass door.

Three feet from freedom, he thought.

From the outdoor amusement ride area, he would run to the nearby remains of the show room. Police protection was at hand. Then, just as quickly as they had started revolving, the doors halted and the lights went out. Someone had shut down the backup system. Tommy was trapped. An immovable glass door locked in front of him, another behind. Sandwiched between them like lunch meat on rye, he had nowhere to run from the eager gunmen.

Four men, who had been sprinting after Tommy, slowed. He watched them saunter toward him, knowing what they were thinking. *No need to hurry, now.* Casually, they strolled to the doors and raised their weapons.

"On my call," one of them said.

Tommy saw the four men were going to execute him with semiautomatic pistols. Each man loaded a fresh ammunition clip. Tommy's shoulder plowed into the door, trying to budge it.

Even if I can only move an inch or two, he thought, *maybe I can break free.*

One man made the slow and deliberate call. "Ready."

Tommy strained with all of his might.

"Aim."

He gave up. No hope of breaking free, he realized. Tommy listened for the last word he would ever hear, facing outward. He didn't want the last thing he saw on earth to be gun flashes from bullets ripping his body apart.

"Fire!"

Gunfire roared. Tommy didn't feel the bullets sting. *In fact*, he suddenly thought, *I don't feel anything.* Slowly, he turned round. There, laying on the ground, were four khaki-uniformed men. Standing above them with a smoking M-16 in his hands was a man with a familiar face. Through a three-day growth of beard, Darnel smiled a warm greeting.

Tommy heard more men shouting inside the darkened casino. Darnel pointed his weapon toward them. Tommy whacked on the glass door to draw his attention. As Darnel looked, Tommy moved to a corner of the area where the doors trapped him. Then, he pointed where he wanted Darnel to shoot. Darnel raised his M-16 and fired at the glass doors until he expended every round. Tommy's ears rang, glass fragments covered him, but they were free.

"After you, boss," the younger man said, pointing outside.

Tommy shook glass from his clothes and turned to Darnel. "How the hell did you get in here?"

Darnel held up his own plastic pass card.

"The guy at the front door turned me away," he said. "So I came in the rear door, here, with this baby." Darnel tapped the stock of his M-16.

Tommy looked at it. "Where did you get that thing?"

"Found it under a limousine hood when I checked

the oil. They stock those cars with the damnedest things."

Tommy knew he would have to pick up on the story later. The two men ran into the night. Gunfire had attracted attention from the police. Sirens on approaching squad cars wailed. Cops in blue uniforms were crossing the outdoor amusement area and coming their way. Tommy looked over his shoulder. A man in a khaki uniform aimed a rifle in their direction as a cop shouted.

"Atlantic City police!"

The deputy lowered his weapon and disappeared into the casino.

Tommy draped his arm over Darnel's shoulder. Together, they walked toward police officers who came from what remained of the show room. As Tommy viewed the devastation, anger filled his heart. He realized at that moment the catastrophes, which had befallen The Megasino, hadn't been accidents. Someone was behind them and Tommy was about to strike back.

Chapter Seventeen

Striking Back

Susannah didn't know where she wanted to spend her afternoon. It wasn't in a drug rehabilitation center, though. She had her bodyguards pickup some clothes for her. The outfit was nothing special, just enough to get her out the door, as she hadn't brought anything with her when she arrived and had been wearing an orderly's outfit during her stay.

A limousine waited for her in front of the Avery-Davis Clinic while she checked out. She was still stiff from her injuries. The pain didn't bother her so much as the shaking. Doctors on the clinic staff just hadn't given her what she needed. Hunger for narcotics came like famine. It plagued her body, overpowered wisdom, and raped her soul. There was nothing she wouldn't do or say for a handful of pills.

As a receptionist typed forms for her signature, Susannah looked out the windows by the main doors. A sunny afternoon called. She wondered, *What's taking this checkout so long?* In the back of the limo a buffet in capsule form beckoned. *Who the hell needs to sign papers? I'm getting out of here, now,* she thought.

A woman wearing a white uniform came close. "If you'll just sign here and over here," she said, fingers dancing between dotted lines, "you'll be free to leave, Miss Halloway."

Susannah grabbed a pen from the woman and signed away.

For Tommy, Darnel, and Manny, time had come to fight back. Tired of rolling with punches, they met in The Megasino board room to figure out the thing. Tommy had also invited someone to join them later.

At first, Tommy had wondered if it was all right to meet there in view of the court orders. Finally, he figured, to hell with restrictions in the orders Grender had obtained. Something about them stunk. Tommy just hadn't determined what it was.

The three men quickly updated each other. Tommy briefed them on his dash through the casino. Darnel relayed the story of his kidnaping. Then, Manny rose. He handed both men contracts, loosened his necktie, and spilled the news.

"I received an offer from Greg Conrad to buy the casino," he began. "The guy even put a bid on The Fantasy in Vegas. He's ready to move on both properties."

"What?" Tommy said, paging through the lengthy documents.

"They're cash offers," Manny continued. "The figures are terrible, but if you factor in the disaster they're probably not all that bad."

Tommy studied the proposals. They were detailed. Somebody had worked overtime to put them together so quickly after the fire. He just wasn't interested. Anger surfaced in Tommy's voice as he paged further. "We have insurance to cover the losses," he said.

Manny paused while his boss read.

Tommy realized his CEO was giving him time to cool. Conrad's attempt to buy the properties at "fire sale" prices was grating. He put the documents aside and took a deep breath. "Go ahead, Manny."

"Boss, there may be no insurance coverage. If Grender can make a criminal charge stick – whether it's for criminal negligence, reckless endangerment or anything else – we're done. The insurance companies will be off the hook. Then, we'll have to swallow our losses. We aren't that solvent."

"That's The Megasino," Tommy said more calmly. "How does The Fantasy factor into the loss? We've set up the casinos as separate corporate entities."

Darnel looked up from the proposals and interjected. "From a legal point of view, we protected the Las Vegas property from the Atlantic City loss, no matter what happens."

"Legally, perhaps," Manny reflected. "The problem is with our finances. We floated a public offering to build The Megasino. To capitalize the offer, we pledged so much stock in The Fantasy that the properties are financially handcuffed to each other. If one goes down, it takes the other with it."

"Why Conrad?" Tommy asked. "Why is he the first guy to bang on our door with an offer?"

"Simple," Manny said. "Only two casino owners in

the country can act on their own – you and Greg Conrad. A major corporation owns every other gambling operation. Those companies also own hotel chains, multifaceted entertainment divisions, motion picture companies, you name it. Their corporate boards don't act so quickly, because their board members don't have the balls. Bureaucracies in large institutions don't allow them to race into anything. Only you and Conrad can operate fast enough to seize this kind of advantage."

Tommy thought a moment. What Manny said made sense. Conrad was cold as a lizard and ambitious as Lucifer. He would have no qualms about making money from Tommy's tragedy. He had a reputation for churning dollars, but something seemed askew.

"This is going to take big money," Tommy said to his CEO. "Even Conrad doesn't have that much cash."

"He claims he was lining up capital for another project, a major construction venture in Chicago. It entailed complete renovation of lakefront property, blocks of it. He says he's willing to divert those funds, here, if he can buy at the right price."

"He's been planning that project for years," Tommy reflected. "I thought it didn't pass the Chicago planning boards. Even political hacks, who cozy up to him, couldn't net the approvals he needed."

"Maybe," Manny said. "He claims financing was ready for the project. Now, he can shift it here."

Tommy peered at the proposals again. He knew he wouldn't find a better offer, though the sale price would leave him virtually penniless, almost as if it was calculated to do so.

"I don't want to lose either property. Somehow, we have to keep both."

The three men sat silently until Darnel cleared his throat and conveyed more bad news. He laid out The Fantasy sports book problem. The casino was going to take a tremendous loss if Nashville lost the championship series.

Tommy looked around and said, "There's a radio in here somewhere. Manny, tune in game three. Let's catch the score."

As Manny fumbled with the dial, a new face entered the room.

"Darnel," Tommy said to introduce him to the woman, "this is Helen DeMarco. I fired Douglas Hooper after he fell asleep on me last night. I'm hiring Ms. DeMarco, right now, as our new chief counsel. You and Helen will tackle the Atlantic County prosecutor for me. Something about his investigation smells. You're going to find out what it is."

Helen's dropping jaw told them she hadn't been prepared for the offer. "I'm sorry, Mr. Brucker. I can't leave Mr. Hooper's firm like that. I wouldn't even have a staff to take on the case."

"I'm assigning Darnel to your staff. He knows the gaming business and he's a member of the Nevada bar. You'll be the lead attorney."

"Well, that's not the only consideration. Your case will need round the clock attention, at least initially, and I have to think about –"

"Your son will be fine with your mother," Tommy interjected, "and we'll provide extra day care so long as you need it."

Helen smiled. "You really check out your staff before hiring, don't you?"

"I've already arranged for payment of your retainer."

Tommy slid an envelope across the table containing a check. Helen opened it and nodded. Fire igniting in her eyes told Tommy he had picked the right person for the job. He passed a business card to her.

"Call this woman for a support staff."

Helen read the card aloud. "Prell Gardner, Specialized Employment Services?"

"Just tell the young lady who your client is. She'll send all the secretaries and paralegals you need."

Tommy continued to study the lawyer's eyes. They displayed astuteness upon which he was counting.

"You're going to have one client. One case. Are you in?"

"I'm with you, sir."

Tommy turned toward Darnel. He was entrusting two young attorneys to slay courtroom dragons. Helen was a more experienced advocate than Darnel and carried herself with self-assurance that only came from racking up her share of legal victories, something he had taken time to verify. Both were bright and had tenacity to fight what was going to be a tough battle. Yet with everything Tommy had was at stake, including his freedom if Grender pushed for an indictment, he wondered: *Am I throwing youngsters into water too deep?*

Manny called out. "Nashville's down. The score's eighty-eight to forty-nine in the fourth quarter. The Wildcats are going to fall in the series three games to none. One more loss to Chicago, and the series is over. We're going to take a heavy hit at The Fantasy."

Tommy couldn't figure it. He asked Darnel, "How could our sport's book be so far off on this series?"

"No one figured the Wildcats superstar would choke

this badly. It's almost like he's throwing the game."

The offhand comment bothered Tommy. "What are the chances of a guy doing that?"

"Doing what? Throwing a professional basketball championship," Darnel said incredulously. "Why would he?"

"I don't know," Tommy answered. "Where's the next game?"

"Nashville. If the series goes beyond that, they'll play game five there, too. The last two games are slated for Chicago, but it doesn't look like the Wildcats can take it that far."

Something didn't seem right to Tommy about the series either. "Wasn't Dion Brown here with some of his teammates for the casino opening?"

"Yeah," Manny answered, "but for some reason, he took off before the place blew all to hell. I remember, because I checked our celebrity roster. Somebody said he had just left early without giving a reason."

Tommy didn't like it. "Anyone have a connection in Tennessee to check this out?"

Manny's answer surprised him.

"Sure. In the Marine Corps I served with a guy who became a Tennessee State Trooper. I think he's a captain on the force, now. I'll place a call."

"I have a Jewish accountant from with friends in the State Police," Tommy mused.

"Hey, this is the guy who turned me on to Jack Daniel's bourbon," Manny said with a grin, "the pride of Lynchburg, Tennessee."

Tommy was already standing. Conrad's contracts were in his hands, and he was ready to set his people loose. "Give your buddy a call," he said to Manny. "In fact, fly there, now. I want to know what's happened to this kid."

Susannah had barely glanced at the release forms she had signed at the reception desk. Her body ached to climb inside the limousine where pills waited with a chilled cocktail. She scurried to the clinic door that her driver held open.

"Umph," a little man said as he bumped into her in the doorway. The delivery man couldn't see where he was going. Bouquets he carried blinded his view as he tried negotiating his way to the front desk. Susannah didn't know why, but something about the scenario seemed familiar.

"Ready, Miss Halloway?" her driver said.

"Just a second." She watched the delivery guy set his flowers on the reception counter.

"Hey," the receptionist blustered, "you can't leave them here. I need room to work."

Blossoms consumed all the counter space, and the delivery man looked too exasperated to pick them up again.

"They're for Miss Susannah Halloway," he said.

Peach roses, she thought. Without checking the card Susannah knew who had sent them. She walked to the six-dozen roses and savored their fragrance.

"I have a whole truckload of these things to drop off," the man said.

The flowers reminded her of happier times so many years ago. Like an elixir for the heart, they gave her hope where mind and soul had failed. Tears welled in her eyes. Still shaking from the icy chill of drug withdrawal, she looked at the waiting car, then at the blossoms lighting up the counter.

Her driver, as if sensing her indecision, softly offered, "Rehab's for quitters, Miss Halloway."

She called to the discharge clerk. "Rip up those papers and have the roses delivered to my room."

For Susannah, time had come to strike back, too.

Chapter Eighteen

Hoop Schemes

Dion "Stuff Daddy" Brown was having his ticket punched in basketball hell. Game four of the seven game series was about to tipoff. A loss would cost his team the championship title and Dion could do nothing to help them. Instead, he would pull them down with his every move, allowing himself to be beat physically and psychologically on the court. Opposing teams normally had to rotate defenders against the premier player. He was too big, too fast, and too talented for one man to contain him through a whole game. During the series, though, it was as if Chicago didn't need to defend him at all.

In game one, they had double-teamed him through the first half of play. Dion stunk up the court with lackluster play. By half time, the Chicago head coach made a switch, assigning a single defender to the Wildcats star. That tightened the reigns on Dion's teammates and gave Chicago the edge it needed. They continued to play that way through three consecutive playoff victories over the Wildcats. Chicago would employ the same tactic again.

Dion lined up at half-court for tipoff. He stood four inches taller than the opposing forward-center, had longer reach and a higher vertical leap. The smaller man, who stood 6'11", stared into Dion's eyes.

"You ready?" he said with a smirk.

Dion realized the man had lost respect for his playing ability. Even sportscasters had keyed on him. A wave of television, radio, and newspaper reporters had splashed the story across the media. They called his subpar performance what it was – the key to the Wildcats failures in the series.

A whistle blew and both men jumped for the ball. Dion missed. Chicago's center tipped the ball where he wanted it to go. A Chicago player dribbled downcourt to score the first bucket of the game.

The referee handed the ball to a Wildcat to inbound. As Dion ran downcourt toward the other hoop, his defender dissed him.

"A little late on that tipoff, weren't you? That all you got today?"

Frustrated, Dion jabbed the man and sent him reeling to the floor. An official's face filled like chipmunk cheeks as he raised his whistle and blew. Less than one minute into the game, Dion was called for his first personal foul. He watched the shooter sink two easy free throws, knowing his unprofessional play had already set his team down 4-0. It was going to be another bad day for the Wildcats.

A Chicago player inbounded the ball to the man he was covering, but Dion wasn't guarding tightly enough and his guy charged toward an easy two-point dunk.

The Wildcats trailed 6-0.

A restless crowd began to grumble. When Dion took the ball and missed an easy shot from ten feet out, calls from boo birds cascaded. He had never heard that sound directed toward him by his own fans. Heartbreak surfaced on his down-turned lips; bewilderment clouded his unfocused eyes.

Dion wanted to play at his unique level and considered busting a move, one of his classics. The ball came to him again. He zigged past a befuddled defender, then saw something from the corner of his eye – an empty seat at center-court where his biggest fan usually called his name and cussed his opponents. "Gramzie," he huffed. Lackadaisically, he passed off and a defender intercepted the ball. Dion chugged in the opposite direction as Chicago players set into position, preparing to drive toward the hoop.

The charge came by the Chicago point-guard. Dion reached out, collared him, and watched the smaller man bodysurf on hardwood. A whistle trilled as Dion raised his arm, signaling he had committed another foul. Then, it dawned on him. No matter how badly he played, his own coach wouldn't bench a superstar. Maybe he could foul himself out. Perhaps then his team would stand a chance.

Dion looked for another opportunity. Under the basket it came when a Wildcat hurled a shot. The ball danced around the rim, almost sinking before teetering off. Bodies sleek with sweat jostled for position, muscles strained on outstretched arms, and fingertips extended for a prize only one player could seize. Dion grabbed what he wanted – two opponents struggling for the ball – and set both on their tails.

Two officials whistled a foul so flagrant fans in nose-
bleed sections of the stands spotted it. Gladly, Dion
took the call, lifting his hand to signal the foul was his as
if reaching for clouds, then lowering it to droning boos
that filled his ears.

Propellers hummed as Manny's plane landed. The
early evening flight touched down in "the Athens of the
South," Nashville, Tennessee. Manny checked his wristwatch and shook his head.

"Damn shuttles," he complained.

The first plane out of Atlantic City had been a junket
flight, returning rated players for whom casinos provided complimentarily transportation. But its takeoff had
been delayed and he was running late for his appoint-
ment.

Manny dashed to a car rental desk, steered a midsize
sedan out of the airport, and barreled along the west
side of the Cumberland River. His casino position entitled him to drive more luxurious wheels, but he didn't
know where the trip might take him. He had researched
the basketball star's background. The kid came from
humble roots and stayed close to home even after he
picked up big paychecks in the pros. If Manny had to
make inquiries in Dion's poor rural hometown, he didn't
want to show up in a fancy car that might make folks
resentful.

A central tower atop the Capitol building dominated
the Nashville skyline. Like so many public structures in
the city, it was of classic Greek design. The stately
building was in view when overhead lights on a city
police car flashed in his rearview mirror. A siren wail

alerted him to pull over.

Manny yanked his license from his wallet, rolled down his window, and waited for the officer to approach.

"In a hurry, sir?" the officer asked while taking Manny's license.

"I'm sorry, officer, but I have a meeting at the state capitol."

"Mister," the cop said nonplused, "I stop people heading there all day. What kind of business?"

"A meeting with Captain Andy Jackson of the State Police. He's been assigned to special duty on the governor's staff."

"Business or pleasure?"

"A little of each. We served in the First Marine Division together."

"I'll be with you in a minute, sir."

The cop returned to his car. Manny spotted him in his rearview mirror, calling on his radio. *Must be checking on the car plate numbers*, he thought, *before writing the speeding ticket.*

When the cop returned, he gave Manny his papers and a down-home welcome.

"Mr. Levine, your story checks out. Enjoy your stay, here. You can follow me to the capitol."

Manny titled his head. He had no idea his service buddy had so much clout even city cops would do him that kind of favor. The officer's face transformed, lighting with genuine congeniality.

"Captain Jackson's a good man," the cop said. "He's the namesake of his famous kin, President Andrew Jackson. Around some parts of the state, he's as well known."

Manny realized he was seeing the right person. If

anyone could help them learn what was happening in Tennessee, it was Andy.

"Strap on your seat belt, Mister Levine," hailed the officer. "I'll get you to that meeting on time."

He returned to his squad car and led the way, siren blaring and overhead lights twirling.

Dion squirmed on the bench. He had fouled out before the first half even ended and could imagine what sports pundits were saying about him. *Oh*, he thought, *who cares?* All that mattered was the Wildcats play sparked soon as he left the court. They were on fire. As so often happens in team sports when a key player goes down, his teammates rose to the challenge. They picked up slack and overachieved.

On offense Wildcats made plays to the basket instead of looking for their superstar to drive it in. Their little man, a 6'1" guard, found his "zone," sinking nine out of fourteen three-pointers. Intensity burned in the eyes of every cat and their play sizzled. With under a minute in the game, it wasn't even a contest anymore. They stuck it to Chicago hard. Nashville was pulling out a victory and taking the series further. Somehow, though, they had to win all of the last three games.

Dion lowered his head. Good as the players were on his team, they couldn't sustain that level of play through the entire series. They needed help, his help. The buzzer sounded to end the game and fans gave their Wildcats a standing ovation.

Two days, he mulled. Dion had two days to figure his next move before taking the floor for game five. He traipsed to their locker room with a heavy heart. If he tried fouling out again, he was certain the hoods, who held his grandmother, would extract revenge on her. He followed a tunnel from the playing court, consumed by a question that had no answer: *What can I do?*

Along the way he spotted a familiar face that he couldn't quite place. They only allowed team personnel and reporters in the tunnel. He wondered, *Who's the little guy?* It wasn't that the man was actually small. When you played a game on a court filled with six-and-a-half and seven-footers, men of average size just look little. Dion racked his brain trying to recall as the guy waved for him to stop.

"Dion," he said. "I'm Manny Levine from The Megasino. We met, just briefly, a week ago."

"Oh, yeah. How did you get back here, man?"

"Connections," Manny said with a smile. "I'd like to talk to you."

"Sorry. Don't have time. I'll catch you back in Atlantic City, though, if you ever reopen that casino."

Dion wanted to shower and take off fast. He turned his back but before he could get away, Manny reached out and grabbed him.

"If you've got a problem," he said, "I can help."

"Hey, Dion," an arena security guard called. "You want this guy outta here?"

"Yeah. Sorry, man," he said to Manny, "I just don't have time to talk."

Dion headed to the locker again as the guard approached Manny.

"You'll have to come with me, buddy," directed the guard.

Suddenly Dion stopped, not knowing why. Then it occurred to him – all his problems stemmed from Atlan-

tic City; maybe the casino honcho could help. Longing
to talk with someone, he turned round and called to the
guard.

"Hey, let that guy wait around. I'll catch him after I
change."

Manny liked stadium food. After so many fancy din-
ers and affairs at the casino, it was always refreshing to
chomp something simple and wash it down with a brew.
Without time to eat all day, even on the shuttle flight
where they had only served salted nuts in mini-bags, he
savored a tray of burgers and fries. With each bite he
reflected on the trouble that showed in Dion's eyes. It
wasn't just basketball that bothered him, but what was
it? Manny didn't know if he could help the kid. He
didn't even know if he could help himself. Manny had
his own problems, which had danced into his life at a
time when his guard was down.

Manny was a career casino man. *No*, he reflected, *I
was a casino man before I had a career . . . and inside
casinos before I was a man.*

His father, who had been a gambler most of his life,
sneaked Manny into race tracks as a kid. Whenever his
dad hit a lucky streak, he trotted – faster than the horses
that filled his pockets with winnings – to the glitter of
Las Vegas. Often, he took his only son. Manny grew
up feeling good about casinos and pursued his livelihood
in Las Vegas gaming palaces after finishing college. He
had a natural knack for figures, a solid reputation for
competence, and devotion to his work that propelled
him up the ranks.

He married his childhood sweetheart and swooped

her to the desert town where they raised two beautiful children. But Vegas wasn't Long Island. Veronica yearned for her family, friends, and roots. Manny's work consumed long hours and perhaps that's why he hadn't realized how troubled Ronnie was, not until he came home one night to an empty house. He scoured every room until he spotted a note taped to the refrigerator.

"Emanuel," it read. "If you want to see me and the kids again, come home to New York. I've taken the children to my mother's house. We won't be back."

His first inclination was to call and beg her to return. Surely he worked long days, but his rearing had taught him: "Today's restraints bring tomorrow's rewards." They lived a good life in Vegas and Manny couldn't imagine himself in an ordinary job. The thrill of casino work churned his blood. He told her that and more. Manny spoke from his heart, but the tone of Ronnie's voice let him know she would never submit. He had to make a choice.

Manny mailed alimony checks until she remarried a Long Island boy who, like Ronnie, would stay anchored. Meanwhile, Manny remained married to his work, the most demanding mistress he had ever known, until Tina came along.

He took her east just once, during their brief engagement, to meet his parents. It was a traditional gathering of family members at Passover. Tina didn't even try to blend into the close-knit Jewish family.

"Tell me you're not going to marry that *shiksa*," his mother wailed.

He was marrying soon as they returned to Las Vegas. Already Tina was planning a small affair for more friends than family to attend. He turned to his father for support. After all, Dad had always said, "Jews are just like everyone else, only more so." Apparently, they weren't enough like Tina, because his father remained silent while his mother *kvitched*.

"Son," she pleaded, "I tell you this woman is no good. Trust a mother's intuition. There's a dark heart inside her."

At the time he remembered thinking that his mother's words were simple expressions of prejudice, no matter how well intended. Mom was deeply religious and had whisked him to services when he had arrived. She had rightly surmised it had been a long time since he'd attended synagogue. His fiancee, who claimed to be "some kind of Protestant," went shopping in Manhattan's exclusive Fifth Avenue shops, instead.

Manny had passed off his mother's words. She was always outspoken and made no excuses about telling him whom he should marry.

"Find someone more like yourself," she proclaimed, "a nice Jewish girl. Your aunt knows a girl, a school teacher, Emanuel. Very pretty, I hear. She's just right for a man who . . ."

His mother was the perfect *shadchen*, but he wasn't looking for a matchmaker. He had found what he thought he wanted in a woman. Tina didn't complain when he worked lengthy hours. Moreover, unlike Ronnie, Tina had no ties to New York. She wouldn't urge him back. He wasn't going to make the same mistake twice; instead, by ignoring his mother's instincts, he made an even bigger mistake. Too late he discovered practice doesn't make perfect when it comes to marriage.

Tina was a catlike shrew, but it really didn't matter. He just devoted himself more deeply to his work. Even after a career opportunity took Manny to Atlantic City, he avoided the frigid atmosphere of their nonexistent home life. Sometimes, he didn't go home at all, preferring to nap six hours at the casino where he worked, then return to the job.

As his career spiraled upward, his marriage descended further into hell where Tina was most at home. She enjoyed saying she was Mrs. Manny Levine. Top casino officers and their spouses were treated like royalty in casino communities. Though he was never certain her background measured up to what she claimed, he knew she savored the lifestyle he could afford to give her.

He no longer cared about rumors of what she did behind his back. Marital infidelity didn't matter where there was no love. Still, if he had just pulled his nose from his work long enough to straighten-out his life, he may have ridden himself of her long ago. The few times he had broached the subject with Tina, she'd shown her claws.

"Divorce me and I'll take every dime you have and every cent you'll ever earn," she threatened. "I'm not like that stupid bitch you married the first time. I'm not going to remarry and lose my alimony. You'll pay big-time if you ever try to get rid of me."

He didn't care about the money. His upbringing glued their loveless marriage together. It told him: Family is important. Avoid divorce, if possible, any way at all.

Sometimes Tina came to him with fickle expressions of feigned kindness. For a while that had been enough to sustain him. Manny was no fool, though. He knew she always arrived with an agenda when she seduced him with her body and her lies. Still, he was a sucker so long as hope might spark, hope that she would open her eyes to the good life they could share if only she'd give it a chance.

Manny had thought he could forgive Tina for anything. At last, her indiscretions may have exceeded his high threshold. His wife had delivered Conrad's offer to buy the Buckman's casinos. Manny wondered how closely she was tied to Conrad. What had she done? How far would she go . . . for whatever she wanted? He would never learn from her, but those questions begged for answers. Manny feared what they might be.

"Mr. Levine!" Dion Brown called.

Manny looked up at the well-dressed young man and wondered where he found clothes. He knew the size twenty-three basketball shoes Dion wore were custom made by a manufacturer who paid millions for his endorsement. A man so big must have all his clothes custom made, Manny supposed. He felt dwarfed beside the kid, but Dion's wide smile and alert eyes conveyed an impression of kindness and sagacity. Up-close, Dion was more than just a big kid who could play hoops like no one else. He was also a big-hearted man with a wise and sensitive soul.

They took Dion's Chevy Bronco for a ride, so they could talk without fear of being overheard. What the basketball star explained about his grandmother's kidnaping let Manny know why the young man was troubled and how badly he hurt inside. Then something Dion said hit a nerve.

"You a god-fearing man?" the kid straightforwardly inquired.

Manny didn't answer.

"God will give me strength to pull through this, Mr. Levine. That's something Gramzie drilled into me as a kid. Without the Almighty's assistance, we can't succeed. With it, we can't fail."

The words sparked Manny's brain. He realized both he and Dion, who rose from such different heritages, lived by simple credos found in time-proven adages. Dion's words also told him how much courage the young man derived from his faith and gave Manny pause to reflect upon his own. The kid was going to need more than blind faith, though. The people, who held his grandmother, weren't on God's team; they played in a different league altogether.

Manny wasted no time taking what he learned back to his service buddy. On their second sit-down, he was ready to cash every chip he had ever earned in their friendship. His words came fast, much faster than his friend's reaction.

The narrow faced and long-jawed state police captain pushed his chair away from his desk. He tipped backward on the rear legs of the chair, rested his head against the wall behind him, and rocked as he deliberated. Andy kept a straighter poker face than Manny had seen at any gaming table.

Will he help? Manny wondered. While the man reflected, Manny momentarily marvelled at how much his friend's features resembled the famous frontiersman, turned iron-willed politician, for whom Andy was a namesake. A framed print of the former president, which was taken from an oil-painted portrait, hung behind his friend's desk. *Will Andy show the same tenacity?* Manny wondered.

Finally, a Tennessee drawl cracked the silence. "You

want me to find a kidnaping victim *unofficially*."

"Andy, I know what kind of people are holding this woman. I worked in Vegas years ago when racket guys still had a hold on the casinos, there. They'll kill that kid's grandmother the instant they suspect police involvement."

"Then," Andy reflected, "they'll kill her soon as the series is over, no matter who wins."

"An official investigation will also end the kid's professional career. The league will ban him for tossing the series, regardless of his motives. He could even face criminal charges." Manny paused as he recalled all he and Andy had been through together, as kids themselves on their way to becoming men, sharing the uncommon bond of combat. "We go back a long way, Andy. Do it for the days we trekked through –"

"The An Hoa Valley." Andy was sharing his thoughts. He reached into a lower desk drawer, pulled out a familiar-looking bottle and two shot glasses, then poured a round of Jack Daniels. "To those who didn't make it back," he said.

They raised their glasses and tossed them back. Manny savored a taste that sweetened with good company.

"Folks, here, are loyal to their local heroes, Manny, and Stuff Daddy is a big one."

Andy paused for another sip, then thought aloud.

"Maybe," he said, "I could muster some Tennessee volunteers. Maybe, but still. . . ."

As Andy weighed the options, Manny realized how fast time was running out. The hoop star and his grandmother had no more time than Tommy. He considered what the kid had said to him, and realized something else. Manny still had time enough to say a prayer.

Chapter Nineteen

Running Blind

Chapter Nineteen

Binding Intent

Documents can torture, Tommy thought. He sat behind his office desk in The Megasino reading Conrad's offer again. The contract would legally bind him to sell The Fantasy and The Megasino. Parting with his dreams would hurt but selling would cut losses. Sometimes, he realized, you have to fold a losing hand. With a stoke of his pen the properties would belong to Greg Conrad. He pondered how the man had so quickly obtained massive financing to capitalize on the tragedy. Tommy also wondered how everything had stacked up so neatly against himself.

His one chance to survive was in the hands of a judge, who would rule on a motion to lift the restraints closing the casino. Helen DeMarco and Darnel had quickly assembled a legal support team with assistance of a woman whom he'd once helped. He reflected on their chance meeting and pondered, like all who embrace fate, just how much luck, good or bad, you make for yourself.

Certainly it had been his good fortune to find Prell. Who would have thought their brief encounter could ever pay off that way?

Years ago, Tommy had spotted the young woman at The Fantasy. As she strolled into the main lounge and sat at the bar, every head in the room turned toward her. A mop of dark hair surrounded what might have been the sweetest face on the planet. The twenty-year-old was a picture of loveliness and obviously aware. *When you know what you have and how good it is, confidence exudes from every pore*, he thought. She dripped it.

A middle-aged man, wearing shabby jeans and a ripped tee shirt, neared her. His droopy jowls and extra chin lent a walrus-like appearance. She smiled to him though he seemed to approach as a stranger. *At her age*, Tommy observed, *everything is possible and every face looks friendly*. Without a word spoken between them, the walrus slapped handcuffs on her.

"No! That's not fair," she shrieked.

Tommy signaled the bartender to call security personnel. As the guy led the struggling young woman away, Tommy walked toward them.

"I own this casino," he said. "What's the problem here?"

The man kept one hand on his captive and reached into his pocket. "Vice squad," he said, flashing his badge and a grin too big for Tommy's likes. "This hooker just propositioned me."

Tommy turned his attention to the young woman in the undercover cop's custody. She was right; it wasn't fair. Neither of them had spoken. A vice arrest couldn't stick without exchanging words establishing the prostitute offered sex for pay. Tommy didn't condone what

the young lady was doing, but that didn't justify the
cop's tactics. He was fabricating a false charge to send
the young woman to jail and Tommy couldn't let injustice pass.

"Officer, do you know who I am?"

"Yes, sir, Mr. Brucker."

"I'm not saying you're lying. But I will swear in
court that you and the young lady never engaged in a
conversation if her attorney calls me to testify."

The vice officer glared at Tommy; the Buckman didn't
flinch. Their standoff ended as cop's face flushed and
his feet shuffled.

"Officer," Tommy said, "do what's right."

The vice cop removed the cuffs and released his captive. Tommy watched the man slink away. He didn't
know why he had intervened. Maybe it was because he
innately knew the judicial system doesn't always work.
A prostitute's testimony against the word of a police
officer wouldn't beat a criminal charge.

Later, Tommy had received flowers from the young
woman with a note introducing herself and promising to
return his favor someday. When he opened The Megasino, she even sent a reminder with a business card for
her firm's specialized employment services. He sensed
there was more to her temporary employment agency
than met the eye, but knew he could count on Prell to
find eager assistants for his lawyers.

Funny, he reflected, *how even small acts of kindness
generate rewards. Maybe there is such a thing as karma.*

He wondered if his stacked high enough to generate
the court ruling he needed. Conrad's contract and a
cellular telephone waited with him for a call from the

courthouse, a phone call that would let him know if he had to sign away his dreams.

Darnel sat at the counsel table next to Helen. Peering around, he realized courtrooms in New Jersey weren't any different from those in Nevada. Familiar trappings were in their places – the flags of the nation and state, the blindfolded statue of justice holding scales. He wondered which way those scales would tip.

He hadn't expected so large a crowd. It was only a preliminary hearing, but the implications would be far-reaching. Local press provided coverage. Even national news teams followed the disaster story. Five lives had been lost and many more had been injured. It wasn't the worst casino disaster the country had ever faced. That had occurred when fire struck a Las Vegas casino hotel a decade earlier, snuffing out more than eighty souls. Fortunately, they had designed the Megasino show room with exits directly to the outdoors or casualties would have been higher.

Helen pointed out plaintiff-lawyers scattered in the audience. They were easy to spot with yellow legal pads in their hands, looking eager to take notes. Lawyers could make money from that tragedy, like any other. Those leaches of the law extended their noses as if sniffing for some good thing in the air. They listened intently as proceedings commenced and clung to every word uttered by Atlantic County Prosecutor Horace Grender.

Grender basked in the sudden glow of celebrity. Squat as a squash, his suit jacket spread wide and seemed cut off so it wouldn't drag on the floor when he walked.

Impressive looking, he was not, but his soliloquy was killing them.

"That casino is a death trap," he wheezed. "Management simply rushed into operation. They cared more about earning money than about public welfare."

Helen had warned Darnel about the man's courtroom style. His high-pitched voice grated the nerves. Annoying as it was, she was right about something else. Grender was an aggressive and effective warrior.

"There's no way to justify reopening the property, merely so big business can make profits. For the public's sake, which this Court cannot ignore, the State seeks continuation of the injunction. The casino must remain shutdown until indisputable proof establishes the public will not be endangered by walking in its doors."

Judge Wilkins looked down pensively from the bench. The silver-haired jurist flipped a ballpoint pen in his hand as if he were a baton-twirling cheer leader wearing a black robe. Then, he checked his notes and asked a single question.

"In your estimation, Mr. Grender, how long might it be before the Court should allow the casino to reopen?"

"So long as the property remains in control of current management, I don't see how we could ever condone reopening it, your Honor. They have demonstrated a pattern of wilful disregard for welfare that's criminal. I'm taking the matter to a grand jury before the end of the month and indicting the principal officers."

Even the judge flinched. The State's investigation was moving at breakneck speed if indictments were coming so quickly.

"Your reply, Ms. DeMarco," the judge called.

Darnel wondered how the young lawyer would react. Helen had what lawyers call a strong "courtroom presence" that was felt even as she rose. Her words came calmly, cohesively, and indefatigably. After high-pitched rants from Grender, Helen's style was refreshing, her words compelling. The judge listened intently. They had been right to jockey the case away from the jurist to whom it had been originally assigned. Judge Wilkins would give them a fair hearing.

Helen pointed out more was at stake than the solvency of a business. Thousands of employees counted upon the casino to feed their families. Tax revenue, which the property generated on a daily basis for the state and city, was astounding. Most important, the prosecutor failed to demonstrate how management improperly ran the casino or how its officers and employees had acted negligently in any way. Public safety officials had inspected the resort before granting Certificates for Occupancy and Public Usage. There was no reason to believe those public servants were biased in any way; nor was there any reason to believe those officials were wrong in their independent assessments that the property was safe and fit.

She entered documents into evidence attesting to the facility's compliance with safety codes and regulations, then took her seat. They waited for the judge to rule. No matter what happened, win or lose, Tommy Brucker would face tough days ahead. The prosecutor was clearly out to nail him with a whirlwind force his office had power to muster.

Judge Wilkins sifted through briefs both sides had submitted. The staff Prell furnished had swiftly put together the paperwork. They had toiled around the clock with the lawyers to prepare for the hearing. Darnel realized he was about to learn whether their hard work would pay off. He sat back as the judge cleared his throat.

Tommy heard his cell phone buzz and knew the judge had ruled. He lifted it, slowly placing it to his ear, knowing everything he owned was riding on the call.

"Judge Wilkins granted our request for increased on-site personnel," Helen began, "to avoid future incidents like the one that cost lives of casino security officers.

"And," said Tommy, pressing for more.

"That's good as it gets, Mr. Brucker. The judge won't lift the injunction banning the public from the premises, but he did enter a new order allowing us ten days to renovate damages and show just cause to reopen the property.

"Meaning?"

"We can present our case again, but . . . . Well, let me read my notes. These are his words: 'In the face of highly probable indictments against company officers, it's unlikely anything current management does will compel the Court to reverse its decision'."

"Helen, what are our chances on appeal?"

"Do you have time? You're looking at eight to twelve months before a full trial on the merits, longer for an appellate review."

Tommy set down the phone, picked up his pen, and signed three copies of the contract. He was selling the properties to Conrad. With the deal done, Tommy didn't want to remain in the casino another moment. He was going somewhere and where didn't even matter; his days in Atlantic City and Las Vegas were over. As he readied to leave, Tommy heard a rap on the door.

"Come in," he called out. He couldn't imagine who was knocking. *Who could have gotten past security?*

Tina Levine poked her head in the doorway. He recognized her sheepish grin as a precursor to trouble. After losing the legal battle for his casinos, though, what could the woman say to faze him? She walked to his desk and glimpsed at the contracts.

"Are you accepting Mr. Conrad's proposal?" she asked.

Tommy never liked the idea that Tina had access to confidential information that came her husband's way. He sat silently as she continued.

"Because I promised to get the signed contracts back to him quickly as possible. With Manny out of town, I'll be glad to run them over to The Pyramid for you."

Tommy shoved them into the woman's hand and watched her turn to leave. She was almost out the door when he called, "Tina, wait a minute."

She stopped and looked back. Her catlike eyes had always said she was ready to play around with him, but that flirtatiousness was gone.

He walked toward her.

"I'm not interested if you're thinking of making a move on me, Tommy."

"No," he said. "I never suspected you were one to hang onto lost causes." He came close and stared into those cat-eyes.

"You could've had me, once, you know," she teased.

Tommy put his arms around her waist and held her tight. Their lips were only inches apart. Her breath grew steamy as he softly whispered, "How did you know Conrad sent that offer?"

Tina softened in his embrace as if she were ready to toy with him before leaving him unfulfilled.

"Greg had me deliver it to Manny."

As her lips, moist and ripe, touched his, Tommy snatched the contracts from her hand.

"That's all I needed to know, Tina."

Her connection to Greg Conrad was calculated. Everything about Tina was shrewdly orchestrated, just as it always was with Conrad. Tommy needed time to piece it together, but he knew for certain. Conrad had been involved in setting him up.

"Be out of here in two minutes," he told her. "If you ever step foot on this property again, security will arrest you."

Tina stiffened her posture and lashed. "You're a loser, Brucker. Don't worry. I won't be back – until Greg takes over this place. You'll sell to him. You don't have a choice, anymore." She snarled and let him know just how closely involved she was with Conrad. "Fuck with me and I'll see Greg reduces that offer. Don't waste time delivering it."

Tina cackled on the way out the door. "If you're a good boy," she said, "maybe I'll find you a job here – as a waiter after you're released from prison."

Tommy picked up the cellular telephone. Perhaps there was another way out. He could try, but first he needed special information, the kind one person he knew might find.

"This is Tommy Brucker," he said into the phone. "Let me talk to Prell."

Chapter Twenty

Nose to the Grindstone

In the cabin basement, Chichi stroked his neatly-trimmed beard and watched his partner flex tattooed arms. Sitting on a stool next to a workbench, Petey Pets pumped the foot pedal that spun a greyish stone wheel. Over racket rising from the clanking grindstone, Petey shouted.

"Where'd you find this thing?"

"Same place I found the TV. The store that sells 'used notions and such'. Hillbillies useta use these things to sharpen axes and knives. Some yokel tried to pass this piece of shit off as an antique when he sold it to me. It still works good, though."

"I like it. In fact, I really like it."

Petey thumped up and down on the pedal, driving the wheel faster.

"Here," Chichi called, "try this on it."

He sprung his eight-inch switchblade and handed it over. Petey fed its blade to the wheel and watched sparks fly.

"I fucking love it!" he yelled.

As Petey worked the pedal, Chichi peered through the slot they had cut into the furnace room door. Gramzie rested in the empty coal bin. He wondered, *How can she sleep through this commotion?*

"Wake up, Sleeping Beauty," he sang. "We're gonna call your grandson."

Chichi watched her stir. The woman moved more slowly. That wasn't the first time he had trapped someone. They always slowed down after a day or two of mistreatment. It was just a matter of showing them who's boss and letting them know they didn't have a chance of escaping. Oddly, captives even began to depend on their captors. They waited for their meals like anxious dogs, thankful for any crumb tossed 'em. Even that spicy woman had fallen into line. Like a caged bird, stolen from the treetops, barely a peep emerged from her mouth.

Soon she would do more than chirp. In a few minutes, she'd be squealing like a hog at the slaughter house. He and Petey had set up the grindstone in front of an old workbench. They would tie her to the bench facing the wheel, then grind down her nose. Not only was she going to squeal like a pig, she'd look like one when they were through. Chichi knew firsthand how that kind of stuff worked. Blood would splatter allover. He already had a pile of dirty towels waiting. Afterward, she could hold them over the hole where her nose had been if she wanted to keep from bleeding to death.

"Wipe those sleepers from your eyes, sweetie pie," he crooned. "We've got a surprise for you."

As Petey's foot thumped harder, the wheel revolved

faster, elevating the clanking sound to a deafening level.

"Hey, easy on that thing," Chichi shouted to him. "Easy, boy. You're gonna wear yourself out before we even start."

Petey left his stool and joined Chichi by the furnace room. They nodded to each other and swung the door open. Gramzie didn't have time to react. Each man grabbed an arm and dragged their captive toward the workbench. Her strength surprised them. She threw Petey Pets across the room. Chichi smacked Gramzie over the head with just enough force to disorient her as Petey leaped to his feet. His eyes scoured for something he could use to wallop the woman. They settled on an old wooden mallet. Raising it to her face, he panted heavily, ready to strike.

"No," Chichi shouted. "We need her alive and conscious."

Petey glared at Gramzie, then turned to the mallet. Next, he looked at the grindstone. Finally, he turned back to Gramzie's nose.

"Yeah," he said between heavy breaths.

The men's faces glistened with enthusiasm as they threw her atop the work bench, forcing Gramzie to lay facedown with her head extending over its end. Petey grabbed leather straps and bound her to the bench with her left arm tightly lashed to her side. Chichi reached for some clothesline rope underneath the bench. They used it to tie her right wrist to a rusted iron vice mounted on the workbench. Chichi had plans for Gramzie's hand. They could grind down fingers nicely, too, one at a time. Her head fell over the bench at just the right level, so her face rested on the grindstone wheel.

"Perfect," Chichi said.

He would grab her hair and lift her head until Petey had the wheel zipping. First, though, Chichi would call her grandson on the telephone. They hadn't gagged the woman. More than anything else, they wanted Dion to hear her screams so he wouldn't think about fouling out of the evening game or dreaming up any more tricks. Dion would keep his nose to the grindstone, just like they'd leave his grandmother's on it.

Chichi punched Dion's home number into their telephone. He didn't like making the call over a cellular phone, but no telephone lines ran to the remote cabin. He'd have to keep the call under fifty seconds to avoid a trace. Still, they could call more than once. The basketball star would get intermittent updates as they ground his granny.

"Dion, baby," Chichi yelled into the phone. "Guess who?"

Chichi paused.

"That's right, you big doofus. Now, guess what?" He laid the telephone on the table near Gramzie's head and smirked at her.

"Don't worry about me, child," Gramzie yelled. "They can't hurt me!"

Without saying another word, Chichi yanked Gramzie's hair to lift her face off the wheel. His smile grew wider as Petey Pets pumped the foot pedal. He beamed as the wheel spun even faster . With her face only inches above the revolving grindstone, Gramzie screamed in horror.

Good, Chichi thought. *She's finally cooperating with the damn program.* "Hold your head up, woman," he roared.

He released her hair. Gramzie struggled to keep her

head raised above the spinning grindstone, while Chichi released the restraint on her right arm. He grabbed her pinky finger and took it to the wheel.

Gramzie wailed in agony as her finger nail disappeared and blood splattered.

"That's right. Squeal, pig!" Chichi shouted.

She struggled to yank her hand away from Chichi's strong grip.

"Pull that hand away and I drop your face on the wheel," he screamed at her. "What's next, bitch? The rest of your finger or your nose? You want us to take your nose off, right now?"

Chichi saw terror fill the woman's eyes. He dropped her arm to wipe the blood that had splashed his chin. Gramzie's horrid wails rang in their ears. Petey slowed the wheel to a stop so Chichi could rest the woman's head while he picked up the phone.

"Know what we're doin' to your grandma, numb nuts? We're grinding her away a piece at time. I've got a Polaroid camera. We'll send you souvenir pictures later."

Chichi paused to let his words sink in. He didn't have much time left on the call. After he hung up, they would grind more and call back.

"You know what we want, don't you? I'm going to make it real simple. Don't foul out. The series doesn't go another game. Tonight the Wildcats lose the championship. Understood?"

Chichi nodded for Petey to restart the wheel and yanked Gramzie's head up. It was time to take that pinky down past the joint, then the rest of the way. Gramzie cried louder. They were saving the best for last. After a few fingers, the nose would go. He took her hand in his own and heard the woman's shrill cater-waul. Petey mimicked her cries. Chichi laughed so hard he had to drop the bloody stump.

He picked up the telephone again and shouted into it: "Tell me you understand!"

The wheel hummed as Petey pumped the foot pedal more rapidly. Chichi could barely hear Dion beg as his grandmother cried.

Now they're both squealing like pigs, he thought.

"I understand," he heard the big man scream. "Stop it!"

The spinning stone roared, beckoning for more blood.

The telephone died in Dion's ear. They had hung up on him. His hands trembled so badly he couldn't place the receiver back in the phone's cradle. It banged onto his kitchen floor. Quickly, he dove for it. He had to hang up in case they called again. He stayed on his knees and clasped quivering hands together.

"Lord, what have I done?"

Dion realized he should have never toyed with those bastards. He would throw the game for them. In fact, there was nothing he wouldn't do for them.

"Why aren't they calling back?"

The telephone didn't ring. Not hearing from them was even worse than receiving another harrowing call. Every fiber of his being ached to reach though the phone and strangle the scumbags who held his grandmother. Not knowing where to find them, Dion placed his mighty strength into prayer.

"God," he prayed. "Sweet Jesus. . . ."

"Shuuuuut uuuuup!" Chichi screamed.

He grabbed a handful of Gramzie's short natural hair. Petey stopped pumping the wheel and gagged the woman with a dirty towel.

The sound came again. Both men heard it, a bang on the front door to the cabin.

A guy screamed, "Anybody home?"

"Who could that be?" Chichi said.

He turned his head as if facing his ear toward the voice would tell him. Petey Pets shrugged his shoulders. They weren't expecting anyone and the nearest neighbor was miles away.

"Keep an eye on her," Chichi told Petey. "I'll get the door."

The knocks came louder. Chichi grabbed his pistol and held it behind his back. If there was trouble, he would blast away. Thuds were relentless. Chichi swung the door open wide and the odor of whiskey filled his nostrils. His lower jaw dropped agape.

"Happy coonskin cap day," an old man slurred.

The guy wore a buckskin jacket, faded jeans, and worn-out moccasins. His big toes poked through holes in their fronts. A cap made from raccoon fur with a tail dangling in the rear perched unevenly on his head. Chichi peered around. It didn't look like anyone was with him.

"Whadda ya want," Chichi snarled.

"Don't you know what day this is?" Eyes glazed, the old timer leaned against a flintlock musket for support. "It be Davy Crockett's birthday."

Chichi looked the guy up and down and figured he was two-hundred years old.

"And you're the actual Davy Crockett?"

"That's a good 'un, son," the old man chuckled. "Hell, no. I'm your neighbor. Live next door, just a couple of miles through the woods."

"Whaddya want?"

"Someone to go a huntin' with. For fifty years, me and Clem have hunted on coonskin cap day to celebrate the birthday of Tennessee's finest native son. This be the day."

"Who the hell's Clem?"

The old geezer scratched his scalp under his cap and asked, "Ain't Clem home?"

"No, you senile old fart! The realtor who rented this dump to me said the coot who useta live here died a year ago. This joint's been empty while the estate's being settled."

"Clem be dead?"

The old man reverently removed his cap.

"Wherever the Lord's sent you, Clem, may the huntin' be easy, the whiskey kegs full, and the women bowlegged."

Chichi looked over the grey head, searching for movement in the forest surrounding the cabin. Dense woods made it difficult to see far, but the dirt drive that led to the cabin looked empty.

"Anyone with you, old man?"

"Nope. Just be me. Me and Clem always hunted alone, but now he be dead."

He wiped away a tear with the tail sewn to his coonskin cap, then plopped it loosely atop his head. With a simple grin quickly restored to his wrinkled face, he lifted a canteen from the leather pouch clipped to his belt. Chichi watched him pull out a cork stopper, swig hard, then wipe his lips on the sleeve of his jacket.

"Want some sippin' whiskey, son?"

Chichi took the canteen uncertainly and sniffed the top. Then, while keeping half an eye on the aged frontiersman, Chichi sipped from the steel flask. Instantly, its spit out its vile contents.

"What's in there?"

"Moonshine."

"Moonshine?"

"White lightening. Got my own still."

The old man retrieved the canteen, took it to his own lips, and swallowed a mouthful.

How do these hillbillies drink this stuff? Chichi wondered. "Scram, old man," he said. "Clem ain't around, no more."

Chichi watched the guy stumble as he turned around. Using his musket like a walking stick, the old man trudged down the path leading to the woods.

As if levitating under its own power, Chichi's pistol rose. He stared down the length of his arm, along the black barrel, and across its sight into the back of the sluggish codger. Effortlessly, Chichi's thumb drew back the hammer. With slow-building pressure, his finger tugged the trigger.

"Ah, screw it," he muttered, lowering his hand cannon. "Let him live. Afterall, it's coonskin cap day, whatever the hell that is."

Compassion never canceled Chichi's kills. He just didn't want anyone to come looking for the guy. Closing the cabin door, he called downstairs to Petey Pets.

"Better put Gramzie back in her room until dark. May be more hillbillies in *dem dare* woods." He pulled draperies back from a window by the door and scanned far as his eyes penetrate the lush timbers. "Come night-fall," he shouted over his shoulder, "we'll go at her again."

Chapter Twenty-One

Love Can Be Cruel

Conrad's chest heaved as he fought to catch his breath. Beneath him Tina lay naked and spent. Her arms wrapped his ankles; her chin rested on his feet. He savored the contours of her long back veering up and out from a slender waist. Tina's hair, matted with perspiration, covered her face. Kicking free of her grasp, he walked to his desk and opened a drawer. A hasty hand grabbed what he needed. While Conrad cleansed with an astringent-soaked cloth, she crawled to collect her clothes.

Their relationship worked better than he had ever imagined. He would enjoy having her around until the deal was done. In fact, he considered keeping her awhile afterward, though not as his wife.

Tina was a brilliant schemer, who had put new ideas in his head.

"So I dump Joey," he reflected, "and deal with the Philly mob?"

"That's the smart move. You pay them once. Joey's local family wants a long term partnership with regular splits. After you have his financing, and no longer need his muscle, why keep paying? Philly will take the action and they're big enough to finish off the Atlantic City family if Joey makes trouble."

Conrad nodded in agreement. "Joey gets blown out of the deal faster than a fart in a fan factory."

He had already placed feelers to the Philadelphia crime family. The stakes were too tempting to ignore. Enticing their move into Joey's Atlantic City territory wouldn't be hard. Oddly enough, he owed the plan to the man he was cutting out. The half-faced hood had talked him into spending time with Tina Levine and she had craftily seduced his mind as well as his body.

The time had almost come. Information Tina had brought him about Brucker's finances let Conrad know the man couldn't hold out. Every day his properties remained closed, Brucker sank deeper into debt, and soon The Fantasy would take a monstrous hit on the basketball series. If Brucker didn't deliver a signed contract by the end of the week, Conrad would reduce the offer just as Tina recommended. By delaying the inevitable, Brucker dug himself a deeper hole.

"To think" he told Tina, "this all came as a germ of an idea from your diseased brain. Joey's out and I sit pretty with you to thank."

"And to enjoy." Tina looked up through eyes that were swollen to slits. Already they had blackened from his blows.

Conrad wondered who was savoring Brucker's downfall more. Was it him or the woman whose devious mind he was fast coming to appreciate? Conrad

looked her over. A woman like Tina could be a valuable
asset. Perhaps he would dump Francoise afterall. Conrad contemplated the thought.

Who knows what will happen in the days ahead?

Joey watched Letitia DeLuca shuffle tarot cards by
the glow of a single candle. Her dim chamber off the
boards was laden with the woman's musty odor. Letitia
wedged a cigarette in the corner of her mouth. She
exhaled smoke laced with a stale rancor as if it had
touched the bottom of her aged lungs. It filled the small
room and made his scarred eyes water. Joey rubbed
them with both hands, then watched the first card hit
the table. It seemed to laugh aloud.

"*Jolly,*" she observed, the jester.

The card surprised him. "Who's the fool, old woman?"

She didn't answer.

Joey's voice boomed through the room. "Who's the
fool? Is it me?"

Her silence made him ponder. Was he the buffoon or
was it someone else who tangled in his schemes? Joey
had heard about Conrad's advances toward the Philadelphia family. What did the tycoon take him to be? He
didn't engage in Wall Street dealings; mob disputes didn't
settle in a boardroom or a courtroom. Conrad was signing his own death warrant and the crime boss was ready
to execute it. He had already planned ahead by approaching Conrad's wife. Francoise would be a business partner upon whom he could count. He could see that she
controlled the financial empire his crime family was placing in Conrad's hands.

Letitia dealt two more cards. They lay side by side, telling him what he had come to learn. Gramzie Brown was also on his mind. Time had come to determine the fate of the woman who had raised the basketball star.

"*Regina*," said Letitia.

The card on the left was the queen. Next to it was what he had expected – the smiling face of death.

"*Pericolo di morte*," she observed.

"*Si*," he said. The woman was in mortal danger. He would convey an order to his soldiers. When the basketball series ended with a loss by the Tennessee team that evening, they would kill their hostage.

The old woman dealt another card. Death stared again. He wondered what it meant. Letitia sucked hard on her cigarette. Smoke stayed inside her body longer with each drag. As the old woman started dealing again, he reached across the table and grabbed her wrist.

"The last card," he bellowed. "What does it mean?" He sensed her fear.

The mob boss screamed, "*Cosa significa*?"

Tears welled in the old woman's eyes while he squeezed tighter still. He would snap her brittle bones if she didn't answer fast.

"Uh," she moaned.

Her lips parted with a painful grimace, exposing the whitish hue of her gums. Smoke retained in her lungs involuntarily expelled with a peculiarly rancid odor. Her eyes were deep-sunken and sullen. Looking into them stirred an uneasy feeling in his stomach as she uttered fatidic words, the words he had hoped to hear.

Tina primped in Conrad's private bathroom. She applied makeup to blackened eyes and bruises he had just given her. Swelling was barely noticeable. She stepped away from the mirror to get a look from another vantage point. The lavatory was good-sized and Tina had already decided how to redecorate it.

She pulled sunglasses from her pocketbook. Gently resting them on her face, Tina bore no trace of having catered to Conrad's cruel brand of lovemaking. She could take whatever he dished for the moment, knowing how quickly she would seize the upper hand. She intended to wield her power ruthlessly. It wasn't enough to be Conrad's wife. She had seen how he treated Francoise. Tina would wear the pants – and put him panties – in their upcoming marriage.

Though she had talked Conrad into betraying Joey Bonivicolla, she would tell the hood what Conrad was doing. Then, she would make a better deal with the mob boss. Conrad was going to make a nice figurehead, while she served as the mob watchdog over him. Tina would deliver Bonivicolla whatever he wanted. In return, he would see she reigned over her new husband's empire like a queen.

When the tables reversed on Conrad, she would administer the thrashings. Chuckling at the thought, Tina considered buying a bullwhip and boots. The idea seemed a little preposterous, but she might enjoy making Conrad grovel just to teach him who was in charge.

"*Missis* Tina Conrad," she said to her reflection in the mirror, "whip mistress of desire." She laughed and straightened her dress. "Maybe I'll even give Manny a good whip licking as a going away present."

Tina strolled from the bathroom into Conrad's office. She sauntered to his desk and perched her sweet derriere atop it. He looked up as she gave him a peck on the cheek.

"See you later, sweetheart," she cooed.

Tina caught him grimacing. He did that whenever she called him sweetheart.

"Now, there's a little habit we'll break," she said with a chuckle, "and replace with a new one."

Letitia DeLuca wondered, like never before, about what the morrow would bring. With the mob boss gone, she dealt again for herself. The card reader pulled a cigarette from her mouth. Smoked to a stub, Letitia didn't even bother replacing it. She was too absorbed by the question she asked herself repeatedly.

"Why am I blind?"

She had drawn death's card and told the mob boss what he wanted to hear, but something shrouded her vision of the future. Something about the queen she had drawn for the mobster puzzled her. Whom did the card really represent? When she had dealt it, Letitia saw something that frightened her as much as the man seated across from her. For an instant, the face on the card was her own, as clear as a mirrored reflection.

Dealing for herself in dim light, Letitia laid the first card down on the table – the queen. The card told her nothing. She closed her eyes and concentrated, searching inside her soul for the window that opened to divination. *Perhaps*, she thought, *my answer will come with the next card*. Ever so slowly she turned it. Death's portrait bared a grin that gripped her with uncertainty and fear.

"Yeah, yeah," she stammered. I see you, my friends,

but for whom do you bring your unearthly salutations?"

Chapter Twenty-Two

In Your Face

A baby sky hook sailed from the hands of the Chicago shooter. Dion watched it arch over his head and swish through the net. Customarily, the big man blocked dinky alley oops, but his hands never reached for air. They stayed glued to his sides.

"In your face," the shooter called to Dion, showing him up as they ran down court toward the other hoop.

The Chicago joyride was nonstop, having started the game with a four-bucket run. Dion found himself back in basketball hell as the Wildcats trailed 8-0.

"Come on, dog," Dion heard his man call. "You can keep up with me, can't you?"

Dion was getting toasted again. He tried closing his ears. Stuff Daddy had to look like he was putting an effort into the game, but he knew what he would do. He would see his team lost. It was game five. Nashville trailed in the series by three games to one. That night the Wildcats would lose the series.

Their little man, a speedy point guard, made his trade-mark crossover move, lining up a shot. Before he could take it, Dion called for the ball. The smaller man tossed it to him. The pass went through Dion's hands and out of bounds.

"Another turnover! Chicago gets the ball," the television play-by-play caster called.

Chichi and Petey Pets cheered. They had left Gramzie confined in the furnace room. She wasn't so much fun after they had whittled her down a bit. They watched the small black and white television screen with smiles on their faces. The picture came in clearly and everything was going their way.

Chicago players set up around the perimeter for an offensive play. The man Dion was guarding charged toward the basket. He breezed by Stuff Daddy for a rock-your-world slam. As the hoop sprang up and down, the score flashed on the television screen, 10-0 Chicago leading, and the two hoods leaped to high-five.

Gramzie heard thuds as the twosome hit the wooden floor directly above her. Old beams supporting the floor rocked with their weight. She looked up at the rotting wood and listened to the blaring television. The exposed floor beams were brittle and decayed. As the hoods bounced up and down, she noticed splinters at the seams of the beams. An idea came to Gramzie. She wanted to reach those beams, yet she had nothing to stand on. Before they had caged her inside, the two hoods had swept the furnace room clean of anything that might provide comfort or serve as a weapon.

She wondered if she had the strength to leap. Gramzie rested on the damp concrete floor with her hand wrapped in a towel. She had ripped a strip of it to use as a make-shift tourniquet. It tied off the open-finger wound since she had no way to suture or sear it closed. Like many country folk who grew up in areas too remote for near-by health care, Gramzie knew something about first aid. She suffered from shock due to loss of blood. The stub throbbed. Her skin was clammy. She was shivering from her body temperature dropping and her breathing was becoming irregular. Gramzie knew she had to sear the wound to avoid bleeding to death. She also knew she needed a tetanus shot to fight off gangrene.

Those problems weren't foremost on her mind, though. She had heard her captors talk. Their sounds fell through the wooden floors. They had received a telephone call with their orders; they were to kill her soon as Chicago won the game. At halftime, they even planned to torture her again. The two men had joked about strapping her back on the workbench to grind down her nose.

Gramzie peeked through the slot in the door. She saw the bloody grindstone, then spied the workbench. *I have to break free*, she thought, *but how*? The furnace room had no windows. Its walls were solid and the door was too thick to pound down. With no way out, her only chance was to attack her attackers. She need-ed a weapon to even up the odds.

The television blared more bad news for the Wild-cats. "Two points for Chicago. That's 16-4."

As the hoods jumped again, Gramzie studied the long splinters on the beams. She had to force herself to leap.

If she could reach the beams, maybe she could pull a splinter long and sharp enough to use as a dagger.

Gramzie lunged and fell. Her behind bumped on the concrete floor, leaving her woozy but determined. She made it to her feet and waited for another Chicago score. As the hoods jumped up and down to celebrate, she garnered all her strength. Gramzie sprang upward with a powerful jaunt and came down with an eighteen-inch long splinter. It didn't have a point on its end, but she could rub it against the floor to sharpen the tip. She scraped it against the concrete with her good hand, all the while listening to the game.

"Time out, Nashville," she heard the announcer call. Heavy thuds pounded onto the old flooring as the two hoods jumped up and down again.

More high-fives, she thought. Thinking of them celebrate at her grandson's expense irritated Gramzie even more. She rubbed the splinter against the concrete harder and faster. Gramzie wanted a mean point on her bodacious evil stick.

While on her knees, she offered two prayers. First, she prayed for her grandson, asking the Lord to look after him when she was gone. Then, she prayed for herself.

"Please, sweet Jesus, take me fast rather than slow," she beseeched, "and another thing. If you can, Lord, let me see those two heathens catch a vile dose of justice before I die."

"A spectacular play for Chicago from. . . ."

The game had resumed. It was moving too fast. Soon, she realized, those two men would descend the stairs to fetch her. Gramzie remembered the drone of the old grindstone. The memory chilled her spine. She dropped the stick and placed her good hand on her nose. She couldn't see it, but at least she could feel it while it was still there.

At the end of the first quarter of play, Chichi bounded downstairs to the basement. He ran to the furnace room door and stared at his captive through the slot. She was holding her wounded hand upward with the towel draped over it.

"That's a dear," he chirped through the hole. "Raise your hand above the level of your heart. You won't bleed so much."

"Hey," Petey Pets called down the stairs. "Are you comin' back up or do you want to mess with her now?"

Chichi thought a minute. He wanted her on the grindstone so badly he considered ignoring his orders. They weren't supposed to kill her until the game was over.

"Yeah, why not?" Chichi called out. "Who's gonna know if we play with her early and whack her at halftime? That way, we can get out of here when the game's over. Nashville doesn't have a prayer."

As Petey bounded down the stairs, Chichi called to Gramzie through the slot in the furnace room door. "Hey, sweetie pie. You like sports, don't ya? Guess what we're gonna do when we're done with your nose?"

He paused.

"We're gonna stick our fingers in your head and use it for a bowling ball."

Their laughter boiled her blood, and her rage energized her. Gramzie rose from the floor with the towel draping her wound. She lumbered toward the door. A beady eye peered through the slot at her.

"You don't look so good Grandma," she heard Petey say from the other side of the door.

He was still laughing when Gramzie pulled her bodacious evil stick from under the towel. She jammed it through the slot, deep into Petey's eye socket.

"Oh, my God! Oh my God," she heard him scream. "She took out my fucking eye."

Gramzie fell to the floor and said a prayer of thanks. She still held the stick in her hand. If only she could find the strength to use it again.

"Now, you've done it," she heard Chichi yell into the furnace room. "I may have gone easier on you, but not now. I'm going to whittle you down, a little at a time, until nothing's left of ya. You hear me, bitch? I won't even use a bullet to finish you off."

"Oh, my God," Petey continued to cry.

"Sit down, you asshole," she heard Chichi say. "Flop on the stool by the grindstone. I'll get a towel you can hold over the eye. You'll pump the pedal while I feed the broad into it."

Gramzie was growing faint. If they didn't come into the room to get her soon, she would be too weak to strike again.

Chichi swung the door open with his pistol drawn. He peered inside the furnace room cautiously. He saw Gramzie lying on the floor with the stick in her good hand. She was no match for him. With his gun pointed at her head, he walked close.

"Put the stick down," he said.

When she ignored his order, he stomped on her injured hand and heard the woman shriek. The stick fell to the floor as she lamely tried to remove his boot from atop her wound. Chichi pounded the pistol grip into the top her skull and watched her pass out.

When Gramzie awoke, she was strapped to the workbench. A strong smell filled her nostrils. She was groggy, but quickly recognized the odor. Puddles of gasoline were all over the basement. Her clothing was sopping wet. They had dowsed her, too. She could hear gas canisters clanking upstairs. Aghast at the thought, she knew their plan. When they were through torturing her, they would burn her body and the cabin to destroy all evidence of the crime.

Her head rested on the grindstone wheel. Suddenly the wheel moved, slicing a laceration down the left side of her face. Gramzie raised her head and saw the man she had stuck with her stick. Petey held a blood-soaked towel to his eye. It was no cleaner than the one they had given her.

"You're gonna wish you never did this to me," he groaned. "You'll see."

The television blared. She couldn't have been unconscious long. The second quarter was just beginning. Chicago maintained a seventeen-point lead. She listened until she heard footsteps bounding down the stairs. Then, she knew; they were about to start.

Chichi grabbed Gramzie's head by the hair and lifted it above the grindstone. "Crank up this thing," he said to his companion. "We'll trade her nose for your eye. Then, we'll take off her Goddamned ears."

Petey pushed the foot pedal and the wheel began spinning. Gramzie looked down on its rough edges. She could tell they were going to rip her apart. Skin, cartilage, and bone would disappear, one layer at a time. The clanking wheel grew louder. As it picked up speed, it wailed.

"Stop," Chichi shouted. "Stop the wheel."

"What for?" whined Petey. He took his foot from the pedal and the wheel slowed.

Then, they all heard it, a loud knocking on the front door to the cabin. The old-timer was back, screaming at the top of his lungs.

"Come out for coonskin cap day, Clem. It ain't the same without ye!" His boisterous call was slurred.

"Go up and plug him," Petey said. "I want to get this over with."

Chichi nodded his head. He grabbed his pistol and checked to see it was fully loaded as they heard the old man yell.

"Clem, where be ye?"

Chichi ascended the stairs, bounding two at a time, as if deadly purpose hastened his strides.

The mobster opened the door and faced the old man leaning on his musket again. The old geezer's eyes were bloodshot; his breath reeked of moonshine. Looking up, he posed a question.

"Ya know Davy Crockett's motto?"

Chichi raised his pistol to the guy's head.

The old man didn't even seem to notice as he babbled, "Be sure you're right, and then go ahead."

Gunfire roared as the old man's musket blasted, opening an entry hole under the mobster's chin and an exit hole out the roof of his skull.

Suddenly men in buckskin and coonskin caps burst through every window into the cabin. They rushed downstairs to the basement where Petey held a lit match. Gramzie lifted her head.

"Don't shoot him," she cried too late.

A man fired and hit Petey squarely in the chest, the impact reeling him backward. The lit match in his hand sailed high into the air. With her arms strapped to her sides, Gramzie was helpless to stop it. She watched it go up, as if in slow motion, and descend like a glistening snow flake. Its fiery tip floated toward a gas puddle on the floor directly underneath her face. Gramzie stuck out her tongue far as it would go to catch it. The match drifted a fraction of an inch from her reach. When it hit the ground, her face would be the first thing roasted in a roaring inferno. Her eyes widened with fear. The match touched the ground and a black alligator dress-shoe stomped on it. Gramzie looked up at the man on its other end.

"I'm Manny Levine," he said to her. "I'm with Captain Andy Jackson of the State Police and fifteen Tennessee volunteers to get you out of here, Gramzie."

Men were cutting the leather binding straps with their hunting knives. One cleaned her wounded finger and wrapped it in a sterile bandage.

"We'll take you to the nearest emergency room," Andy said.

Gramzie wasn't interested. "How close are we to the basketball arena?"

"Thirty minutes or so," a man called out.

"That's where your taking me," Gramzie screamed.

"Get me there in ten minutes. I want to be there before the second half starts."

The men looked at each other. Andy made the call.

"Put her in my car. We'll blast the siren all the way. Manny, sit in the rear with her. Johnny, keep working on her hand while we drive. One carload can follow me. The rest of you secure this place. I'll send some troopers out here."

As they placed Gramzie in the rear of the car, she looked at the old timer who had feigned drunkenness.

"Are you the guy who was screaming that its coon-skin cap day?"

"Yes, ma'am," he replied.

"What in the Lord's name is that?"

"You'll have to ask Captain Jackson, ma'am. It be his idea."

Manny told her the story en route to the game. Andy had initiated a word of mouth rescue effort that had quickly spread through the Tennessee countryside. Mustering volunteers to find someone prominent as Gramzie Brown wasn't difficult. Most folks had seen her on television at Wildcats games. The feisty grand-mother was something of a local hero herself. The old-timer had heard her wails as he was hunting in the woods. When he checked things out, they'd seemed suspicious enough to call Captain Jackson.

Their car sped along the interstate highway.

"Gramzie, I'll give you five minutes at courtside," Andy said. "Then, I'm taking you to a hospital."

With a smile brightening her face, Gramzie told them, "That's all the time I'll need."

Charlie Walton had benched Stuff Daddy Brown. The coach couldn't take it anymore. A coaching maxim flashed through his mind, "When you get to playoffs, do what you did to get there." That was conventional wisdom. Playoffs weren't the time to try a new game plan, but Dion was hurting his team. Maybe they could still pull out the game without him.

Bullied and tired, Charlie's team had taken the floor for the third quarter without their superstar. The level of their play picked up as they fought with everything they had. They elbowed, tripped, and trash-talked. Along the way they defended hard and sunk shots they had to make. Nashville fans were getting back into the game. They cheered for the feisty team that scrapped for its playoff life.

Charlie ripped off his suit coat and tie. Jamming the clipboard that held their plays against his puffy belly, he flipped notes until he found what he wanted. Then he tossed the board to an assistant coach, marched the sidelines, and barked directions to his players. Charlie was putting everything he had into the game, too. He caught a glimpse of his big man stirring on the bench. Something had been bothering Dion throughout the playoffs, but the coach didn't have time to think about the kid. Instead, he watched his team get physical on the court. Normally they weren't a team to bang, but they pulled out all the stops to dent Chicago's lead.

A referee's whistle sounded. Their new nastiness had cost them. Two free throws sent the Chicago lead to ten points with five minutes to play.

Charlie felt a tug on his arm. He turned to see his big man standing by his side.

"Let me back in coach," the kid said.

"Sit, Dion." He never thought he'd hear himself say those words.

"Coach, I can do it."

Dion was smiling. Charlie hadn't seen that grin through the entire series. He thought a dose of championship series jitters had choked the kid's play. As the coach looked into Dion's face, he saw sparks. He wondered if Stuff Daddy was back. Charlie didn't know what to do. If he put his superstar into the game, would the kid ice a victory or a loss? The coach had to make a quick call. Charlie tapped Dion on the rear.

"You're in for two minutes," he said.

The whistle blew and Dion raced onto the floor.

What have I done? Charlie asked himself. He heard fans boo as Dion took the ball. Then, the big man dashed across the three-point line and launched his body toward the hoop. Twisting in the air to avoid two defenders, Dion flipped the ball from behind his back without glancing at the basket. The ball never touched the rim. A two-pointer found nothing but net.

Dion shouted to his teammates as he blistered down the court. Trumpeting a call to arms, Stuff Daddy led the charge.

Charlie turned to the crowd. *Where are the boo birds now*? Behind him he saw what must have sparked Dion's smooth moves. Gramzie Brown sat in the stands, cheering for her grandson and cussing out every Chicago player on the floor. Men dressed like Davy Crockett surrounded her and a huge white mitten wrapped her hand.

Cheers tuned Charlie's attention back to the game. Dion had blocked a Chicago shot and was racing with the ball downcourt. At the free throw line, his knees rose to his waist as he leaped high. One hand sent the ball home for another score.

The Chicago lead was down to six points with four minutes to play. Charlie wasn't worried. The hottest gun in the game was on target again. The crowd rocked the arena. Above all the cheers, Charlie heard the screams of Dion's biggest fan. Gramzie Brown was back in town.

Chapter Twenty-Three

Big Words . . .
Come from Little Men

Prell was back at it, handling a day date. She entered the main doorway to the casino without fear of being recognized by security personnel. It had been a long time since she had turned a trick, yet Prell remained a portrait of desire. Flowing brown curls still framed one of the sweetest faces on the planet. A strong and lithe body, punctuated by curvaceous hips, completed the picture.

A well-heeled gentleman, who liked to watch young women do themselves, had arranged for her companionship. Once, "show and tells" had been her specialty. She had writhed and moaned with assorted adult toys from her oversized handbag, while her date found pleasure peering at hers.

She alighted an elevator, then traipsed down a long hallway, whistling a tune. Its lyrics rang in her ears,

"Whistle while you work. . . ." Cheery as an elf, she approached a private suite the way her date desired, wearing a full-length mink and high heeled boots. His tastes were specific and easily satisfied. The John expected her to drop her fur on the floor. Underneath she was to be wearing nothing but earrings and boots. Prell would be an eye-feast to drive his sensations over the edge.

Long ago, she had enjoyed the work. As Johns stuffed her palm with cash, her heart would sing, "I love being a girl." Standing there, however, a range of emotions suddenly overwhelmed her, running from uncertainty to revulsion. It was then that it struck her; the thrill was gone. She had only come for one reason. Tommy Brucker had asked her.

She rapped on the penthouse door and sensed an eye focusing on her through the door's security peep hole. Her date was taking his time. Sometimes men with his proclivity liked watching through the peep hole as a prelude to the voyeuristic experience to come.

So you want to start this way, she thought. It began as she tossed back her cinnamon locks and ran long red fingernails over the single clasp holding her coat closed.

"Come on, sugar," she purred in contralto. "I know you're there."

From the other side of the door, he watched her spread the top of her fur, exposing glimpses of a porcelain paradise. Unable to resist the urge, he opened his bathrobe and touched himself. He felt his knees bend, his legs grow rubbery.

Her lips parted. The coat opened farther to expose only the hollows of her cleavage. He imagined those breasts as ripe melons. The fur parted no wider, but lower, revealing a pierced navel. A golden charm hung above a passion mound still wrapped in mink.

His engorged member throbbed. He would let her enter and rip that coat apart. A soft moan escaped his lips as he released himself to turn the doorknob. Mr. Wu opened the door to greet his date but instead found Tommy Brucker.

"Forgive me, Mr. Wu," Tommy said. "I was afraid you wouldn't meet me any other way."

Mr. Wu quickly closed his robe, peered into the hallway, and looked in both directions. Tommy was discrete enough not to mention Prell had only come as a personal favor to him, nor did he mention how quickly she had disappeared; fur had never flown so fast.

Prell had let him know her service had received a call to satisfy the special needs of a Hong Kong businessman. When Tommy had been a young executive, specially assigned to the premier highroller, Mr. Wu's people asked him for the name of a reputable service that could cater to his voyeurism. The man had an aversion to intimate touch and instead bore a strong yearning to watch.

Tommy had sensed Wu's involvement, as financier, in the deal Conrad presented. When Tommy had sought funding to construct The Megasino, one of Wu's business agents approached with an unsolicited proposal, which Tommy rejected, fearing financial entanglement with the extraordinarily wealthy Asian crime boss, who so enjoyed passing himself off as a businessman on his gambling junkets. Deals with mobsters were laced with hidden strings, the kind that tightened into a noose around the neck. Prell had removed any doubt Tommy had about Wu's association with Conrad when she let him know Conrad's staff had arranged the morning tryst.

Tommy watched Mr. Wu's face flush as he stammered, "Come, oh, come in." Men, even men who run operations nefarious as Wu's, have the aplomb of a thirteen-year-old boy when caught with eager genitalia exposed. Tommy knew, however, that Wu's composure would quickly resurface; he was accustomed to being in control.

Following the man into the livingroom of his suite, Tommy was eager to ask frank questions, but knew he could not appear overanxious. With his every ounce of reserve straining, Tommy waited for Mr. Wu to take the lead. He would have to approach him slowly, perhaps even circuitously, if he was to learn what he so desperately needed to know. Taking seats on separate couches across from each other, both men remained perfectly still, as if both were playing a game to see who would be first to slice through the tension born in silence.

"It's been some time since we've chatted," the diminutive man finally said.

"Since your marriage in Las Vegas. How is Mrs. Wu?"

Initially, Tommy observed, the question made the man squirm, as if ill at ease, but he relaxed when he began speaking.

"That young lady is no longer my wife."

"She was lovely."

"Indeed, but she was not a good Chinese wife. She quickly became fat like a married American cow."

Tommy easily pictured the robust platinum blond putting on extra poundage.

"I divorced her on a trip to Thailand. Have you ever been there, Mr. Brucker?"

Tommy shook his head.

"Pity," Wu continued. "The rural countryside is beautiful. The customs, ah, they're so very quaint. One marries there by handing a clerk a bottle of liquor and divorces by handing the clerk another."

As he told it, the story was nearly charming. Yet Tommy assumed the hapless bride had been "divorced" even less ceremoniously by Wu's henchmen.

"In our country customs are not so quaint," he said.

"Oh, really. I recall marrying a Marilyn Monroe look-alike, after a forty-eight-hour courtship, in a twenty-four hour a day wedding chapel, following a nuptial ceremony performed for an Elvis Presley impersonator in full regalia. Don't be so smug, Mr. Brucker."

An icy edge returned to Wu's voice, control of his faculties being fully restored. The man had an uncanny knack of removing himself from himself, as if he were looking at himself. It was an eerie yet highly intelligent capability, which equipped Wu with more than mere resilience. Somehow, he led an immoral life without a trace of immorality seeming to attach. Tommy knew the man's wealth came from illicit drug connections all over the Orient. Thailand drug lords probably had been his real connection to that country. Though a highly complex man, there was no mystery about his love for gambling. The deal Conrad must have offered Wu was, no doubt, a compelling lure. Would the man feel secure enough to reveal those plans? Tommy was counting on it.

"Let's get to business," Mr. Wu said. "What will you

be doing with your troubled casinos?"

"I thought," Tommy ventured cautiously, "that you might know."

Mr. Wu just smiled as three Chinese men, wearing grey business suits, entered the living room from an adjoining suite. They dressed as Hong Kong executives, but moved with the swagger of men accustomed to exercising brute force. Bulges inside their jackets weren't from plastic pocket liners holding pens and pencils. Tommy surmised the contours concealed handguns in shoulder harnesses.

"These are my associates, Mr. Brucker."

One stood behind Mr. Wu and the other two behind Tommy.

"Now, why have you come to see me?"

Tommy had come that far. He decided to go all the way.

"I sense you are connected to offers Mr. Conrad recently made to purchase The Megasino and The Fantasy. He needs financing for the deal and your interest in owning a piece of a large gaming operation is well known."

Mr. Wu showed no emotion. "I'm an investor who always maintains an open eye for legitimate ventures."

"The tragedy at my Atlantic City property raises questions. One has to wonder how legitimate the venture is."

Still, Tommy thought, *there's no reaction.*

"The endeavor may also be connected to an extortion attempt," he continued, "to influence a sporting event in which millions of betting dollars will be exchanged."

Mr. Wu finally stirred. "Big words often come from little men. In your case, Mr. Brucker, I surmise they're coming from a small and desperate man. I'm a businessman, here to enjoy legalized gambling and salt water taffy on the boardwalk. If a business opportunity arises while I'm here, I'll convey it to my American lawyers and financial consultants."

Mr. Wu signaled his men.

"Time for you to leave," Mr. Brucker.

The three men gripped Tommy by his arms and lifted him from his seat. He elected to leave without resistance, knowing Wu would respond more favorably to poise than force. Tommy had come with a proposal that might be the bait he needed to lure the man. As he reached the door, Tommy called back.

"Just one moment, if you please. I'm prepared to offer a better deal than Conrad."

Wu's men tossed Tommy into the hallway. He straightened his jacket and walked toward the elevator. *Have I guessed wrong*? he asked himself. Maybe Wu shared no part in the deal afterall. Whoever was involved in Conrad's scheme was furnishing plenty of muscle. It seemed unlikely Wu's Hong Kong associates, though ruthless, could pull off so sophisticated an operation in the United States.

The elevator arrived. He entered and pushed a button for the ground floor. As the doors closed, almost all the way, two gloved hands reached inside to force them open. Mr. Wu's three associates greeted Tommy with their handguns drawn. They didn't speak. Instead, the man closest motioned with his gun barrel for Tommy to walk back down the hall.

Perhaps now, Tommy thought, *I'll learn the truth.* If he kept guessing correctly, Wu could reveal everything – or kill him.

Chapter Twenty-Four

Before the Next Morning's Dawn

"*Emposebele!*" she exclaimed.

Letitia DeLuca couldn't believe she had slept so late. She bolted upright. That day of all days, she did not wish to spend resting. *So much to do*, she thought. Letitia had fallen asleep with rosary beads clutched in her hand. She kissed them, genuflected, and considered the vision that had come to her with such clarity.

"Get ready," she told herself. "Move!"

She fluttered as if drunk on a brew dredged from the cauldron of hysteria – and for good reason. Letitia knew what would happen before the next dawn.

Tommy shifted his weight uneasily on the same cushiony sofa, knowing why he felt so uncomfortable. Across from him, Mr. Wu, still wearing only a bathrobe, sat flanked by armed associates. Once more, Tommy waited for the other man to take the lead.

"I invited you back," Wu began, "because there may be merit to a joint venture, as you suggest. What terms are you prepared to offer, Mr. Brucker?"

So your nerves sense stimuli, afterall, Tommy thought. Wu looked anxious to hear the plan, but how would he react? Tommy outlined a proposal to make Wu his partner in exchange for funds to keep his casinos afloat. He pulled duplicate copies of a contract that would seal the pact from his coat pocket.

"The contracts only need our signatures," he said.

His own words chilled him. Tommy never wanted to become entangled with the hood. Wu would use their legitimate business deal to enter the casino doors, then find a way to force Tommy out. The Buckman knew the perils but also knew he had no choice. He needed funding fast, the kind traditional lending institutions wouldn't extend. He also needed to deprive Conrad of his source for capital to acquire The Megasino and The Fantasy. Most of all, Tommy needed time to figure the thing out. Entering a pact with Mr. Wu could accomplish those ends. Later, Tommy would face an inevitable showdown with the Hong Kong crime lord.

He handed over the contracts. As Wu read them, the man's smile said he knew the two casinos were in the palm of his hand whether he associated himself with Tommy or Conrad. Tommy wondered if he had offered enough and Mr. Wu told him by lifting a pen. Quick swirls covered both copies of the document. One of his men returned them to Tommy for his signature.

A cellular telephone buzzed in Tommy's pocket. He pondered whether he should answer, then reached for the mini-phone. Under Wu's watchful gaze, he took the call to delay what was inevitable. So many thoughts raced through his mind, as Manny's voice beckoned on the phone, that he had to stop his CEO in mid-sentence.

"I'm sorry, Manny. Run that by me again."

"Boss, I have news from my buddy in Tennessee. The bodies of the two men, the guys who held Dion Brown's grandmother, were positively identified. The state police sent their photos and fingerprints to the FBI. These guys have lengthy criminal records."

Tommy didn't understand the enthusiastic tone of Manny's voice. "That's expected," Tommy said, nonplussed.

"The Bureau organized crime unit recognized these guys," Manny continued. "They're reputed members of the Atlantic City crime family. Know what that means?"

Tommy knew. It was coming together. Conrad was part of a well-orchestrated scheme to steal Tommy's two casinos. He had combined local mob muscle with Hong Kong drug money for an explosive mixture.

"We may have enough evidence for a fair courtroom fight to reopen the casino," Manny offered.

Tommy considered the implications. "If we lose that fight, we lose everything."

"Boss, are you still willing to gamble high?"

"Mr. Brucker," Wu interrupted, "business is at hand." Tommy nodded to him.

"Where are you?" he said into the phone.

"At home, catching some rest after the Tennessee trip."

"Stay there. I'll reach you later."

Tommy set the phone down and looked at the contracts. He pulled a pen from his pocket and put it to the signature line. "Void," he wrote. "Deal not made." Then, he ripped the contracts in half.

Wu's eyes widened.

"You've made a grave mistake, Mr. Brucker. You will regret it only once, but that will be for the remainder of your life." Wu gestured to his men and added, "Short, though, it shall be."

Tommy didn't move from the approaching henchmen. He remained on the couch, stared into the eyes of the drug lord, and spoke with more confidence than he felt.

"The young lady, who saw me greet you at the door, is waiting outside in a limousine. If I'm not inside the car in ten minutes, she'll have cops swarming this suite."

"And you expect the police to accept the word of a prostitute? Such a naive notion."

Wu pointed his finger at the smallest of his men. The man pulled his pistol from its shoulder harness and strode close to Tommy.

"Silently, please."

Wu directed the murder as casually as ordering lunch in a restaurant.

"And no mess."

Tommy's mind raced. The gunman picked a silencer from his jacket pocket and affixed it to the pistol barrel.

"Mr. Wu, this afternoon my lawyers are meeting with the Atlantic County Prosecutor."

Wu's man leveled the handgun at Tommy's forehead to take him out at point-blank range.

Heart pounding, Tommy talked fast. "They'll have a lot to discuss, especially now that the FBI has established an organized crime connection to these dealings. You may wish to reconsider your association with Mr. Conrad."

Tommy's eyes fixed on the pistol. Its barrel stared like a single eye into his. Wu clapped his hands together just once. A thumb cocked the hammer for a deadly blast. With nothing else to say Tommy readied to leap at the gunman. He couldn't avoid taking a bullet, but he'd fight anyway. A bead of perspiration trickled from his brow. *Now*, he thought, rising from the sofa with all of his might.

Wu clapped his hands together again. The man lowered the gun and reset its hammer. Tommy looked over the smaller man's head and into Wu's eyes.

"You may go, Mr. Brucker," Wu told him.

Tommy stood still, too shocked to move.

"I wouldn't waste my time making it to the door if I were you." Wu lifted a newspaper from the sofa and flipped to the business section. "Goodbye," he said with his head buried in stock listings, "for now."

Tommy moved toward the door. He felt the watchful gazes of Wu's three men. He noticed the gunman had removed the silencer from the gun but hadn't put the pistol away. As he glanced at Mr. Wu one last time, the gunman quickly aimed at Tommy's head. Tommy froze but didn't flinch as the man cocked the gun hammer.

"Bang," the man said to the amusement of himself and his associates.

The Buckman quick-stepped into the hall and hurried toward the elevator. He pushed the elevator button and waited. It didn't seem to be coming. He looked back the hallway toward the suite, fearful that Wu might dispatch his men again. When the elevator arrived, Tommy pushed a button for the lobby, breathing hard. He wouldn't feel safe until the doors closed all the way. Tommy considered what he had told the drug kingpin. His position wasn't nearly so strong as he had alluded, but the Buckman was gambling high.

Dion felt painful spasms twitch. Soaking in the training room whirlpool bath, he battled severely strained back muscles. Hot swirling waters brought little comfort. His lips clenched a cigar big enough for a man his size, while his hands leafed through sports pages from local and national newspapers.

After the Wildcats had won game five in Nashville, they had roared into Chicago to play the remainder of the series. He had injured himself late in game six while struggling for the ball under the boards. Fortunately, Nashville had taken a big lead, so they had coasted when their star left the floor. The Wildcats victory evened the series at three games apiece. They would play the final game that evening in Chicago.

Coach Walton entered the training room, came close, and looked Dion in the eye.

"Can you play tonight?"

Dion knew he would have to play through pain if the cats were going to take a trophy back to Nashville. "No problem," he lied.

"How long can I keep you in the game?"

"I said it's no problem."

Charlie Walton didn't look so certain. "Dion, trainers lifted you off the court last night. Lucky for us, you didn't get hurt until we had game six wrapped up. But, the doc says you won't be able to play – even if he pumps you full of steroids and pain killers."

Dion blew a smoke ring. "No back injury is benching me. We've earned this championship. I'm not sitting out."

Charlie's eyes followed the smoke sailing to the ceiling. "Maybe you'll make it to the floor, but how well are you going to be able to play?"

As Dion reached around to turn the whirlpool off, he groaned. His coach waited for an answer he didn't have.

Francoise hurried into the finest restaurant at The Pyramid. Instantly, the maître d' approached and tipped his head.

"I'm meeting my husband for lunch, Elio," she gushed.

"Of course, madame. Follow me, please."

It had been so long since Gregory had invited her to dine with him that she followed the maître d' in eager anticipation. Francoise had spent extra time applying her makeup and dressing, wanting to look just right for her husband. She yearned for things to be right between them and hoped their luncheon date would be a start.

Her meeting with the scar-faced hoodlum had troubled her. Francoise had listened to the man but knew she could never betray her husband, no matter what his transgressions against her had been. She had no family since her father's death, just Gregory. More than anything in the world, she wanted their marital wounds to heal. Francoise still wanted the relationship to become all she had dreamed she would find in marriage.

She spotted Gregory seated at a table for two. As she neared, waiters rushed to the tableside in a flurry. One pulled her chair. Another unfolded her linen napkin. A third filled her water glass.

"*Bonjour, amie*," she said with eyes aglow.

Conrad didn't return the warmth of her greeting. Instead, he was businesslike and straight to the point. "I have something to tell you," he said.

"Me, too," Francoise bubbled. Recently I met with a man who asked me to betray you. I came close to –"

"Fuck who you want," Conrad interrupted. "We're through. I arranged this meeting for a public place, because I'm not in the mood for your tantrums. You'll meet with my lawyers in ten minutes. The prenuptial agreement you signed will satisfy your basic needs. I've also authorized my attorneys to give you something extra if you get out of the country within forty-eight hours and never come back. Take the extra money. You'll need it."

Conrad sipped his wine and rose from the table. "*Au revoir*," he said, turning his back on her forever.

Francoise's eyes moistened. "*Rat d' egout*! *Batard*!" she called after him. He would always be a rat bastard.

Conrad felt good about himself, and he had Tina to thank for his auspicious fortunes. He entered his office and sat behind his desk. Tina rose from the same chair in which she had met Joey Bonivicolla. She came close to Conrad, then went to her knees by his side. Her head rested on his thigh, the touch of her slender fingers warming his loins.

"You should let me go with you, tonight," she said.

Conrad shook his head. "No, I'll meet these people without you. They've already accepted the deal in principle. The Philadelphia family will push the Atlantic City mob out of the picture soon as the deal's done. Brucker can't hold out. I've got a grip on him like a vise on sore testicles. By tomorrow, his two casinos will be mine and I'll make a single payoff to the Philly mob to handle Joey."

Conrad paused to reflect. "A single payoff," he marveled, thinking aloud, "the scheme that germinated in your diseased mind."

His deal with the South Philly crime family would save him billions of dollars in years to come. He stroked the head that had hatched the stratagem. Increasingly, he relied upon Tina's advice. More than shrewd, she was streetwise with a colorful past. His investigators had thoroughly checked her background when he had hired Manny Levine. What they had learned always intrigued him. He had even paid to have them surreptitiously pry into juvenile criminal records, which courts seal to the public.

An alcoholic father had deserted her mother when she was thirteen. Mom remarried and the rebellious teenager resented her stepfather. Young Tina seduced the man and began a long-term sexual relationship with him, first in exchange for modest allowance increases and later for much more. She arranged for her girlfriends to catch them in bed together. Then, she blackmailed the man with photos her friends snapped. Tina had threatened to expose their affair to her mother and turn him into the police. The man faced ruination and jail on statutory rape charges for having sexual relations with a minor.

Her stepfather paid handsomely. Tina even continued the sexual aspects of their relationship to spite her mother. Inevitably, Mom discovered, then threw Tina out of the house. By the age of sixteen, she was selling dope and turning tricks on the Sunset Strip in Los Angeles. Arrested, juvenile authorities brought her to "juvie" court where she told her story. A judge sentenced Tina to a California reformatory for young women when her mother wouldn't take her back. There, she learned new tricks. Tina was an extraordinarily bright and devious young woman without the baggage of a conscience. In her early-twenties, she arrived in Las Vegas to become a part-time exotic dancer, part-time hooker, and full-time schemer.

Tina had beauty to attract men and the cunning to choose those who would do the most for her. She ran through a series of marriages, always walking out on her own terms and ahead of the game. Tina wasn't just a man-eater. She was a carnivore with an insatiable appetite and a brilliance for surreptitious designs. Conrad was ready to take advantage of that devious mind. He would also enjoy the beautiful face and lush body that were part of the package.

"I'll be back for you after I close the deal in Philly."

She looked up with lips puckering for a kiss he wasn't primed to surrender.

"Later," he told her.

"Consumed in thought?" she said, while stroking his thigh.

"Consumed with *the art of the deal*," he said. "I could write a book about it."

He considered the deal that would enrich him while

nailing Tommy Brucker and the deformed Atlantic City hood and returned her warm smile.

"I'll want you tonight," he mused. "There's no greater aphrodisiac than closing a deal that fucks your enemies."

Darnel watched Helen DeMarco in action at the county prosecutor's office. *The practice of law is a high testosterone occupation*, he thought, *and this woman has big balls*.

Originally, they had planned meeting Horace Grender with a different agenda. The prosecutor's office had sealed police and fire department records connected to the casino fire during the pendency of Grender's official investigation. They had merely hoped to see them. The information Manny had provided, however, sent Darnel and Helen on a different mission.

"Don't take my word for it, Hoss," Helen insisted, while driving her point home. "Contact the FBI yourself."

Grender turned pale. His sweat glands pumped in overdrive. Darnel saw how badly the heavyset man wanted to prosecute Tommy. He wondered why the guy seemed so personally involved. No matter, evidence linking the mob to Gramzie Brown's kidnaping put a new wrinkle in the State's case against Tommy.

"Organized crime figures were behind the casino disasters and the security guard killings at the casino." Helen pressed.

"That's just a theory," Grender wheezed. "Anyway, the guard killings were part of a major larceny, not incidental to an organized crime scheme. The casino vault was emptied."

Helen didn't retreat. "If your office refuses to look into an organized crime connection to these incidents – and fast – we'll ask the FBI to launch a probe."

"I'll contact the FBI," Grender said, "to independently verify what you've told me." He held a ballpoint pen, clicking it hard, as if it were the switch to an electric chair reserved for Tommy Brucker. "But, nothing you've told me so far will cause my office to redirect its investigation. Now, get out of here."

Joey rested his sunglasses atop the bridge of his nose. He listened to waves crash against the shore as he strolled along the boardwalk. His loyal underboss, Teko, followed close behind. Joey stopped to observe pitch-black skies far out over the choppy ocean.

"A storm's coming," Teko said. "Even the sea gulls have run for cover."

Joey looked. "Yes, my old friend," he said. "Tonight a storm will brew like a deadly potion. And, for some, there will be no rest until dawn."

Chapter Twenty-Five

A Storm in the Night

Fans roared, a whistle trilled, and the basketball sailed above them for tip-off. The Chicago center-forward leaped sky-high, but Dion reached through the stratosphere and tapped the ball to a teammate. His point guard rocketed down court, braked, and drilled the ball toward the hoop. That quickly, Nashville drew first blood in the final game for the trophy.

Dion chugged upcourt and set on defense. A cortisone shot, which had been administered by the team physician, controlled his pain. Knowing he would get less play time than he'd like, every minute on the court had to count. Defending the passing lanes, Dion spied an opportunity for piracy. He stole the ball from a confounded Chicago player, tore down the floor on a fast break, and crossed the three-point line with a teammate by his side. With only one defender in their way, Dion charged for a two-on-one. He flipped the ball behind his back where it floated and waited – the perfect dump-off to his teammate who slammed the ball through the basket.

Frustrated, the Chicago defender bumped Dion and sent him reeling. Hardwood floor smacked his spine, sending a jolt of pain up his back, which radiated to his skull. As Dion tried rising, he stumbled backward and pounded the hardwood again. A referee blew his whistle, stopping play for the personal foul.

"I can't get up," Dion groaned.

Even cortisone wasn't helping. Teammates stood above him as Coach Walton and a trainer rushed to his side, each setting a knee on the floor, leaning close.

"My back," he murmured through lips drawn tight. "Reinjured it."

The trainer blurted, "Don't move yet."

"I'll be all right in a minute," Dion said. He took a deep breath and lifted himself into a sitting position.

The trainer gripped his shoulders and spoke into his ear. "Want something to mask the pain?"

Dion was too disoriented to answer.

"You can play in pain," Coach Walton offered, "but playing seriously hurt can turn a minor injury into a permanent one. Only you can make the call, son. What do you want to do?"

The big man peered into the stands and caught a glimpse of Gramzie. Her eyes were fixed on him. He knew what she would say; she wouldn't want him doing it. Dion turned to the trainer.

"Help me to the locker-room and shoot me up, fast."

In the stands another man watched Gramzie, while she focused on her grandson leaving the floor. She was

oblivious to everything else, including the man whose
eyes never left her. Stage makeup matching the Chicago team colors covered his alter boy face. A cap with
the home team logo was set far down over his eyes. His
hand, stuffed into an oversized pants pocket, held a small
pistol. Joey Bonivicolla had sent Matthew to whack
Gramzie. The assassin cheered for Chicago and pa-
tiently waited for the right moment.

The mob had to silence the feisty woman who might
have heard Chichi and Petey Pets talking. There was no
telling what she could tell police. If an opportunity arose
during the game, Matthew would take it. Otherwise,
he'd whack her at the final buzzer and escape into throngs
departing the jammed arena. The game clock ticked
away and, with it, her lifeblood.

He watched Gramzie adjust her high-stacked hairdo
and reach for her handbag. She started for the isle.
*Probably headed toward the locker room to check her
grandson*, Matthew thought. She would even pass him
on the way, making his job easy. Matthew tightened his
grip on the gun and pulled back its hammer with his
thumb.

The crowd roared as a Chicago player tossed a three-
pointer from near mid-court and the ball arched high.
Gramzie turned round for the action, then raced back
toward her seat as it descended.

"Goddamn," Matthew exclaimed, an expletive lost in
crowd noise. He reset the hammer, realizing his target
would catch more game action before catching his bullets.

"That's a three-pointer from way downtown!"

The television play-by-play announcer screamed as Conrad walked into a neighborhood tavern. He shook his umbrella to dry it. Outside, heavy rain and strong winds had emptied Philadelphia streets, while inside the packed bar rollicked. Whoops rose for another score. Sentiment strongly favored Chicago and the team was heating up with Dion in the locker room. Just three minutes into the game, Chicago mounted a lead.

A bartender waved for Conrad's attention, then guided him through the building. Conrad never felt comfortable in that kind of cozy environment. He glanced with disdain at beer guzzlers on bar stools. Everything about them was common – the way they spoke, dressed, even what they drank. He intended to conclude his business and leave fast.

"Come on Don," he beckoned over his shoulder. His burly driver followed awkwardly through the throngs. Conrad hadn't taken a limousine to the meeting, fearing unwanted attention on narrow South Philly avenues. Instead he had come in a sedan driven by the big man who made him feel more secure.

The bartender led them to a narrow flight of stairs, which Conrad eyed suspiciously. "You first," he told his driver, who lumbered up rickety steps, blocking Conrad's view of everything but the man's broad hind quarters. When he reached the second floor landing, his eyes scoured a shabby banquet room. The place was empty except for two men sitting at a table in the rear, whom Conrad recognized as the Philadelphia mob boss and an underling. They sipped dark-red wine from goblets and raised their glasses as if toasting his arrival. Conrad took a seat at their table with his back to a wall. His driver, armed with handguns in both coat pockets, sat

beside him. Rowdy cries from the barroom traveled up
the stairway. *Must be another Chicago score*, Conrad
thought. At least they were rooting for the team on
which he pinned his hopes.

Conrad watched the hoods drink heartily. The boss
was in his early fifties. Compared with his Atlantic City
counterpart, the man was handsome, if only in a dark
and ethnic way. He wore an outdated three-piece suit.
A necktie, too flashy for the ensemble, hung low under
the man's open shirt collar. The underling by his side, a
youthful and more casually attired version of his boss,
seemed eager to please everyone. He had the mentality
of a bus boy, Conrad observed, and jumped at the older
man's every word.

"Some wine, Mr. Conrad? It's homemade," the crime
boss said as he pointed to a large jug.

Conrad's glare unveiled disdain. "I'm here for business," he replied.

"So are we, but first we'll drink to our new partnership. You'll join us in a custom from the old country,
will you not?"

The younger hood poured two more glasses. He
handed them to Conrad and his driver. Then, the boss
called out a simple toast. *"Alla salute,"* he said, cheers.

Great, Conrad thought. *I'm dealing with two drunk-
en dagoes.*

The Philadelphia crime boss had quickly responded
to feelers Conrad carefully placed, just as Tina had said
he would. For a moment, the thought of Tina's face
and lithe body flashed through his mind. She could put
an impish pout on her lips that was childlike. That's
how he liked to take her. Soon as the meeting conclud-
ed, Conrad's driver would jet him back the expressway

so he could whip that pout all about.

While he and the mob boss discussed their venture, Conrad contemplated how much more he had been prepared to pay for riddance of those Atlantic City clowns. Mobsters were morons. They had no idea how much casinos were worth. Tina had been right. Dealing with them was far easier than he had anticipated. He laughed inwardly at just how effortlessly he was ridding himself of Joey Bonivicolla.

As they spoke, Conrad grew warm and weary. He wondered why they kept the room so hot. His driver removed his coat and Conrad loosened his neck tie. The talkative hoods didn't seem to notice the stifling temperature. Instead, they became more animated as he slipped into an opium dream. A vision of Tina, lusting for his manhood, made him sway. Her pouting lips called from every corner as room angles became irregular; her long legs danced across a titled floor.

Suddenly, it occurred to Conrad. He hadn't seen the two mobsters pour their wine from the open jug. His driver was asleep, head tilted sideways, and he was drifting off as well. He started to rise, but the younger hood came close and simply pushed Conrad's weakened frame back into his chair. Then, the man pulled a two-foot rope from his pants pocket. Expertly, he tied a knot in the middle and wrapped the garrotte round the driver's throat, the knot resting on his Adam's apple. With a quick tug, the garotte tightened and the driver's eyes bulged. Conrad didn't know that a neck cracked so loudly – or that a man's tongue could stick out so far.

Next, the hood approached Conrad. He laid the garotte on the table and gently brought Conrad's drowsy eyelids down.

"Time to rest, sleepy-pie," he said.

Conrad began to slumber.

From the other side of the table, the mob boss sipped wine and watched his young associate place both hands over Conrad's face. He rested his fingertips on Conrad's forehead, then placed his thumbs over Conrad's eyelids. Quickly and forcefully, he pushed Conrad's eyeballs out of their sockets. He wiped his hands on a napkin and pulled a stiletto from his pocket. With another swift motion, he expertly slit Conrad's throat from ear to ear. They watched Conrad gasp. Air entered his nose and open mouth, but escaped through the severed esophagus, unable to reach his lungs.

The mob boss checked his near-empty glass and called for another drink. His underling reached for the jug on the table.

"Not that one," the boss reminded him. "Get a bottle from the bar. While you're there, tell the boys to dump this guy in the bay, now."

Conrad's twitching head rested atop the table. While he bled and suffocated, the mob boss spoke nonchalantly.

"I promised Joey we'd feed this *cafone* to the fishes before the second quarter of the game ends, but tell 'em to drive careful. It's raining awfully hard."

Woeful groans escaped Conrad as the boss pulled a pocket watch from his vest. If his soldiers hurried, they could keep his promise. Conrad's corpse would be dumped into Absecon Bay by The Megasino, where it would be quickly found with the incoming tide, just as Joey wanted. Conrad had attempted to humiliate the

Atlantic City mob family, so it was important he be found bearing the death mask that was Bonivicolla's trademark. That would serve as a warning to anyone else who considered welching on a deal with the mob.

As Conrad's spasms subsided, the boss lifted his glass for another toast, which he offered with greater fervor.

"For every man, rich or poor, life is a fatal adventure."

"Two more points for Stuff Daddy Brown!" the television play-by-play caster shouted. Dion had reentered the game but was playing hurt. Announcers had picked up on it and Manny could see the big man wince whenever cameras caught him in a closeup. The kid was hot, though. The Wildcats hadn't fallen too far behind when he'd gone to the locker room. With Dion back on the floor, they were cutting into the Chicago lead.

Manny sat behind a desk in his home study, watching a TV across the room and sipping Jack Daniels. The bottle rested atop a stack of papers on his desktop. He regretted having left Tennessee without taking the famous distillery tour. But not having time, he had promised Andy he would return for it. That wasn't an idle vow. Manny liked Tennessee and yearned to spend time there under more leisurely circumstances. Eyes closed, he pictured the lush hills and countryside. When he opened them, a familiar and curvy form blocked his view of the television screen.

"I thought you'd show up," he said.

"Manny, I'm back," Tina announced.

"I see, but I'd appreciate your moving to the left or right. I have an interest in this game."

Tina turned off the television. "I'm sorry," she said
with eyes downcast, "but I think our marriage is more
important. Darling, I have a confession to make."

Manny suddenly realized that he hadn't made the last
drink strong enough. He reached for the bottle.

"I – I've been unfaithful," Tina blurted. "God, I'm
so sorry. How could I have ever done this to you?"

Tina rushed to his side and fell on her knees beside
his chair, face tipped down.

"I'm so sorry," she choked. "Please, sweetheart,
forgive me."

She tilted her head upward. Breaths came in near
convulsions. Tears welled, then cascaded.

"A tidal wave of tears?" Manny said. "Darling, you're
a human tsunami."

"Don't tease. Please don't."

His eyes peeked inside her open silk blouse. Creamy
teats lured from a black lace bra. It had been so long
since he had felt the comfort of a woman's body. Old
feelings stirred inside him. If he wasn't careful, they
would spring free, unstoppable as flowing lava.

Tina rose. Her hand beckoned for him to leave his
chair. Without thinking, he found himself on his feet,
close enough to her that they shared the same breath.
Bewitching eyes and an impish pout extended an en-
chanted invitation from his demon-lover. Her arms held
him back while her hips reached forward, teasing his
loins. The tip of her tongue rounded ruby lips and opened
the floodgates of passion. Driven insane, he wrestled
her to the floor. They rolled across the carpet in a twisted embrace of arms and legs, while her tongue jammed
down his throat as if reaching to steal his soul.

Crashing into a wall where they could roll no farther,

she breathed deeply, her bosom heaving. She pulled away. Yet having cornered her and fuelled by lust so long unfulfilled, he wouldn't let her escape.

"Oh, Manny, Manny, Manny."

She cried out his name as his hands ripped apart her blouse and hers reached behind her back. She unlatched the bra that held what she'd kept from him. Her eyes penetrated his as she allowed the lace bra to dangle. Pink nipples taunted, daring him to try holding back. She chuckled as his face buried between her breasts and his hands tugged at his belt, struggling to open his trousers at the same time. She laughed even harder as he lifted her skirt and wrapped his hand round the top of her pantyhose. Not even taking time to remove them, he lowered her hose and string bikini just far enough to penetrate her. At first she pulled back. Desperately he plowed into her.

"That's right, baby," she cried. "Take me. I'm all you want. I'm everything you need. I'm what you have to have."

Her cries propelled him to swift fulfillment. For a moment, he lay atop her, listening to her breathy coos. Then, he rose and reached for the bottle. Instead of pouring another drink, he grabbed the papers under it. A cough cleared his throat; a single deep breath cleared his mind.

"Thank God," she panted. "Thank God we still have each other."

"I wouldn't say so. You have five minutes to pack your things and leave this house."

"What do you mean?"

"I saw the same news report about Conrad's body washing ashore that you saw. It interrupted the game.

On your way out the door, you can sign these divorce papers my lawyer, Ms. DeMarco, prepared while I was out of town."

Tina looked at the document Manny handed her. Sight of the words, "Property Settlement Agreement," instantly dried her tears and restored normal breathing. She was well acquainted with the term and scoured through the pages.

"This Goddamned thing gives me nothing," she screamed.

"That's right. You'll leave this marriage with less than you brought into it."

Tina roared, "I sue you for every dime you –"

"Sign, right now, or I'll notify the county prosecutor's office of your involvement in Conrad's takeover dealings. You won't need much money in prison, will you dear?"

"You wouldn't dare!"

Manny watched Tina think. It was an amazing cognitive process, much like watching a computer evaluate ten-thousand possible chess moves in a fraction of a second.

"I'm not signing shit," she screamed. She walked toward the door.

Manny lifted the phone and dialed. She stopped in her tracks as he spoke.

"This is Manny Levine from The Megasino resort. Can you connect me with Horace Grender? If he's not in the office, I'll talk to the assistant prosecutor on night duty. I have information connected to Greg Conrad's death."

Tina scampered to the phone and pressed down the receiver button to hang up the call. "You motherfucker!" she screeched.

He watched veins rise in her neck and sweat bead on her brow as he handed her the property settlement agreement again.

"Sign both copies," he said.

"Oh, who the hell cares," she said in a quaking voice.

Tina took a pen to the papers and signed.

"I won't need your money, anyway, you fucking loser. Do you really think I don't have another man waiting in the wings? Look at what you'll never have again."

Tina slowly caressed her body. She ran slinky fingers up to her face and over the top of her head. Shaking her hair, Tina preened like the intoxicating vamp she was.

"I can have any man I want," she sneered.

She went to the telephone and dialed. "Sweetheart," she sang into the phone, "baby wants to see her daddykins. Are you free?"

Her smile broadened when she hung up. "He's a stockbroker with a zillion frigging dollars. And the best part is, he's already had his first aneurysm. That's right, darling. I'm dating a million-dollar heart-attack."

Manny watched Tina leave. He turned his old friend, Jack Daniels.

"Nah," he said. "All my troubles just walked out the door."

The game entered its final quarter with the Wildcats trailing. Dion nursed his injuries on the bench, a trainer massaging his tight back muscles. Coach Walton was resting the star so he could play the last minutes of the game. That gave Gramzie the break she needed. She trudged up the arena steps past the concession area and entered the nearest ladies' room. Women entered ahead of her, but they were gone when she left her stall. She heard someone moving inside another stall until a roar from the crowd drowned the noise. *Hometown score*, she surmised as the house rocked.

Gramzie pulled a comb from her purse to fix her hair. That was no easy feat with one hand still bandaged. Though the wrapping was smaller with her finger healing, it still limited dexterity. She teased her hair with a long four-prong fork and tried hard to redo her lipstick with her left hand. "Damn," Gramzie cussed for applying it so far around her lips. She was beginning to look like a clown.

If I'm not careful, she thought, *I'll look like the woman who slipped into the bathroom behind me with the Chicago team colors painted on her face.*

As the woman came out of the stall, Gramzie spotted her in the mirror. Then she noticed something without turning. The woman was a guy and he held a pistol. Gramzie shrieked and ran for the door.

Matthew was faster. Diving at her with a gun in one hand and the other extended, he caught Gramzie's shoulder, then raised the pistol to her head. He jammed it against her temple to pump bullets into her brain. Gramzie jabbed him with her teasing fork, causing him to scream and release her. But she couldn't run fast enough. As she darted toward the door, he yanked the trigger. Gunfire echoed off the bathroom walls.

Gramzie went down. She looked up into the smoking barrel of a gun that had just fired. Andy held it. Two of his men stood behind him. They were still protecting the treasured asset of the volunteer state. One trooper went for a local police officer while Andy examined the body of the man he had slain. Gramzie didn't have time to wait around. With the game clock ticking down final minutes she hustled to her seat, accompanied by another of Andy's men. Behind her, a teenage fan with an air horn let loose a mighty burst that rang in her ears.

Winds howled. Raindrops whirled, more sideways than down. Tina hustled through the storm and ducked into a crowded bar. She waved to her new boyfriend. The gentleman's silver hair imparted a distinguished look. He wore a classic navy blazer, tan pants, and a striped necktie from his alma mater. Tina rushed to his side and pecked on his cheek.

"Daddykins," she cooed, "it's so good to see you."

He beamed with pride while soaking in her charms. She saw how much he enjoyed having an attractive woman on his arm. He motioned for the bartender to serve Tina a glass of champagne. As the barman uncorked a bottle, she realized that she must look a mess. She barely had time to put herself together after rolling on the floor with her loser husband, and the storm had blown her around. A hair out of place wasn't her style. Tina excused herself to freshen. She gave her daddykins another light kiss on the cheek but nothing too dramatic. She didn't want him to have that heart attack, yet.

She pushed through the crowd toward the ladies' room and entered in a huff. Having the place to herself, Tina pulled her makeup kit from her purse and bustled. She placed some concealer over the slight scar line from her second face lift, then admired skin that was butter-smooth and wrinkle free. When through, Tina stood back from the mirror, studied her handiwork, and liked what she saw.

Returning to her date, she snapped a mental survey. First, she always focused on a man's teeth and finger-nails. She liked his clean smile and professionally man-icured nails, but he dressed too conservatively. The blue blazer look was tired. She would show him how to dress. Updating a man's style was something for which she had a knack. When Tina clung to a man's side, she liked outshining him without being embarrassed by his appearance. Daddykins needed her as his fashion coor-dinator.

Then, she observed something peculiar. The bar had emptied while she was in the bathroom. The only peo-ple remaining were her date, the bartender, and a hand-ful of men hovering in a corner watching the end to that damned basketball game on television.

"I'd like to introduce you to some of my friends," he said, as she took her place on his arm.

They walked toward the television set. Tina was accustomed to being shown off by men, especially old-er ones, and liked being an ego bolsterer. As they neared his cronies, he called to them.

"Hey, I want you to meet someone special."

"Hold on," one of them shouted back, "there's just two minutes left in the game."

Men and their silly games, Tina thought. *They're all the same. Predictability is one of the things that makes men so easy to manipulate.*

"Commercial," another said. "Time for another round of drinks." He called to the bartender. "Put it on my tab."

"Maybe now," Daddykins chimed, "you guys can take a minute to meet my Tina."

"I already met her," a guy said without even turning around.

Tina had to laugh. That one even stayed glued to commercials. His voice sounded familiar, but she couldn't quite place it.

Daddykins grabbed his shoulder and urged, "Come on. It'll only take a second."

The man turned and Tina looked into the hideously scarred face of the boardwalk boss.

The men, who had been standing with him, surrounded her. Tina's head turned in all directions. Frantically, she realized that she had nowhere to run and no one to call for help. The bartender locked the door and began turning out lights. Her date stripped his clothes. He was down to his sleeveless undershirt and the khaki pants from his sheriff deputy's uniform. The disciples were about to engage in their unholy work.

"You remember what I told you, my dear," Bonivicolla said. "Our deal was simple, but you didn't keep your end of the bargain. I promised something if you failed. Perhaps you recall; I promised to give you a face like mine." The mob boss came close and bellowed, "Look at me."

She turned her head and closed her eyes. His strong hand grabbed her chin and forced her head around to face him, nose to nose.

"Open your eyes!"

"I – I can't," Tina cried. "You're too ugly."

"*Vedere*!" he screamed. "Look at what you are to become."

Tina opened her eyes inches from the acid-seared

face. "No," she cried, to the scars crisscrossing his eyeballs and pus filling the corners of their sockets. Tina howled into the night as five men dragged her to the backroom and set her atop a pool table with a ripped velvet top.

The scoreboard told the tale. Its clock displayed 15.7 seconds remaining in the game. The score read, "Chicago 104, Nashville 102." Coach Charlie Walton had called his last time out. The Wildcats would inbound the ball and go for the final shot. What play was he giving his players? Everyone in the arena knew Nashville would try to run down the court and launch a single shot with no more than a second or two remaining. That way Chicago wouldn't get another chance to score before the buzzer sounded, ending the fourth quarter. Yet everyone wondered whether he would call a two or three-point play. Was he telling his team to drive to the basket for a two-point shot that would tie the score and send the game into overtime – or was he gambling in a three-pointer? Would he risk losing by trying to win the game and the championship with a single long shot? Walton was a conservative coach. Would he follow conventional wisdom? The rules of thumb said try a two-pointer for a tie on your home court. Launch a three-pointer, trying to win, on the road.

Dion rested his aching back, sitting on the bench as his coach made the call. The timeout expired. Dion's teammates lifted him. Coach Walton didn't give him a familiar fanny tap, fearing his superstar would collapse.

Five Wildcats walked onto the floor knowing the play. Five Chicago players lined up against them, ready to defend any call. The crowd stood as the whistle blew.

"Dee-fense," hometown Chicago fans chanted.

The Wildcats inbounded to their feisty point guard who had a hot three-point hand. He dribbled upcourt. The cats set for a play. Dion moved slowly, but had plenty of time to position himself. Would the little man hold and shoot? Too much time remained on the clock. Nine seconds, it read.

Chicago played sticky defense. Players on both teams bumped hard. Referees wouldn't blow their whistles. Unless a foul was flagrant, officials would let athletes play the game out. The court became a combat zone and there wouldn't be a truce until players on one team were crowned champions.

Dion looked open, but he looked free whenever he wasn't double teamed. Their point guard fired the ball in his direction. Dion took it with six seconds remaining and dashed toward the boards. Chicago players immediately reacted. Three men converged to contain the stronger and more athletic star. That gave Dion the opportunity for the play Coach Walton had called. He fired back to their point guard. Four seconds were on the clock. The man was open to fire a three-pointer for the lead, but that would still give Chicago the time for a last ditch effort for a score. He delayed just an instant, but an instant too long. Chicago's players adjusted. When the little man tossed the ball toward the basket, high reaching hands of a defender deflected it.

A cloud of arms followed its path in the air. The weight of the crowd roar seemed to send the ball down. It fell into the hands of a single player. He took the ball wherever he found it and tossed a turnaround jumper in the direction of the basket.

Crowd cheers drowned out the final buzzer. Dion lay facedown on the floor, looking at the painted three-point line. He didn't know if he had thrown the ball from in front or behind it. He didn't know whether he had sunk the shot or missed. Dion dragged himself to his feet and caught a glimpse of the score, Chicago 104, Nashville 105. His teammates hugged, shouted, and jumped. Chicago fans looked dumbstruck. Everyone had figured Dion was human. After that three-pointer, some weren't so sure.

Stuff Daddy sprinted around the court, high stepping with his hands in the air, feeling no pain. He stopped when he saw Gramzie and leaped into the stands. He lifted her above his head. They had shared the dream of that moment from the day she had put his first basketball in his crib. Tears of joy stained her face. Gramzie had won a championship, too.

Horace Grender put in a late night. Slated to take The Megasino probe to a grand jury in the morning, his staff had worked alongside him. They had sorted hundreds of documents, photos, and graphics as evidence. Witnesses had been prepared to testify. Law enforcement officers, structural engineers, and public safety experts were ready to take the stand. The case looked good, and Grender had a reputation for leading a grand jury down any path he paved. He had a knack for framing indictments.

"Here's the paperwork you wanted," his first assistant prosecutor said. Like him, the woman appeared weary from long hours devoted to the task. She handed a form to him slowly, as if she were reluctant to do so.

Grender reviewed the document and considered whether he should sign it. He had called the FBI. Their information intimated that reputed members of the Atlantic City organized crime family may have been involved in the casino mishap, but it wasn't clear. Probably no one would ever learn for certain. The mob family had a reputation for strictly maintaining *Omerta*, its code of silence. No one talked because the tough mob boss quickly silenced those who might. Anyone who could tell law enforcement authorities something meaningful about the affair was probably already dead.

The prosecutor could indict Tommy Brucker or let him go. The document in his hands would officially established his call. Grender signed the paper and handed it back.

"File it," he said. "There's insufficient evidence to establish criminal wrongdoing. This investigation is closed."

"But that means Tommy Brucker will reopen The Megasino," the woman exclaimed.

Grender's bark was gone. "That's exactly what it means." His words came like the whimper from a beaten dog. He wasn't taking chances. An indictment or further courtroom challenge to open the property could lead to an investigation that tracked back to him. Grender shut down the official inquiry and canceled the grand jury session. On the way out the door, he turned out the lights.

The toe of her high-heeled pump tapped the floor. Francoise stood in the center of Gregory's office, staring at the desk where he had so often cavorted with women. She knew all the stories. Still, that made it no easier for her to forget his *masque mortuarie*. Francoise had identified the remains of her husband. Even the medical examiner's warnings, hadn't prepared her for the horrible death mask he wore.

She had returned to The Pyramid Casino. It was hers, together with all of Greg Conrad's real estate and businesses holdings. Looking around the office, which had been a den for his perversion, she dictated to casino executives who eagerly took notes from their new boss.

"Get that desk out of here. In fact, chop it into bits and feed it into a shredder. We'll turn this room into a high rollers lounge."

No one would dance on a desktop in there again. Francoise walked toward the windows that displayed unbridled views. She peered outside at a new world that nocturnal cloudbursts baptismally cleansed.

"*Vivre*," Francoise heralded. "So good it is to be alive and free."

Tina heard air whirl and hard-driven rain pound against concrete. *They must have let me out on the street*, she thought. She stumbled into a wall and fell backward. Tina could hear voices, but couldn't see through seared eyes. They had dripped something onto her face from a large syringe. She no longer felt the agonizing pain. Her body was in total shock, as if all her nerve centers had shut down.

"Somebody, help me," she called. "Anybody, please. I can't see." Tina listened to approaching footsteps, then heard a blood curdling cry.

"Oh, my God," a woman wailed.

Tina guessed she was on Pacific Avenue, outside the Atlantic City Medical Center. She had heard Bonivicolla tell his men to leave her at the hospital. He didn't want her to die. He had said she was to suffer the penultimate torture: she would survive.

"Get a doctor!" screamed a man.

Hands grabbed her arms and directed her movements. Tina sensed they had ushered her indoors. She could hear sounds of bustling movements, voices calling, and phones ringing. Needles jabbed her arms.

"Who are you?" she said.

"You're in an emergency room," the same voice told her. "A doctor is on the way. You're going to be all right. We've given you something for pain."

Although she didn't feel hurt, Tina realized she must look like she needed the shots. She wondered what was happening. Voices that had surrounded her hushed. She sensed people were near, but they had stopped talking for some reason. What had Bonivicolla's men done to her? How bad was it? She hoped her plastic surgeon could quickly correct any minor flaws. Then, she heard whispers.

"What happened to that thing?"

"Is it a man or a woman?"

"Not sure."

"I can't look at it."

Tina reached to her face. It was numb to the touch. Whatever they had poured down her cheeks had burned horribly until her skin numbed and shock set. Tina felt herself.

"What the fuck?" she mumbled.

Something felt hard where her cheeks had been so soft. It felt like bone. Her hands fell straight into her mouth. Tina shrieked loud and long. She felt the jab of another needle. It was then she realized they had dissolved all the flesh from her ears to her mouth.

Heavy rain delayed takeoffs at the Atlantic City International Airport. Flights backed up awaiting go-aheads. While some passengers dosed uncomfortably on waiting room chairs, Darnel spoke on a public telephone. Talking to Jasmine, he realized nothing would ever part them. Separation had only brought them closer.

"My plane's already boarding," he said. "I'm on my way home, baby."

"I never thought I'd hear those words. You know, every day our little lady calls out for her daddy."

"And her momma?"

Jasmine paused, then whispered reflectively, "Without you, I'm an orphan. Get home fast."

Her words were soft and bed-warm as her breasts in the morning. Darnel had never felt such a strong yearning to be anywhere.

"I'll be home, soon," he promised. "Pick me up at the airport. I'd rather not take a limo."

Mr. Wu watched a young black man dash from the phones toward the departure gate.

"Last boarding call for Flight 534, departing for Las Vegas," the airport public address system announcer called.

"Someone's in a hurry to reach Vegas," one of his men said.

They also waited on a flight. Wu had sized up his

adversary. The man's face just didn't bear the scars of a losing streak. The Buckman displayed the strength of will to fight and win.

As the young man bounded around a corner and out of sight, Mr. Wu answered another boarding call. He was traveling to a different corner of the globe. For a man like him, new opportunities always rose with another dawn.

Chapter Twenty-Six

The Future Ain't
What It Used to Be

At daybreak the winds died. Showers, which had driven so torrentially through the night, stopped as if the Almighty simply turned off a spigot. Begone, the heavens declared, to the roars of thunderous whitecaps that had crashed against the sands. Peaceful ripples, swelling on the low tide, hummed a genteel wake up call.

Seabirds warbled their joyful chorus while sampling a smorgasbord of delicacies washed ashore. Joey watched them from a boardwalk bench as golden sunbeams thrust over the horizon. He fixed on three gulls fighting over a crab carcass. The largest bird won and proudly warbled. Its smaller brethren cowered, but quickly found fresh morsels to tug from thousands of beached clam shells.

"That's how it is after a storm," Joey mused. "The strong scarf up the best of the spoils."

He looked over his shoulder at Teko, who covered his back, and refashioned the sunglasses on his face. His eyes could take no more. Time to find solace in darkness, he realized. Joey rose. He and his sentinel strolled past construction crews that roped off sections of the boardwalk, readying for the workday. Hammers and mallets were about to strike.

"They're replacing the rotten boards along here," Teko observed.

Joey watched a robust laborer wedge the tip of a crowbar between planks. With a mighty thrust the boards rose, cracked, and splintered.

"That's what I should have done, long ago," he said. "The old woman failed me. Her gift to foresee is just as rotted."

As the last piece of business in his aborted affair, he would snuff the life of Letitia DeLuca for failing to tell him what he had needed to know. He approached the card reader's shop on the boardwalk. That would be her final resting place.

The bell above her door rang as he entered. Though the cramped quarters looked the same all the years he had come, its musty odor had grown stronger as the old woman aged. Rarely did she open the windows and on his visits the drapes were tightly drawn.

She's expecting me, Joey thought.

Already the drapes were closed. He removed his sunglasses and reached for the pistol in his pocket. Joey sensed her presence in a strange and icy way. He cocked the hammer as his eyes focused. Then he saw her. Letitia rested beside a single lit candle, her lips stretched tight and curled up at the corners. She drew not a breath.

"Only when you meet death on your own terms," he

observed, "do you lay in such peaceful repose. *Arrivederci*, old woman."

He bade Letitia DeLuca farewell. For so long, he had been her benefactor as well as her torturer. Joey set down his gun and fell into a chair next to the body. He was so tired. Yet he peered and silently paid his respects.

Letitia had laid herself out in a long black dress and had pinned the toes of her stockings together to keep her feet upright when rigor mortis set. Her hands were clasped as if in prayer. Rosary beads were clenched between her fingers.

The old woman had not well-predicted the outcome of recent events. Joey thought back to the superstitions of his youth. Those who could foresee, it was sometimes said, lost their gift when life's breaths grew short. Yes, she had failed him. But she had known when death would collect her in its grim tally.

Wind suddenly blew. The room rattled as if the gust came from inside. For an instant, he thought he could smell her garlic-laden breath and hear the raspy tones of her voice.

"*A presto*," she seemed to say, see you soon.

Then, all was still. The spirit of Letitia DeLuca had departed.

A man so intimately acquainted with death was not one to regret the passing of life. Joey sat comfortably, longing for rest after the busy night. He closed his eyes and drifted to sleep.

Tommy knocked on Susannah's door at the Avery-Davis Clinic. From the first day her doctors had permitted her to receive them, he had sent fresh clusters of peach roses. At last, she could receive visitors, so he delivered the blossoms in his arms. He entered feeling the pangs of a nervous schoolboy picking up his dream date for the prom.

The room swelled with a floral sea. Amid its cascading surf, Susannah beamed, the top of her white robe his open invitation. Their eyes locked. Each stood captivated in silence, knowing words were superfluous for two who shared the same thoughts.

An attendant peered into Susannah's room and called, "Will you be going to breakfast, Miss Halloway?"

She waved the woman away. Tommy shut the door; Susannah drew the blinds. Then, as if carried on notes of an unhurried waltz, they slowly closed all distance between them. Their embrace came with the tenderness and innocence of an infant's grasp. Her heartthrob matched his own. Each engulfed the other completely, two bodies aching to be one.

Joey Bonivicolla opened his eyes to the agony of daylight.

"Hey, close the drapes," he called to whomever was there.

Still seated in the chair beside the old woman's corpse, Joey covered his eyes with his hands. Yet the glare tormented pupils that couldn't dilate. He bellowed again.

"Close the damned drapes."

"No can do Joey," he heard Teko reply.

Joey recognized other voices, too. His men buzzed all around him. He couldn't see them, but he could sense their movements.

"The light's killing me," Joey wailed.

"No, it ain't," Teko said, "This is."

Joey felt a knife blade slice his side. It penetrated his flesh, but not a vital organ.

"And this," said another of his men.

Again, Joey felt himself being sliced.

"And this."

Another stab, but none would put him to death. In horror he realized they were ritualistically carving him.

"There, son of a bitch," he heard another man say. "You get one wound for each person who died in your scheme."

"Like this," called another.

That time a blade penetrated his spleen. Blood from internal injuries filled his mouth.

"I'm your boss!" he gurgled.

"The future ain't what it used to be," Teko said.

Joey understood. The killing of a boss required sanctioning by the heads of other families. Just as he had feared, he was paying for the failed scheme with his life. The harvest of so many casualties at The Megasino would bring too much heat on the mob to allow him to live. In his world, it could only end that way.

He roared in pain, then writhed and slunk forward in the chair. Still, knives pierced his back.

"No more," he moaned.

His spirit exhausted, Joey Bonivicolla slumped to the floor. He died without enmity, knowing he would meet all his men again in hell.

The big man lay still beside the old woman. Peculiar life mates became bizarrely joined in death. Before leaving, his men closed the drapes as a final tribute to their former boss. They disappeared, heading different directions along the boardwalk, all but one.

Teko remained outside the card reader's shop. Turning westward, he observed the majesty of The Megasino tower. Then, he faced the surf, staring listlessly as if sated by the milk of nirvana. Sparkling waters glistened under warm sunshine, delivering a message for anyone who took the time to see and hear. Each wave that rushed ashore encouraged a brighter morrow.

Before the backdrop of soft hued and fragrant blossoms, their lips parted. Tommy and Susannah peered into each others hearts through wide-open eyes. Hers, Tommy saw at long last, were the same clear pools ingrained in perfectly carved images that were his most cherished memories.

Instantly carried to far shores of the paradise they had once shared, he relived tropical breezes, swaying palms, and promises of enduring rapture. Love, he had learned, is never long gone when measured by beats of a remembering heart.

Their arms bound them in a secure velvet world. Her breath brushed his face when she whispered.

"My dreams lead nowhere without you."

Her lids lowered, her eyelashes kissing his own. Then, Susannah trembled as she uttered what he knew was her only fear.

"Is it too late for us?"

Tommy didn't wait for words. Emotion erupted. It surfaced in a million-dollar smile. Then his covenant, whet with meaning, told her all she would ever need to know.

"My love, fate is a wildcard in a deck full of aces."

MORE FROM FREDERICK SCHOFIELD

The Boardwalkers

"Schofield has stories to tell, good stories."
–The Press of Atlantic City

Excerpt from Chapter One: Close Your Eyes

Sarah stood in silent surrender. Eyes cast low, she turned over cuffs that would tenderly restrain her wrists. Welcoming their familiar touch, she stroked satin straps that would bind her ankles. Sarah's hands joined behind her back. The cuffs closed. A soft cord wrapped round her body like a comfortable second skin. Leg restraints clasped her ankles. They nuzzled silk stockings drawn taught over her willowy legs by a lace garter belt. She felt secure.

A long red feather gently caressed her cheek, then swept auburn curls from her brow. The sensation consumed her with promise. Towering in spiked heels, she was gently lowered to sit in cramped quarters. The quill kissed her bare breasts. Her back arched so erect nipples could converge with tingling swirls. As a coo escaped quivering lips, which glistened from expectation, she closed her eyes for the next loving stroke.

A tickle chilled, then dribbles warmed her chest. All her senses piquing, curiosity rousing, Sarah raised dreamy eyelids and screamed as a razor-sharp blade slashed her again. Gashes followed, slow and unyielding, deep enough to draw blood, too shallow to kill. She howled, knowing no one would hear, and struggled, knowing she could never break free. Panic broiled her brain until all sensations numbed. Head bowed and life draining, she drifted into darkness. Blood oozed down her legs, onto her shoes, and across the floor.

She stared into the crimson puddle that was hers and took life's last breath without a struggle. Air rank with the odor of alcohol and thick with cigarette smoke filled her lungs. As her heart pounded its final beat, she thought of him. Knowing he would be accountable for her death was her last earthly satisfaction. Her own iniquitous compulsions would send him on a journey he had neither the soul nor heart to take. Mad laughter echoed in her mind. It ricocheted off the walls of her skull, til all that Sarah Cameron was – was gone.

A telephone ring broke the icy stillness that February night. One week out of four she took night calls as a member of the major crimes unit. Seasoned with twelve years' experience, she was an Atlantic County Assistant Prosecutor. Getting roused in the dark was an occupational hazard, but that kind of call churned her adrenaline. A voice pierced through murky sleep dust.

"Miz Resnick?"

"What time is it?"

"Three fifteen, ma'am."

"In the morning?"

"Wake up, Miz Resnick. It's your week on rotation. We have a homicide on Brigantine Island."

Carol sat upright in bed, stretched her limbs, and tossed her blond hair off her face. She finished the call and leaped to her feet without even yawning. In less than five minutes she had a cup of black coffee in her hand, dressed in a black suit with a long skirt and high heels. The homicide cops had nicknamed her the Mistress of Major Crimes and she was on duty.

A murder mystery rips on a hot romp to a steamy end . . . when evidence stacks against a trial attorney charged with gruesomely slaying his wife. Without an alibi, an innocent man faces a death sentence, while a crime boss shares the same fleeting breaths. Unaware their fates are uniquely joined, they only see that the salvation of either can cost the others life.

Take a romantic sixty year stroll beside the surf. Walk where saints and sinners . . . wives, husbands, and their lovers . . . judges, lawyers, cops, hoods, and street people . . . are tender life mates, eager bed fellows, and deadly foes. A seaside town as never exposed, on and under its boardwalk, casts shadows where drama slices with a razor edge. Only in this lush cosmos can you learn about love from a killer with a heart, search for your soul among the soulless, and pray to find an elusive murderer before it is too late.

Creatures like the ones strolling through this story

made the author's former law office their second home. Whether they told their tales through laughter, tears or stuttering fears, their irrepressible passion is imprinted on every page, passion that triggers the starting pistol for THE BOARDWALKERS.

became under Satan's dominion

PRAISE FOR A RUN TO HELL

"This exciting tale grabs you from the first page . . .
packed with secrets, intrigue and adventure – something
for everyone."

–*Book Dealers World*

"Tom Clancy and John Grisham's fans will REALLY
love this one! It is extremely intense! Fiction and fact
are mixed so well that I cannot tell where the truth ends
and the lies begin. HIGHLY RECOMMENDED READ-
ING!"

–*Huntress Book Reviews*

"It's the way mob stuff really ran."
                    –Joey "A" Altimare, alleged former
                    longtime Philly mob member

"When Schofield says, 'everyone adores a new twist on
a dead princess,' he's right on the money, telling how
the Mafia murdered Monaco's Princess Grace Kelly
Grimaldi, her Philadelphia city councilman brother, and
their brother–in–law, a story known through his family
ties and criminal clients."
          –Roger Cheetham, Jack Kelly classmate, *O'PC 45*

"*A Run to Hell* jabs like a pitchfork through your heart."
                    –Don Cannon, *WOGL-FM*, Philadelphia